Pirates of Savannah

The Complete Trilogy

The Birth of Freedom in the Lowcountry

Tarrin P. Lupo

Porcupine Publications

Available in print and ebook editions at www.Lupolit.com and other online retailers.

Second Edition
ISBN 978-1-937311-00-1

Published with the spirit of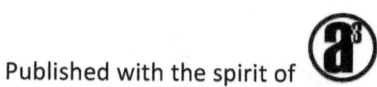

DEDICATION

This book is dedicated to all the past, present and future liberty activists who found the courage to say no to authority.

PREFACE

Pirates of Savannah is a historical fiction novel that takes place in a forgotten and fascinating time of history. This book is loaded with adventure and reminds folks just what it took to survive in such a rugged, harsh time. I have seen hundreds of great fiction novels written about the Civil and Revolutionary wars, but almost none use pre-Revolutionary days as their backdrop. This book brings forward many obscure historical events that were censored or forgotten by time.

Unless you are from South Carolina or Georgia you might have no idea where the Lowcountry is actually located. It originally started out as a little section of southern South Carolina coastline and then grew to include the whole coastline of South Carolina and parts of Georgia's coast. These days it has been pretty much bastardized to the point where people all the way from Cape Fear, North Carolina to Saint Augustine, Florida also say they are from the Lowcountry. Perhaps in my lifetime the entire east coast will be absorbed into the Lowcountry as well.

Most of the events in the book really happened and the famous characters are all real. I wrote this so the fictional characters weave in and out of real history so much, that unless you're an expert in Lowcountry record, you will not be able to tell where the true past begins and ends. You can always check the epilogue at the end of the book to find out what was based on history and what was fictional.

A map of the locations in the book

I thought it would be interesting to write an entire book accurate to the speech and writing patterns of the time. That idea lasted about one hour. After I plowed through tombs of writings of 1700s' lexicon, I realized how difficult and time consuming that style is to decipher. It slowed the story line to a crawl and took away from the enjoyment of reading it. So I have stayed true and used words from that time period, but not the confusing writing and speaking styles. You need to remember; standard rules for grammar did not come into play until the 1800s, so pretty much anything went. One could spell the same word five different ways and use them all in one giant run on sentence. If you are the kind of person with grammar and spelling OCD then you would have never survived back then.

One last thing about spelling, some spelling was changed over time. When the book talks about Charles Towne instead of Charleston or Jekyll Island Instead of Jekyll Island it is not a mistake. Even some of the famous people in the book have multiple ways to spell their name. So if a name looks different than the way you remember, it is because I chose the version I came across the most.

Here are other things you might need to know before diving into this book. The 1700s were filthy! I mean really, really disgusting. Think of the grossest college rugby or frat house and multiply it by one hundred times. Any personal hygiene was a luxury and most common folk only bathed once a season. Average people owned only one set of clothes and would have never even seen soap. My father even asked me to include a warning about the vividness of the first chapter in the book. He wanted me to tell you that the rest of the book is not that squalid. Oh, everyone is a critic!

I'm sure you have heard the saying "History is written by the winners". I never realized just how true that was until I dove into stacks of old writings. People forget in this day in age how writings which criticized the powers that be was the fastest way to a noose. Most of the writings that survived that time period were the king's correspondences, militaries' records and propaganda. When I was doing research, I tried to look past the flowery good reports and extrapolate what was really going on behind the scenes.

Most people in school learn a watered down version of why colonists came to America. I was always told they came over so they could practice their religion without fear of being killed by the king. Now, it is true that many did escape from the king's religious persecution but that is not the full story. Many others came over to escape the rule of government all together.

Some of those settlers were this nation's first freedom activists. They fled from generations of government tyranny in their homelands and came to the colonies hoping to just be left alone.   To finally live a life without some government or authority telling them how they must live.

The strong anti-government and pro-individual freedom message of the first settlers was censored over the years, especially after the Civil War.   When people think of the Revolutionary War, the first images that come to mind are the Boston Tea Party, Boston Massacre, First Continental Congress, the signing of the Declaration of Independence, and the Constitution. Did you happen to notice that all these celebrated events happened in the North? Interesting since two thirds of the Revolutionary War was fought in the South. How come all the events people celebrate are Northern victories?

Part of the reason was Ben Franklin had his hand in most of the printing during that time and wanted to promote himself and northern states.   However, the big reason for this is because after the South lost the War of Southern Secession, or the Civil War, the North purposely erased as much Southern history as it could.   A propaganda campaign played out to change Southern minds so they would stop seeing themselves as independent and instead see themselves as part of one new nation. That held over and continued forward, even today. Just pick up a public or government school's history book and see what events are celebrated and what events are omitted.

I hope to do my part to re-teach that bit of missing rabblerousing history through an exciting and interesting story instead of a boring, crusty history book.

Check out all the video, audio and other extras that accompany this book at www.Lupolit.com!

Good Hunting,

Tarrin P. Lupo

CONTENTS

ACKNOWLEDGMENTS

Editors:
Final Editors: Sandi Britt & Ruby Nicole Hilliard
Copy and Layout Editor: Ruby Nicole HIlliard
Creative Editors: April Reed & Reagen Dandridge Desilets
Editors: Marc Emery & Margie Jaques & Sky Reed

Illustrators:
Ruby Nicole Hilliard, Scott A. Motley & Lori Messenger

Cover Art:
Ruby Nicole Hilliard, Johnson Rice & Dawn Etheridge

Consultants:
Cannon, Musket, Charles Towne and Lowcountry Historical
Consultant: Reagen Dandridge Desilets
Sword and Blade consultant: Mark McMorrow
Archeological consultant: Audrey Salem

Contributors:
Teresa Warmke, Michael Sansone, Aziza Seven, Julie Chessher
Stone, Jim Davidson, Mariana Evica, Luthor Freeman and all my
great friends on Facebook who helped along the journey.

CHAPTER I

DEBTOR'S PRISON

Debtors' Prison

Patrick and the crew watch Isaac drag a dead body out of their cell to the fire pits

Like a religious experience, the sun flooded the prison cell blinding the young man. A thick black cloud of buzzing flies poured out the door as they rushed toward the light that now bathed the young man. He rubbed the darkness from his eyes. He squinted at the intrusion of light, only being able to make out the blurry cloud of black flies that seemed to resemble smoke madly escaping from a burning building. For what felt like minutes, thousands of flies swarmed out of the doorway as the man's eyes adjusted to the first light they had seen in two long weeks. Fourteen days without a hint of light, sealed in complete darkness, is not quickly erased from the eye. But after a few moments, he could see the guards.

Tattered rags had been tied tightly behind the guards' heads, covering their noses, revealing only their eyes. Their eyes were wide with fear of the disease that had swept through the prison so quickly. Even their hands were wrapped thick with cloth like filthy mittens. No chances would be taken this close to the foul of the cells that were littered with emaciated, diseased, and dying prisoners. The man watched dispassionately as a guard barked a muffled command to another inmate, ordering him to drag the dead from the cells to the fire pit to be burned.

The man smiled weakly and thought, *It must smell rosy in the barracks.* He knew the guards only allowed the prisoners to remove the dead bodies when the festering smell of pox would creep up into their quarters. The prison cells used to be sanitary, but that was before the rampant pox. The only thing that had spread faster than the pox was the fear of the pox. In response, the dungeon had been sealed and unlucky, frightened guards were assigned to leave food and water by the door once a day.

A selected few inmates were allowed to go to the door to retrieve the food and dispense it among their fellow prisoners, but the guards made sure only the healthy received the poor excuse for nourishment in this pit. The sick were too weak, unconscious, or dying to waste vittles and water on.

The cell had become the dumping ground of those who did not have the minor great pox or, rather, the more deadly smallpox. A few unfortunate souls suffered from the malignant variety or worse yet, the dreaded black pox. In a place where human refuse reigned, it was no surprise that smallpox struck the prisoners with such fury. Already twenty of the twenty-five imprisoned men had succumbed, their bodies breaking out into papules filling with opalescent fluid. It was only a matter of time until the remaining sick would join their fellow inmates in the deep fire pit in the yard outside the prison.

The extremely massive but emaciated prisoner dragging the corpses was handling his job with slight grace, but soon became nauseated by the thick fumes of ammonia that were emitting from the foul on the floor. He became overwhelmed and, gripping his stomach, he paused to expel his only meal all over the bloated, pus-filled bodies that were at his feet. His vomit, which did not get stuck in his long beard was an added spice to a floor already covered in a black and green slippery slosh of feces, urine, blood, dried, crusted semen and other diseased vomit. This vile sludge, as the prisoners referred to it, covered the floor an inch thick.

The man had almost forgotten about the floor being alive until he saw it again in the rare sunlight beaming in from the open door. He recoiled from the sight; the throngs of maggots, fungus, and flies laying their nests in the filth. He had grown so accustomed to the constant buzz of flies and beetles coming from below his feet that he no longer heard them, but their squirming bodies, now illuminated, gave the illusion that the floor was a living, moving organism.

There was a time that chamber buckets would have served to keep the cell sanitary, but they had since become overfilled and obsolete. The guards, so sickened by the smell of prisoners dumping the buckets, simply let the pots succumb to the vile sludge over time until they were simply two, large mounds of fungus and shit.

"Hurry it up!" a guard commanded to the prisoner who was puking instead of dragging bodies. The man could see horror in the guards' eyes. They wanted to be exposed to the filth and disease of the cell as little as possible and it was already taking too long. The man could almost hear the guards desperately wondering if they made a mistake, questioning if the prisoner they chose to drag the bodies was sick himself.

The man smiled again, blinking in the blinding light, and thought, *Serves the bastards right.*

To add to the madness of the cell, most of the prisoners were touched in the mind from the prolonged fevers they contracted. Their bodies would rebel from the smells of the floor until even their physical senses left them. Soon, they would crumple like wet paper mâche to stew in their own bile. Weakness would overtake their wills and they would eventually fall into the puddles of decaying and fresh human waste on the floor.

The man would listen from a bench with his knees drawn up to his chest and his arms wrapped around his knees, hearing the wet, flat sound of bodies hitting the floor. The only reason he was not dead from infection was the sanctuary of the bench he sat on. It was the only bench in the cell and it was like an island with just enough room for six castaway prisoners. The old, wooden bench had been broken so many times in the past, it was now barely held together with a rigging of thighbones and rags taken from dead prisoners to keep it standing.

Now with an empty stomach and his chest and beard covered with brown vomit, the nauseous prisoner soon regained his composure enough to finish his chore and dragged the corpses into the hall one by one. The man closed his eyes and rested his head on his knees drawn to his chest as the guards closed and locked the heavy cell door, leaving him once again in darkness.

With only the constant wails and moaning of the dying to keep him company, the man, just as he had every day for the past seven years, returned to thoughts of home and the fateful day of his arrest. He rubbed the long scar on the left of his jaw and silently vowed he would live to meet William Potts again.

* * *

His name was Patrick Willis and he was once an aspiring jeweler. His father was a jeweler to the high society in the outskirts of London. Sadly, his father died of consumption when Patrick was fifteen. It was a horrible, slow death of hacking coughs, phlegm, and blood. The fever lingered a long time and the elder Willis lost his mind, inevitably sinking Patrick's family in debt. Patrick's family placed the patriarch in a sanitarium that promised to cure him, but the money ran out before a cure was found. Then the sick, old man had to be moved back to home where he was cared for by Patrick's mother and his three sisters.

Before his father's debts were called, Patrick made a desperate move to keep him out of prison, still hoping he would recover. He took every scrap of valuable jewelry the family had left and went to make a deal with a competing, ruthless jeweler named William Potts to buy their family's interests out. He hid the jewelry well and disguised himself as a pauper while traveling to Potts's shop so as not to arouse suspicion.

Fortunately, Potts recognized Patrick as soon as he entered the shop but he did not throw him into the street, as he normally would of any true pauper. Potts invited Patrick to the back of the shop so that the young man could display his wares which he kept in a hidden bag concealed on his person. The swag was mostly bits of wire scraps of silver with a few rare stones. If he had the luxury of time, Patrick could have found buyers fetching a decent price for the swag, possibly just enough to pay his father's debts. Sadly, this was not the case. Patrick did not have time and he had to desperately acquire as much money as he could before his father was sent off to debtors' prison.

Mr. Potts scratched his chin, taking painfully long to examine the swag, and could see the sweat beading on the young man's brow. He relished Patrick's desperation and anxiousness. The older Potts assumed correctly this was Patrick's first financial transaction. He also heard the rumors of the elder Willis's plight and was quite happy to see his competition sinking into illness, debt and desperation.

Mr. Potts slowly examined every stone, rolling them in his fingers and occasionally sighing for affect. The master jeweler took far more time then he needed considering the level of his expertise. It was all a game, to test young Patrick's patience and to judge the depth of his desperation. Finally, after what seemed like a painful eternity, Mr. Potts simply grimaced and stated flatly, "No," without any further explanation.

Patrick grabbed Potts by the sleeve and begged, "Please, sir. Reconsider. I will give you a dandy of a deal."

"No, boy," Mr. Potts smiled coldly. "Now release me and get out." Patrick's jaw went slack with shock. He released the older man's arm and felt as if the hope of saving his father from debtors' prison was slipping through his fingers. Brushing off his sleeve as if Patrick's touch had soiled him, Potts reiterated, "Go on now. Out with you!"

As Patrick staggered through the shop's front room towards the door, he looked over his shoulder to take a glimpse of Potts one last time. Maybe his father's competition would change his mind. Perhaps this was all a ploy to lower the cost of what he would have to pay for Patrick's valuable snippets.

Potts had strutted to behind his shop counter where another man in a rich red coat was casually leaning. Both men grinned maliciously and spoke to each other in cutting, hushed tones. Embarrassingly, Patrick was startled by the sound of the tiny bell that hung above the shop's door when it chimed softly as he made his exit. The two men roared in laughter and Patrick could only hang his head and walk out with a defeated gait.

Humiliated, Patrick slowly began his dejected ambulation home. His mind scrambled trying to find the words he could tell his poor mother that his last, desperate plan was a failure. He thought about his poor little sisters and how they would fare in a life of poverty, with no dowry and no prospects for betterment.

Then suddenly, Patrick felt a red, hot burning sensation flash across his jaw. It felt like he had stuck his face in a fire. Grasping at his jaw, he fell to his knees writhing with pain. To his astonishment, he realized that a puddle of blood forming on the ground around his knees was from the blood dripping off his own chin. He then felt a hard boot slam against his back forcing him prone into the mud. Immediately, Patrick felt hands rummaging inside his shirt. The thief knew right where Patrick's pouch of valuables was hidden and deftly ripped it from his clothes. Looking over his shoulder, Patrick could only see the backside of the thief running quickly down the street. For a brief moment, Patrick was sure he had caught a glimpse of a red, rich coat as the thief darted around the corner.

It took the assaulted young man a few sands of time to figure out what had just happened. His head spun and his face throbbed with pain. He called out for help but strangers just ignored him. The man appeared as a seemingly lowly pauper bleeding in the street, so the witnesses continued to walk by without even making eye contact. The strangers knew it was entirely too dangerous to get involved in other people's business. The locals knew that exposing a thief was the fastest way to put your own family in danger and find a dagger in your back.

With no one to help, Patrick collected himself and tried to stop the crimson from gushing from his left cheek by pressing his sleeve against the gaping wound. He knew chasing the thief was futile and that he had better get home as fast as possible to control this blood flow and clean the wound. Nothing killed a man as slow and painful as sepsis.

When he finally made it home, Patrick's entire family sat around the kitchen table and cried as he told them what happened, how Potts offered him nothing, laughed him out of his shop, and how Patrick fell victim to the road agent. When he was done telling his sorry story, the whole family was silent. His small straw haired sister, Garland, came over and held his hand. Patrick's family knew what this failure meant and that the consequences were ghastly. The Willis family owed the sanitarium a great deal of money.

Since his father was a prominent jeweler, the sanitarium assumed Mr. Willis had plenty of money and extended him credit. After a few months, the sanitarium wised up and threw Patrick's father into the streets, demanding payment. Immediately, the sanitarium lodged a complaint with the officials and it was expected that soon the elder, sick patriarch be dragged off to debtors' prison.

Two days after Patrick failed to sell the jewelry scraps to Potts and was robbed by the road agent, his father died at the humble home they were renting. With tears in her eyes,

Patrick's mother sold the wedding ring her husband handcrafted for her to pay for his funeral services and for the following month's rent.

It was a simple and solemn funeral poorly attended from fear of catching the consumption from the corpse of old man Willis. The service was heart wrenching. The sobbing of Patrick's mother and sisters who were grieving openly and loudly was muffled by the sound of heavy, falling rain. Garland wept loudly and hugged Patrick's leg as their father was entombed in the earth.

Then, as Patrick made his way from the grave, two agents of his majesty, King George II, grabbed each of Patrick's arms. He knew then he was out of time. By the king's law, it was decreed that the oldest son became responsible for the father's debt. This statute was usually not enforced on one as young as Patrick but unfortunately, his family's debt was sizeable. He sadly said his goodbyes to his family and he calmly walked away with the agents escorting him. The sobbing sounds that came from his huddled family broke Patrick's heart. Although his mother and sisters vowed to work hard and pay off the debts to free Patrick, they all knew it would be impossible to come into such a large sum of money.

* * *

Patrick's first prison cell was nowhere near as bad as the one he was currently residing in. The people demanded of their king that mercy be shown on debtors and the poor. More and more, the king and his parliament were expected to pay for people's incarceration. Initially, debtors would be charged room and board at a private facility in addition to the debt they owed. Families on the outside were expected to work harder or sell off their belongings to pay off the debt for their imprisoned loved ones as fast as they could so as to not incur an insurmountable sum. The longer a prisoner was incarcerated, the larger and larger the debt grew due to daily fees. Once a prisoner's debt became too unmanageable, the private facility quickly realized they would not make a profit and moved the debtor to the king's debtors' prison.

These government prisons were worse than hell and Patrick resided in the most infamous of them all. When he was young, Patrick's father read to him the illegal papers of the Enlightenment Doctrines. These ideas were radical and talked of such things as a man being born with rights and that these rights were not bestowed on him from king or church. His father told him, "As history has always shown, any government program will be run far worse than the private market would."

The king's prisons were no exception to this. The Crown begrudgingly spent as little as he could on these hellholes. In times past, the king simply executed the troublesome, poor prisoners who were nuisances to him. Now, however, he was not so openly tyrannical. George the II wanted to give the appearance that he was a compassionate king, so he created social programs. He hoped to avoid the negative gossip in the socialite circles stirred by executing so many poor, non-violent subjects. He did not want to be publicly exposed as the tyrant he truly was. The king determined it was far easier to keep his subjects within his law if they felt their concerns were being heard by a sympathetic ruler.

Recently, King George was pressured by powerful socialites to show compassion and extend his benevolence to the debtors' prisons. Many subjects' families had at least one relative in these dungeons and this was a popular societal concern. But soon the king discovered he was quickly going broke being compassionate.

Patrick was imprisoned in September of 1728. When he was still in the private system of prisons, he met a good fellow named Robert Castell who was a publisher. Castell had published a book on architecture and he was imprisoned for the debts he incurred by publishing it. Robert told Patrick that there was so much excitement about the book, that private investors practically threw money at him through loans. The book was called *The Villas of the Ancients* and it focused on ancient Greek and Roman architecture. Greek and Roman architecture was then all the rage in upper-London society. Sadly, it was poorly timed. Robert took too long to release it and by the time it was published, the frenzy for Greek and Roman architecture had fallen out of fashion. The book was a total failure and Castell incurred a tremendous amount of debt.

Robert was a real nice fellow. Patrick and he quickly became friends. Patrick assumed he must have reminded Robert of a little brother or maybe a nephew, but never confirmed this notion. The young prisoner did not care what the reason was; a friend was welcome in this lonely place. They rotated watch so they could sleep safely and unmolested. Robert even taught Patrick to play chess in the dirt with some rocks he collected. He used to tell Patrick that this was the game of kings and royalty. It did help the time pass which dragged on. Patrick's family never paid one shilling towards his debt. He imagined his mother and sisters needed everything they could get just to pay for rent and to put food on their table.

After they earned each other's trust, Robert shared a secret with Patrick. The day he was incarcerated he dispatched a message to his friend James Edward Oglethorpe. Oglethorpe was a high-ranking military official and an old friend of Robert's. Robert promised his old friend would help but sadly, before Oglethorpe could do anything for the men, Patrick and Robert were moved from the clean, private prison to the den of stench that was the king's debtors' prison.

Upon entering their new cell, the offensive, dank stench announced the squalid condition immediately. Robert pleaded with the guard to move them back to their private jails. Angered by this request, the vindictive, cruel guard had Patrick and Robert moved to the filthiest, most infested cell in the entire prison. The sadistic sentry seemed to enjoy prodding Robert and mockingly asked, "Will the *privacy* of this cell suit your delicate disposition, sir?" After the heavy, cell door clanged shut and the lock clicked, Patrick could hear the laughter of the guards echoing down the hall as they walked away.

This same watchman seemed to delight in torturing Robert.

He would purposely add inmates to their dark cell whose minds were violent or touched with insanity. Among raving lunatics and violent men who were more like animals, Robert and Patrick had to fight just to keep a piece of moldy bread or a ladle of water. The worst of the insane cellmates would smear themselves with their own feces and at night, would toss their urine or semen on other cellmates while they slept. Many of these demented souls were murdered in their sleep, especially the ones who had lesions on the brain, who were touched and made mad. They so disgusted and annoyed the other prisoners, they were commonly strangled to hell their first night in the cell.

Robert was surviving as well as expected until the corrupt, cruel guard decided to make their cell the infirmary for the smallpox victims. Robert soon fell sick from smallpox and died a terrible death shortly thereafter. The prison rumor mill told Patrick that when Oglethorpe finally arrived, he was furious about his friend Robert's death. It took Patrick a while to piece all these fragments of information together but this is what he gleaned:

Oglethorpe had enough political favor to initiate an investigation of the jails after the death of his dear acquaintance Robert. He even boldly took a committee to investigate the king's prisons. The findings were eventually reported to Parliament and the king, who were either truly shocked about the deplorable conditions or they faked their disgust well. When the news broke about the investigation, the subjects and powerful socialites demanded something be done immediately. Oglethorpe's report was used as a pawn in the political chess game and it caused a resounding rally cry for reform. In fact, the crooked jailor that made Patrick's and Robert's lives hell was publicly called out and taken to trial. It was such big news; it made it into the monthly periodical and was not even censored away from the public.

Of course nothing really changed at Patrick's jail. The officials merely cleaned up a few cells and a handful of prisoners, then invited the authorities to inspect their new "reformed" prison. Once the official inspections were over, the prison returned back to one giant pestilence and pox factory.

Over the years of his imprisonment, Patrick heard more of this Oglethorpe character attempting to reform the prisons. He assumed Oglethorpe was so upset by Robert's death, that it ignited a burning in his soul for a sense of justice. The military officer lobbied Parliament to consider a Bill for Relief of Insolvent Debtors. He also was selected as a director of the Royal West Africa Company. Patrick later heard that directing this company put a bitter taste on his tongue for the practice of slavery. The prisoner even heard a strange rumor that Oglethorpe was trying to teach Indian heathens to accept Anglican beliefs. The thought of seeing all those savages wearing their feather head dresses in a church would make Patrick laugh heartily.

Eventually Oglethorpe and his friend, Lord Percival, came up with a notion to take all debtors' and other criminals filling the prisons in England and move them to the colonies in America. They made an appointment with King George II to bring this idea in front of him. Patrick was later told that Oglethorpe tried to win favor with logic. He sold the idea that it would solve a few of the king's problems with one move. He argued that the Royal colony of Charles Towne in South Carolina was being harassed and harangued by the Spanish and savages from Florida and that a new colony could act as a buffer against such attacks.

He went on to explain the advantages of having sub tropical crops for the Crown to exploit. Many merchants were getting very rich trading commodities from the colonies because England's soil was too sandy to grow most crops. Nevertheless, what really sold the king on the idea was relief to his burdened treasury. Oglethorpe suggested that the king provide relief to the debtors and poor by removing them from England and freeing them to work in the colonies. He knew if all reason failed, he could appeal to his majesty's coffers. The king was rumored to have ruminated over this for a while but Oglethorpe closed the deal with one capital idea. He offered the king that if he would let him establish the new colony, Oglethorpe would name the territory after him and christen it "Georgia." Appealing to his purse and now his ego, the king loved the notion and instantly took all credit for the idea, like all politicians do.

So on June 8, 1732, the king signed the charter for the colony of Georgia. This charter planned for a clutch of politicians and board trustees, which would manage the colony for twenty-one years until it would be recognized as an official colony. Although the king and Parliament directly appointed these boards of trustees, they would become difficult to control due to the vast expanse of ocean between the colonies and the mother country. Corruption became wide spread on these boards making many trustee members very wealthy through nefarious side deals.

As with all governments through time, it was a game of rewarding one's friends and punishing one's enemies using the legitimacy of state powers. The first ship called the *Anne*, with a little over one hundred settlers, had landed in a place in Georgia called Savannah. They dropped anchor on February 12, 1733 and the settlers began working immediately. They were trying to build a viable infrastructure in the settlement before they opened the floodgates to all the prisoners about to be shipped over. Moreover, those first in and positioned properly, stood to make the most profit. Moving debtors to America took a long while; many fell ill and died of disease while waiting for their turn.

Shuffled from one shit-and-maggot-infested dungeon to another for years now, Patrick could not believe he had defied death for so long in that stew of filth. He had miraculously survived five whole years since the new colony of Georgia had been established, still clinging to hope and waiting for his turn. Just to entertain themselves, each day the guards would lie to Patrick saying that he was next to leave. The watchman continually promised everyone that they were on the next ship leaving. Patrick had almost stopped believing there was even a place called Savannah and any hope of escape. What kept him going was the two friends he had made in his five-year nightmarish ordeal.

Massive gambling debts brought Isaac Swartz to his cell two years before. Built like a bull, he was a Jew who was once employed as a debt collector. Swartz was in his late twenties and had scars all over his body from a lifetime of knife fighting and beatings. He was certain he would wake up dead if he did not make friends fast because he was so reviled. Over the years as a debt collector, Swartz had broken and beat many of the men he was now imprisoned with as a debtor himself. Patrick was too frightened of the hulking Isaac to point out the irony of it all. Since Isaac was so massive and strong he always seemed to get the horrid duty of dragging the corpses from the cell. The Jewish man was getting weaker with each body he moved to the fire pit because he was getting so emaciated and thin.

Patrick's other friend was a wiry, Irish fellow named Shamus Red. He had flame crimson hair, ghost-white skin, freckles, and very few teeth. He had arrived about half a year ago after he took a large loan out to start a bar. Later he told Patrick more of the truth; Red was from a wealthy family and used their good name to obtain credit. His father was so infuriated, that he paid off the debt of the bar and then transferred the debt to his son. By king's law, Shamus was now legally indebted to his father and could be held accountable for it. His father disowned his prodigal son and reported him to the collection agent. Soon after, Shamus ended up in the cell with Patrick, hopelessly waiting for his father to regret the decision and buy back his freedom.

Shamus made one fatal mistake when he opened his business; he forgot to calculate the cost of his love for the Devil's piss. The doors of his bar were only open a short time before Shamus ran out of beer and spirits. Some people are angry drunks, some people are happy drunks. Shamus was a generous drunk, and a fool. When he would become inebriated, he gave away too much of his stores. He made many friends, but little profits. The bar seemed to flourish with crowds every night but that was because the patrons knew if they got Shamus drunk, the drinks would flow freely all night.

Like vultures, they would circle Shamus waiting for his speech to slur and his grin to grow wide, the tell tale sign that spirits were about to become free.

Neither Patrick nor Isaac knew how the Irishman was still alive. He was much thinner than the rest of the inmates and his breath smelled of rotten eggs and death as if he was a talking corpse. Patrick and Isaac theorized Shamus must only be surviving on pure spirit. Even in this dung palace, he still smiled and joked like a man with no worries.

CHAPTER 2

OUT OF THE MUCK

One hot morning, something was different. Patrick helped the weakening Isaac complete the chore of dragging three more bodies into the yard to be thrown on the fire. Patrick did not enjoy being picked by the guards to help his Jewish friend drag puss-oozing bodies to the yard. Often the pox-stricken only appeared dead when they were thrown into the fire pit. Their screams were animal-like and unnerving, but they were silenced quickly enough. Patrick reasoned the hasty death was the only sign of mercy in a pestilent pit like this. He and his gaunt Semite friend learned to appreciate the few, fleeting moments they could enjoy the sunlight of the yard.

When the two men returned to the cell, Patrick, Isaac, and Shamus were ordered to take the food by the door and dispense it to the other inmates, as they had a hundred times before. This day, however, a guard barked, "Hurry up and eat. Your ship is leaving today and I ain't fooking larking ya this time."

Patrick froze in his place with the bucket of gruel and ladle and stared at his two friends. Shamus was so stunned, he dropped the water he was carrying and asked, "Did you just fookin' hear that, laddies?"

The guard grew impatient with Patrick and Shamus who were taking too long to dole out the food and hissed, "What's wrong with you damn fools?! Would you prefer to stay in bloody London? I said hurry it up! Now move!" He then addressed the entire cell. "Any man healthy enough to walk

16

and who is pox-free may leave the hospitality of this cell and take their chances in America, but I am not going to wait all day for you criminals to enjoy your breakfast, so eat!" Every cellmate that was healthy enough quickly ravished their food down their gullets as fast as possible and ran from the room before the guard changed his mind. Five prisoners in total sprinted out of the cell and left the dying behind with no regard.

It had been some while since Patrick had taken a good look at himself or the others. The light revealed how the inmates were now only shells of men; ribs, thin skin, green or missing nails and rotted teeth. Their hair was matted across their emaciated bodies and gaunt faces. The watchman was disgusted by the prisoners' appearance and pungent reek. All of the guards stayed a generous distance away from the men.

The sergeant of the guard grumbled loudly, "This will not do. The first thing we must do is take you all down to the river for a bath. If you cannot clean yourself up good enough, gentlemen, your captain will never let you aboard his ship. Try to not look like you've been sleeping with death and pox or back to the cell it'll be." Each man nodded their heads empathetically with wide eyes. They would scrub the skin off their bones to stay out of the cell if they had to.

The ragged prisoners were escorted down to the river. The river was slow-moving and downstream from the main city. It was filthy by most people's standards, but it was like a fresh mountain spring to the grimy men. Isaac and Shamus were wearing tattered loincloths and piss-and-shit soaked rags they took off dead prisoners, using them as tunics. Patrick still had pantaloons with the common bloodstained thighs that he had recently lifted off a dead prisoner. He was not ashamed by the blood stains on his crotch. Commonly referred to as "peasant stains," most people Patrick knew had the same blood pattern on their trousers. One would labor many days in the hot sun and the sweat would drench their pantaloons. At night while they slept, the bottoms would dry leaving a layer of salt on the pantaloons and skin. After days and days of the salt collecting, the thighs would tear each other raw and bleed. Eventually, after many painful months, one would develop hard skin on their thighs and not bleed as much. Patrick was told if one could bathe every three days and wash their clothes, they could avoid the condition, but only royalty had the means for such a luxury.

As all five undressed, they looked like a parade of the undead with their long, matted beards and hair tangled with feces and dried blood. One guard cautiously approached them, taking care to avoid their stink, tossing Isaac a small brown and yellow bar.

Isaac looked suspicious and asked, "What's this?"

"It's soap," the guard responded flatly. "One of the prisoners had it on him when he came to the prison." The guard then smiled, "He got the pox so we decided best not use it ourselves." Isaac looked betrayed given the affect of one who had died of the pox. The guard, sensing the big man's growing anger, sneered, "Go on, Jew, and scrub yourself good. Maybe then the captain won't keelhaul you right away because of your stink."

Isaac started to splash water on himself, continuing to stare at the sentry. He had used soap once as a boy, but forgot what it looked like or how it felt. The other fellows bathing looked equally befuddled. He began to rub it on his body and immediately it stung his sores and cuts. After a good hard minute scrubbing his arm, he noticed the color of bright white skin peeping out of the black scum all over his body. He scrubbed and scrubbed, but the best he could do was only free a few patches of filth loose. He passed the soap on and continued to scrub himself raw with his hands. The massive man had forgotten how pleasant water felt on his body and sat in the river until the guards called them.

Patrick's clothes were a total loss and he was instructed to set them in a pile to burn. The guards gave them new clothes they said were donated by wealthy socialites. Of course, these clothes were really just old hand-me-downs of the guards. The watchman and their wives stole the first pick of donations leaving their tattered, old clothes to the prisoners.

New clothes for the journey

Although poorly fitting and patched together here and there, the five men were thrilled to have clean clothes and begun to smile and even giggle. Patrick was even lucky enough to receive some hand me down boots that actually fit. All five of the men even found old hats and vests that fit.

The guards still maintained their distance. One bath does not remove years of stink and filth. The sergeant addressed the prisoners loudly, "It is a three hour march to the docks. You lovelies need to be there before sun down. So let's go!" The guards escorted the stinking and ragged men at a safe distance behind, making certain nonetheless that these pathetic creatures left English soil by nightfall.

Patrick thought there was plenty of time to get there and was confused by the sergeant's haste. It was still morning after all. What Patrick did not consider was that the prisoners, from years of entropy of living in a cramped, hellish cell, were all too weak to walk that far. Patrick barely had any muscles left in his legs from years of inactivity. It just seemed he had only shin, knee, thigh bone and skin. The other four suffered terribly as well and hobbled like cripples on the road. One of them even suffered from rickets from being in the dark so long. He winced in pain with each step, but damned be if that would stop him. Shamus leaned into Patrick's ear and whispered, "Look at dat one. I bet Sam Scurvy be a fine fookin' dancer, eh?"

The fifth man in the procession of skeletons was simply known as Jessup. He had been spared only one week in the cell. Jessup never spoke and no one knew anything about the stranger.

The guards and the prisoners both knew well that if the men looked too frail, the captain would send them back to the certain death of the prison cell. The prisoners knew this was their only chance for life. The sergeant of the guard mercifully did not push the men too hard either. He wanted to be rid of these prisoners as much as the prisoners wanted to go, so he walked the hobbling men ten minutes then rested them. The group repeated this rhythm of walk and wait for almost six hours before they finally arrived at the docks where sun hung low. Patrick had never seen a ship this big up close before. It seemed impossibly gigantic and he was completely taken aback by the sheer scale of the vessel. The salty air of the docks immediately stung his sore riddled flesh, the pain bringing him back to the here and now.

As ship standards went, it was actually a small vessel but Patrick knew nothing of ships and was impressed nonetheless. He had seen a few in his time but all he recently knew was the dark closeness of the dungeon he had been reprieved from. Many of his memories were lost in the deprivation.

This ship was a modified galleon and the name *Robin* was painted on the stern. It had ten guns on carriages but four of the guns were Quakers, or fake cannons. These were old or nonfunctioning guns placed to give the appearance that the vessel was more formidable.

The *Robin* had three square-rigged masts and after many voyages, was still in very seaworthy shape. She did not appear battle-scarred as many vessels of the Royal Navy ships seemed. Most Navy vessels had obvious mismatched wood, patchwork sails and rigging with hurried cannon shot repairs. It seemed

The *Robin*

odd that a ship this small would make an open ocean crossing, but the profit that could be made in the New World was worth the risk. Crossings were attempted with just about anything that could float these days.

The sergeant who was in charge of escorting the skeletal five walked to the dock and waited. Soon one extremely well-dressed man and another tall man, dressed in a hodgepodge military uniform, came down the gang plank to meet the sentry. The sergeant and the men spoke in hushed tones pointing at the five prisoners. They bargained for a long while until an agreement was reached. The shine of silver coins caught the setting sun's light as the sergeant gleefully accepted them from the well-dressed man. The guard waved for the five to come over and join them. He beamed, "Take a good look at 'em, Cap'n. They be fetching a good price after you fatten 'em back up."

The well-dressed man looked over the scraggly five he just purchased and stated flatly, "You have procured yourself a very dandy of a deal, sir. You are dismissed." The sergeant quickly took his leave and hustled off, rubbing his silver rounds between his fingers and grinning.

The five men stared with exhausted but hopeful eyes at the well-dressed man. The fancy man proclaimed loudly and arrogantly, "I am the Captain Gibbons of this vessel and you five now work for me. For some ungodly reason the king has shown mercy on you criminals and has given you a second chance in the colonies. This will be the only and last time I will speak to any of you directly. All communication or concerns will go through my quartermaster, Mr. Mandrik. Understood? You're his problem now." The captain then took his leave and strutted like a peacock down the dock to inspect the bumboat which was cleaning the filth of the *Robin*'s stern.

Mr. Mandrik was a tall Greek man with olive skin and full lips. He looked young and refreshed for his station; not the sort of face one would expect of a quartermaster who lived a hard life at sea. The sailor was a very religious man who always carried a small, wooden, painted icon of St. Nicholas, the protector of sailors. He also wore around his neck an ancient, blue, glass-blown, apostrophic talisman known as the Mati, or The Eye. The Greek man was always afraid of his vengeful and disgruntled crew cursing him. The superstitious Greek would check if he was the victim of the Evil Eye, using the ancient olive oil test. Once a week he would drop some oil in a glass of water, if it floated he was curse free, if it sank he would have to perform secret rituals to remove the hex.

He spoke with an extremely awkward accent. Even after years of sailing he still could not get a grasp on the king's tongue and spoke very slowly. It also did not help that years of sailing the Earth caused him to fuse many other cultures' inflections into his own accent, which could only now be described as worldly. "I am Mr. Mandrik," he introduced himself in broken English, "and it is me job to keep yas alive until we gets to Savannah." He examined the men closely, looking them up and down before continuing to sound off loudly. "First thing we dos is gives ya jobs. Ya will take great care of this barky and show her love."

"What da hell is a g'damn 'barky'?" Shamus wondered

aloud.

"It be a ship well loved by her crew," Sam Scurvy barked back. "Now shut da hell ups! The quartermaster be speaking."

Mr. Mandrik then interviewed the slaves one by one, about their past, occupations, and skills. No quartermaster in his right mind would give a novice unsupervised responsibilities, so all five were assigned the roles of mates, making them apprentices on the ship. As mates, the men's new roles would be taught by others who were more experienced at sea life. The men could expect to be assigned only the most menial of labors and back-breaking grunt work. Isaac was first to be questioned by Mr. Mandrik. The quartermaster smiled as he looked at Isaac's wide shoulders and his hulking size. Impressed by Isaac's stature, he wistfully observed to no one in particular, "If I fatten dis Jew back up he do work of two." He then grinned and smacked Isaac on the shoulder, "Ya look strong, so ya go and work with da heavy cannons." And just like that, Isaac was assigned to Master Gunner's mate.

The enigma, Jessup, it was later discovered, had a strong knowledge of sea life, but he refused to talk to anybody, including Mr. Mandrik, about his past. Since it could not be determined what his past profession was, he was assigned to common crew or as it was better known as A.B.S, or able body sailor. The A.B.S. were the true backbone of the ship and mostly dealt with riggings and sails. They also had to be like storm crows, able to smell the wind and the coming weather.

Sam Scurvy had a history at sea life as well. He was a talented fisherman before his incarceration. He was thrown into debtors' prison when he lost his ship to a rough storm which he still owed a great deal of money on. Assigned as the galley mate, his job would be fishing and cooking his fresh catches for the officers of the ship.

When Mr. Mandrik stood in front of Shamus, he did not know what to make of the skinny, yellow-eyed Irishman. Before he could ask one question of Shamus's past, Mr. Red asked, "What be your full name?" Shamus had a peculiar habit of calling everyone he met by their full names.

Patrick was certain Mr. Mandrik would beat down Shamus for the insolence and leave him bleeding on the docks of London. He was surprised when the quartermaster seemed to almost smile. Patrick could not tell if the Greek was annoyed or entertained. "My name be George," Mandrik spoke.

"Ah... Very good George Mandrik," Shamus smiled warmly. "I be Shamus Red and I can't wait to learn ye Greek sea shanties over some devil's grog."

"Luckily fer ya, Mr. Shamus Red," the Greek man growled, "ya not the first mick I had to deal with on the *Robin*. So dis one time, I will allow dis lack of respect. My name is Mister Mandrik." He continued slyly, "Since ya skinnier than wet rat and loose in da mind to think you can talk to me in dat way, I, sir, have da perfect job fer ya." Mr. Mandrik was the one smiling now as Shamus started to look nervous. "Ya will be assigned as a rigger mate."

Rigging was the most dangerous duty on the ship. Countless riggers had fallen to their death after losing their footing on a slippery spar but Shamus reveled in the idea of being a rigging monkey high above the deck. His wild Irish smile returned to his gaunt face.

Lastly, Mr. Mandrik sized up Patrick. Patrick was well built and muscular before he became a bag of bones but he was nowhere near the size of Isaac's goliath mass. He had dark, wild hair, a long unkempt beard and had darker skin then most Englishmen. "What skills ye done in yer past living" Mr. Mandrik asked Patrick.

"I was a jeweler," Patrick replied.

"Not much need for dat out here." Mandrik scratched his chin, "But I bet ya be good wit da tools."

"Yes, sir," Patrick answered quickly. "Very good."

"Fine," Mandrik decided. "So ya go be the carpenter's and surgeon's mate."

Mr. Mandrik belched out the names of five members of the crew and commanded them to hurry to the decks. Five men scrambled from all parts of the ship everywhere from the rigging to below deck. They quickly scurried down the gangplank onto the dock. Mr. Mandrik made brief introductions and handed the mates to their newly appointed teachers, who they were informed would also be quartered with. Daylight was running out and the quartermaster was in a hurry to cast off before it was night. The five were rushed up the gangplank and split up to watch their new instructors perform their casting off duties.

The dock was in a mad frenzy of activity with everyone hurrying to load supplies as the sun set. Extremely large and heavy barrels were being rolled up the gangplank and lowered into the cargo hold. The crew lowered the barrels using a system of a large wooden anchor wenches called windlasses, with ropes attached to the yardarm. When the supplies were all loaded and their bumboat was paid for its cleaning services, the gangplank was finally drawn in. Sam Scurvy and Jessup helped the crew take shifts ratcheting the anchor up. Even with four men taking shifts ratcheting, the process still took an hour and a half. The ship was finally untethered from the dock and was cast off. The *Robin* slowly drifted off into the sunset as the last light of the day danced wildly away on the water.

Even though the ship was not that large, Patrick quickly lost track of his friends. His mentor was a man named Mr. McLain. Mr. McLain handed Patrick a patch of cloth with string attached to it.

"What is this for?" Patrick asked.

"This is an old sailors' trick. Put it over one eye. We spend a lot of time going from the deck to the bilge so this will help your eyes adjust faster going in and out of sunlight all day long. You wear the patch over an eye of your choosing in the sunlight. When you go below into the darkness you take it off and you will be able to see faster than if both eyes had been in the sunlight," Mr. McLain explained.

"Thanks for the trick. I will give it a try," Patrick smiled as he pocketed the eye patch.

He then took Patrick all the way down to the bilge, the lowest part of the hull. It was musty and rat-populated but seemed like a king's quarters compared to the filth of debtors' prison Patrick recently inhabited. On all fours with only the light of a whale oil lamp, the two men crawled around the floor looking for leaks. "The light's not needed at all," McLain explained. "You can simply feel for water and trace it back to the leak." Patrick nodded that he understood.

"What about the rats?" Patrick asked, worrying about being bitten by the vermin as he was back in prison.

"Pay them no mind," Mr. McLain responded. "We had a cat that was a great hunter. Kept this barky so pest free we never got any poison. But he went missing at our last port stop. As far as I know, the captain ain't got a new one yet but refuses to buy poison, too."

Mr. McLain wasted no time showing Patrick what he needed to know. He informed his new mate that a few times a day, an inspection would be made to keep the ship watertight. The planks of the hull would be inspected and oakum would be placed in seams that needed it. Wood constantly changes shape with different temperatures and the vessel continuously leaked. Every shift they had to check the water level in the bilge with a stick. If the water level was too high they would have to wrestle with a large bilge pump. The pump was cranked with large a lever, which caused the water to be sucked out of the bilge and jettisoned off the boat through a hole on the topside.

The carpenter's duties also consisted of plugging leaks with wooden pegs and repairing the mast and yards if needed. Since the *Robin* was a smaller ship, the carpenter was also expected to be the surgeon. Unless the ship was very large, it would not have a trained, full-time doctor. Typically, most ships only had poorly trained surgeons, which were basically glorified carpenters.   Their duties included routine basic health inspections to control outbreaks or setting up a quarantine if needed. The only actual surgery a ship's surgeon normally performed was amputations.

It was a flurry of information to understand but Patrick was quickly learning. The lack of nourishment made it very hard for the ex-prisoner to focus and he was tempted to fall asleep where he stood. When Mr. McLain became unsure if Patrick was nodding because he understood or because he was falling asleep, he sent Patrick to his quarters to get some much needed rest.

Patrick was lucky to be in quarters with a hammock. It took him a few tries to learn how to lay down in it without it flipping over and dumping him out. The veteran crewmates took great delight in watching Patrick fall repeatedly while trying to steady the hammock. Eventually, a crew mate took pity on Patrick after a good laugh and held it steady while he mounted it. In a few seconds, the gentle swaying of the ship rocked the hammock in a rhythmic motion. It was a strange sensation. It was the first time in years he could lie down to sleep. There were no buzzing noise of flies or the overpowering ammonia smells from the floor covered in the vile sludge. He closed his eyes with a grin and took a long, deep breath before passing out from utter exhaustion.

Patrick later woke by the violent shaking of his shoulder. Mr. McLain was standing over Patrick's hammock shouting. "Finally! You've been asleep for two whole days. Time to wake up! How the hell did you sleep through all those damned bells and whistles anyway?" Patrick rubbed the sleep from his eyes as Mr. McLain informed him, "The quartermaster wants to see your whole lot. Now!"

Patrick was in great spirits, but was incredibly sore. Every movement hurt. He was excited; in just two months on the ocean, he would step onto Savannah a free man. He hurried up to the deck as fast as his aching bones would carry him and saw the other four former prisoners assembled and waiting. Smiles were exchanged as Shamus laughed, "Patrick Willis, I see yer da g'damn bilge rat now, eh?"

The men attempted to stand at attention as Mr. Mandrik walked up. The group immediately stopped talking. The quartermaster explained their situation to them. "Let me remind ya. Ya criminals are two days out to sea already. I hear ya talking about freedom, it just be two months away but me thinks ya not understand yer situation. Yer not just going walk out a free man when you step off dis ship. No." He paused to allow the five men to understand the gravity of his words. "Ya have to *earn* yer freedom and passage." The five men looked at each other, wondering exactly what Mandrik meant. When he was sure he had their full attention again, the quartermaster continued, "When we port this ship, ya will be indentured to a local merchant. Five years of service. Ya will learn a trade and *then* ya be free."

The shoulders of the men stooped. Their hearts were crushed. Patrick gasped, "Five more years?!" Isaac starred stoically off, past the rail of the ship and into the horizon.

Noticing their lowered morale, the quartermaster explained that being an indentured servant was not as bad as being a slave, unless of course you were a woman or worked indentured to a tyrant. They would be provided with food, a place to sleep and a job skill. After the contracted work was over the master was expected to send them off with some money and the tools of their new trade. Two thirds of the colonists bought their passage with this arrangement, so there was very little social stigma in being an indentured servant.

Feeling as if his words did not reassure the men, he released a great, big belly laugh. "If you don't think dis arrangement is fair, feel free to swim home," he stated as he pointed to the open ocean. At that exact moment, Shamus started walking to the railing, took off his shirt and readied himself to jump overboard when Isaac grabbed the skinny Irishman by the scruff of his neck and pulled him down to the deck.

"Shamus!" Isaac yelled in his face. "You'll be dead in minutes, you stupid, lousy drunk. Do you even know how to swim?"

Shamus flailed his arms trying to get Isaac to release him, rolling into an angry rant he was infamous for. "Dose dirty, English bastards fookin' lied to us! And dey have some damn greasy Greek do dere bidding. Fookin' cowards!" Isaac grabbed Shamus by his arms as the Irishman's face flashed with angry crimson. "Lemme go! I plan on swimmin' back to England and kicking George the Second right in da cherries!"

"Settle down, Red," Isaac coolly warned.

The Irishman grew hot with anger, but Patrick knew Isaac's anger was cold and not to be toyed with. Shamus continued, "Fooking never trust the g'damn English for any g'damn, fooking thing! If I get a chance, I'm going to piss in all dere mouths tonight when dey be sleepin'! Those pieces of dog squeeze fooks! I can't wait to mmmm..."

Isaac had enough. He put his giant hand over the irate Irishmen's mouth and held him down like Shamus was a small child.

Mr. Mandrik was amused at the Irishman's fire and vitriol. He smiled as Shamus ranted and the bigger Isaac handled him. When he felt the show was over, he commanded, "Gets backs to work and remember to do as we tell ya!" Pointing at each man, he warned, "I wants no trouble from you five."

As the five scrambled to their duties, Mandrik turned to McLain, "Mr. McLain, I need you to double their rations. They won't fetch a good price looking like drowned kittens." McLain nodded as the quartermaster continued, "Da one with da bow legs, see he gets triple the birch beer and limes. He won't fetch no good price if the cripple can't ambulate."

The quartermaster then took his leave and left the angry men all staring at each other from their positions. Jessup later angrily admitted to Isaac, "I agree with Shamus. He deserves a good kick in the balls."

Isaac calmly reasoned, "How quickly you forget the death sentence we just escaped from. Use this opportunity. Appreciate our new positions. Enjoy the fact we now get double rations."

The idea of double rations did bring smiles to the former prisoners' faces. For years, Patrick had survived living off moldy bread, rats he could catch and scraps of bone. He could not remember what real food tasted like. Anger over being indentured servants was quickly replaced with dreams of food. Patrick was happy to discover that the crew always ate as much food as they could the first two weeks out of port while they still had fresh fruit and vegetables. Soon enough, the sailors would be surviving on heavily salted meat and fish. Patrick was practically drooling on his way the first time to the galley. It was small and cramped in the galley and the food was shuttled out in wood bowls, but it seemed like a holiday feast.

Patrick sat with the other four former prisoners as they received bowls of fish, potato and turnip stew. They started slurping it down immediately. Patrick could not even remember what hot food tasted like and his taste buds were in shock. When his belly was full, Patrick had a difficult time keeping his food down but fought the urge to expel it. In just a few minutes, he started to feel his body come alive again with energy. He thought to himself how truly amazing his body was when given proper food. When their bowls were empty, the five were told to come back at sunset for their second meal. Sam Scurvey was informed he would get two limes instead of one during the second meal.

Above deck, Quartermaster Mandrik could be heard shouting commands, reminding the crew that being this close to the coast was the most dangerous part of the trip. There were a few cabin boys running around but two boys were covered in black powder. They were known as the powder monkeys and their job was to run gun powder to the cannons from below deck. The master gunner had his mates and powder monkey on high alert and they practiced drills relentlessly. The cannons were cleaned and oiled with a religious fervor.

The loud whistle of the boatswain's call interrupted all work. Each man knew that the distinct whistle meant that all crew stop what they are doing to hear what message the captain had. The entire crew assembled on the deck and listened quietly as the captain addressed them from the raised poop deck. Captain Gibbons cleared his throat and spoke loudly over the constant sound of the waves lapping at the ship's side, "Gentlemen, we are now in pirate waters. The ship will be on high alert until she reaches open sea. Night watch patrols would be doubled as well. Spanish privateers are infamous for attacking at nightfall." Patrick swallowed the fear that was creeping up his stomach into his throat as Gibbons continued,

"We will be flying the Yellow Jack until we land in Savannah." After the captain dismissed the crew, the men hurried back to their duties.

Patrick, being a true landlubber, had no idea what most of the captain's message meant. Sam Scurvy saw Patrick was bewildered and stated in his raspy sailor's voice, "'Privateers' are mercenaries, commissioned by the crown. When two countries be at war, the navy allows private ships to attack any enemy vessel. They be basically pirates, they loot and steal without fear of reprisal since they carry Letters of Marque. Both Spain and England use the Letters of Marque."

"Ah," Patrick nodded as if he comprehended all that Sam explained but he only really heard 'pirate'.

"The captain will fly the Yellow Jack. It's a warning flag meaning the ship is infected with yellow fever." Sam Scurvy grinned with his broken smile, "Hopefully that'll keep us from being boarded by privateers."

Captain Gibbons had some luck in the past flying the Yellow Jack. Most privateers would not take the chance and would leave his ship unmolested, but Patrick knew none of this. He only knew the tales he heard about pirates in the prison and had never actually seen one. His family had run in the upper circles of society and was never subject to such gruesome things. Images of bodies being tied to a yard arm and heads hung on the ship's bowsprit now filled his head, but these visions evaporated once he was called away to return to his duties as a bilge rat.

* * *

Surprisingly, life on the ship quickly became routine for the ex-prisoners. Patrick saw most of them between shifts and while they were eating their double rations. All of the men had already put on weight. Patrick quickly discovered on the ship that, besides being a surgeon and a carpenter, he was also expected to be a barber. Mandrik informed Patrick that the captain was complaining about the smell of the former prisoners and ordered him to sheer all the hair off his friends. Patrick had no idea how to actually do this and employed the help of Mr. McLain. The surgeon took a very sharp blade and sawed the mats of hair away roughly. Yanking, pulling, tearing, and sawing the thick mats was slow, tedious work. It was painful and he spied some blood coming from the nicks suffered when he was removing Sam Scurvy's long, mangy beard.

Isaac was ready to fight when Patrick and McLain came to trim his beard. Protesting, he complained that his religion forbid him from shaving his beard. Patrick calmed his friend down and a compromise of a trim and a wash was made after much negotiating. Isaac also seemed to have fashioned himself a little hat out of leather that he pinned to his hair. Such an outright display of Judaism would not have been tolerated by most captains' standards but Gibbons seemed not to care. The crew was intimidated by Isaac's monster size and gritty attitude and not one man worked up the courage to say anything derogatory to the Jew about his new hat.

When it was Patrick's turn, it seemed to take hours. Removing seven years of matted and tangled hair was a slow and agonizing ordeal. Blood flowed from his scalp all over the makeshift barber's chair, down his shoulders and down his back. When it was finally and mercifully done, Patrick felt lighter, cooler and reborn. Free from hair, his scarred up face was now apparent. Being mugged in London and fighting for seven years in prison had left their mark on his portrait. When he looked at his reflection in the bottom of a brass pot, he did not recognize the face that stared back at him. For the first time he saw himself as a full grown man, not a teenage boy. The food and sun had agreed well with him and he was already looking much healthier.

Later that day Patrick heard a ruckus when he was walking about the main deck. He was told by Isaac that Shamus had been trading away most his food for extra grog. Shamus was now madly skipping along the slick spars in the rigging singing a happy shanty. No one knew if he was really drunk or if this was just part of his normal behavior. Shamus was now lobster red with large patches of burnt skin peeling off his body. He wore only a loincloth. The skinny man had complained his long clothes, or 'land clothes', were being caught in all the riggings. To be fair, very few riggers would ever wear long clothes and usually wore skintight clothes to avoid entanglement. To the crew's horror and delight, they were taken back in seeing a sailor working in nothing but his skivvies. Shamus recklessly hopped around in the rigging and seasoned sailors were shocked that he had not fallen to a broken back yet. Most quartermasters would never tolerate such dangerous behavior, but Mr. Mandrik had started a wager with members of the crew to see when the fool would fall.

"I need to see ya tonight," Shamus yelled down to Patrick, "to take a wee look at me bite."

"Come see me when your shift is done," Patrick called up, "if you live through it."

Patrick was above deck to join Mr. McLain for a routine health inspection walk. They would lexically examine the crew looking for signs of pox or fever. They then went below to check the surgeon's chest. The chest was mainly a collection of bottles of rum and opium. It also had some blades, saws, braces and bandage rags. As Patrick was being instructed in the finer points of how much opium to administer for various conditions, Shamus's bright red, burnt body walked in. Since entertainment was lacking on this vessel, Isaac followed the Irishman down to watch the surgery.

"My God, Shamus! Let me put olive oil on that burn," Patrick exclaimed.

"I don't need no g'damn fooking Roman-horse-orgy salve all over me skin. I am 'ere for me bite." Shamus began to rub his jaw. "I gots so much fire in me front tooth here I can't sleep or even tink. I needs ya to yank it out, lad, but I gets real nervous when people gets near me mouth." Shamus lowered his voice sincerely and somberly said, "Perhaps a wee bit of the creature could help me relax."

Mr. McLain fell for the ruse. "We got plenty of rum. I think we can spare some to make this go easier." Patrick actually had never seen Shamus drink before but he knew he loved Satan's nectar. Thinking Shamus would take only a few swigs of the bottle before they pulled out his rotten, green tooth, Mr. McLain made the foolish mistake of handing the entire bottle of rum to the Irishman. The master surgeon turned his back to Shamus to dig through the chest and find a small tooth hammer. Shamus lifted the bottle straight up and begun to guzzle it down. When McLain found his hammer and turned back around and was shocked to see one entire bottle empty on the table and Shamus was downing a second one. He shrieked, "Christ! Stop that man before he drinks all the rum!"

Patrick and McLain grabbed for the Irishman but Shamus dodged and weaved deftly trying to finish the bottle. Isaac laughed heartily as he watched the two men try to catch the wiry, sunburned man squirm and wiggle until the last of the rum disappeared.

"Damn you, man! The whole crew might need that later," McLain shouted angrily. "We can't waste all this medicine on a damn tooth." With the bottle of rum drained, Shamus finally stood still and belched. McLain was breathing heavy through his nose like an angry bull, "Don't just look at me dumbly. Sit the hell down and let me knock that damn tooth out."

In response, Shamus let out another loud, long belch and confessed, "I'm not fookin' ready yet, doctor. Me needs more rum to relax."

Patrick tried to tackle him again, but to no avail, beginning the chase once again. Isaac laughed even harder as Shamus somehow kept away from the two men chasing him with a hammer in the small chamber. Every so often, Patrick would catch him but Shamus would easily break free and the wild chase would start all over again. Patrick and McLain would become exhausted and give up. Shamus would then continue begging for them to remove the painfully rotten tooth initiating the chase all over again. The chase highly entertained Isaac but he knew that he had to help end this game. Tapping Shamus on the shoulder, the Irishman turned around to be met with Isaac's heavy right hand punching him in the teeth. When Isaac pulled back his fist to inspect his knuckles, he saw two of Shamus's rotten teeth stuck in them.

"Fook ya! Ya goat-humping bastard!" Shamus yelled as he spit blood on the wooden planked floor.

"Do you got any other health issues you want me to fix while I am here, Irishman?" Isaac smirked. Patrick and Mr. McLain immediately began laughing.

"Fook all of ya shite eaters!" Shamus cursed.

"Your breath already smells better," Patrick laughed. "And you're welcome."

The laughing was interrupted by the sounds of the watch bell ringing madly and the ship sprung to life. The bell rang over and over until the entire crew was hastily mustered on the deck. The sun was setting in the West, but a small outline of a ship could be seen quickly approaching.

"Man battle stations! Pirates amidst! Man battle stations!"

CHAPTER 3

PIRATES AHOY!

News from the crow's nest

All hands were madly scrambling and manning the stations. Patrick was frightened. He had hardly done any battle drills. Nervousness could be seen in all of the eyes of the new crew members, green sailors who had only performed some basic war maneuvers. They all questioned their abilities in real action.

Reports from the crow's nest were shouted down. "She fly no colors, Captain! I see no jack at all!" The approaching ship was still very far away and cresting the horizon, but it was plain to see from her mirroring movements the *Robin* was being pursued. Using his folding spy glass, the captain could tell it was

Spanish Sloop

a sloop about the same size of the *Robin* with one large mast and a smaller secondary mast.

The mystery sloop was gaining on the *Robin* but not by much. Most pirate ships stayed within a few days sail of the coast and traveled light to increase their speed. These ships were stripped down to the essentials and modified for speed. What pirates do not ever reduce is the size of their crews and cannons. Though the *Robin*'s compliment was fifty souls, a pirate ship of the same size would have around two hundred men. The *Robin*'s crew was keenly aware of this fact and knew if the ship was boarded, all would be lost.

Captain Gibbons finally came to life in an authoritative role, usurping that of the quartermaster's. Until now, Mr. Mandrik was in charge of all the ship's daily activities, but when danger was abound, the captain ran everything with supreme, authoritative power. Captain Gibbons barked a stream of orders and the crew quickly fell into a sort of organized chaos. The rigger men were quickly dancing high in the masts as the sailors wrestled with line and tacking, trying desperately to get full sail.

Mr. McLain shouted at Patrick to get under deck and prepare. Patrick froze and McLain saw the fear in his wide eyes. "Get a hold of yourself, man! Focus on your duties. We'll be fine." Patrick nodded and rushed below deck with Mr. McLain.

While rushing along below deck, the master carpenter/surgeon hastily explained what was expected of Patrick. "You'll heat this tar and oakum and be ready to patch holes. The rest of the crew not fighting or sailing will be helping you peg down spare planks and bail water. After the fighting be over, the real fun begins and we'll start treating the dying."

Patrick knew he should be paying close attention to McLain's words, but horrible visions of his head hanging off the mystery sloop's bowsprit kept invading his mind.

Back topside, the sun was quickly being swallowed by the sea and it was becoming hard to make out the pursuing ship in the long shadows on the water. Captain Gibbons yelled to Mr. Mandrik, "Darken the ship and make haste! All lights are to be extinguished immediately and no sailor will talk over the level of a hummingbird or I will have his tongue."

"Aye, Cap'n," the quartermaster confirmed his orders. "I will blacken dis ship like night fall, sir."

The moon was now half waxed and with good eyes, one could make out the dark shadow of a ship against the shimmering blue reflections of the moonlight. Even with his spyglass, the captain could not make out the style of the rigging to determine its weaknesses. Captain Gibbons attempted hard turns and angles to lose the pursuing ship in the darkness. The *Robin* desperately zigzagged for hours in hopes the pursuing ship would be lost in the darkness. The deck crew worked silently, only occasionally speaking in hushed tones, as they wrestled with keeping the sails full. Every so often, a stream of Irish accented obscenities would drift down from the riggings cracking the silence. Shamus did not seem to understand the concept of a hushed voice and the sounds of cursing would carry across the black water. Barely keeping his temper, Mr. Mandrik reminded the Irish fool to control himself or his tongue would be nailed the mast.

Two hours after sunset the *Robin* was rewarded with a bit of luck as a bellow of clouds rolled in covering the moon and starlight. The overcast blessedly lasted until sunrise. The deck crew was drenched with sweat as they responded to the captain's every order. The captain took the *Robin* hard off course in the hopes that it would be lost to the pursuing ship's sight come morning. The approaching vessel had also darkened herself and was lost to the black of the night. Both ships would have to wait till sunrise to see the results of this seafaring chess battle of strategy.

The *Robin*'s crew waited in paralyzing fear as the sun slowly overtook the water. The first ray finally caught the water and in minutes lit up the sky. The captain and the crow's nest lookout were shouting back and forth to each other. The lookout now was very sick and had vomited bile all night into the barrel he was standing in. The sea's sickening motion was strongly amplified in the crow's nest and very few sailors could take more than a few minutes let alone an entire night's watch. The crow's nest was commonly employed as a punishment device by Mr. Mandrik for disobedient sailors. The lookout, sickly and green, shouted weakly, "Captain Gibbons, I can't find her anywhere. I think you sigoogled her." Indeed, the captain did outflank the mystery ship and could not find her on the horizon.

A great shout of joy went through the crew, but the captain sternly warned them, "Stay focused, gentleman, and stay on course."

Captain Gibbons then ordered the sailing master to join him on the poop deck. On the highest deck on the ship, the sailing master pulled out an antique astrolabe, held it up into the sun and stared. He then turned his back to the sun and held up a Davis backstaff determining the altitude of the sun. Then the practically blind man pulled out his old quadrant and determined the *Robin*'s longitude by staring directly into the sun with it. With extreme caution, the sailing master gingerly removed the sextant from its protective case. The sailing master knew it was the most valuable item on the ship and if ever dropped, the sextant would be ruined and he would be punished harshly. Because of this, he always attached his sextant to a make-shift lanyard around his neck for safety.

"How far off course are we now?" Captain Gibbons questioned, "How many days did I just add on to our journey?"

As with almost all sailing masters, his eyes were filled with white, cloudy fluid and could barely see in daylight. He held aloft the sextant and sighted the sun and horizon. He looked through the telescope and dropped the shade glass in place as he stared directly into the sun. He knew his eyes would burn and itch hours later for this daytime reading, but he also knew the captain needed it quickly. He would have preferred to wait till the night, relying on the stars for better accuracy, but the grave circumstances demanded a day reading. The sailing master then took a reading with a sundial and compass. He then did a dance, consulting his charts and instruments repeatedly. Never trusting just one instrument, he utilized a combination of old and new navigation technology.

After a few minutes of studying, he looked at the captain with his cloudy, white eyes and reported calmly, "Captain, we be about three days off course now, but I think I can plot a new course across open waters to catch some of the time up."

"Very good, sir," Captain Gibbons barked. "Get to plotting!" The Captain knew how risky to chart straight across the open ocean rather than island and coast hop, but he feared pirates more than storms right now.

The crew settled into an uneasy state of alert with all eyes continuously fixed on the horizon. The captain finally relieved the seasick lookout and gave him time to sleep and slowly, the crew returned to their normal watches. With no sight of the pursuing ship to be seen, Captain Gibbon's knew if he could just get a few more days out to open waters, the *Robin* would be safe.

They followed the sailing master's course throughout the day and the seas became choppy. As the sun began to set, the seas became even more uneasy and the sky filled with menacing gray clouds. Angry winds filled the sails and started bending the masts sideways until a steady rhythm of rocking was established.

Patrick was woken up by the surgeon's chest violently sliding into his hammock. The hammock was swinging wildly and Patrick abandoned it as fast as he could. The scarred man was unnerved as heavy items shuffled across the floor while the ship careened. He had taken to sea life fairly well but had not yet earned his sea legs. Until now, he had only felt mildly uncomfortable by the rocking of the sea, but now he was rapidly getting sick. Curiosity took him up deck side to see if they were under attack.

As he came through the hatch, he was pelted with stinging rain. The deck crews had just pulled the sails down and were tying down everything on deck. The crew screamed orders at each other through the howling wind. A sailor was moaning, like a prophet of doom, that crossing the ocean during the late spring was dangerous. Rain came down in blinding, sideways sheets and Patrick could only see a short distance around the ship. The nightfall was not helping. Against the judgment of the captain, the quartermaster was frantically dropping anchor to no avail. They were now in deep waters and the anchor would find no home.

Patrick realized very quickly that things had just turned treacherous for the *Robin*. The wheel was spinning wildly as the ship rocked back and forth and started spinning in a circle. Two men grabbed the wheel in an attempt to steady her but even with their collective strength, they could not hold on. Isaac seemed to materialize out of the darkness and rain and he grabbed the spinning wheel. The three men were joined by the captain and they collectively slowed the out-of-control helm. A scream came from the wooden rudder but it held together. For the rest of the pitch-black night, the crew wrestled with the storm to stay afloat. The quartermaster soon realized what a horrible mistake it was to try and drop anchor and it was causing the *Robin* to list wildly. In less than an hour a frenzied crew managed to ratchet the anchor back in place.

While struggling against the wheel and the angry sea, Isaac was arguing with one of the sailors when a giant wave crashed over them. When Isaac opened his eyes, the man had simply vanished. Isaac scanned the deck and found the lost man nowhere.

"MAN OVERBOARD!" Isaac screamed as the crew began to echo the call. Men scrambled to help Isaac with the wheel, while others ran to the rail to scan the black waters. A voice desperately screaming for help could be heard from below but he could not be found in the blackness. Fortunately for the man in the drink, flashes of lighting cracked illuminating the dark waters and he was spotted off the starboard side. The crew quickly threw a rope down to the man who was fighting desperately to stay afloat. The sailors missed the throw repeatedly. He was just out of reach of the line, but then Shamus tried and threw the rope so straight that it hit the flailing man in the face. The sinking man quickly tied the wet rope under his arms and around his chest.

A wave rose up and swallowed the man. He sank into the dark and out of sight. The *Robin*'s bow then swung wildly and slammed into the man. As the deck crew pulled the rope, a limp body rose out of the water. The body was unceremoniously dragged up the starboard wall and on to the deck. The saved man was groaning and his eyes could not focus. "Crewman Willis," Mandrik called out, "take dis man down and see to 'em."

The remaining sailors frantically tied themselves to a rope which was lashed to a tall mast for safety.

Patrick was ordered to return below deck just as they battened down the hatches. Endless screams and shuffling could be heard from above deck. Patrick tried to focus on his patient but the man passed out on the hammock and was snoring. The surgeon's mate joined most of the crew below in rotating moments of fear and vomiting in the dark. He mustered his constitution and then took to his bilge pump duties. The night was long and frightening, and the men kept their minds off dying by bailing bucket after bucket of water that had seeped in from the heavy rain.

* * *

The ship was finally settling down and the hatches were opened. The sun would be rising soon but it was still raining and pitch black. The waters had finally settled and the ship was no longer rocking wildly. The constant state of fear had kept the exhausted crew up all night.

Patrick wanted to escape the vomit smells from below so he went up topside. He saw that the dead-tired crew was still tied to the mast on long ropes as they performed their duties sluggishly.

Finally, the clouds became patchy and a little moonlight could be seen dancing on the water. Patrick walked to the railing, stretched his arms over his head, yawned and looked out across the waters. Moonlight was slowly becoming daylight and the water illuminated quickly. Patrick's eyes grew with fear as he saw a silhouette of a sloop become visible five hundred lengths off the larboard side. He screamed in a panicked voice, "Captain! Pirates! Larboard side!"

The deck immediately sprang to life with activity, shouts, and bell ringing. "Battle stations!" the quartermaster commanded in his awkward slow broken Greek accent. "Be ya reedy on da cannons!"

Captain Gibbons hurried to get the sails up on the modified galleon. The *Robin* had three masts with larger sails and a crow's nest. Most private captains modified the ships to their tastes, and the *Robin* was no exception sporting fore and aft jib sails as well.

The pursuing ship was easier to see now and it was more of a large coastal style sloop with one large mast and a smaller aft mast. The pirate ship was also taken off guard and was quickly raising its massive sail as well. The storm had unknowingly brought to two vessels together in the night. It would now be a footrace to see whose crew could catch the wind first.

An exhausted Captain Gibbons immediately took the helm. He steered the ship the best he could away from the pirates, still getting full sail. The wind was helping the *Robin* but unfortunately, was also giving an advantage to the mystery vessel. Captain Gibbons still was unsure if this vessel in chase was an English privateer, so he ordered his true colors to be flown. The yellow jack was pulled down and replaced with the English Jack. Gibbons waited nervously as he watched the mast of the pursuing ship.

The Captain felt his heart sink as the enemy vessel did not slow or even raise a jack.

For a brief moment, Captain Gibbons considered giving the order to jettison all extra weight to gain speed. He realized this far out to sea, with the size of his crew, they would be dealt a slow death of starvation and thirst if their supplies were abandoned. They would have to stay and fight. It was a grim thought that made Gibbons uneasy.

The quartermaster yelled for silence and the crew listened attentively. Faint echoes rode out across the water. The Greek listened for a minute and then muttered under his breath, "God damn it... That's Spaniard piss dey dribbling out der mouths." He then yelled, reporting to Gibbons, "Spanish privateers, Cap'n. I will see da crew be ready for fightin'."

Captain Gibbons did have some knowledge that gave him a little bit of an upper hand in this chess match. He knew most privateers relied on fear and not actual force. It was too costly and not wise to have holes blown into the prize you were trying to take. The captain calculated they would not shoot first; they would try to cower the *Robin* into surrender. The Spanish might take on his crew, but Gibbons was well aware that captured captains were usually killed or ransomed. Either way, this would not end well for his skin.

The Spanish sloop was now quickly closing the distance. With his spyglass, the captain could see over a hundred armed men on the sloop's deck preparing to fight. The captain knew his ship was out manned and out gunned. The *Robin* only had six carriage-style French garrison guns which actually worked. They were poorly retrofitted on the deck and below. The *Robin*'s cannons rested on Vauban marine carriages so they would not fly backwards off the deck when fired. The carriages had thick mahogany cheeks and large wood-banded wheels. Captain Gibbons's plan was to bring the Spanish sloop as close as possible and cripple the sails with the *Robin*'s smaller cannons.

A fake surrender would be staged to bring the Spanish close. Mandrik instructed all men above deck to raise their arms in the air as the Spanish vessel closed in tight. The ships were now turning broad side to each other as the Spanish crew could be seen preparing their grappling hooks to throw into the *Robin*'s rigging. Captain Gibbons was putting enormous trust into his master gunner's hands and waited for his gunner to start firing. Gibbons was making a big gamble. Only four of the *Robin*'s cannons were in range of the Spanish sloop.

Below deck, Isaac was loading the gunpowder in the gun tube with a ladle and watched as the other gunner's mate loaded the 12-pound ball. A loud metal-on-metal screech pierced Isaac's ears as the ball was shoved down with the ram rod. The Master Gunner then used his gunner's gimlet and poked it into the vent on the cannon to make it ready for the priming powder. He then broke open his dry powder bag and used his powder horn to prim the seat. He carefully loaded the priming quill, which was really a spirit-soaked wick, into the gun tube and down into the powder. The master gunner lined up the cannon, aimed it high at the Spanish sloop's mast and took the smoldering linstock from his gunner's mate. He moved out of the path of recoil and blew on the slow match of the linstock until it was bright orange. The master gunner turned the linstock sideways and lit the quill. Calls quietly went out under deck to light the wicks of the other cannons.

Isaac had tied rags over his ears to protect him from the deafening blast of the cannon, but still had to cover his ears with his hands. *BLAMM!* Even Isaac, with his hulking mass, was blown a step backwards from the violent, concussive force of the explosion. Gray smoke blinded all three men manning the

The Robin opens fire!

gun while the master gunner immediately ordered a reload. Two other explosions were heard from the belly of the *Robin*.

At the sound of the first volley, Captain Gibbons turned the ship's bow hard and started to make an expedient escape. Five Spanish cannon shots rang out in return. Crewmen of the *Robin* screamed as they picked up the hidden weapons from the deck and began firing. A gray fog hung between the two ships.

The Spanish privateers took two hits across the deck. One fantastic shot hit the poop deck and damaged the helm. The other shot missed the mast and just skimmed across the deck. One shot missed completely and another cannon never even fired because of damp powder. In return, the *Robin* took considerably more damage. One of the jib sails was ripped completely off. A hole was punched into the galley and one of the Quaker cannons on the deck was hit and had blown into the sea.

Men were firing muskets with little luck. Both sides missed just about everything they fired at. The battle scene grew quiet as both sides focused on reloading. The *Robin* turned away hard and the sloop did not turn to match its movements. The Spanish vessel's steering wheel no longer worked and they were already drifting aimlessly.

Isaac frantically wormed and then swabbed the cannon so

not to pour gunpowder down a smoldering barrel. Another gunner mate then hastily ladled powder down the barrel. Isaac then loaded the cannon with another ball and the gunners mate rammed it into place. The master gunner repeated his last ritual and readied the fuse, aimed and lit the wick. He took careful aim this time, trying to time the rise and fall of both ships. The master gunner knew this would be his last chance from this cannon before the angle of attack changed too much. All three men covered their ears, closed their eyes and prayed for a direct hit. *BLAMM!* A deafening crack filled the compartment and the cannon blew backwards. A loud creaking and crash could be heard from the Spanish sloop. As the smoke cleared, Isaac could see the Spanish vessel's mast hanging a kilter and wailing in the wind. "Fantastic shot! You shivered her timbers!" the gunner's mate yelled in excitement. "Huzzah! Huzzah!" The three men cheered wildly not believing the lucky shot they landed.

Up on deck, cheers from the *Robin* could be heard as they watched the sloop's mast flail in the wind. The *Robin* now completed its turn, so only its stern was a target to the sloop as it made its hasty get away. The two ships exchanged cannon fire with not much avail. It seemed that both crews' gunners were very inaccurate. The *Robin* only took some minor damage to the railing as it fled away.

The Spanish vessel soon became a small shadow until finally it was swallowed by the horizon. The crew of the *Robin* was in a mad rush to make repairs. Captain Gibbons knew that he had to increase the distance between the Spanish privateers and themselves as fast as possible. He knew that the Spanish ship would already be rigging up a make-shift jolly mast out of the shattered one. Patrick and the master carpenter busily jumped to work patching the damaged galley. Sam Scurvy was covered with blood and had a large cooking fork sticking out of his shoulder. He was ignoring the large fork and trying to clean his galley. Patrick summated that he was in battle shock and could not feel the pain of the skewer yet.

"Samuel, don't forget that pot in the corner there," Patrick pointed.

As Sam Scurvy turned, Patrick made his move and yanked the fork free. With a tearing of flesh, a large splash of blood showered both of them. Sam Scurvy howled and then stared at the large fork in Patrick's hand and stated, "Arrr... Dat's where dat fork be."

Mr. McLain insisted that Patrick take Samuel to the surgeon's chest and clean the wound with spirits. As Patrick was treating Samuel, Shamus crashed into the room.

"Fook ya two! Why aren't yas lookin' for Brian?" Shamus yelled.

"Who is Brian again?" Patrick questioned, "Where is he?"

"He be a gunner's mate," Shamus belted back. "And if I fookin' knew where he be, ya goat fooker, I wouldn't be inquirin'! We tink he be blown into a drink when the Quaker cannon blew off."

"We will be there as soon as I finish defestering this lesion," Patrick replied.

Shamus stormed out as noisily as he could with a string of Irish obscenities.

Brian would never be found as the days passed. The crew still kept looking long after the *Robin* was patched back up. Still uneasy from the battle with the Spanish privateers, the crew continued to nervously scan the horizon for days after the attack. A few days out in the open sea, the captain finally relaxed and turned his command back over to the quartermaster, Mr. Mandrik. They would not have to worry about pirates again until they closed in on Savannah.

CHAPTER 4

PASSAGE TO A
NEW WORLD

The ex-prisoners adapted to sea life well, rarely getting sick. But as soon as it seemed they earned their sea legs, the fresh food ran out and then their diets only consisted of salty meats. Their knives scarred their pewter plates because salted pork and fish was so tough to cut. The ship was gripped with constipation and a constant, overwhelming thirst. To complicate matters, the fresh water was becoming scarce and the stores were dangerously low. Water was collected by any means possible. When rains came, any item that could hold liquid was placed topside to collect the precious run-off. Mandrik devised a very clever method to recover water out of the sails.

Most mornings, dew would collect in the sails and he would instruct his rigger monkeys to tilt the cloth at just the right angle so that the dew would bead together and run down the sails into a waiting cistern, which was nothing more than a modified barrel. If the sails were shaken and rung out as well, they yielded an astonishing amount of water. The quarter master proudly boasted to the crew it was an ancient Greek sailing trick to collect water. Most of the men ignored this claim since Mr. Mandrik was notorious for attributing credit to the Greeks for every single good idea on the ship. If a crew member invented something as small and simple as a new knot, Mandrik would proclaim loudly in his awkward Greek voice, "Dah! The Greeks did this first!"

The longer at sea and the longer the crew sailed, the more efficient each man became at their jobs. Soon the crew had a fair amount of free time on their hands the gambling started and although it was against the captain's policies, everyone gambled. Well, just about everyone. Isaac had finally learned his lesson from the debtors' prison and swore it off for life.

Liar's Dice was the game of choice and Patrick watched some of his crewmates make and lose a small fortune flipping cups and making dubious claims. Too nervous to play a game he knew nothing about, Patrick watched his fellow sailors play for hours. When Patrick became familiar with the game, he still did not try his hand at Liar's Dice. The carpenter's mate had no money, nor valuables. All he had to bid with was his rations of food. He was just starting to feel strong and look healthy again and considered his food too high of stakes to lose in a game of dice.

But Shamus saw things very differently. Except for his grog, the wild-eyed Irishman immediately started betting all his food in game. By betting large amounts of his food, Shamus somehow negotiated his way into a game with real silver. The Irish drunk had a real gift for lying. He told Patrick in confidence he was descended from a race of storytellers, natural liars, and was quickly amassing a small fortune in silver.

Patrick watched in awe as Shamus entered a very high stakes game where the winner would walk out with one-hundred-and-fifty ounces of silver doubloons. Shamus had somehow won an exotic hat and clothing from his last few games and now wore them as trophies. To complete the image he now sported a small beard and mustache which he had grown with astonishing speed for an Irishman.

As Shamus sat on the deck with two other sailors in a triangle formation, a gasp went up from the crowd as all the silver rounds were slid into a pot. One of Shamus's opponents wore a fancy gentleman's blue hat. The other gambler was shirtless and only wore a hempen necklace tied with shells. The three men each had five dice in front of them on the deck and a worn, wooden cup. Holding each other's gazes, the three men collected the dice carefully, dropped them in their cups, and then wildly shook. A thunderous crack echoed above the waves

Shamus playing liars' dice and Sam Scurvy watching.

lapping the bow of the *Robin* as all three men in unison slammed their cups down on the deck.

All eyes watched as the combatants peeked under their cups.

"Open with four twos," the shirtless man stated.

"Dar be four sixes on deck," Shamus corrected, upping the ante.

"I will have to follow our shirtless friend's lead," the top hat man countered with a confident smile and a well-educated English accent. "I believe there are five twos."

"There are six twos on the floor," the shirtless man offered with a grin.

"Ya two a bunch of fookin' liars," Shamus screeched. "I am callin' ya out!"

The three men lifted their cups revealing their dice so that the counting could begin.

The shirtless man had four twos.

The man wearing the top hat revealed two twos.

"Crap! You fookin' liars and cheats who fook their father's horses," Shamus cursed as he revealed he also had a die showing a two.

"Well that is seven," the educated gentleman informed Shamus. "Cast your die in, sir."

"Fook you! I can do numbers, you pig kook-sooker," Shamus pouted as he tossed one of his die into the pot.

The men collected their dice but Shamus now only had four dice and the others still had five. They shook their cups. *Crack!*

Shamus quickly lost two more obscenity-filled rounds and was now just down to two remaining dice. Although he was down in dice, the toothless pale man used the opportunity to study his opponents closely. The gentleman always opened with a bid with a bluff, lying about dice he did not have. He hoped his opponents would bid too high and then he could call their lie out. The other man seemed more honest except when he would toy with his necklace, a subtle tell. Shamus continued to cuss like a madman, but it was all theater now. He knew he had all the information he needed to quickly turn the game around.

Crack!

"I open with four threes," the gentleman coolly stated.

Shamus immediately pounced on him and challenged, "He's fookin' lyin'! Call him out!"

"I think ya may be right," the shirtless man agreed with Shamus before turning to the gentleman. "You be a liar!"

The gentleman's mouth was slightly agape as he

questioned, "It is opening bid. Are you sure you want to call?"

"Stop fookin' off," Shamus called out pointing at the gentleman's cup. "Show ya damn dice."

The business of turning cups began. Shamus's cup revealed he had one three. The shirtless sailor had two three's. The top hat man had none.

"Only t'ree fookin' t'rees," Shamus howled in victory. "Cast ya die, dog humper."

The game went back and forth with lies upon lies until all three men only had one die each. Shamus wondered if he should open with a lie or actually be honest and play his die true. Honest to his nature, he decided to lie. "I open with one five, ya sheep shaggers," Shamus cooed happily.

"What is it with you and all the bestiality? Do you think of nothing else?" the gentleman questioned. He was frustrated losing so many dice to two such lowly characters and was becoming quickly disgusted with Shamus's outbursts.

"I grew tired of fookin' your mom and moved on to her livestock," Shamus snapped. "Now make ya bet, ya shite eater."

"Very well," the gentleman pompously conceded. "One six."

The shirtless man quietly stated, "Two threes," without fondling his necklace. Shamus's eyes widened. He knew he was holding a three and assumed if this man was not lying, he must also have a three.

"Ok, ya two horse kooks." Shamus confidently proclaimed, "I am calling the bid spot on." A hush fell over the very large crowd which had collected around the high stakes game. All eyes eagerly waited.

Shamus had a three. As Shamus predicted, the shirtless man also had a three. The top hat man told the truth and actually had a six.

The bid was spot on. Both of Shamus' opponents grumbled. They cast their losing dice into the pot and the crowd erupted with roars and cheering.

Shamus could barely lift the pot full of silver and threatened the crew, "If any of ya humpin' badgers touch this silver, I'll run ya through and throw ya into da drink!"

The crowd laughed and made mock threats to steal Shamus's fortune when he slept. So happy to see a common man win, the crowd continued cheering and thumping the deck with their feet, howling and clapping, long after the shirtless man congratulated Shamus and the gentleman sulked off.

Only a few days were left of the crossing and to the crew's pleasure, it had been relatively uneventful. It was commonly known that crossing the ocean in early summer can be very treacherous because of the wild weather but the ship had been lucky to not have the ocean's wrath affect them. The crew attributed the good weather and good luck to the proper care given to the old sea rituals.

A bottle was successfully smashed on the hull to ensure a safe return and a horseshoe was properly secured to the mast to keep storms away. A black cat was kept on board, ensuring the sailors would safely return home from sea and rum was generously poured on the deck and in the ocean to offer the sea god a bribe for safe passage. Most of the sailors wore earrings to prevent them from drowning and were properly tattooed for protection as well. The ship was adorned with a figurehead of a bare-breasted woman with a robin's head. This was so the naked woman could calm stormy seas, offer an eye to see the way to their destination and the robin's head was added so that unlettered sailors could easily identify the *Robin*. All these precautions convinced the sailors of safe passage. When a family of dolphins was spotted off starboard side swimming with the ship, the crew was confident that they and their ship were blessed.

Patrick was woken by the sounds of excitement and rushed topside to see what the commotion was. The imposing sun blinded him immediately, but after he rubbed the darkness of his cabin from his eyes, Patrick could see the hazy coastline lying far off in the horizon. Captain Gibbons could be heard praising the sailing master for such a deft job. The *Robin* was but one day's sail up the coast. Straying so far off course after the battle with the Spanish privateers, the captain's gratitude of

The figurehead of the *Robin*.

* * *

the impressive navigation was well deserved. Morale amongst the crew was high. Each man bragged how they would soon be spending their hard-earned silver on women, fresh food and strong spirits.

"Quartermaster, muster the crew," Captain Gibbons ordered. "It is time we made them understand the rules of shore leave."

Immediately, the boatswain's whistle blew and the excited crew gathered around the captain.

"Before you men get so excited you lose your focus, I need to remind you of your obligations," the captain stated sternly, looking at each man in turn. "You will have only one week to enjoy shore leave but you must check in with the quartermaster at high noon every day. Remember you have sworn contract to this vessel and if you do not return to honor those commitments, the consequences will be severe." The captain allowed the men their moment to grumble. He understood their excitement because the crew had been stuck on a ship for weeks, but he would not suffer any indiscretion. When the men quieted again, he continued, "There are certain rules and protocols in Savannah you must follow or you will disgrace this ship and its captain."

Quartermaster Mandrik was quick to drive the point home and shouted, "And any of ya crew break da laws and disgraces da cap'n, I will flog ya to da devil!"

"Now then," continued the Captain, "Savannah only has four rules you must remember. One: No strong water, spirits, rum or brandy is allowed." A loud rumble of objection quickly overtook the crew. "But beer, ale and wine are just fine," Gibbons explained.

"Two: absolutely no lawyers are allowed. The city understands that lawyers create divisiveness, encourages clients to seek causes. So if you do get in trouble while ashore, you will have to plead your own case. Then you will have to come back and deal with Mr. Mandrik," the captain warned.

"Three: there is no slavery in this town. The Negroes you meet will be free men and we expect you to keep your peace with them.

"Fourth and finally: No Papists and Roman Catholics are allowed to worship there. Savannah doesn't want to worry about its Catholics sympathizing with the Spanish Catholics, so that sect of religion is outlawed."

"Fook, this is gonna dun break me mutter's heart and make Jesus cry, ya bastards!" Shamus barked up.

"I would normally have ordered you beaten close to death for that outburst," the captain cautioned, "but since you are being sold tomorrow, I can't have you blackened."

"Also, there are no Jews allowed," the captain pointed out. "They don't really enforce this one but it is their law. So, Isaac, be mindful of that and lose that little Jew hat of yours.

"Unfortunately," the captain addressed the crew and former prisoners, "we have some unpleasantness we have to take care of before we land. Let this serve as a demonstration that I am not a captain you want to embarrass in Savannah." He then turned to Mandrik and ordered, "Bring them up!"

Two hoodwinked men were brought out and forced to kneel before the captain. Their hoods were removed and both men had tears streaming down their faces.

Captain Gibbons announced so all the crew could hear from their positions, "Mr. Michael and Mr. James, you have denied your odd behavior in the past. I have heard complaints from crewmates that you two spend unnecessary and copious amounts of time unclothed around each other. Others have heard noises of a sexual nature deriving from your bunks. You two dress like colorful dandies, not sailors. I had overlooked all of this to keep peace in my crew until Mr. Mandrik caught you two mounting each other in the hold."

One of the accused men openly sobbed while the other merely starred at the planks of the deck.

Gibbons continued, "It is unnatural and an insult to your crewmates and to God! Do you have any words before I pass your sentence?"

Mr. Michael quivered. He wiped the snot off his nose on his shoulder, gathered his courage and then pronounced, "I can't help it. I love him, Cap'n. I am tired of hiding it. I don't care who knows anymore." Upon confessing his guilt, Mr. Michael continued a deluge of tears. Snickers could be heard from the crew.

Mr. James was older than Mr. Michael and starred defiantly at the captain, "Ya group of Judases! Hypocrites! Men have been fucking each otter on ships since da beginning of time. I have even been fucked by some of yas, but I don't see you kneeling down here with me now. Ya didn't mind kneeling down for me before when we be alone, but now ya be cowards and not stand up for us when it counts!" With that condemnation, James spit on the deck.

"Enough!" Captain Gibbon's eyes were burning as he dispensed, "For that outburst and unremorseful statement, I pass the sentence on you two, disgusting Sodomites. Two rounds of keelhauling for the both of you." The crew gasped at such a harsh punishment.

It was at that moment when the Greek man felt his

wooden St. Nicholas icon fall out of his pocket and hit the deck. The religious man tried to grab it as it dropped but he watched in horror as the edge of the icon broke off as it bounced around the planks. A deep sense of dread overtook him and he realized this was a warning sign from his protective saint. He knew the captain's orders were much too extreme and down deep he knew he should not follow this order, but years of strict obedience overruled his gut feeling. Instead of not following the harsh order he tried to convince Gibbons to reduce their sentence.

Mr. Mandrik drops his icon as Mr. Michael and Mr. James are presented for punishment.

Mr. Mandrik cleared his throat, nervous to question the wisdom of his superior, and asked, "Cap'n, couldn't ya just introduce dem to the cat-o-nine tails or tie dem to da mast? Keelhauling for dis might sit bad wit da crew."

Gibbons shot his quartermaster a steely glare. "You heard me, Quartermaster. Execute my orders!"

The sentenced men shook with fear. Mr. Michael wailed like a woman as they were both tied to the keelhaul rope. The line ran from the starboard side deck, under the ship, and back up to the larboard side deck. The long rope was normally used to scrape barnacles off the keel. Now the two offending sodomites' bodies would be used to clean the razor-sharp shells from the bottom of the ship. Mr. James hissed, "Bastards!" as Gibbons nodded to Mandrik.

With that cue, Mandrik bellowed, "Send them into the drink, men. Pull them down!"

A group of sailors pulled hard from the larboard side and the two condemned lovers flew off the deck, over the side and under the ship. A loud thumping of kicking could be heard on the ship's hull. The sound made Patrick shudder. After a few seconds, the two men emerged on the starboard side drenched in salt water, gasping for air and screaming in pain.

"Quartermaster, that was too fast," the captain smiled maliciously. "Have your men slow it down this time!"

Mandrik swallowed hard and nodded to his captain that he understood. His voice cracked as he barked the command, "You heard the cap'n, boys. Slower." The torture procedure was then reversed pulling James and Michael over the side and into the sea. The men pulling the ropes pulled slower this time, drowning and dragging Michael and James across the sharp barnacle shells attach to the belly of the ship.

When they were finally pulled from the water, over the rail and back on the deck of the *Robin*, the clothes of the two men were blood soaked. They were both coughing up water and Patrick cringed at the sound of two men whimpering like children. Once untied from the rope, both James and Michael doubled over, holding the deep lacerations, futilely trying to stop the bleeding. The crew was silent.

"I am not completely heartless," Gibbons explained with a sadistic delight. "See to their wounds. Then tie them each to a barrel and set them a drift. If you wait a few hours, the tide will be moving towards the shore and they might even be lucky enough to drift into land." The two howling men were dragged to the surgeon's quarters, leaving a line of crimson soaking into the deck. A young crewman ran over to quickly mop up the trail.

The excitement of landing had somehow vanished for

Patrick. He just wanted to drift to his station, make his himself busy with work and forget the horror he just witnessed when Mandrik reminded, "Hold on, lads. The cap'n wants more words wit yas."

The captain rubbed his hands, as if wiping away the dirty business he just had overseen, and spoke, "You five will be sold as indentured servants, work hard and take this opportunity to learn a craft. You will be set free in just five short years."

Shamus was confused. "I thought I just heard your kook-sookin' mouth say slavery was forbade."

The captain replied, "Ay fine sir, you are *not* slaves since one day, you *will* be free. Until then, you will get living quarters, food, a small salary and even a little time to enjoy yourselves in the town in exchange for your labor. But you will not be allowed to court women or start a family until your contract is finished." The captain paused to give his next words greater gravity, "Let me explain the consequences, gentlemen. I expect to get top gold for you five and *you* want to make sure that happens. If you do not sell, you will spend the rest of your days doing dog's work on this barky."

"We already be doin' da shite jobs!" Shamus exclaimed.

"One more outburst, Mr. Red, and I will let Mr. Mandrik teach you to respect your captain," Captain Gibbons warned coldly. After holding Shamus's eye for a long moment to emphasize his seriousness, the captain continued, "We have written ads for you that will be posted in town. Local merchants will come to inspect you and question you. You want to put on a good show and you hope they purchase your services. Otherwise, your life will be unbearable on this ship and you will curse your mothers for ever birthing you. Do we have an understandable agreement, gentleman?"

"Aye Aye, Captain," Sam chirped.

The quartermaster questioned, "Are any of yas versed in words? Raise yas palms if yas can read!"

Patrick and Isaac raised their hands.

"Yas two go over da descriptions of duties proclaimed in da notes," Mr. Mandrik explained in his heavy odd Grecian tongue.

"Make sure everyone knows da skills we say day are learned at. I am given yas da proclamation of sale notes. Don't dare soil dem and I be back shortly."

As the quartermaster walked away the five men gathered around to read the advertisements written about them. Patrick read his own advertisement first. The advertisement was written on hemp paper and in elegant penmanship it read:

Just Arrived

June 21st The sale of this indenture will commence at noon in Market Square. Patrick Willis is versed in word and numbers and is well learned. He hast skills of a jeweler and silversmith. The indentured is very skilled with delicate hand work. This man can adapt to other metal work such as blacksmithing and forging. He also has served as a ship carpenter and surgeon's mate. Terms be a seven year service. I will sell on bid for ready money or Tobacco and the Credit, Bond and Security will be required.

Inquire with Mr. Mandrik of the Robin for inspection and sale.

Patrick reread this advertisement and quickly panned through the others. "All of these are seven years, and none at five!" Patrick stated angrily. "We been lied to again, lads!"

"I thought it be strange," Sam Scurvy piped in. "Most prisoners be indentured seven to ten years, only free men serve but five." Sam thought for a moment and then continued, "The cap'n is going to try and pass us off as freeman, I says. He made no notice of our transgressions in the advertisement."

"You can fook that fancy-coat cooksooker. I be going to shove his wig right up his arse! Fook this whole fooked-up, monkey-humpin' situation. I had enough of this dog squeeze!" Shamus shouted irately.

Isaac held out his hands and calmly resolved, "I will suffer two more years as to never go back to the crap hole we were rescued from."

"Let us ask Mr. Mandrik about this when he comes forth," Jessup injected.

"Agreed, we will have him change this," Patrick conferred.

The heat of anger continued to build among the huddled men until the quartermaster returned.

"What da fook is dis seven year crap you Greek goat-eater?! You's all lied to us and ya best change da notice back to five years!" Shamus barked as he pointed his angry finger at Mandrik's chest.

The quartermaster began to breathe heavy through his nose like a bull that had seen red. He spoke loudly so there would be no questions. "Da captain changed da terms and ya all better be marketed now. You're to never mention yas jail time or I will throw ya into the drink on da way back to London! Now get back to yas duties and mention dis no more!"

The quartermaster angrily stomped off, leaving the five men staring at each other with dismay. Patrick sighed. "I guess I must suffer seven more years until I can truly live free." The five former prisoners nodded quietly in agreement as Patrick continued, "Lads, much confusion will happen in the next days and this may be the last time we are in league together. So let's all concur: one day on a harvest moon, years from now at the dock we arrive at, we have a reunion at their best pub."

The grumbling group accepted Patrick's idea.

After the men accepted their new fate, the feeling of excitement started to swell again. Tomorrow morning they would finally see Savannah. The men retired to the duties with a sense of newfound hope.

CHAPTER 5

SAVANNAH

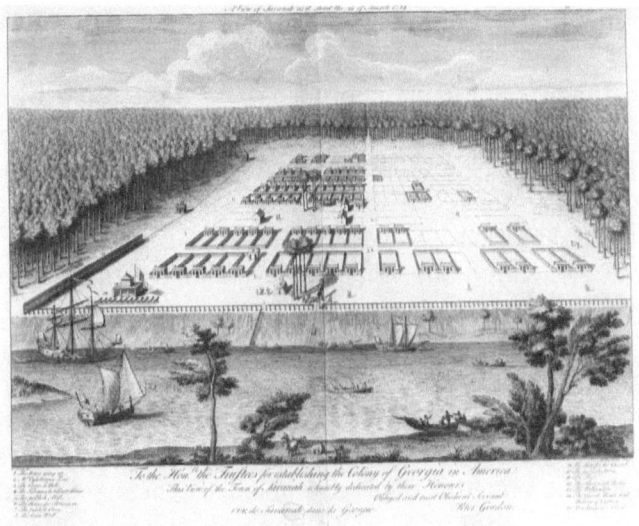

Savannah, 1734

Patrick woke up to loud hoots and cheering. He sprung out of his hammock so fast that his foot caught in the netting and he fell. His cabin mates roared with laughter that after all this time, he still could not maneuver his simple hammock. After gathering himself up from the floor and untwisting his ankle from the hammock's netting, Patrick rushed up the deck to the jeers and hollering of the crew already gathered. Off in the far distance, docks could be seen as well as steps climbing up a steep hill.

The boatswain's whistle blew loudly and the entire crew

was materializing topside. The men wore smiles from ear to ear as they slapped each other's backs with joy. A loud Greek voice proclaimed "Prepare da *Robin* fur shore, pretend yar Greek so ya will dos it the right way dis time."

The crew hollered like a church choir, "Huzzah, Huzzah, Huzzah!" as each man scurried to their job like ants on an apple. The deck exploded with excited activity.

Patrick smiled at Jessup, Sam Scurvy, and then Isaac. All the men were grinning at each other in anticipation of landing in Savannah, but a wave of odd feelings washed over Patrick. Something, or someone, was amiss. He wondered, "Where's Shamus?"

Savannah was slowly approaching; a bluff could be seen with a dock jutting from it. A long flight of stairs was cut from the steep slope. The stairs ran from the dock to the upper plateau of the town. There was a large wooden octagon ratcheting crane that was very similar to the windlass used to raise the anchor on the *Robin*. The crane was used to slide heavy cargo from the docks up a skid to the top of the bluff. Most of the town was difficult to see beyond the large protective palisades, or the wooden fences, circling it.

The crew was a fevered frenzy of activity. If the crew could swim, pushing the ship to increase speed, they would have. A call went out and the men scrambled, reporting to docking stations, as they drifted closer and closer to the bluff. More calls went out across the deck to drop the rigging in order to slow the approach of the speeding galleon. As land grew closer, the calls became more frantic, "DROP THE RIGGING! DROP THE RIGGING!" with no response. Furious, the master rigger questioned, "Where da HELL is da

Calls echoed across the deck, "Shamus, you toothless potato eater, get to your station!"

This commotion immediately attracted the attention of Mr. Mandrik. "Mr. Willis, go find ya drunken mick friend and get 'em to his station immediately," he demanded sternly. Patrick recruited Isaac to his aid and they went below deck searching for Mr. Red's passed-out, drunken corpse. They looked rigging

mate?"

Savannah dock in 1789

everywhere; every bunk, every crawl space, even the bilge. No sign could be found of him. What's worse was that all of his belongings, including his wooden pot of silver winnings, had vanished as well. Both Isaac and Patrick felt a growing dread. They knew the quartermaster would be murderous with this news and neither man relished the thought of reporting it back to him. They both drudgingly climbed above deck to report to Mr. Mandrik with the news.

As they told him what they found, Mr. Mandrik seemed to grow taller as his rage consumed him. His face became dark and fire blazed in his angry eyes. The two messengers were frightened and recoiled as their eyes sunk to their feet. Both men were struck in their faces with one stinging backhand. "Ya two best hope he is on dis ship! Summon the boatswain to call another meeting, NOW!" the imposing Greek bellowed loudly.

The sound of the boatswain's whistle could be heard screeching across the deck. The crew quickly assembled in excited curiosity. The quartermaster spoke in a harsh, angry tone. "It seems dat Shamus Red is missing dis morrow from da *Robin*. No man is getting off dis ship until he is found. All da crew search dis ship and find him. NOW! Or dare be no shore leave for nobody!" Except for the few men essential to docking, the entire infuriated crew immediately began a high-speed and panicked search.

In the meantime, as Savannah came closer into sight, Captain Gibbons ordered, "Quartermaster, signal the harbor master that our barky is ready for the mandatory pox inspection."

Mr. Mandrik produced a solid iron mug with a finger-sized hole drilled into the middle of it. The signaling cannon looked more like a beer stein than a cannon. "Cover ya ears, sailors. Don't let its small size fool yas, it packs a hell of a crack. They call this cannon a thunder mug for good reason." He carefully loaded the powder into the tiny cannon and then took a linstock to it. A loud, thunderous crack filled the harbor and within minutes, the harbor master could be seen rowing small jolly boat out to inspect the vessel.

Some formalities were shouted back and forth between the captain and the dock master. After some quick discussion, the harbor master boarded the *Robin* and quickly inspected the crew for disease. He returned to his jolly boat, waving the *Robin* in and leading it to the dock. The harbor master then gave a quick thumbs up motion to call off the cannons on the bluff, which were quietly trained onto the *Robin*.

The *Robin* drifted in perfectly and was gently docked; a true credit of the captain's abilities. The *Robin*'s crew and the men working the dock snapped to life, working in a fluid unison to tie the ship down. A large steel ruckus was made as the *Robin* unleashed its noisy anchor. Wasting no time, the crew slid the gangplank to the dock. Before any man could dash off, the quartermaster blocked the way of the crew. "Nobody touches land until da dirty mick is found!" The crew let out a collective groan, like children who were not allowed out after finishing their chores.

Ignoring this order, the captain walked down the gangplank to barter with the dock master over the price and terms of his stay. Summoning one of his cabin boys, the captain instructed,

"Boy, post this notice for the auction of the indentured in market square. You'll see the other postings and figure out where to nail it up." The boy silently and solemnly nodded he understood and ran off. The Captain then strolled up the long stairs and disappeared into the town hidden behind the palisades.

Mr. Mandrik continued to make the crew search futilely for Shamus for the rest of the long day. The men searched until sunset when they started to collect on deck to approach Quartermaster Mandrik. "We done torn dis ship apart, sir," the rigging master stated. "There is no sign of Red. I doubt the drunk was washed overboard; his belongings vanished mysteriously as well. He must have jumped ship, Quartermaster."

The Greek man was seething with rage. "Listen good!" he shouted as the crew was silenced. "Whoever drags that mick, Irish bastard back to da *Robin* get's his weight in silver. Go find him in dis damn town. Check every last piss-stinking booze house and in every penny-whore's bed. But remember da captain's rules: make no mention of his sordid past or I'll make ya wish ya you were in a shit-hole prison in London."

The flood of excited men pushed past each other as they shoved their way down the gangplank. Patrick only got one foot on the gangplank until he was shoved to the deck by the angry Greek. "Ya four ain't going anywhere. We no lose anymore of ya slippery fucks. Ya will stay locked below until da auction." The four men surrendered to their fate and begrudgingly shuffled below deck escorted by six armed crewmen. Each of the four was locked into a cabin, instructed to sleep and clean up. Two days from now they would be auctioned off and they could not look dirty or tired.

* * *

Two long hot slow days had passed. Just a skeleton crew was left to help resupply the *Robin*. Boxes of cargo were removed while new barrels and boxes were loaded in the cargo hold. The full crew was only seen once a day while they checked in. The *Robin's* bell would ring loudly at noon and hung-over and sleepy sailors would slowly materialize on the dock. No returning sailor reported any sighting of Shamus yet. The captain was furious about the loss of so much income. The profits of the *Robin's* cargo only covered for expenses of the trip. Gibbons made more gold from his servants than all the cargo he dragged with him across the ocean. The indentured servants were all profit to his war chest. The captain knew he was on a tight schedule and had to have the auction without the foul-mouthed Irishman.

The quartermaster now presented the newly well-dressed, clean and healthy looking men to the captain for inspection. The extra food rations had done well in restoring them from their past skeleton-like bodies. Mr. Mandrik reminded the four men standing before the captain, "Remember whats da cap'n say: no mention of prison or ya find yourself swimming back to England!" Mandrik then escorted the men to the gangplank and down to the dock.

Patrick, with his feet finally on steady land, felt punch drunk. He stumbled and staggered, trying to make it to the stairs. After finally earning his sea legs and adapting to the constant movement of life on the ship, he now found the solid earth disorienting as he adjusted back to land.

The four men and Mandrik climbed the long flight of stairs and crested the bluff. They passed through the palisades, staring at the town. Savannah welcomed them with a blast of oppressive heat and rancid smells. The ocean breeze was stifled by the high walls of the palisades. Patrick was taken aback. He had never felt heat like this. He could actually see the heat dance in the air and felt the sticky, wet haze soak his shirt. The heat was not the only welcoming present Savannah gave to the men. Patrick swatted at the swarming insects that were biting his hands and face. It was bewildering. He could not see the insects but felt their incessant biting. The men were all swatting and scratching madly as they wandered into town.

Savannah was a town under occupation; the king's military

were everywhere. It seemed half the town was redcoats. This immediately made the four uneasy. In England, the king's army were feared and reviled. They followed and executed the king's orders without mercy. They were no different than the violent gangs of bandits that roamed the streets of London, except they had nice, bright, uniforms and the government's blessing. Patrick wondered if the military would still be just as terrifying in Savannah, so far from the king's iron grip of control.

The men started up the street and were immediately immersed in all the activity around them. It seemed most of the town was moving toward Market Square to watch the auction of the new arrivals. Patrick noticed the stark differences in the layout of this town compared to London. It had more of a military fort feel to it, especially the way it was designed. He was told Savannah was the colonies' first planned city. The men turned a corner and smelled the livestock. They then passed the livery where travelers' horses were being boarded. There were many black merchants selling goods from carts along the road. Once entering the square, Patrick immediately noticed all the business owners in the square were white. The men approached the livestock area where a large crowd had gathered. The four men were then led by Mandrik to a small wooden block and were instructed to wait.

The awkward Greek man started negotiating with the owner of the livery about the cost to display the men on stage. After a long session of haggling, a silver round was exchanged and both men smiled. Captain Gibbons seemed to materialize from nowhere and motioned to Mr. Mandrik to start the sale.

"Patrick, ya be up first. Get up dar," the Greek said as he shoved him up onto the block. Patrick stood on stage and stared out nervously into the crowd. He was offended to be sold as a mule to the highest bidder and he grew indignant.

Captain Gibbons piped up in a loud, pompous voice, "You may now inspect this man before the auction starts!" A group of men shoved their way to the block and manhandled Patrick. They poked and prodded him; one man grabbed his mouth and examined his teeth like a common horse.

"What the hell are you doing? I am no slave," Patrick angrily protested and smacked his hand away. Mr. Mandrik became furious and then made a swimming motion to Patrick to remind him that he would be swimming back to England if he did not sell.

The buyers returned to their bidding positions and started conversing with each other. While all this action was occurring, Patrick's eyes caught a vision. A woman was removed from the arguing and trying to keep her distance. The woman had jet black hair flowing down her dress. Her pale face stood out of her worn red and black dress. She adorned a large red hat with a black lace ribbon tied on the backside and draping down her back. Red gloves, red shoes and a red parasol completed the outfit and protected her from Savannah's merciless sun. Patrick had not seen a woman in almost eight years and was completely dumbfounded. He stood and outright gaped at her while the auction started. He hoped nobody could see the full erection he was now harboring.

Captain Gibbons began his pitch. "Patrick Willis worked for one of the finest jewelers in all of London. His metallurgic skills are unmatched and would be a wonderful addition to any craft that requires delicate hand work. Mr. Willis also has performed very well as our ship's carpenter and surgeon's mate. He is lettered, numbered and ciphered. Remember, this is a 7 year term, so dig deep gentleman. I am opening the bidding at 10 pounds."

Three men in the crowd tried to open with the bid and their fingers shot up. The bid rose fast as the three men started their bidding war.

"The bid is now twelve! Fourteen! Eighteen! Twenty and twenty-two!" Gibbons exclaimed.

A man wearing a leather bib and covered with black soot spoke to Patrick, "Can you make gunshot and nails quickly?" Patrick was completely oblivious to the events going on around him, he was only fixated on the red gloved lady.

Mr. Mandrik yelled at Patrick, "Lad, answer the man!"

"Ohhh yes, I have made shot before but not nails," Patrick

said hesitantly.

"Very good. Twenty-four," the man in the bib chimed in.

"Twenty-five," another man in the audience replied.

The man in the bib came back with "Twenty-five and a barrel of Carolina tobacco."

A hush fell over the crowd.

"Last chance at Twenty-five and a barrel of Carolina tobacco. Going once, twice and sold upon agreement of the parties." Gibbons clapped his hand smiling, "Sold!"

"Let's go over there and work out this contract," the captain motioned.

Patrick was then escorted off the stage and shown the contract. "This is a voluntary contact so both parties need to agree. Look it over carefully and make sure you two meet on the level," Captain Gibbons stated.

"What are you known by, good sir?" Patrick asked.

"My name is Archibald Freeman and I am glad to know you," he extended his filthy black hand to Patrick.

"Name's Patrick Willis," he responded and then shook Freeman's hand firmly.

"Good. Let's take a look-see at this contract together," Archibald proposed.

The Contract read:

This INDENTURE Witnesseth that Patrick Willis a Jeweler doth Voluntarily put himself Servant to Captain Gibbons of the Robin to serve the said Captain Gibbons and his Assigns, for and during the full Space, Time and Term of Seven Years from the first Day of the said Robin's arrival in Savannah, during which Time or Term the said Master or his Assigns shall and will find and supply the said Patrick with sufficient Meat, Drink, Apparel, Lodging and all other necessaries befitting such a Servant, and at the end and expiration of said Term, the said Patrick to be made Free, and receive according to the Custom of the Country. Provided nevertheless, and these Presents are on this Condition, that if the said Patrick shall pay the said Captain Gibbons or his Assigns 25 Pounds British and a barrel of Tobacco in twenty one Days after his arrival he shall be Free, and the above Indenture and every Clause therein, absolutely Void and of no Effect. In Witness whereof the said Parties have hereunto interchangeably put their Hands and Seals the 21st Day of June in the Year of our Lord, One Thousand Seven Hundred and Thirty Nine in the Presence of the these men.

Addendum

Captain Gibbons of the Robin assigns this agreement to Archibald Freeman of Savannah.

Signatures of

Patrick Willis of London
Captain Gibbons of the Robin
Archibald Freeman of Savannah
This document is lettered in triple.

Patrick snickered at the notion this was a voluntary contract, as if he had some sort of choice. He could voluntarily choose to say "no" and be cast out to sea or accept this one chance to eventually be free. He forced his heavy hand to sign the next seven years of his life away under duress. Mr. Freeman then handed a bag of money to the grinning Gibbons and arranged delivery of the tobacco. Both of the men, the captain and the blacksmith, then signed and sealed the deal in spittle.

They were then interrupted by the sounds Mr. Mandrik and Isaac arguing.

"Take ya little Jew hat off for da auction," Mr. Mandrik barked angrily.

"I will not," Isaac replied stoically.

"I will rip the goddamned hat from yar Jew head if you don't!" the quartermaster threatened hotly.

Isaac on the auction block

Isaac stepped on the block and stated coolly to the captain, "I am ready to start. Open the bids." The captain, annoyed with it all, just went along with Isaac's notion and called for inspection, but no man approached. The crowd of buyers stepped back in silence.

The captain continued anyway, "Isaac Swartz is a large, hulking man with a very strong back and could do the lifting of two men. He was trained to collect bad debts and is a trained pugilist who is very handy with his large fists. He would be excellent in security or as a sentry. On my ship he was trained as a gunner. I enthusiastically open this bid at twenty pounds."

The crowd was silent as awkward stares fell upon the captain.

Gibbons went on, "Anyone? Anyone at all? Very well. I will keep him as my gunner. Going once, going twice..."

A shout came for a frail, tall gray haired man wearing a yarmucle, "Wait, I bid twenty pounds!"

"Very good. Going once, going twice... SOLD!" the *Robin's* captain shouted.

The three men came together to examine the contract. "Shalom. I am the town Doctor, Dr. Daniel Nunis. Glad to meet you," the doctor offered politely.

Isaac replied, "I have no training in treating aliments, sir. I have no idea why you would bid on me."

The doctor grinned, "Anyone brave enough to refuse to remove his yarmucle to these Christians is a man I wish to call friend." Both Jewish men then smiled and quickly signed the contract with Captain Gibbons.

Next up on the block was Sam Scurvy. Although his legs were bowed, he was very able now. Once the crowd found out he was a master fisherman a furious bidding war started and ended at 23 pounds. Purchased by a local fisherman, Sam was happy to get hired for a job he already knew and loved.

The last man was Jessup, who even still, nobody knew anything about. He refused to talk of his past so Captain Gibbons embellished his sailing experience. Jessup had the weathered look of a seasoned sailor so the tale seemed believable. When the bidding opened, not one soul in the crowd placed a bid. As Gibbons was about to close the auction and walk away, a colored man approached him.

"Captain, I will buy him for fifteen pounds," the black man said. Some of the crowd jeered and stayed to watch.

"You want me to sell you a white man? What possibly for?" Gibbons was befuddled.

The colored man answered flatly, "I own a whaling ship and need men. Does my money spend?"

The Captain looked at Jessup, "It is up to you, Jessup."

"Well, if I go back with you I will be swimming back to London, so what choice do I have?" Jessup offered sarcastically.

"Fine. Let's do a contract, your money spends with me," the Captain snipped. The crowd watching was outraged but could do nothing about the sale but grumble.

Patrick and Archibald observed this sale and Patrick asked, "Is an African savage really allowed to be a ship captain in these colonies?"

"The colored folks are not slaves here," Archibald answered. "At least for a little longer, but rumors be that is changing. Yes, a black man can be a captain, but only in whaling. Whaling is the only profession where a man is not judged by the color of his skin, but his performance." Archibald continued, "It is so dangerous, that most of his crew will be dead within just two years. When a job is that grave, every day a flirtation between life and death, a man's skin doesn't seem so important." He then instructed Patrick to say his "goodbyes", then they had to get to the shop.

Patrick shook his friends' hands and exchanged partings, agreeing to get together in their free time if they could. He also reminded Isaac, Sam and Jessup of their promised meeting years from now at the inn. Patrick could not help but smile as he walked away and saw Captain Gibbons fade off in the distance into the crowded streets.

Archibald led Patrick through some winding alleys and then stopped in front of a house. In the yard were a covered fire pit and a large anvil. The house looked like all the others around it.

It was a small, humble building with a pitched roof and two windows on each side of the door. A small building used as a workshop was in the back yard. Opening the front door of the little house and smiling warmly, Archibald offered, "Come in and meet the family. I bet you're ready to rest a spell and eat some fresh vittles."

CHAPTER 6

A NEW LIFE

Patrick was greeted by a pair of women and a pair of boys sitting around a stone table. The older woman was wearing a sky blue dress, tied from the waist to the chest. Despite the oppressive Savannah heat, every inch of her was covered except her face. The younger woman could not have been more than fifteen; she had young skin and was wearing a shorter, yellow dress. Her exposed forearms and hands were covered with red mosquito welts. The two boys were dressed in matching tricorn hats, simple black vests and buckle shoes.

"Finally," Archibald announced, "this fine man is the indenture we have been planning to take on." The family sitting around the table sprung to their feet and cheered. Patrick was taken aback by this display of appreciation and could not find his tongue. Archibald continued with the introductions. "This is my wife, Marian; my daughter, Heather; and my twin sons, Maximilian and Amos."

Amos walked over to the new indentured and said in a haughty accent, "You, sir, shall polish my shoes before bed every night."

"And I demand you empty my chamber pot every morning," Maximilian said, matching Amos's mocking tone.

"Patrick, I'm sorry for these two. They joke even when it isn't appropriate." Archibald then turned to his sons and threatened, "You twins better behave or I will drop you off at the Bethesda Boys' Home for Wayward Children."

"I wish you would! Did you see how nice that building

looks?" Amos snapped back with sarcasm. Archibald shot him a look and he immediately apologized to him and Patrick.

Turning to his wife, Archibald asked cheerfully, "What's for dinner, Mrs. Freeman? Our new friend must be starving."

"Mr. Freeman, we are dining on a bucket of crabs your two men, Maximilian and Amos, caught this morning in their traps," Marian replied in a formal tone.

"Well done, lads," the father beamed with pride and asked, "Where did you trap them?"

Amos replied "A short skirmish south of the palisade, off a small outcrop, where that large rotted palmetto tree is."

The Father picked up a snapping crab and chased after his boys with it saying, "Shall we eat them raw or introduce them to the kettle pot?" The family laughed at the scene of giggling boys running in circles around the stone table, just barely escaping the pinch of the angry crustacean. "Oh right! I forgot our manners," Archibald stated, ending the chase. "Wife, be a dandy and cook these crabs while I show this jasper to his quarters."

"Nice to meet such a lovely family," Patrick said humbly as he departed, smiling at Heather.

Patrick followed Archibald to the shed. It was tight quarters and there was not one bit of space wasted. A hammock attached to the walls, and under that, boxes of metal scraps. There was a workbench full of tools, strange contraptions hanging from the rafters and a small window mostly blocked by even more tools.

"The shitters are positioned on the north side of town against the palisades currently, but they will be moved again shortly," Archibald instructed. "You can always shit just outside the palisades in the swamp; nobody will get up in arms about it. Just bring a bucket of water and sponge with you. It is hard to find foliage to clean your backside that won't redden your ass skin. It seems everything green is poisonous out there," Archibald continued as Patrick tried catching every word he said. "Water is abundant and everywhere. You can get water out of the rivers, but it is best from any of the streams around,"

Archibald explained.

"I have had a very long journey, but I am ready to work if you like," Patrick stated eagerly.

"No. Not tonight. Tonight we get to know you and determine if we wasted all our family's gold coin or not. Shall we have some grog before dinner and watch the sun slowly retire, Mr. Willis?" Mr. Freeman grinned.

Patrick sighed happily, "Yes sir. That would be dandy good."

Both men sat down on stumps in the yard, staring at the sky. Archibald called for Heather to fetch him drinks and the men began to relax, getting to know each other better. Archibald removed his tricorn hat revealing his white curly wig. Patrick suspected he shaved his head, like most men, to avoid lice and wore a wig to stay stylish. As Archibald scratched at the wig in the warm Savannah heat, he asked very seriously, "Tell me, Patrick, how did you venture up here in Savannah? Truthfully."

Patrick anguished. Should he tell the truth or do as Mr. Mandrik instructed and omit the prison section of his tale? He drew a breath and spoke, "Well my Father was a prominent jeweler in London and I studied the craft. I took to the skill fast and made my father proud. Bad fortune fell on our family and he became a lunger." Patrick embellished a little, "After he died, I decided to earn my fortune in the New World with hope of sending for my family one day."

Heather appeared smiling with two wooden mugs of grog. She made a polite bow and handed the first cup to her father and then repeated the action for Patrick.

"So did you take a bride back in London, Patrick?" Heather chimed in. Her father shot daggers out of his eyes at the girl.

Patrick had not even seen a woman in eight years, never mind spoke to one. Nervousness overwhelmed him. He fumbled "Um, no ma'am. I've never took a woman. I mean bride. I mean, I have never been sealed in nuptials, with a woman. Not that I mean I took nuptials with a man." He hemmed and hawed, "I mean, uh... I mean, I never had the chance to, um..."

Archibald rescued the floundering man, "I think he means he is still trying to meet the right lady."

"Yes, yes and yes," Patrick agreed quickly, adding, "That is true what he be saying."

Heather laughed at Patrick's awkwardness and strolled slowly back inside the house.

"Well Patrick, let me tell you what you will be doing the next few years." Archibald went back to his instructions and his grog. "I am a blacksmith if you could not tell by my bib. I make my fortune mainly on making nails, horse shoes and tools. Times are demanding more of me lately and I cannot keep true to the demand. So I am hopeful you will take to iron as well as you take to silver and help me stay level with said production." The wigged man queried, "Do you think you can adapt your skills with your hands?"

Patrick nodded in agreement, as he guzzled his grog.

Archibald continued, "It is pretty simple but very repetitive, the real silver to be made is in gunshot and muskets. The king's forces constantly demand shot. They drop their casting equipment off for the day and we custom make shot for their muskets. The redcoats keep careful watch that the colonists don't make too many guns for themselves or they'll simply confiscate them from us non-military locals. If you plan on getting your own musket soon, you'd be careful to keep it hidden until you go hunting. It's best not to tempt those red demons."

"I can't even fathom being able to afford my own firearm. I was a fine shot with a sling in my boyhood," Patrick joked. "These days I could not even afford a rock to throw."

Marian interrupted them, announcing that dinner was now ready. She insisted that the family dine outside because she did not want her home to reek of crab and low tide, so the family gathered in the back yard under the dogwood tree. The tree was in an unusual second, yellow bloom and provided refuge from the sweltering sunlight. The shade extended over one large stump that was surrounded by eight logs sitting upright.

The family sat on the make-shift, wooden seats and dropped the cooked crabs on the large stump table from a steaming pot. To add to the feast, Heather set out some fresh cornbread, presented in a small basket and wrapped in a cloth napkin to protect it from the clouds of flies.

Sitting down, around the great stump covered with boiled crab, the family started giggling as Archibald cheerfully counted, "One, two, three!" The family playfully grabbed at the food as fast as hungry orphans and competed for slices of the cornbread. Boisterous laughing ensued as Marian and Amos played tug a war with a crab until it broke in two. Such a ridiculous and vulgar display of manners only increased the family's joy and laughter.

Patrick was taken aback by this odd display. No prayer was said, no proper rotation of hierarchical serving was observed, just chaos. He sat there with a stunned look on his face as the family grabbed for crabs. Maximilian smiled, presenting Patrick with a crab and large piece of yellow bread. "I am faster than my father," the twin stated slyly. "Here, take these." Patrick laughed loudly and dove into the cornbread, smearing it in his beard. The family chuckled as the smashing sounds of crab shells and wood hammers echoed in the air. Much laughter was heard from the dogwood for the rest of the evening as the libations continued to flow.

Later in the evening, Archibald led Patrick to his hammock in the moonlight and bragged, "Be ready for a tour of Savannah tomorrow. I want to show you off."

Patrick slowly mounted his hammock clumsily. "Months on a ship and I still can't figure these damn contraptions out," Patrick confessed with a grin as the two men laughed warmly.

"You will," Archibald promised. "You can rest during second sleep until the seasons change."

As with most cultures around the world, the night was split into first and second sleep. This tradition was carried over from the old world to the colonies. First sleep was about an hour after dinner until the witching hour of midnight. Second sleep was from midnight till sunrise. The late hours where used for just about anything. Many chores were done as well as hobbies. Many times the women knitted or prepared food for the next day's meal. The men completed chores that were too difficult to do in the day's heat like late night wood chopping or hauling. In the Freeman house, it was also a great time to read and they burned through barrels of whale oil in their lamps.

As Archibald retired to the house, Patrick smiled as he gently swung himself fast asleep in his hammock.

* * *

A mosquito bite on his nose welcomed Patrick to the waking world. The bite was already welting up. He noticed his hands and face were covered with more bites and angry welts. With an ungraceful maneuver, he fell out of his hammock and onto the pile of scrap metal with a cacophonous crash. Amazed he found no lacerations from his fall, he considered himself protected by good spirits.

Patrick took himself around the back of the shed and made water. The merry libations were now draining his fluids. Although the sun was just rising in the morning sky, the heat already overtook him and he immediately started to sweat through his linen vest. The new blacksmith amused himself by trying to pee on flies in a stagnant puddle. Mr. Freeman soon came around the corner and joined him in the morning urination.

"We start early around here to avoid the heat," Archibald explained. "I want to give you a tour so when I send you to fetch errands you can navigate the town. Let's explore Savannah, or as the rest of the colonies call it, the Scoundrel's Haven. This small swamp-town has also been called the Sanctuary for the Bandit, Swindler, Murderer and Whore. Shall we go explore this convict's paradise?"

The men walked out onto the dirt thoroughfare and started their walk into town. "Savannah is set up as a Military base. All the lots are about the same size. It is supposed to promote equality, no man be better than his neighbors."

Archibald smiled, "Unless of course you're a high ranking officer." He continued, "Oglethorpe knew about all the fire problems in London so this city is mainly grids and open spaces. This also is smart for defense from the Spanish and the savages. The town pretty much revolves around four main areas called wards. There are also two new Wards being developed. Each ward has a central square and is surrounded by trust and tything lots. The trust lots are for government builds and churches and such. The tything lots are used for homes and each home also gets a lot of five acres at the edge of town. I will take you around the wards and give you a guide of each.

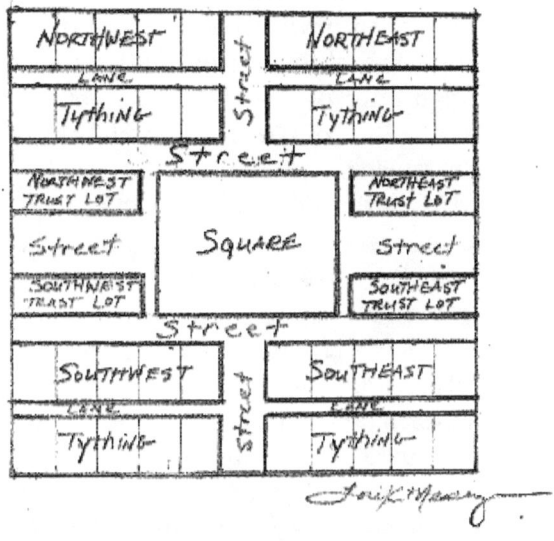

The layout of Savannah's wards

"The ward we live in is called Decker Ward and we live here on the Strand. The square in the middle is called Market Square and all the town's commerce comes through here. You see all the carts of vendors setting up, mainly they are African freemen. This colony does not allow slavery. It has the town split. The king's subjects are jealous of all the riches that the

Carolinas are now enjoying on the backs of slaves. Others of His Majesty's servants found the practice morally appalling. Every year the people try to bend the ear of the trustees that run this town to allow the practice. I fear the Trustees' are turning sympathies to the slavers." As Archibald cautioned, Patrick nodded. Freeman continued, "Basically any kind of foods, services, or commerce can be found in this square and Ward and you will spend most of your hours here.

"If you go down over there into the tall grass a ways, you will come to a large crepe myrtle that has been split in two by a lightning bolt. Never seen anything like it. The tree is still alive and growing as two trees now. Ever since that myrtle got burned in two, the townsfolk call that area Thunderbolt."

Freeman motioned down a corner to Patrick, "Let us turn down Mr. Thomas Broughton's street until we come to Derby Ward. It is named after one of those fat cats, the Honorable James, the Tenth Earl of Derby." Archibald mocked the pompousness by bowing.

Archibald led Patrick down a dusty road to a square that opened in front of them revealing a large dirt space. The area was busy with activity; surveyors pulled string between wooden stakes marking lines, a crew of shirtless and sweaty men were digging a large hole as a group of well dressed aristocrats and a minister in a black smock and white wig patted each other's backs and shook each others' hands. Archibald informed Patrick of the Johnson Square. It was named after the generous and well-liked royal governor of SC and it was the hub of Anglican activities. They watched as a congregation of devout Anglicans was breaking ground to build themselves a church.

"I am not a gossiping kind," he ensured Patrick, "but so much scandal has occurred in this Ward around those pastors." With a sly smile and wink for Patrick, he continued, "So let me not tell you what happened. The very first minister named Henry Herbert died when he was returning on Oglethorpe's favorite ship, the Anne. He was heading back to England and his merciful God struck him down for reasons unsuspected. Then they had Mr. Quincy stand a short tenure till the third pastor arrived. His name was John Wesley, and lad, let me tell you this scandalous tale!" The wigged man laughed. "Well the beautiful Sophia Hopkey was to be married but a misunderstanding and folly caused Pastor Wesley to refuse to publish her banns of marriage in the church. Thereafter, she ran over to South Carolina in disgrace and got nuptials done there. Pastor Wesley was made the fool by this and refused the new couple communion when they returned. Such a public insult this was that Sophia's husband sued the pastor for defamation. Have you ever heard such a thing, suing a man of God? The resulting and embarrassing controversy caused such uproar in his parish that they asked him to return to England in thirty-seven. Funny thing is, a man told me he is starting some new Methodist Church in England that is already wildly popular. Oh those religious folks and their stories make me laugh."

As Archibald collected himself from laughter, he changed the subject and suggested, "Let us turn up this street until we run into the Heathcoat Ward." The men slowly walked on with Archibald continuing to point out the sights and characters of Savannah.

"The ward is named for George Heathcoat. I know, not very original. He is also one of the trustees. Although Savannah preaches the merits of equality, this is where all the high society resides. The square we are walking by is called St. James and at night is home to some wonderful music and arts. My favorite wandering bard sings here. His name is Wes Loper. We must remember to try and catch him one night. I'm sure you'll enjoy him very much. Rumors also bound that a troop of actors might come and perform here in the square."

Patrick could only nod. So much information of his new home town was beginning to overwhelm him but Archibald continued on.

"Well then let's make our way to the Percival Ward. This ward and square are named after Viscount Percival. Again, I know our founders were not very creative with the names," Archibald cracked. "This is Jew territory and where the ladies of pleasure reside. There's not supposed to be Jews here at all, but that Dr. Nunis, the man who purchased the services of your goliath friend, he is the common man's town doctor and won favor for his kind. If you have bags of silver and are of the proper social class you get an appointment with Dr. Tailfer, but he would never be seen with the likes of us. It took no time to break that no-Jew law because the second boat to land had forty-two Jews on it. Oglethorpe and the trustees' never made them leave because these Jews were refugees from Spain and Portugal. They had sympathy for their plight. The trustee's then decided to only ban Roman Catholics, in fear of them assisting the damn Spaniards that keep attacking outside of this town."

Archibald then straightened his shirt and spoke as if he was very serious but a faint smile could be seen on his lips. "As far as the whores go, well, officially, there are none here. The upstanding, church-going wives would have seen them in the stocks of course, but all the men deny they are here. To know the truth one just needs to look at all the soldiers and sailors in this town. Of course any military attracts whores like honey to bees."

As if on cue, two of Patrick's former crew mates then stumbled out of a house. A woman in a worn, red dress unceremoniously shoved them out the back entrance. She then escorted them out and exchanged gazes with Patrick. A warm inviting smile beamed from her as she waived her handkerchief at the two blacksmiths. She then hiked up her dress revealing a tattooed ankle, slipping a silver round down the side of her red shoe. She slowly sashayed her backside left to right, left to right, left to right, smiling over her shoulder, giving the blacksmiths an eyeful of motion. At the door, she blew a gentle kiss at Patrick before returning to her duties. Patrick immediately felt his desire swelling in his pants. Such a blatant display of sexuality after weeks on a ship and years in a prison cell overwhelmed him.

Archibald smiled at the younger man, "Ah lad. That is the mysterious April Sky. I know it is an odd name. I've never heard of someone named after a month but I am fairly certain it is not the name she was christened with. With that stated April Sky is the most powerful madam in all of Savannah and no woman dares whore here without her blessing and paying her homage. She is the scourge of Savannah's proper women but the men do really love her girls, so she is left to her craft unmolested. The rumor is she used to run the seas with pirates before all the pirates were hunted down and killed. I am told every inch of her body except her face is covered with tattoos. It is said she is highly superstitious and uses them to ward off the devil." Archibald then warned, "If you want to keep your temple pure you best stay away from that harlot."

Patting Patrick's shoulder, Archibald then announced, "Well that sex parade is over. Come along. There are two other wards under construction I need to show you."

The two men recommenced their journey with Freeman pointing out the sights. "Over that way is the Upper New Square. The other one over that way is another that they have not decided on a name yet, it seems to change every hour. I reckon they must have run out of honorable trustees to bestow the honor on," Archibald poked Patrick in the ribs.

"Beyond there, continuing through the wild to the southwest is Fort Argyle," Archibald continued. "I'm sure you've guessed it's named after someone. John, Duke of Argyle, and personal friend to Oglethorpe. It's supposed to help offer protection from the Spanish and from Indian raiders but it's never been manned properly." Archibald stopped and seemed lost in thought. "A lot of men from the Scottish town of Darien rotate manning and running patrols there." He brought his attention back to the here and now and they started walking again.

"Savannah is growing so fast it seems like they move the bloody Palisades outward every week. Let us walk this way toward the river," Mr. Freeman instructed, "and I will show you the exotic plants over in the trustees' garden."

The men wandered to the bluff and came across a garden adorned with a small herb house. "This is Oglethorpe's pride and joy, the Trustees' garden. It is said to be modeled after the

Chelsea Botanical garden in London. The mental bastard spent a king's ransom on having plants delivered to him from the four corners of the world. All sorts of exotic plants were first soiled

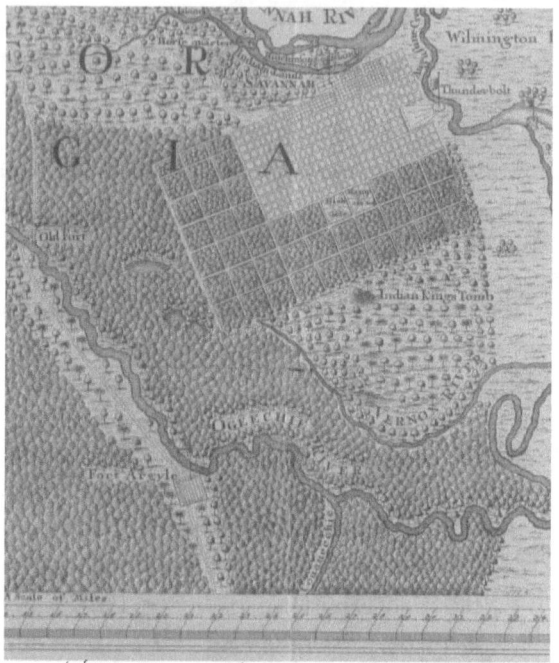

1740 Map of Savannah and Fort Argyle

here, but the first frost killed most of them. There were apple, pear, olive, fig, coffee trees, and cotton. Bamboo plants, indigo, coconut palms, hemp, oranges and many various herbs to assist a doctor. The money crop was intended to be mulberry trees for silkworms. Oglethorpe dreamed he could use them to feed silkworm and spin silk. The garden used to be well tended when Francis Moore was here, but it is now falling quickly into disarray. This is typical of anything owned by government," Archibald spit. "Nobody's ever held accountable and anything the king touches goes to piss. You would never see a farmer let his own land go that way. It's a damn shame." Freeman looked longingly at the failing garden and shaking his head silently with disgust.

"What's that mound of rocks in the middle of the garden for?" Patrick inquired.

"That is a pyramid burial mound of one of the Yamacraw savages," Archibald answered. "The Yamacraw locals were very helpful to Oglethorpe. In return, he respects their ways. He even promised their chief not to disturb any resting souls."

"Ah," Patrick mouthed with understanding. There were so many new, alien customs and strange sights. It was the only response he could muster.

Archibald continued still gazing upon the garden. "Now all that is really growing well are the oranges, apples, and the hemp. Us regular Savannahians refer to this place as Oglethorpe's folly! Now don't let any of the lobsterbacks hear you saying such or you will be hanging from a gallows. That Oglethorpe does not care to be mocked."

Patrick nodded earnestly. He wanted to impress upon his new master he understood. Archibald could sense Patrick's seriousness so he joked, "Well that will be one shilling for the tour. You'll have to pay me in credit I am assuming." Patrick smiled and Archibald concluded, "Let us get you to the tailor now."

The men went to the Broughton side of market square and knocked on the door of a humble house. A large breasted maiden answered the door hastily. Her hair was disheveled and her dress was hugging her sweaty chest. She clutched a stuffed linen ball full of needles close to her full chest.

Archibald removed his hat and politely inquired, "Good morrow, Prudence. Is your father here? I need my friend here fitted for some work linens."

She loudly cussed up, "No, the bastard reds got him working for free again mending their damn coats in their quarters. Those heavy wool red coats are made by that company in Charles Towne called the South Carolina Independent Company. They make fine wear but the buttons are always ripping off or the sleeves been singed by lamp lights. Those red coats catch, they go up like a Viking funeral pyre." Prudence was visibly upset and spouted, "The arrogant bastards! Making him come to them and fix their wares for gratis!"

"Quiet, love. Your tongue is too loose in open air," Archibald hushed Prudence.

"I just hate those red leeches so much! I hope the bastards get cock sores from April Sky's whores," Prudence responded with a little more restraint. She sighed and remembered the business at hand. "What are you two larks standing around for? Well, show him in and I can get his numbers."

Both men looked nervously at each other. "Um, ma'am, we cannot enter the domicile of a lady with no man home," Archibald nervously explained.

"For the Lord's sake!" she exclaimed. "Fine! I'll do it in the yard to reassure the world that you two not be molesters. Christ!"

Patrick was instructed to stand on a stump while she used marked cords of hemp to measure.

"This is Patrick, our new indenture. He will be smithing with me. He needs hemp fiber if possible, something sturdy and protective around fire," Archibald propositioned.

"Yes, I know how to make a bloody smithing outfit for, fuck's sake. You know I am a grown woman?" she snapped.

"Yes, and such a refined and proper young lady you grew into," Archibald smirked.

"Fuck you, damn Scottish, dress-wearing drunk. I hear your Scottish brogue you so desperately trying to conceal," she warned him.

"Stand still will you!" she snapped at Patrick as she ran her hand up his inseam.

This was the closest a woman had ever been to his crotch and he was instantly erect. It was so unnatural for a man of his age to be completely inexperienced in the ways of women. He found his impure thoughts overwhelming since the moment he landed in Savannah. Being exposed to so many of the soft gender was wreaking havoc on his senses and concentration. He tried his hardest not to squirm on the stump.

"I got all I need," Prudence stated. "Come back in two

weeks for a final fitting and me father will figure out the silver with you. Also, I would like to come call on Heather tonight to join Mari Anna and me in listening to Wes's fiddle," she half asked, half told.

Archibald responded, "If she is finished with her chores, I see no discord. Mentioning Mari Anna, is she baking today?"

"I smelled that heavenly corn bread in the air this morning. You best hurry. I know she is low on corn flour, it might be the last of it for an age," Prudence urged.

Patrick pointed to a long line of redcoats at a nearby house. "What is that huge line for?"

"Ah, lad. That is the food line for the government workers. They stand in this sun for hours to get some rancid meat and rotting fruit. The first few years of the colony were the worst. I remember when everyone was forced to take Oglethorpe's handouts to live on. The founding settlers quickly over hunted the area and were completely dependent on what the traders brought in. They paid very little money to the local Yamacraw tribe, so the Indians only sold them only the worst meat and fruit." Archibald explained. "In short time, the populace discovered how poorly their needs are handled if they trust the government to take care of them. A free market exploded very quickly and the quality of everything got better. Still those tied to the king, like the soldiers and bureaucrats there, are completely dependent on that disgusting slop. I guess we could still get the spoiled meat if we wanted to but no self-respecting man I know would take it. Do not forget how the food is actually paid for; silver is taken from the rest of us to pay for it. I can't take that grub in good conscience because I know the funds to buy it were stolen from my family and neighbors by redcoat threats and force."

The men departed with a wave to Prudence and continued back into the square where a small covered booth was standing. A queue five deep was waiting to purchase warm bread. The line was intoxicated with the smell of fresh bread. A father and daughter worked behind a table and were quickly running out. The blacksmiths waited anxiously in line hoping to buy some before they ran out.

The old, heavy man behind the counter then barked, "Your timing is that of a hawk, Mr. Freeman. We are down to our last loaf."

"I have always had outstanding luck, Mr. Dandridge," Archibald playfully responded.

"Good morrow, Mr. Freeman! Who's your companion?" The daughter queried.

"Miss Mari Anna Dandridge, let me introduce you to Patrick Willis, our new indenture," Archibald proclaimed and then bowed.

Patrick took in the beautiful young lady. Dark braided hair fell out of the cooking hood and onto her shoulders. She had a thin linen white dress and a cooking apron. She wore no gloves but her hands were not bug welted like everyone else. Working around a fire all day kept bugs from biting her delicate hands. Patrick bowed formally and stated, "My honor, lady."

Archibald then interrupted the formalities. "My daughter and the *lady* Prudence," he snickered, "Would like you to join them tonight to go hear the bard sing. If your goodly father bestows his blessings, I will escort you ladies to and fro."

"Yes, I grant my blessing, but those three are like molasses. Enjoy yourself escorting them, Freeman," Mr. Dandridge grumbled. Mari Anna then threw her arms around her smiling father and hugged him like a black bear.

Changing the subject, Archibald asked, "Mr. Dandridge, how did you get corn this early in the season?"

Mari Anna answered for her father. "The redskin deer pelt traders brought it up from the south. I suppose the winter was mild enough to plant early down there. Sometimes, if they are real lucky, they get two grows out of one season." Silver was then exchanged for the bread and the blacksmiths walked off as they split a piece of hot bread.

"Ok, lad, it's time you earn all this food and clothing. Let me go teach you how to make nails," the wigged man said as the returned home.

* * *

The men came home to an empty house but Archibald was not alarmed.

"Every morning the family goes out to collect fallen wood to supply the pit. First thing we do is restock the fire. Grab some of that dried hay and that there stirrin' stick. There are usually hot embers still alive from last night, so reheat them with the bellows," Archibald instructed. Patrick pumped the bellows until the embers grew orange. He then tossed some hay and kindling onto the smoldering pit. With the kiss of air pumped from the bellow, flame was immediately summoned and the pit sprung to life. The men stacked some drift wood in and tended the fire until it glowed. It took a half an hour of burning wood to get it hot enough for their purposes.

"Here, lad. You can use my old apron and gloves," Archibald offered. "They are thick buckskin and will keep you safe." Archibald then helped Patrick tie the heavy apron on.

"Now I have already melted some of the scrap metal and drawn the metal out into rods. Take this rod and heat it until it glows orange." Archibald demonstrated, "Put it deep into the embers like this. Now, pull it out before it melts and quickly bring it to the anvil."

The seasoned blacksmith began to forge and shape the glowing end of the rod into a four-sided point. He worked very quickly and then placed the nail shape end on the chisel sticking up out of the anvil. He proceeded to turn the rod over and over as he struck it against the chisel. He then took the chisel-weakened section and bent it until it broke off from the long rod. Finally he grabbed the glowing nail with a circular pair of pliers and inserted the nail into a hole in the anvil. He quickly pounded a flat head onto the nail and dunked it in cool water. With his adroit craftsmanship, the whole process was over in less than a minute and there sat a fine looking nail. Patrick was impressed with the speed and skill Archibald possessed.

Archibald sensing Patrick's distress reassured him, "Don't worry, son. After a few thousand nails you will be just as fast.

You ready to try your hand at it?" To that, Patrick nodded. He worked until sundown with Archibald's close supervision. At the end of the day, there were fifteen mangled, misshapen nails and ten that were passable. It was hard hot dirty work but at least the heat drove off the mosquitoes and annoying, biting sand gnats.

Patrick was beginning to feel confident in his vocation of pounding out nails. When Mari Anna and Prudence arrived to call on Heather, the disruption caused Patrick to smash his thumb with his hammer. The two girls laughed at Patrick's misfortune. Archibald, the veteran blacksmith, had to laugh as well. "Mind your hammer, lad!" Patrick's thumb turned almost as red as his cheeks. The elder Freeman then patted his shoulder and suggested they break for supper.

That day, Maximilian and Amos had caught four decent sized fish and Heather and Marian had readied them for cooking. The visiting ladies graciously brought a basket of fresh apples with them and they all dined under the dogwood. After their bellies were full and good conversation was shared, the anxious young ladies prodded the wigged smith to escort them to St. James Square.

"Daddy, it's starting. Can we please go?" Heather whined.

"Yes, my dear," he answered and then turned to his apprentice. "Would you like to hear some music this evening, Mr. Willis?"

Patrick nodded eagerly.

The three young women checked their appearances, fixing each other's hair, as the group started on their stroll to the square. The three giggling girls held hands and walked ahead of Archibald and Patrick, making jokes the two men could not hear.

"If I can be so direct," Patrick boldly asked, "it seems odd, sir, that three adult women are not already bonded to men and baring children. This colony has many single men. Are they not being courted?"

"Oh, lad, these three be the most courted women in the colonies but they never accept any man's advances. They treat the men like toys and accept their gifts but they seem more focused on being with each other than finding themselves in a family way."

"Savannah is an odd colony. I have never seen women so carefree and not bound by social graces," Patrick carefully noted.

"Lad, the king's military and upper crust socialites act nothing like us working colonists. You will take a bloodcoat's musket butt to the teeth if you do not adhere to their strict social protocol. Our friends are very careful about who and where we speak openly around," Archibald warned.

"So how do you know you can trust me?" Patrick inquired. "How come you already speak freely around and with me?"

Archibald stopped in the street and turned to face Patrick. His face looked grave yet sympathetic. "Because you spent some time in the king's prison. I know you must hate the government that did this to you."

Patrick stopped in his tracks and the color ran from his face. He then hung his head shamefully and muttered, "It's true, Mr. Freeman, but how did you know I was a convict?"

"No free man would indenture his time so long. A freeman would only do five years at most for passage. Your debt is seven years, so I reckoned only a prisoner without a choice would accept those terms," Archibald reasoned.

Patrick confessed, "It is true. I will tell you anything you want to know. I hated being clandestine with you. I was under mortal threat by Captain Gibbons to conceal the truth from you. Just please, sir, don't return me. There is only death for me back at sea."

Archibald put a caring hand on Patrick's shoulder and begun to walk. "Lad, you have no worries by me. Just tell me your story and speak the truth without fear."

Violin music was heard as they rounded the corner. St. James square was now being illuminated by the setting sun. The three young ladies picked a prominent spot to be seen while listening to what they thought was German music. They

Heather, Prudence and Mari Anna milk courters for free gifts

perched and displayed themselves like peacocks welcoming their suitors. It did not take long either as all kinds of men strolled by and found reasons to converse with the comely, young ladies. Mari Anna even brought a basket to carry home all the gifts the ladies would receive from hopeful men.

Patrick watched slack-jawed as a line of men tried to catch the ladies' fancy. "Well, I guess we have time for me to tell you the true story of how I came to be here in Savannah," Patrick conceded. Patrick spun the heartbreaking tale and even had to hold back the tears as the grief poured out of him. Archibald held his shoulder in support and concern. A new trust and understanding was forged when the tale was done.

CHAPTER 7

THE ANGRY LOBSTERBACKS AND TOMOCHICHI

18th c. drawing of Tomochichi and his nephew Toonahawi while visiting London

The flirtation of the young ladies entertained their line of courters. Savannah's socialites would have been horribly offended by this vulgar display, but they would not be seen in this section of town, especially at night. Torches were lit by nearby patrons who sat in their yards to enjoy the music. Mr. Loper was doing well tonight and his violin case glittered with silver in the torchlight. All was going pleasantly until the crowd parted and became uneasy as a group of bloody backs marched in. The music stopped and the crowd began to drift away into the darkness.

"Don't stop on my account," the commander spouted sarcastically. "Go on Mr. Loper, play that old Irish noise you keep trying to pass off as German. Please continue."

Wes Loper nervously picked up his fiddle and peeped, "Of course, Commander Kingsley."

The tall officer wore a formal commander's uniform everywhere. He had a collection of wigs which he changed daily and wore like an arrogant rooster. He smiled slyly to the crowd and warned, "Yes, yes! Everyone stay. I would consider it a personal insult if one soul left this party on my account."

The crowd held their ground in a hushed uneasiness keeping their distance. Archibald grabbed Patrick's hand and pulled the confused blacksmith away.

"Archibald!" A condescending voice rang out, "Who is your new lover you lead into the dark?"

A shiver shot up Archibald's back as he froze in his tracks. He spent most of his time staying invisible when the lobsterbacks came into sight. He knew he would lead a longer and happier life the more he could avoid the king's government. Slowly turning, he dropped Patrick's hand.

"This is my new indenture, Patrick Willis," Archibald reluctantly surrendered.

"Patrick, eh? Strange. You don't look like a filthy Irishman," the commander observed.

Patrick replied, "Not Irish. I was named after my mother. Her name be Patricia."

"Ah that would explain your feminine hair and build now," Kingsley mocked. He then turned to another lobster back and mused, "Sergeant Luthor, do you think Mr. Patricia here fancies himself men?"

"Of course, Commander. He looks like he is no stranger to the livestock either," Sergeant Luthor replied.

"Daddy, it is time for us to be escorted home," Heather interjected. She looked worried. "Mari Anna has to be home now."

"I will escort her home, Freeman," Commander Kingsley offered as he leered wantingly at her.

"No. I promised her father I would escort her home, and we were just leaving," Archibald stated as he begun to herd the young women away.

"Perhaps then," Kingsley laughed, "I will have to come to her father and court her at home."

The three young women and the blacksmiths quickly slipped into the night as the commander was asking them to stay.

"That fucking bastard!" Prudence cussed. "I want to run him through with a knitting needle one day."

"Let's just retire back to my house overnight until we know we are all safe," Archibald commanded.

When the families returned to the Freeman home, the ladies were hurried inside. Marian demanded, "Good Lord! What is all this haste you bring into this home?"

"Damn lobsterback commander making eyes at these ladies. You keep them inside and on the ready," Archibald ordered his wife.

The blacksmith then went into the shed and closed the door. Clanging and clamoring rang out until finally the door swung open. He returned now brandishing a firelock, a large ax, broadsword and a thin wooden box. He laid the box on the stump and carefully opened it. The box was lined with deer hide and contained two gun shaped recesses. In the recesses sat two dueling flintlock pistols with a bag of shot and a ball caster.

"Lads, you remember how I taught you to use these?" Archibald asked his sons. "Keep it clandestine until you're up close and personal." The two boys nodded obediently as their father continued, "Now check the flint and prime the flash pan with this powder. I want those Queen Anne's primed and ready, lads."

Maximilian and Amos each checked their flint and rammed their muzzles. They finished priming while Archibald got his musket ready. The blacksmith then tied on his sword and handed Patrick the axe and warning, "I hope you know how to swing this thing. Aim for the neck. You only will get one chance, so keep your aim true."

Patrick had never been in a fight with weapons before in his life and was now panicking. His hands shook and the axe vibrated with fright. The master blacksmith quickly noticed Patrick's nervousness and thought an errand would distract him from his fear. He then pulled out a large bag from his coat and instructed, "Go arm the women."

Patrick took the heavy bag into the house and emptied its contents on the stone table. Five Scottish dirks splayed across the table. Each of the women took one and Mari Anna took two. They practiced thrusting them in the air.

"Aim for the leaders," Mari Anna encouraged.

"Leaders?" Heather questioned.

"The neck veins. Where did you say you're from again?" Mari Anna questioned. The three friends nervously giggled. The matriarch then shot them an intense gaze to remind them of the seriousness of the trouble coming.

Patrick returned from arming the women. The boys were directed to watch the front yard as the men hunkered down in the back yard under the dogwood. Archibald and Patrick doused their torches and cautiously scanned the darkness for hours. Aside from the chirping of frogs and locusts, the camp grew eerily silent. Confident the threat had passed, both men fell asleep under the dogwood tree in the early hours of the morning.

"Ah... At least ya still sleep under a tree like a proper Scot!" a booming Scottish voice woke the men.

"Damn, lad! I damn near burned ya down with my firelock! Waking me like such," Archibald replied to the kilted man with the Scottish brogue.

Heather came running from the house and threw herself around the kilted man. "Uncle William, it has been so long!"

"I see you be carrying a proper dagger, lass. This makes an old man proud," her Uncle William smiled. "Maybe we will finally make you into a proper Scottish woman soon enough."

Behind the large, bearded, kilted man, a mule drawn wagon was parked. William grabbed Archibald and led him to the wagon speaking a combination of Scottish, English, and Gaelic. The wigged blacksmith grew irate and shook his fist at William.

"What are they talking about?" Patrick asked Heather.

"William told Father that he has been gelded because he no longer wears his kilt and he speaks in English tongue," Heather responded with a smile.

Archibald returned to speaking English and asked, "William, are you going to just keep insulting me or are you going to buy some nails?"

William roared with laughter. "Both! Darien is booming with growth and we can't keep up with the demand for timber there. We are building sawmills to handle all the yellow pine and cypress. Check out all the wood in the cart. We are having a good harvest. When are you finally going to join your kinfolk and come to Darien, brother? You won't have to be sneaking around pretending you're English."

Archibald's eyes lit up with fire and he mumbled in an angry hushed tone, "I reminded you to hold your tongue about my family life."

William laughed, "Ah, finally your Scottish blood is flowing. You *are* still alive in there!"

"How many nails you buying, you drunk?"

"All you got, of course! And I need some 'other' provisions," the kilted man asked in a whisper.

"I am out of 'other' provisions but I can make some in two weeks' time," the blacksmith offered.

"Aye. I take it. I pay you after inspection. If anyone asks, tell them that Captain McPherson at Fort Argyle has commissioned you. These 'other provisions' are not for the fort, as it's well stocked. McPherson is not coming into town anytime soon so no one will be the wiser."

"I'll do that. How are our clansmen at Fort Argyle?"

"They are fine. We hate having to man that useless fort. Nothing ever happens."

Patrick recalled Archibald talking about how the men at Darien manned the fort and it suddenly occurred to him that Archibald was concerned about family stationed there.

A barrel of nails was loaded onto William's cart. The giant Scot then tossed Archibald a bag of silver, reminding him, "Be back in two weeks, Archibald '*McIntosh*.'"

Archibald replied with angry Gaelic curse words as William rode off.

"Alright, family. Unload the weapons," Mr. Freeman instructed. "I think the danger has passed. Patrick, I need you to escort the ladies back to their homes and explain to their fathers why they stayed the night. If they feel you not be trusted, tell them to come see me."

Patrick then walked the ladies to their houses and watched as each were met with angry fathers. Patrick explained what had transpired, but it was not well received. On the walk home, he noticed the *Robin* sailing out to sea. Patrick wondered why they had left so early. Captain Gibbon's crew already hated him. Surely cutting their leave short would increase the captain's chances of not making it back to England. *Good riddance to the whole lot*, he thought.

* * *

Five months had passed and Patrick welcomed the fall air. Savannah was very beautiful in the fall and was a stark contrast to the filthy dark, gloomy city of London. After living so long, wasting away in a disgusting dungeon, he now took time to appreciate the simple blessings in life. He sat for hours staring at sea birds he had never before seen. His favorite was a black bird that looked like a large gull. The bird would skim across the ocean with its bottom orange bill slicing into the water. When the bird's lower bill hit a fish near the surface, it would snap it up and fly off, never losing its balance. He also grew to respect the strange pelicans and their fantastically awkward hunting skills. Most of the harvests were now coming in and the blacksmith's apprentice could see all the rice fields surrounding the town being prepared for winter. It was a bountiful harvest this year and he found himself falling in love with Mari Anna's corn breads.

The scars on his face were softening over the months. He worked long hours but had grown quickly skilled in making nails, hinges, locks and various tools. He was proud of his Scottish dirk that Archibald had showed him how to make. The blade was well balanced and true but a bit longer than a traditional Scottish knife. He had even grown bold enough to wear it as he traveled around Savannah. The British troops gave him a curious eye but left him to his own devices.

Patrick had quickly grown close to the Freeman family. He was especially enthralled with Heather and found himself unable to focus on any thought in her presence. She even caught him staring at her voluptuous breasts while she was serving him dinner. He was horribly embarrassed but she just smiled. She seemed to enjoy his discomfort. Archibald was like his father he so badly missed. He convinced his employer to help him send a letter back to London to his family, explaining to them that he was alive and well in the colonies. Both men knew it had little hope of ever finding its mark but it was written and sent despite the chances of making it home.

Tensions with the British troops had eased some since Commander Kingsley and Sergeant Luthor had been deployed to fight skirmishes with the Spanish down south, at least until the searches started. Patrick had still never seen the infamous James Oglethorpe in town but the young blacksmith heard the he was infuriated because somebody dared to steal his imported winder they used to spin the silk cocoons raised in his beloved Trustees' Garden. All his silk cocoons would now just go to waste like most of the rest of the garden. He ordered a town search and his troops tossed all the colonists' homes.

Strange men rifled through wives' unmentionables supposedly searching for something the size of a small cannon. This created a hornet's nest of animosity from the common folk toward the military.

He also saw Isaac occasionally in the morning buying a special kind of bread from Mari Anna. Mari Anna informed Patrick that a Jewish dictate forbade him from eating bread with yeast in it. She did not understand what the Jewish god had against yeast, but she baked flat bread and was happy for the extra money to be made for the unusual bread.

Patrick loved the new work clothes that Prudence had delivered to him. He had never had anything custom made for him. He had been washing them every three days because of the excessive sweating, but Savannah's heat was breaking a little and he only had to wash his clothes every ten days now. He desperately did not want peasant bloodstains on the thighs of his brand new outfit. The Freemans made jest of his excessive washing, God forbid, two times a week! The indenture took the jokes in stride though. He had spent so many years living in the putrid squalor of the debtors' prison that he took any chance he had to clean himself. Patrick washed himself every Sunday, while most of the town was at church. Oddly, the Freemans never attended the services held in Johnson Square. One day he thought he might ask why but he loved the alone time he was given and frankly did not care.

Patrick was quickly realizing that Savannah was like a huge melting pot. It was made of British, Irish, Scottish, African, Redskins, German, Polish, Portuguese, and a collection of stragglers from all over Europe. This made the religious worship an interesting mix. So many beliefs all in one place yet most people were tolerant.

Patrick was also combining the gossip from different criers, as well as the news from all over the colonies. He was told nothing of Savannah back on the *Robin* and was finally beginning to understand his new environment. He reasoned that many immigrants were promised freedom and the escape from the iron fist of the king. To a degree, they were indeed freer. They were allowed to own land and the tax burden was much less than in England. Some families were already creating wealth quickly, which would have been impossible back overseas. Some things had not changed at all though. Colonists were still subjects of the king and his soldiers could do anything they wanted to the colonists without fear of recourse. Patrick believed that the allure of the power the government offered attracted the worst kind of people. Most all of the soldiers were men following power-hungry politicians without question. The soldiers who disobeyed found themselves victim to mortal consequences. As a result, the worst of the worst rose to positions of power. The further up the ranks, the more corrupt and touched in the mind with power they became. Horrible atrocities would befall those that did not accept this situation. Patrick also discovered that people took dangerous risks anyway. Behind closed doors, words of freedom and personal sovereignty were spoken with whispers. He even stumbled upon an entire underground network of people and businesses that worked around Oglethorpe's rule. A disgruntled disobedience was on the wind.

One early morning of October 1739, Patrick woke to the sound of a ruckus. Heather was pounding on the shed door shouting, "Wake up!" She informed Patrick that Oglethorpe had commanded that the entire town attend his savage consort's service that day. "If you had not heard yet, Tomochichi and his savages are doing some heathen ceremony for Oglethorpe today." Heather mocked, "Be ready to join the family as we stop work and march ourselves down to Percival Square to console poor Oglethorpe's feelings."

The family adorned their most formal outfits and started the walk to Percival square. While walking, Archibald stated to Marian, "We should have gone anyway. I was fond of Tomochichi. I resent being ordered around like a mule." He kicked at the dirt in the road. "I think it soon be time to really think about joining our kin in Darien."

Marian shushed him and warned, "Let's not discuss this now with so many 'red' ears around."

The family turned a corner to view a huge crowd surrounding the square. The entire Yamacraw tribe attended in full dress. Even though Tomochichi had a falling out with the Creek tribe, many Creek still attended out of respect. Putting their differences aside, the Creek and Yamacraw met each other with traditional strong handshakes. The body of Tomochichi had been honored with a full military parade earlier and now sat in the center of Percival square on a horse drawn cart. Patrick was taken aback at seeing so many savages in one place. They were in full ceremonial dress. Huge headdresses, bright colors, fur, and feathers were everywhere. Many warriors were there. They had their hair cropped with a long central lock representing the traditional style of the Creek Indian. The warriors were also covered with ritual tattoos and pierced earlobes. He sensed the gravity of the event and, as far as he knew, no white man had ever witnessed the secret Creek Indian burial ceremonies.

Heather leaned over and whispered to Patrick, "The rumor circling today is this is only the internment ceremony. The Yamacraw already did a vast array of private rituals no white man may witness over the last few days. As part of Tomochichi's last request, he asked to be buried in Savannah to foster peace between our nations. I think he just loved all the white man's praise and attention. It made him a big fish to his people."

Four loud blasts sounded from a cow horn to summon the Yamacraw to the center of the Square. Five elders were holding large feathered ceremonial staffs that had broom ends. They then used the broom/staffs to sweep the crowd of groups. Patrick found it very odd how the tribe elders directed people to sit by pointing their lips.

The indenture then saw the esteemed Oglethorpe for the first time when the elders allowed the white leader to speak before they would begin with their scared rituals. He wore a formal military uniform with a new white wig. He solemnly walked to the center of the Yamacraw crowd and spoke sincerely to them. Oglethorpe kneeled in front of Tomochichi's wife, Senauki, and his nephew, Toonahowi, and spoke respectfully. Oglethorpe's friend, Mary Musgrove, translated English to the Yamacraw. She was the widow of a prominent South Carolina Indian trader who traveled with and was befriended by Tomochichi. She was born of mixed blood to a Tuckabachhee lower Creek Indian woman and Edward Griffin. She was married off to John Musgrove to foster peace between the Creek and the English. John met the Coweta headman, Brims. The English had earlier designated as "emperor" so that, in the eyes of the English at least, Brims could speak for the other chiefs or headmen. She was held in a position of prominence with her people and, even though the trustees of Savannah did not like her, Oglethorpe adored her and trusted her. She was now remarried to her indenture which was considered scandalous by Savannah upper-class socialites. She translated Oglethorpe's words to the stoic Yamacraw crowd.

"Tomochichi was a great chief. The counsel in sky will welcome him with the pipe of peace. The king and the people of Savannah owe him a great debt for all the help he gave us settling this town. Let us not forget his greatness and wisdom which helped us negotiate a treaty with the lower Creek. He was a great warrior and a noble savage."

Patrick was surprised when he eyed Commander Byron Kingsley in the crowd. He grew nervous knowing that muckraker was back in town. The commander rolled his eyes in disgust and disrespect while listening to Oglethorpe's heart filled speech.

The white leader continued, "I got to know him and his family well when we traveled to England together back in the Lord's year of thirty four. He was the toast of England and his majesty the king considers him a great loss.

"Let us not forget the noble work of John Wesley, Benjamin Ingham, Peter Rose, The Salzburger community and the noble chief. They all worked together to establish the Indian school at Irene to help teach Indians of the Lord and abandon their savage ways. I want to proclaim to all, Yamacraw

18th century painting of Tomochichi and Oglethorpe visiting London

and Creek: so honored is this great chief that Savannah will forever know his name and his grave will rest here, undeterred till the end of time. A pyramid will be erected with an inscription in brass, so all generations will know his name and deeds." Oglethorpe bowed to the tribe and sat in an honorary position next to Senauki and Toonahowi. As Oglethorpe sat down, a line of redcoats in full dress came up and presented arms. They raised their muskets into the air and fired an honorary volley of shot.

Heather whispered to her father asking, "Did they ever find out who killed that nice Indian named Skee?"

Archibald responded, "I know it had to be John Musgrove's servant named Justice because his life was taken by Skee's relative named Essteeche. The whole thing smells of scandal and whenever scandal is involved, I look no further than Commander Byron Kingsley." The father then warned sternly, "You and your lasses stay far away from that commander, do you understand?"

"Aye, father," she obediently responded

Patrick watched as the honored rituals and the sacred ceremony started. As Creek tradition insisted, only the friends of the family could dig the grave. Tomochichi's own family sat and watched while the warriors of the tribe dug. During the digging, the squaws danced and chanted their last goodbyes. This part of the ritual of digging, chanting and dancing took over an hour. To pass the time, Patrick whispered to Archibald, "Why would this savage help the white man bring more white men here?"

Archibald explained quietly, "The Yamacraw have an enemy tribe in the south who have sided with the Spanish. For fear of extinction, Tomochichi befriended the English. When Oglethorpe needed help establishing Savannah, Tomochichi saw the opportunity to win favor for his tribe. It also didn't hurt that Oglethorpe and the trustees stuffed his mouth with gold." He smiled as he continued, "As with most savages, he did not keep the gifts for himself but distributed it to his tribe to reward rank. I also think he was motivated by the fame and respect the white men gave him. He actually liked being referred to as a 'noble savage'."

A group of warriors then lifted the coffin Oglethorpe provided for the chief. They used ropes to lower the pine box into the hole dug in the ground. The chants and dancing continued as the casket was lowered.

The master blacksmith spoke sarcastically, "If that chief be ninety-seven years aged like they say he was, then I am the King of Scotland. No man would still be a warrior at his age. Look how young his skin is. I'd guess he was no older than sixty! Well let's depart. We have done enough for king and country today and I need to be quenching my thirst."

Most of the whites were departing but the natives

continued to mourn at the tomb. As Patrick looked back, he saw the warriors starting to make a pyramid mound out of stones over the grave.

CHAPTER 8

FORT MOSE, LIBERTY AND HONOR

The Freemans approached their home in a hushed walk so as not to disturb the closing ceremonies of Tomochichi's burial. Archibald and Patrick returned to the shed so Archibald could hide his Scottish broadsword he wore for the ceremony. The men froze when they heard a loud crash inside the shed. The master blacksmith drew the large broadsword while the apprentice grabbed an extinguished torch to use as a club. They stood close and Archibald threatened, "Come out with peaceful intent or I will run you through!"

Movement and a hushed conversation could be heard in the shed.

"Come! Present yourself in front of me now or I will raise arms!" the angry blacksmith demanded.

Slowly, a crying black woman stepped out of the shed with open palms. She was followed by a skinny African man who also presented his open hands. He quickly explained in a nervous voice, "I be very sorry. We just searching fo' scraps of food. We done been robbed by road agents and not eaten a ting in days, sir. Please, mister, we stole no wares. Just let us be on way."

"Sit down," Archibald commanded with his sword pointed. The nervous colored couple sat on the stumps for splitting wood outside the shed. "Go take inventory of the shed, Patrick. See if they be speaking true," the smith instructed.

An uneasy truce was called while the apprentice searched the shed loudly. This attracted the rest of the Freemans, who

Alick and Gloria are caught

watched in shock from the backdoor of their home.

"Good sir, I find nothing amiss," Patrick reported.

"Marian, can you bring me that basket of apples we have in haste," Archibald asked his wife.

Marian offered the basket to the shaking couple, "Here, relax."

"I will give you as much food as you desire but in return I want you to tell me your real story. Your fresh shackle bruises tell me your possessions were not taken by road agents. You two are runaways or I am a fool," Archibald offered.

"My name be Alick, sir, and dis be da wife Gloria. It true. We be on da run from Charles Town," the black man stopped to bite into an apple.

Heather and Marian took seats as the tension relaxed. "Tell us more, Alick," Heather prodded.

"We from da Kingdom of Kongo and our friends and family be forced inta service. Many of us from dar. One of Cato's slaves, Mr. Jemmy, stirred up da lot of us. We was treated much worse den all da utta slaves we know. Da beatin's be very bad. Twenty of us slaves rise up and go running from da Ashley River, it be north of da Stono River. A few men used ta be soldiers and started making weapons from whatever we found on da way." Alick boasted, "We kept goin' south and da news spread. We liberated about sixty slaves from der harsh masters."

Archibald looked dismayed, "How many white masters did you kill?"

"We took revenge on twenty of da white devils and took der things and weapons," he said with dismay. "Da militia from da Carolinas caught up wit us at Edisto River and a great battle took place. Dey killed forty-four of da slaves. We killed twenty of da white devils. Da survivors went running and da militia hunt dem down. We be da only ones left I tink. Please good, sir, I never killed any whites in those battles. I don't have it in me ta kill anyone. Dat is why we have no weapons and we run fast. Those were evil men and deserved ta meet da devil." The fugitive slave pleaded, "Please just let us go on our way and forget we be here."

The Freemans looked at each other with concern as Archibald spoke sternly, "We need to discuss this. Do not think about running." The patriarch then handed his sword to Patrick and told him, "If he starts to move, stick him."

The young smith watched the slave couple cry and shake as the Freemans were judging their fates. After a passionate and lengthy discussion, Archibald returned.

"The Scottish have been terrorized and enslaved in sorts by the British for as long as I can remember. I sympathize with your plea for freedom," Archibald grimaced, "but you put my family in grave peril by staying here. What are your plans for flight?"

"We have no's ideas. Maybe run as far in da swamp is we can so nobody can ever find us." Gloria replied.

"What if I told you there is a place you can be safe and free?" Archibald questioned.

"No such a place I be know of," Gloria stammered.

"There is such a place where you can be free. It is called Fort Mose. It is a settlement the Spanish set up to anger the lobster backs. The Spanish made it as a haven for escaped slaves to encourage British slaves to run and then raise arms against the British as free men," Archibald explained in hushed tones.

The black couple stared at the wigged smith in disbelief.

"It's true. The fort was founded last year. It is a little north of St. Augustine in the Floridas. A Creole man runs the fort. I once did some unmentionable business with him. He is named Francisco Menendez. I am telling you this because I have no love for the English or any government ruling over people with force. It is with great risk to my life and family. I would be branded a traitor to the English and hung from the gallows," Archibald warned.

"We bless you for dis knowledge. If you draw us a map, we leave at nightfall. We owe your family our lives and would never speak of you ta anyone," the colored couple sincerely promised.

Alick and Gloria spent the rest of the day quietly eating and drinking upstairs in the small house. Late into the night, Archibald saw them off. "Here, take these apples and this skin to hold water. Here is a dirk for Gloria and an axe for you. Keep these hidden until you have made your way past Darien. Those in Darien would most likely kill you on site for having Scottish weapons. If you do get caught in Darien, beg for your life and tell them to give this note to William McIntosh. The note might keep you from losing your heads."

The two fugitive slaves' eyes were wide.

"After Darien the real danger falls on you. You have to pass through English, Spanish and Indian deer hunting territory. It is a large zone where hatred is set aside to make silver. You two would be a good bounty to the wrong kind of person, so stay silent in the marshes. You need be invisible and only travel by moonlight. Pray no savages or British find you or that will be the end of your lives. Keep steady south and you will find Fort

Mose. Good luck and may the wind be at your backs."

Gloria and Alick were taken with tears at this generosity and said their goodbyes. They quickly disappeared into the night, quiet as mice.

* * *

Patrick was enjoying the cooler air blowing in, even the sand gnats and mosquitoes had slowed their assaults for his blood. He was trying his hand at forging an axe head and was making fine progress when Archibald interrupted him, "Lad, it is about time me and you go have a drink." He then instructed his daughter to bring them rum. The two men sat under the dogwood as Heather appeared with a bottle and mugs. She looked around cautiously and then poured the rum into the mugs.

"Ah, lad! Here is some of the forbidden nectar of the Caribbean. Let us enjoy our sins against Oglethorpe," Archibald mocked. He continued. "Lad, I put you in grave risk when I helped those Negroes. When we thought that bastard Kingsley was going to ascend on my daughter, you came to my family's aid without question. You have given me the truth of your nefarious past so it is time you learned the truth about me."

Feeling comfortable with Patrick and the rum, the master blacksmith let his brogue come out, "Me real name be Duncan and I am from the clan McIntosh from Inverness, Scotland. Life for me family was hard and miserable, we never owned anything. The damn English took so much, it kept us in squalor. I grew up a blacksmith like me father before me. He wanted to leave that hopeless life so when the English outlawed Scots carrying weapons, he saw an opportunity. He learned to make muskets, blades, axes and small shields called 'targs'. He enlisted me help and I quickly grew competent in weapon crafting. Me father made a fortune but so much trade brought the eyes of the British on us. Because of this scrutiny, he gave me all his monies to go out and resupply our shop. One day when I came home, I found me whole family dead. Me father and me mother were hanging from our tree and me siblings met their deaths by fire inside our home, burned alive by British soldiers."

His eyes filled with tears as he confessed, "It was a message to our town about what happens to arms dealers who defy his majesty. I immediately became a wanted man and was hunted. Me clan was outraged and demanded a reckoning. I talked them out of a war on the lobsterbacks. I would not let them spill the blood of me community and clan. Me clan smuggled me to Savannah with money from me father to start a new life. A few in Darien know me true self but I had to take on British mannerisms for safety. I changed me name and me voice to protect all those around me. I concede to live this way until I can escape the English warrant for me."

"So are these your birth children?" Patrick questioned in surprise.

"No. I met Marian and her family when I arrived in Savannah in the Lord's year thirty-six. She was married to a Spanish trader who played both sides of the war but he was executed by the Spanish for selling stolen arms to the British and savages. So her family is not welcomed in the Spanish colonies or Indian Territory. We be a family of outlaws trying to make enough money to get far away from any government. We needed each other, so our marriage was a good fit. The bloody backs ignored her warrant because her husband sold so many guns to them."

Patrick sat stunned and speechless. He then put a comforting hand on Archibald's shoulder and promised, "I will take this secret to the grave. And I wish there was a place that existed without some authority ruling over our freedom, my friend."

"Do you lad? Well I have one more secret you might want to know. There are many others who feel as us, a whole underground world," He smiled as he sipped his illegal rum.

"Will you teach me to make muskets and pistols now?" Patrick inquired.

"His royal fucking majesty's men do not get alarmed when I

make simple blades but they do not allow me to make muskets for anyone but their soldiers. I will teach you but if you're careless, it ends with all of us swinging in the wind. We can only make them when no eyes be watching. Have you ever noticed it takes me weeks to fix a long firearm or a pistol? Working under the guise of fixing a redcoat's firelock, I am allowed to secretly make another one in plain view without suspicion," Archibald taught.

"So now we hang together my friend. You're invited to a secret meeting two fortnights from now. I hope you will join with others who feel the same as you about governments," Archibald offered. Patrick nodded his head in acceptance as Archibald finished, "Oh! One last thing. It is no good making all these weapons if you can't use them. Tomorrow we go hunting in the swamps."

* * *

Crack, BLAMM! The firelock blinded Patrick with smoke as it went off. He coughed and rubbed his eyes.

"Oops! I forgot to mention. You have to keep your eyes closed and hold your breath when you fire," Archibald and the twins howled with laughter. "Maximilian, did he hit the pine?"

"No father," Maximilian shook his head. "I can't find the shot anywhere."

"Let us not try to waste that shot. It be hard to get metal in Savannah. Try to find it. Now Patrick, hold your breath and stabilize it better with your shoulder." Archibald smiled, "Now show me how fast you can load, lad."

"Everyone clear out of the way, I'm loading," Patrick called out to the twins.

Patrick had practiced the procedure repeatedly without ammo all morning hoping it would become second nature. He pulled the charge out of his deerskin pouch. It was shot and gunpowder carefully wrapped up in paper to fit in the barrel easily. He then detached the ramrod from under the barrel and

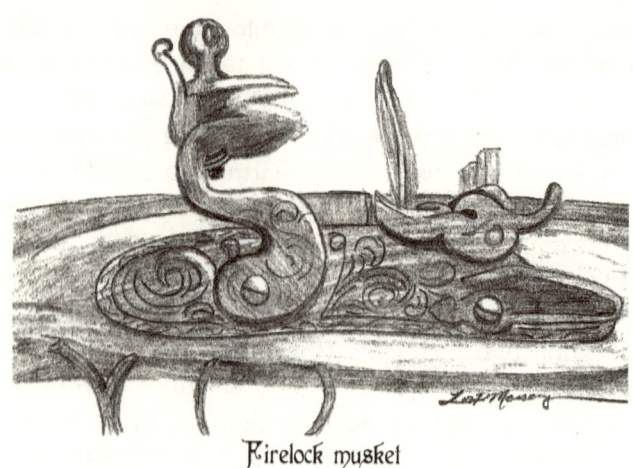

Firelock musket

pushed the charge all the way to the bottom. He returned the ramrod, moved the flint to the half-cocked position, and then opened the flash pan. He poured in a small amount of powder in the pan and then moved the flint to full cock. He then sited at the large pine 50 paces away and took careful aim. He lined up his feet and shoulders as Archibald instructed, held his breath and lined up the sights again. He closed his eyes and held his breath as he slowly squeezed the trigger.

A loud crack could be heard as the flint struck the mizzen. The powder ignited in the flash pan and moved into the chamber. *BLAMM!* A large cloud of smoke covered Patrick and a paper wad flew out of the barrel. When the smoke cleared, he took a deep breath, opened his eyes and asked with anticipation, "How did I do?"

"Father!" Amos shouted. "He hit it!"

"Fantastic, lad! It took me days before I ever hit anything. You need to fire ten more to get a feel for Marian," Archibald said with pride.

"You named your firelock 'Marian'?" Patrick queried.

"Of course, lad. It be bad luck not to name your weapon after your sweetheart. You really don't know a damn thing about fighting," Archibald laughed.

Patrick practiced all morning and hit six out of ten of his

shots with the musket before switching to Archibald's antique Queen Anne dueling pistols. The pistols were wildly inaccurate. Even at fifteen paces, Patrick only hit the tree three out of ten times.

"You boys go now and dig that spent shot out of that pine, we need the metal to recast," their father commanded.

The men went shooting the entire week under the guise of being bad hunters. Patrick improved greatly. Archibald even showed him some basic knife and broadsword skills before his shooting lessons. Once in a while, one of the twins would bring back game he had hunted while Patrick was getting his lessons. They were excellent hunters for such a young age. Both boys had learned to shoot a bow from a savage friend of theirs and were becoming deadly shots.

One morning in November, Maximilian helped his brother hobble to the front door. His foot was bleeding badly.

"What in the Lord's name happened?!" Marian exclaimed. "Heather, fetch your father immediately!"

Amos grunted in pain, "I stepped on a bloody oyster shell and it sliced me good."

"Heather, go fetch that Jew doctor! Hurry!" Marian screamed while she compressed the wound with her dirty hand.

Amos's foot started to bleed less and in a short time, Dr. Nunis and Isaac Swartz were tending the boy's foot. Patrick had missed seeing his goliath friend and once Amos was tended to, they caught up. Patrick had shown Isaac the broadsword he was making and Isaac showed Patrick the exotic plants he had in his medical bag. Dr. Nunis watched the exchange and finally said to Archibald, "Why don't I stay for a while and visit your family? I would be happy to check you all for aliments. It would be nice to let the old friends talk."

Archibald nodded his head in agreement and then showed him Maximilian's forearm. "See the worm is moving right next to the skin, it is growing and almost half the length of his forearm," Archibald pointed out.

"Oh, Mr. Freeman, you need to call me sooner. If you had waited a few months longer, the damn African worm would have come right out of a blister. It would burn like hell and cripple your boy," Dr. Nunis explained. "We need to take this worm out right now. Let me get my worm stick."

He returned with a knife and a small stick that had a hole dug out in the center of it. After that he explained, "We have to cut enough to put the end of the worm through the hole in the stick. Then we need to tie it off." The Doctor then cut a small nick and blood rolled down the brave boys forearm. Everyone gathered around to watch as the doctor threaded the head of the large white worm though the stick. While nimbly attending to his work, Dr. Nunis spoke, "These damn worms are all over lately. I think they came over with some slaves in the Carolinas and now they are everywhere."

After a few moments, the doctor stated, "Okay, I have it tied down. Only give it one half turn a day, anymore than that it will break and kill the worm. If this worm dies in your son, his forearm will become septic and make him very ill. Do *not* over turn the stick! Do you understand?" Dr. Nunis warned. "Now son, continue to hold your hand on the laceration until it clots."

Archibald then took the opportunity to show the doctor a rotting tooth and asked his opinion.

Patrick and Isaac were laughing, reminiscing about the vanishing of Shamus, when Patrick froze in mid-sentence. Isaac watched as his best friend's face lost its color. Two well-dressed men were standing over them.

"You there, go fetch your master," the tall aristocrat demanded.

Patrick stood up and continued to stare at him intensely.

"Are you dumb and deaf? Go fetch your master or I will have him beat you!" the tall man pushed on.

Isaac quickly sensed something was very out of sorts with Patrick and waved Archibald over. Patrick began to close the distance between himself and the two men when his employer stepped in his way and stated, "I am the blacksmith here. How can I help you?"

The tall man replied, "Ah yes. I need a very small hammer made. I am a jeweler just come from London and I seem to have misplaced my hammer."

"Can you draw out the size you need with this paper and quill?" the blacksmith responded.

"I can do my best, good smith." The aristocrat then took the quill and paper.

"I'm Archibald Freeman and can I ask your name, sir?" Archibald asked as the tall man busied himself drawing the dimensions of the proposed hammer.

Drily, the aristocrat announced, "My name is Mr. Potts and this is my associate Mr. Edgeington."

Patrick pushed past Archibald and smacked the paper and quill out of Potts' hand. "We won't help you here," Patrick snarled. "Now get the fuck out!" The entire group was stunned by Patrick's extremely unusual behavior. Archibald tried to step back in and but Patrick pushed him away. "I said get the fuck out!" Patrick screamed.

"Mr. Freeman, you might want to control your hammer monkey before Mr. Edgeington buries a blade in his chest," Mr. Potts threatened.

Tension grew thick in the small house and everyone was standing on toe. Patrick then spit a large ball of mucus into Potts' eye and screamed, "Fuck you, and take that with you!" Patrick's accuracy had benefited from hours of spitting competitions in prison.

Everyone stood stunned and mortified. None believed what they were seeing. As all disbelieving eyes were on Patrick and Potts, Mr. Edgeington skinned his blade, though Potts urged him to hold.

Patrick now took his time to build a large amount of phlegm in his mouth before sending it flying across the distance and landing on Potts' chin. "GET THE FUCK OUT!" he shrieked.

Potts then wiped his face, closing the distance between himself and Patrick. As he was closing fast, he was suddenly smacked in the face with Patrick's deerskin smithing glove. The entire room watched in awe as the glove hit the floor and lay at Potts' feet. Potts stopped in his tracks and looked at the glove. He then looked back up at Patrick with a moment of fear.

"Pick it up," Patrick demanded coldly. Isaac tried to pull Patrick back but the challenge had been made. "Fucking pick it up you coward!" Patrick growled.

Potts hesitated and was terrified as he looked into the rage filled eyes of his opponent. "I want to know your name first before I accept your challenge."

"I am Patrick Willis," Patrick hissed. "You stole my life. You disgraced my father and you're the reason I was in debtors' prison all these years."

Marian and Heather simultaneously gasped in shock.

Potts stopped and examined the younger man closer. "Ah yes... Mr. Edgeington don't you remember this boy who was nice enough to donate those stones to you all those years ago?"

Mr. Edgeington smirked, "Right, boss. I had forgotten. Hey lad, how's da face?"

Both men laughed as Patrick flew at them in a rage. Isaac then quickly grabbed his friend and was only barely able to overcome Patrick, pinning him against the wall and holding him back.

"Well, lad, those stones of your father's were shite," Potts said mockingly. "I had to practically give them away." Mr. Potts slowly bent over and picked up the fallen glove and informed, "I guess I will have to end your whole rutting bloodline and accept your challenge. Stupid boy, I have emerged victorious in four duels."

"Very well. Single combat at daybreak on the deer hunting road to Darien. Meet me under the thunderbolt tree outside of town to avoid legal complications." Mr. Potts challenged.

"You fucking child. Were you not already gelded, you would do it at noon. Dawn is for cowards," Patrick bit back. "Why not a duel at noon? Your death will be devoid of mist and fog."

"Fine," the tall aristocrat answered. "A single combat duel at noon, I will take your life in clear sight, boy."

Isaac pulled Patrick's other glove off his hand and threw it down at Edgeington's feet. "He does not accept single combat, do you second?" Isaac questioned.

The crowd looked on in amazement.

"This man wants to meet his Jewy god. I will hurry your wish," Mr. Egeington laughed as he picked up the glove. "I have killed many more men than Mr. Potts. I will enjoy this opportunity to send another Jew to hell."

As the arrogant men took their leave, Isaac continued to hold Patrick against the wall while the enraged man continued to scream in anger. After a few moments, his rage waned and led to tears. Isaac was able to release his upset friend and the entire Freeman family came to Patrick and hugged him. They held onto him tight as if they knew these would be his last hours on earth.

CHAPTER 9

DUELING AT NOON

Patrick's weeping soon turned to focused rage. He could not stop pacing the Freeman's tiny home. The Freeman family and the doctor were still in shock. The old skinny man yelled at Isaac in Jewish tongue and forbid him to take part in the duel. Isaac stubbornly ignored him and dismissed his orders shaking his head. Indentures were not allowed to make any challenge until their contract was fulfilled. Both servants, due to the egregiousness of the insult, ignored this custom.

Isaac spoke up after being silent for so long. "We need a strategy to level this challenge."

"I have dueled once in my life, but it be with an axe," Archibald interjected. "This Potts is a cur. He lacks the courage to fight by blade. He will choose pistol which in turn will mean pistols for the seconds. This is fortunate though because Mr. Edgeington was wearing a very fine blade and I assume he is a very skilled swordsman. We don't want blade combat. I do assume if Mr. Potts killed four men already, he has more pistol experience than you, lad," he soberly addressed Patrick. "So you will have to get him in an up close and personal duel."

"Agreed. He would never challenge us to blade or fist," Isaac concurred.

"That being the case, let us get as much pistol play as possible between now and then," Archibald resolved. "Boys! Go fetch the dueling pistols and as much shot and powder as we can find."

The entire family marched by torchlight to the shot marked

124

pine tree. Shots echoed through the dark marshes all night long as the two men honed their killing craft. They ran out of shot by mid-morning and returned to the blacksmith's house. Marian and Heather fetched fresh bread and eggs for what could be the duelers' last meal. The combatants sat in stoic silence. They stayed focused, rehearsing the correct pistol firing procedures repeatedly in their minds.

Amos came limping in with a bandaged foot. He stated solemnly, "Father, the noon hour is approaching. We need to depart."

"Lads, do you have any last orders for me?" Archibald sadly inquired. He felt strange calling two men 'lads' as they were about to encounter grave battle, but he needed to comfort himself as much as Patrick and Isaac.

Patrick replied with a dry mouth at last, "I like the ocean. Bury me at sea if it is not too much trouble. And if that letter ever finds my family in London, tell them I was thinking about them in the end." Patrick then stared out the window.

"The doctor knows where to find my sister. Ask her to make sure I get a proper Jewish burial," Isaac asked.

The group slowly got up and embraced each other. The hugs were heart filled as the Freeman's had come to love Patrick as family already. The duelers finished their final goodbyes and walked in lockstep down the dusty road.

"Isaac, you don't have to risk your life as my second. I can still request single combat," Patrick offered.

"You would do this for me. It is an honor to be there for you now. I will be your second, but be sure to demand cross shots for me. I want to see this Jew hater shit his pants while he dies," Isaac smiled. Patrick nodded as they continued down the road out of town.

* * *

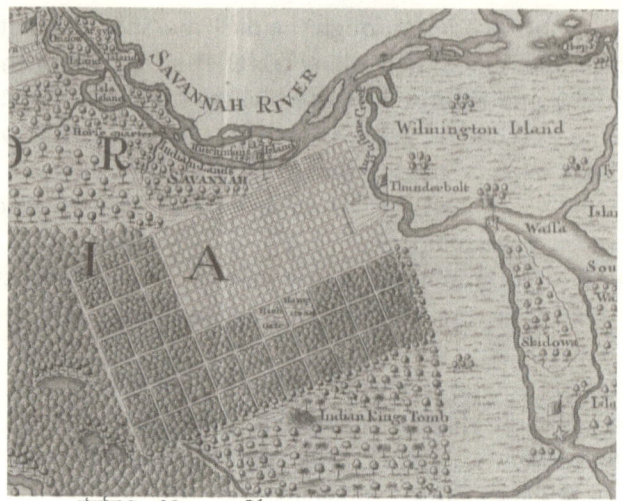

1740 Map of Savannah showing Thunderbolt

As they approached Thunderbolt, they saw Potts and Edgeington sipping tea under the shade of the two lightning scarred trees. A large crowd had already gathered. The tall aristocrat had bragged all night in the tavern where he was staying about how he would "end this heathen's bloodline forever". It seemed that every Jew in the village came out to support Isaac, thanks to the doctor. It was no longer a secret event hidden away from the authorities. Mari Anna, Prudence and their families also showed for support, quietly holding back their frightened tears. On the edge of the crowd, watching intently, was the Madam April Sky and a few of her women of ill repute, painted and dressed for the morbid occasion.

"We thought you had pissed your leg and ran off like a kicked dog," Mr. Potts called out insulting Patrick and Isaac while playing to the gathered crowd. With faces like grave stones, Patrick and Isaac only had cold stares for a response. The aristocrat flourished with a handkerchief in his hand, continuing with his theatrics. "Well, no reason to delay your deaths any longer," he smiled evilly. "Shall we establish the rules to this duel?" He continued, "Blacksmith, we have chosen you to proxy."

"I accept your offer," Archibald responded. "First, an understanding of terms must be met. Do all parties agree this is a duel to the death with seconds?"

"Aye," all four combatants replied in unison glaring at each other.

"The first man challenged has choice of weapon for the rest. I lay these out for your choosing and, remember, you may also pick open hand." Archibald opened the large bag his son was carrying and displayed the arms on the ground. Four hunting swords of similar length, four dirks and four pistols were displayed. Mr. Potts inspected each choice of arms carefully, turning the dirks slowly in his hand but the crowd gasped when he finally reached for the broadswords. Isaac and Patrick both looked at each other attempting to conceal their cold panic, neither had much experience with a blade. Mr. Potts then abruptly changed his mind and picked up a dueling pistol. The Queen Anne flintlock pistols were a proper matching set crafted specifically for dueling. The other two pistols were similar in look but were aged and worn. They were borrowed that morning from Prudence's father, the tailor. Potts looked the crowd over then searched Patrick's eyes, hoping the younger man would tip his hand, and then nodded to Freeman to indicate he had chosen. Archibald then gathered the pistols, dividing the fine Queen Anne's pistols between Potts and Patrick and then gave Isaac and Mr. Edgeington the mismatched flintlocks. The four men then loaded their pistols carefully while listening to the instructions.

Archibald spoke loudly so the entire crowd could hear, "The challenged may set the paces."

"I choose twenty," the smug jeweler announced.

"As I thought, you coward," Patrick snarled. "Too afraid to face me like a man."

"You do not want me to have any challenge at all? Suit yourself, sir. I will oblige. Ten paces," the arrogant aristocrat played to the crowd.

"A brave gentleman would accept the terms of cross shot as well," Patrick baited Potts's ego.

"You make this too easy, boy," Potts smirked. "Accepted."

With the rules agreed upon, Archibald then paced the ten steps and stuck a sword in the ground. He repeated the procedure in the opposite direction.

"I also thought you might like to know what happened to your lovely mother and sisters," Potts began to snicker, smiling at his lap dog, Edgeington. "My associate Mr. Edgeington helped them gain employment at London's most renowned brothel. That is, after he enjoyed them himself."

Patrick started to raise his pistol but Isaac grabbed the barrel and pushed it towards the earth. "Not like that," Isaac whispered, reassuring Patrick. "Soon enough, friend."

Archibald then instructed nervously with his voice almost quivering, "Take your marks, gentlemen. When I drop this cloth, you will exchange one round of fire."

All four men fell as silent as death as they approached the swords sticking out of the ground. The crowd backed away from the line of fire and grew very anxious. It was so quiet that a light autumn breeze could be heard rustling through the leaves of the ancient burned trees above them. The four duelists then took their prospective places. Patrick mirrored Mr. Potts walking five paces over, and behind them were their seconds. Archibald gulped a hard swallow and lifted the red linen handkerchief in the air so all parties could see. Patrick turned straight on, exposing his entire body to the aristocrat as a challenge. To not be branded a coward in front of the large crowd, Mr. Potts reluctantly matched his posture to Patrick's. The duelers were all sweating, perspiration dotting their foreheads and their pistol grips becoming moist with anticipation. Time seemed to slow down, as if swimming through molasses, as Patrick watched the red cloth drop from Archibald's hand. The entire world went silent.

The virgin dueler saw Mr. Potts raise his pistol and was immediately overwrought with panic and fear. Patrick nervously stumbled with his pistol, pulling the trigger and firing into the ground. His eyes and nose burnt as his senses became overwhelmed with white smoke. Patrick then felt a punch to the side of his head. His knees crumpled and he slowly fell to the ground. His head felt afire and his eyesight filled with crimson. As he lay on the ground, he saw Isaac lying next to him. Forgetting his own pain, Patrick became extremely upset to see his best friend was holding his right arm, now covered in blood. Patrick's ears were like church bells on Easter Sunday; the ringing was deafening. Mr. Potts' weasel-like voice was laughing hysterically at the inexperienced dueler and his bloody friend who was lying at his side, moaning.

"Dandy of a shot, boy!" Potts taunted. "Were you trying to shoot the devil before you meet him?"

Patrick shook his head, attempted to collect himself, and slowly sat up. The world seemed to tilt and whirl a little. He then touched his ear which felt like it was burning. When he looked down, he saw his hand was covered in blood. To the scar-faced man's relief, his second, Isaac, was now sitting up as well. The two wounded friends nodded at each other, confirming they both survived, and then turned their gaze down range.

Mr. Potts had stopped laughing abruptly. He was gaping in disbelief at his associate, Mr. Edgeington, who was clutching his bleeding chest and gasping desperately for air. The more the man's chest heaved, the redder his shirt became. Patrick thought he looked like a dumb farm animal, finally aware that slaughter was imminent.

"Reload," Archibald's steely voice commanded. As instructed, Amos and Maximilian ran out and took the pistols from both Patrick's and Isaac's hands. They deftly reloaded as Patrick helped Isaac back to his feet.

Voices in the crowd shrieked at the site of so much blood while others, with a more morbid fascination, clapped and howled for more. Not one soul came to help Potts and Edgeington reload their pistols.

Edgeington, who seemed to gain some of his sense, spit blood and cursed, "Let me kill this horned Jew fuck. Make Jesus happy before I pass on." He then ordered Potts, "Hurry up! Load those guns and get me to my feet."

Mr. Potts paused for a moment. He could see Edgeington's wound was mortal but he moved quickly to follow the instructions. Within a couple of minutes, the four men were again standing at their marks, pistols ready.

Archibald raised the linen cloth again. Isaac's bloody right arm hung limp and he was forced to switch pistol hands. Mr. Edgeington was fading fast. His mouth hung agape and he blinked excessively as if he were falling asleep. He swayed his weight from his left foot to his right foot, wobbling like a drunk. The red of his shirt was spreading quickly and the top of his pants were becoming wet with blood.

Patrick still heard ringing in his ear. Two blurry images of Potts danced before him. Patrick shook his head and rubbed his eyes with his free hand. As Potts came somewhat into focus, he hissed a last promise, "I am going to introduce you to the devil with this shot, boy!"

The crowd grew silent again and it seemed like an eternity until the handkerchief fell. When it was finally released, it was like a leaf, slowly drifting on the warm breeze. Patrick could feel his arm slowing climbing up to his target. A puff of white smoke engulfed Edgeington as a fire eats paper and the man fell like timber that had just been cut down.

Mr. Potts was taking his time, ensuring he aimed true. His head tilted as his steely gaze stared down the barrel searching for a mortal shot on Patrick. As his site pointed directly at his inexperienced opponent, he was blown off balance and spilled over onto one knee. Potts screamed, grabbing his shattered, bloody shin. When the bloody aristocrat looked up, he was horrified to realize Isaac had trained his gun on him instead of Mr. Edgeington.

Patrick seized the opportunity. He held his breath and slowly squeezed the trigger as Archibald had taught him. There was a click, a puff of white smoke, then the explosion of the shot. Patrick felt death in his hand. When he opened his eyes, the hazy smoke of his pistol was swirling away in the breeze. Patrick watched as the tall aristocrat staggered trying to balance himself on his one good knee and grasp his neck, now spewing with blood. Pott's struggled to breathe, wheezing as his neck gurgled like a fountain.

"Send me to the devil, Potts," Patrick pounded his chest with his pistol hand. "I am right here."

Potts raised his pistol, pathetically attempting to stand steady with one of his legs shattered below the knee. His arm shook erratically as he could barely muster the strength to keep the pistol raised above his hip. His pistol cracked, echoing through the woods, creating a small cloud of smoke but the shot was wild. Potts collapsed, drowning in his own blood.

Patrick and Isaac enter a traditional four man duel

Patrick shouted at the fallen man, "I hope the devil makes you his whore, you evil fuck!"

The victorious man was hatefully staring at Potts lying in a puddle of his own blood when he heard his friend screaming. He immediately turned to Isaac who was holding his right hand to his chest as he rocked back and forth. Patrick saw blood running down Isaac's forearm from where his ring finger once was. As he rushed to his friend, he screamed for the doctor. He put his arms around his friend who was sitting on the ground. Isaac screamed, "Fuck!" He gritted his teeth and his eyes were squinting with pain. Isaac looked at his friend, "I'll be okay. It just fucking hurts like all hell." Isaac tried to smile. Patrick nodded dumbly. Isaac could tell his friend was gravely concerned and winced when he spoke, "Forget about me for a moment. Let's make sure we watch those evil bastards die." Patrick nodded again.

They both turned to their fallen enemies. Edgeington was crumpled into a ball like a calf that had just been slaughtered. His eyes were vacant and his open mouth seemed to kiss the ground. The corpse's buttocks were stained brown from where his bowels evacuated when his life left him. Isaac smiled when he realized his prediction came true, indeed he actually made "The Jew hater shit his pants". Potts was still struggling. His body convulsed. Some gathered around him but they all knew he was done. Potts then made a terrible sound, like a cough muffled by a wet quilt, as blood bubbled from his neck. Patrick's vision finally cleared and he could see the pupils of Potts's eyes constrict to the size of a pin head. He gurgled one final, bloody cough and his pupils became as wide as a schilling as the last bit of color left the flesh of his face. Potts finally stopped moving.

Archibald immediately took control of the situation and urged the girls to collect the weapons before the redcoats arrived. He ordered Maximilian and Amos to drag the bodies of Potts and Edgeington into the swamps and to cover them well until they became a gator's dinner. He then instructed Dr. Nunis to bring Isaac and Patrick back to the Freeman home to treat them. The crowd quickly dissipated as the Freemans scurried to work. Within minutes, there was no sign the duel had ever happened in Thunderbolt.

* * *

Dr. Nunis was struggling to stop the bleeding from Isaac's stump of a finger. Isaac had been shot a second time but still had managed to get a miraculous shot into Mr. Potts before the pain overtook him. Both duelers had been overtaken by the battle, numb to pain and to the world, focused only on killing.

Patrick had never killed a man or anything, for that matter. The reality of what had happened began to sink in and he succumbed to emotion. He cried and cursed, occasionally pounding a table or wall, and was wracked with guilt for his wounded friend.

When Patrick had finally calmed, Archibald meticulously cleaned the blood from his indenture's head and ear. Freeman examined his hairline, delicately combing Patrick's hair from the wound, and surmised, "Lad, I see lots of blood but no real injury. This is the luckiest dueling wound I've ever seen." The apprentice's eyes blinked as he listened. Archibald smiled grimly and stated, "You just lost some skin and you might have another scar, but you will be fine."

The doctor walked over to Archibald and Patrick, wiping blood from his hands with a rag and announced, "The bullet passed through the muscle in Isaac's arm. It will be numb for a while but it'll recover." The doctor's voice lowered with seriousness, "The finger though, that's a different and more complicated case. We'll have to take fire to it to stop the bleeding. We should burn it now while his senses are vacant."

The blacksmith's sons were instructed to stoke the fire pit to heat the coals. When the fire was ready, Archibald sunk a cattle branding iron deep into the embers until the steel glowed. He then carefully removed it and handed it to the doctor. The entire Freeman family gathered around the table where the hulking Isaac lay and held him by his arms and legs. Marian parted his jaw and put a wooden spoon handle in his mouth. Once Isaac was secured, the doctor did not hesitate and quickly placed the glowing iron on the bleeding stump. Isaac let out a piercing scream. His back arched with pain as he ripped his arms and legs from the combined grasp of the Freeman family. He raised the smoldering stump of his finger towards the heavens and spat out Marian's wooden spoon. The smell of burnt flesh filled the air. Isaac, now jolted out of his stupor by the pain, stood on his feet and the first thing he noticed was two muskets pointed at his chest.

The group, so busy struggling to hold down the giant Jew,

never noticed the group of armed redcoats that had appeared in the yard. Sergeant Luthor reported, "Commander, this must be them. They be covered with blood."

Commander Kíngsley strutted into the yard and stated, "Indeed, they match the description of the duelers." His face was stern like a statue as he gave his order, "Take them to Oglethorpe for judgment. Shoot any of these barnacle colonialists that resist."

The Freeman family anguished with fear. Their feet were like stone, unmoving in front of the armed British troops. Dr. Nunis pushed his way forward and demanded, "I am escorting these men. I am not done treating this patient."

In an annoyed tone, Kingsley complied, "So be it."

Two pairs of soldiers grabbed Patrick and Isaac by their arms just under the pits and roughly escorted them out of the Freeman yard. They shoved the bloody men through town to the curiosity of many onlookers. They were then dragged to Oglethorpe's gigantic tent near the bluff. Although he resided in the largest structure in the city, the eccentric well-dressed man preferred to operate out of a field tent. Isaac and Patrick stood before the tent as Kingsley disappeared through the flap to seek audience with his superior before presenting the accused combatants. After a long and uncomfortable half-hour standing in the waning afternoon sun in front of the tent, the two were ushered in.

The tent was arranged similar to the King's Court. Oglethorpe sat regally in the back upon a throne-like chair while his minions orbited around him. The man seemed apathetic, as if the proceedings were a nuisance, and announced, "There are no lawyers allowed in Savannah, so you will present your own case." He cleared his throat letting Patrick and Isaac languish in his words. "You two are charged with dueling and the murder of two men. Make your case"

"I did duel two evil men today," Patrick boldly stated. "It was a fair duel and rules were observed."

"Please," Oglethorpe sniffed, "Explain the reason for this duel."

Patrick hoped for reason and justice and threw himself at the mercy of the wigged man. He explained the entire story of Mr. Potts and how it was a matter of family honor.

"Do you have any words in your defense, second?" Oglethorpe asked of Isaac.

"It was exactly as Mr. Willis told it. I was the second and it was a fair fight. Ask anyone that was witness," Isaac pleaded.

Oglethorpe turned to Kingsley and asked, "And what are the witnesses saying about the duel?"

"The rumor is proper etiquette was observed and the fight was fair," Commander Kingsley stated. He then continued, hoping to persuade his superior, "But sir, you have had a very strong stance against dueling and I would advise that you wouldn't want to appear soft on your own rules."

"I want the colonists to feel I am just but sympathetic," Oglethorpe snapped. He made a temple with his hands just below his nose and considered the evidence before he gave his verdict. "My ruling is the challenger is free, but execute the second. Dismissed."

"No!" Patrick protested. Isaac was stunned for a moment but then the two duelers moved for Oglethorpe. They were immediately restrained as six soldiers surrounded Isaac and Patrick with muskets drawn.

"Wait!" Dr. Nunis yelled as he stepped between the guns. "Mr. Oglethorpe, if you damn this innocent man and execute him, I vow I will help you no more. I will not treat one of your soldiers from even the smallest of aliments. I will leave them to bleed out on the battlefield. So Moses help me, I will be your doctor no more!"

The wigged man scowled at the doctor but held his tongue. Instead, he looked long and hard at the doctor and the condemned Isaac, considering his next words carefully. "Doctor, you have been a good friend to the crown and I have long appreciated your services. If you vouch for this man, I will suspend his sentence." The kind Dr. Nunis released a relieved breath as Oglethorpe continued, "But beware good Doctor, you are now bonded to this man, Isaac Swartz. Any trouble and you will both answer for it. Is this understood?"

The doctor's hands were trembling as he cleared his throat and responded, "I understand."

Oglethorpe waved his hand and his soldiers withdrew their guns. The party was allowed to leave unmolested to Commander Kingsley's visible dismay. As Patrick and Isaac walked through Oglethorpe's tent flap, the commander and his sergeant glared at the freed duelers.

CHAPTER 10

JENKINS EAR

After the duel and the ensuing trial, Isaac became a new fixture at the Freeman's home during his free time. His name had become local legend in the Jewish community and his bravery reflected well upon Dr. Nunis. Benevolently, the good doctor gave Isaac ample time to recover the use of his right hand and arm. Patrick found a sort of inner peace after the duel. Normally he was against all forms of violence but this was not a street mugging or bullying. This was a voluntary battle in which he emerged the victor and that fact made the death of Potts and Edgeington easier to bare.

Both men were healing quickly which was a miracle. Many shot wounds were met with amputation or were a short boat ride to the devil. Years of living in putrid filth had made their bodies very resistant to disease. Maximilian had removed his worm successfully as well. It took three long weeks of slow half turns of the stick, but he removed the worm without killing it. He even dried it in the sun and used it for bragging rights to his friends.

Amos was not as fortunate. His foot festered and he had been fighting the infection for weeks. Many times Dr. Nunis wanted to amputate, but Amos refused and bore the infection. It was a long drawn out case of sepsis that never became full blown. The infection would grow fierce and the following day it would recede. Even though he was very ill, he still snuck out to the river to fish every few days when the fever would wane. Amos soon realized his infection felt better every time he soaked it in the cool river. Archibald surmised it was the cold water that helped the swelling or perhaps the brackish salt water cleansed the infection. Whatever the cause, after several weeks, his foot returned to normal and the family was relieved.

With the mending health of the four young men, the next few weeks were uneventful and a happy time for the Freeman home. News had been trickling in from all corners that trouble was brewing once again between England and Spain. Patrick asked Archibald to explain the history of English and Spanish animosity. Being locked deep in a dank debtors' dungeon for years, Patrick had been mostly unaware of the happenings in the outside world during that time. Archibald happily explained what he knew.

"The Spanish hate the English as far back as I can remember. Many years back when I was a child the two countries made a trade agreement. If I recall, it was called the 'Treaty of Utrecht' which gave Britain a thirty-year *asiento*."

"Asiento?" Patrick questioned.

"It is a Spanish word. It means the Spanish government gave permission for other countries to sell slaves to the Spanish colonies. Slavery, being a very profitable business, encouraged many English traders to jump on the opportunity to make fortunes." Archibald continued, "But it was not a treaty that held well. Britain and Spain were at each other's throats and constantly fought, so then it became common for Spanish ships to attack British vessels and steal all their cargos."

"Now, England is frothing at the mouth, like a mad dog for war, to have an excuse to rob the ships of the Spanish. They, and by 'they' I mean the politicians, even dug up some poor bloke named Captain Jenkins, a pawn if you will. They dragged the poor bastard onto the floor of Parliament and the House of Commons to tell the sorry tale of his ear and his ship, the *Rebecca*. It seems the sorry man was captured by a Spaniard named Captain Fandiño who accused Jenkins of piracy and sliced off his ear. He told the man, 'Go, and tell your king that I will do the same, if he dares to do the same.' So the politicos in London propped up this sorry man and made him recite his sordid story to affirm that the Spanish threatened His Royal Majesty. I hear that Jenkins actually pulled out his own

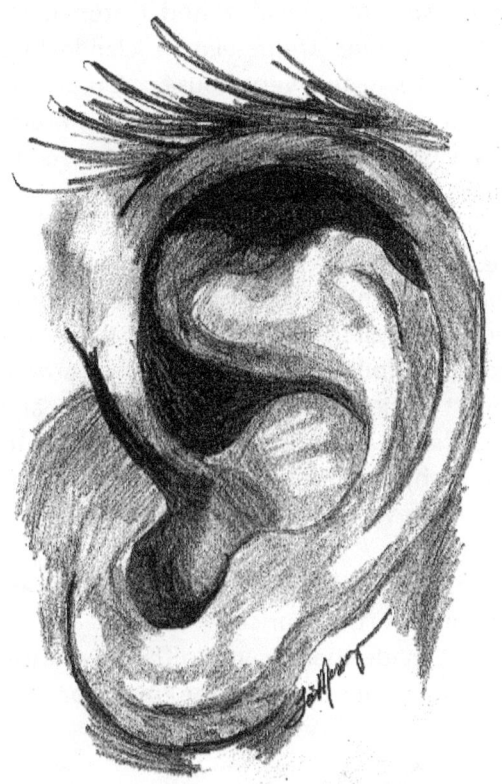

The mummified ear of Captain Jenkins

mummified ear to display to the esteemed council." Archibald laughed, "Foul, eh?"

"Of course," Archibald continued, "the shite rolls down from the top of the mountain and this silly political chess match is rearing its ugly head in the colonies. A soldier in town told me the other day that rumors are circling that the crown is centralizing forces here in Savannah. Governor Oglethorpe has sent word to the Forty-Second Foot Regiment as well as the Georgian and Carolinian Militias ordering them to assemble in Savannah. There must be truth to these rumors. I've received orders from the Governor myself to start making cannon balls and shot. Something grievous is definitely coming this way."

"On a good note," Archibald's toned lightened as he leaned in close to Patrick, "we are having a clandestine meeting tonight, up the stairs in this very house. You are welcome to invite your friend Isaac. He has proven he is mettle worthy of trust but tell no other soul. The meeting will commence an hour after sunset."

Patrick then made off to round up Isaac. Although he was uncomfortable not knowing any details, Patrick was been able to convince Isaac to come along. If anyone else but Patrick had extended such a mysterious invitation, Isaac would have declined suspecting foul play. When they returned to the Freeman property, the two men spied Marian and Heather standing in the shadows of the yard as lookout sentries. Isaac was taken aback by the two women acting as security, but Patrick assured him everything was fine. Curiosity was growing in the large man.

Marian whispered from the shadows, "They are waiting. Knock twice, then once, then thrice."

The two men made their way into the tiny house, then up the ladder to the loft and rapped on the trap door.

Two knocks.

Then one knock.

Then three knocks.

The trap door swung open and the two men ascended into the loft with only one candle to light the way. Four men and two boys sat in a tight circle. Archibald rose, inviting them to sit in the secret circle, but Isaac was so large, he seemed as if he would take up half the circle himself.

"Welcome to the Freeman Society," Archibald announced warmly. "We are a network of men who believe a man is only subject to himself. We believe a man to be sovereign to himself and not a king or ruler of any kind. We also believe the individual knows best how to control his own life and make their own fortune, not anyone else. We can tell you more, much more, but first you have to enter this circle of trust on your own free will and accord. Do you two wish to continue?" Archibald questioned solemnly.

"How could I possibly agree to honor something before I know what it is?" Patrick pressed. "You've got to tell me something."

"We are at an impasse," Archibald frowned. "We cannot tell you any of our secrets until I know you can be trusted. Most secret societies work the same way, Patrick. In fact, a Free Mason will not tell you any details about who they are at all until you take a pledge of secrecy first. It is how it is done. Trust," the blacksmith explained, "begins with you."

Patrick and Isaac looked at each other in the dim candlelight judging how the other would respond. Both men nodded in approval to each other, turned to the men sitting in the circle and stated in unison, "We do."

"Very well. You are welcomed into this circle of trust, founded on the ideas of personal liberty and sovereignty. Here you can allow your true mind to be free, speak what you will. You can ask any question, challenge any idea or belief without fear of reprisal. But there is a price for this freedom of the mind and spirit; you must never speak of this group to any soul without asking the permission of its members first. You hold the lives of these men and their families in your hands as they hold your lives in theirs. Do you understand the full importance of this vow you are about to make?" Archibald asked both men in turn. Isaac and Patrick both nodded in acknowledgement.

"Then show your vow by wearing these." Archibald presented ribbons of black and yellow cloth to Patrick and Isaac. They were then instructed to tie the black cloth around their right arms, sealing the two to their vow of secrecy and to act as a reminder that a loose tongue would bring death to all they knew and loved. They were then told to tie the yellow ribbon around their left arms to seal their vow to follow the path of enlightenment, that the yellow was symbolic of the sun washing away the darkness of other peoples' ideas that attempted to control their lives.

After the ribbons were tied to both of their arms, the small group circled on the floor chanted, "The only ideas we accept are ones that benefit our happiness. We will always work toward breaking the chains of an enslaved mind. So mote it be!"

"Pay attention, lads," Archibald warned. "This is the secret handshake of the Freeman Society." He then locked his wrist to Patrick's wrist and formed a "V" with his index and middle laying them on Patrick's forearm. "There," Archibald shook Patrick's hand and motioned to Isaac. "Now practice this with your brother."

After the two successfully mastered the secret handshake with each other, Archibald stood between both men, took them by their shoulders, and turned them towards the circle. "Gentlemen," Archibald announced, "let me proudly introduce Sovereign Willis and Sovereign Swartz to the circle." The men circled on the loft floor of the Freeman home. All nodded as Archibald gestured to the gentleman sitting. "To my right is Sovereign Quinn. You know his daughter Prudence. To my left is Sovereign Dandridge, Mari Anna's father. The gentleman wearing my clan's kilt is Sovereign McIntosh whom you have already met. I also think you may already know the twins, Sovereign Freeman and Sovereign Freeman," Archibald grinned.

Archibald, Patrick, and Isaac then joined the circle and sat upon the floor. The wigged blacksmith stated the meeting would begin with news from other Freeman Societies and would end upon the study of the writings of John Locke. He turned and asked his brother, Sovereign McIntosh, of the news from the Scottish settlement in Darien, Georgia. McIntosh cleared his throat and spoke. "Many tongues run from the clans in Darien. Da Governor is about to call tis markers and command us to fight fir 'em. We understood that was da exchange for passage here and land t'was. The Scots will come to aid him if he calls. Something be brewing, laddie." McIntosh leaned in towards the circle, emphasizing his grim words, "The clans be preparing for war, just not knowing where or why yet. All men of fighting age are to descend on Savannah when da alarm be sounded."

"What do you think Oglethorpe is planning, Mr. McIntosh," Patrick asked earnestly.

"Lad," Archibald interrupted, "it is our custom to not use 'mister' or any title but 'sovereign.' It is a sign of respect as well as a reminder that the man you speak to is free and serves no one here."

Patrick sincerely apologized as McIntosh continued, "It probably has to do with da damn Jenkin's ear. It is all da town be speaking of. I would be betting we'll soon be fighting the Spanish for that Governor Oglethorpe.

Sovereign Quinn interjected, "Lots of confusion and opportunity happen in battles. It could be a very profitable endeavor for our cause."

"If we can position ourselves near the battle, but not in it, we could scavenge a haul of muskets, munitions, supplies," Sovereign Dandridge added. "In all the confusion, none would be wise to our deception."

"Part of our discussion in this group is about the ideas of property rights, Sovereign Dandridge," Archibald warned. "It is immoral to steal another's property. Only two kinds of people use force to take what they want: thieves and government. We need to take the higher ground here, gentlemen. We cannot take anything from another for any reason, no matter how noble our cause."

"The British has enslaved and tortured our people since I can remember, brother," Sovereign McIntosh posed. "They steal our silver, our property, our freedom, our women and our very lives. Is it immoral to take back your own stolen property? If a thief robs me and then drops some of me silver on the ground as he runs away, is it immoral if I pick it up?"

The circle of men sat and pondered the question. Each looked at each other, weighing morality in the scales of their minds, when Sovereign Freeman finally conceded. "No, brother. Taking back my rightful property from a thief or government is not stealing."

Sovereign McIntosh grinned as Sovereign Quinn continued the reasoning "So by that reasoning, I suppose taking the arms and supplies of fallen British soldiers would be moral. The government *did* steal our monies with those *same* guns to buy all the supplies to outfit their handsome army."

"I would not see that as stealing," Sovereign Dandridge interjected. "That *is* taking back your own money but one would need to figure out exactly how much the crown has indeed stolen in his life and make sure to take not one schilling more."

Sovereign McIntosh was becoming visibly frustrated by this penny-pinching of morality. He asked emphatically, "And what be da exact price would ya say the British owe me for killing me pa?! Should I try to estimate exactly how much me poor father would have made toiling the rest of his life if he was spared? Exactly how much can I take from the rotten English till me clan be fully square?"

McIntosh was fuming. His brother sniffed back a tear and asked calmly, "That is a very tough question, William. I have the very same dilemma as you well know. I would assume you should take as much as you want until you feel whole and compensated for your loss."

Sovereign Dandridge patted Archibald's shoulder with compassion as he chimed in, "Then let us gain riches from the storm brewing. Let us scavenge the thieving British in their next fight. We need to position ourselves close to the action but not in it. I say we hire a savage to guide us in and out of the bloodshed. The redskins are experts at what we are proposing to do."

"I know one I can trust," Sovereign Quinn added. "He's a fur trader and keeps asking for my Prudence's hand. He's willing to do anything to get in my good graces. He's very old though but highly skilled. I will contact him; determine if he will be able to assist us."

"Sadly lads I don't think I can avoid the fighting part," Sovereign McIntosh confessed. "Me clan gave its word to Oglethorpe to support him if he ever needed us. I have to fight or I dishonor me family. I predict he is going to call us to arms soon enough. He visited Darien recently and showed us the respect of wearing a kilt the whole time he was there. He even opted to sleep under the big oak with the rest of the men instead of sleeping in a bed. Showing his ugly knees and sleeping under an oak tree, the Governor is making sure he is still in good favor with the clans. I will help the cause any way I can from the battle lines, but..." McIntosh hung his head slightly but the men of the circle nodded that they understood. It would have been comforting to have a man with the ability of the lumbering McIntosh along, but he was obviously honor bound.

Archibald then instructed each man to keep his ears pinned back and ready to jump when the coming battle arrived. The meeting then turned to study. Archibald inquired of the group who they preferred to study: Algernon Sidney or John Locke. Sovereign Quinn proposed that Sidney was murdered by the government for his words and stated with a mischievous grin, "Let's find out what they did not want us to know."

With the group's approval of Sidney, Archibald reached into a secret compartment in the bottom of his bed frame at the far end of the loft and pulled out a buck skin bag. He opened the bag delicately, uncovering a very worn tome. He explained to the new brothers that these books of his were more dangerous to own than one hundred cannons. If Governor Oglethorpe or his minions were to discover the society's collection of writings, their necks would be stretched and their toes dangling from a tree. He made the new recruits swear to never speak of them. He had paid a good bit of silver to a smuggler to get the books out of London and they were the most valuable things he owned. The newly initiated members of the secret Freeman Society nodded solemnly. Archibald then carefully opened the book and read Sidney's words, reminding the gathered sovereign men as to exactly why the crown executed him 1683.

"If there be no other law in a kingdom than the will of a prince, there is no such thing as liberty. Property also is an appendage to liberty; 'tis as impossible for a man to have a right to lands or goods if he has no liberty and enjoys his life only at the pleasure of another as it is to enjoy either when he is deprived of them."

Archibald continued to read from Sidney's book for a while and only stopped after a section which proposed the right to revolution. This section always inspired the most debate amongst the secret circle of men. Isaac spoke first. He was trying to digest the words of the philosopher. "So, Sidney is saying revolution and freedom are closely linked? That when a people's rights and liberties are threatened, they have the right to rebel, nay, the duty to?"

With no easy answers for such difficult questions, Maximilian asked another. He seemed as perplexed as Isaac. "Does revolution always mean with violence, Father? Can one have a revolution with *other* ways?"

The group began to talk over each other, each man offering their opinion, until Sovereign Dandridge spoke above the clamor. "I have never heard of a nonviolent revolution, but I would suppose there could be one." Dandridge continued proposing that if subjects stopped funding the king by not paying their taxes, maybe then the he would not afford the pretty crown that adorns his head or his army to do his violent bidding. "Many minds have to change and they'd have to reject the king's authority before this could happen. It'd be dangerous to those who were the first to protest but it would eventually encourage others. When enough subjects stop funding the government that oppresses them, it should collapse the empire in financial ruin."

Patrick had not considered these radical ideas before. Before, it was just vague anger but now his thoughts were taking shape. He found it odd that throughout time, people have funded their own oppression, building the very chains that enslaved them. Patrick explored all these new ideas as the group clamored on until Sovereign Quinn's voice cut through the others, "Piss on that! The way to freedom is through the barrel of a musket. You cannot reason with evil nor violence. You must answer violence with greater violence!"

Worried the neighbors or a passing British soldier might hear, Archibald shushed the excited man. When group quieted, Archibald rationalized in hushed tones, "How can one find peace through violence, Sovereign Quinn? In the game of violence, the most violent is crowned the winner. Might makes right, not morality nor reason? You, sir, would simply be trading one violent king for another more violent king."

"No, no, no," Sovereign Quinn countered. "You don't understand. We simply need to install one of our own men. We just need to find the right man to lead us. We have to have someone lead us, otherwise you'd have anarchy, a society wrought with nothing but murder and thievery."

"Maybe a society with no ruler and no government would have less murder and thievery. We have plenty of murder and thievery now. Hell, King George's troops have killed more men than smallpox!" Archibald laughed at his own joke.

"I don't know, Sovereign Freeman," Sovereign Quinn mused. "'Tis true enough but we need some sort of government. Men are too evil to be trusted to their own reckonings."

"You need to use that reasoning a little deeper, you are saying that men are too evil to be trusted, but government is made up of men. So does something magical happen when they become the government that washes away that inborn evil? Lads, remember the most basic thing about all governments: GOVERNMENT IS FORCE! In its simplest form it is one soul making another soul do what he wants by force. It rings true for any of the king's laws and actions. The only reason his subjects comply is because of the threats of force hidden behind the law. So it is the musket in the room that demands obedience. He who has control of the gun cannot resist the temptation and power to use it," Archibald explained.

He continued, "Even if we fight like hell and throw the king and his corrupt government out of power, we are just handing the musket in the room to a new ruler. In time they will not be able to resist the siren's call of its power and will find a reason to justify using it. Perhaps the new ruler will only use the gun to keep the rest of us safe and force his new subjects to pay for a military. Maybe he will force his new subjects to pay for programs to help his kingdom and its people. Over time the new ruler will find more and more reasons to use the musket to take his subjects' silver.

"When a government's only tools are threats and violence, why is it so surprising to its subjects when they use it? If you only own a hammer, everything looks like a nail. Lads that is why it is called a revolution, because it only goes in an endless circle of killing and control. When you use violence to remove a government it is only a matter of time until the new government has to be removed with more violence," Archibald summarized.

"You are living in a world of fairies! You can't use nonviolent methods at people willing to kill you. No thanks! This change has to happen with blood. There is no other way." Prudence's father stood steadfast.

"I like Sovereign Dandridge's idea of a massive tax revolt, using nonviolent resistance to cripple the king's treasure chest. But how do you get enough subjects to risk their lives and do it?" Patrick questioned.

"It has to be in everyone's best interest and important enough to them to take a risk. As far as I know we are the least taxed subjects in the world, so taxes alone won't be enough here. This will come down to an issue of control. The king will not be able to maintain control much longer since he is so far away. There is also no representation but folks still have to pay taxes to some other land. The way to change people's hearts is to sell the idea that they should be in control of their own lives; not some government," Archibald responded.

The men argued until the dawn, much to their wives' and daughters' dismay, about if such a thing as a nonviolent revolution could ever occur.

* * *

It was still hot, even in Mid-December. Although some leaves had turned and fallen, other more robust foliage was still holding tight to their colors. Despite the heat, a cold snap in November killed most of the sand gnats and mosquitoes, a small blessing to all men and beasts. Patrick had a face of fully grown beard and Archibald followed his lead growing a mustache, though it was still hot enough for him to take off his wig when they were smithing. The twins were growing tall and lean and Heather and Marian seemed to not age a single day anymore.

During this strange and balmy winter, Archibald quietly taught Patrick the art of gunsmithing. It was an ideal time to teach since much gun work was coming in. Many repairs and modifications were being made in preparation for the anticipated Spanish and savage invasion, so the making of stockpiles of guns openly aroused no suspicion. Taking advantage of the situation, the blacksmiths worked long hours into the night crafting extra black market firearms.

During his tutelage, Patrick found the most difficult aspect of gun smithing a smoothbore firearm was the barrel. It took great skill in fabricating to get it smooth, even and straight. The lock was dissembled into its parts; hammer, trigger, springs and flash pan. Patrick would delicately dissemble a flintlock and copy each part one by one. He would first take the hammer and set it in a clay sand mix to make a mold. Then he would pour molten iron into the mold and create a close replica. He then would file and shape the hammer to the exact dimensions of the original. He repeated this process until all the parts of the gun were finished but the barrel could not be cast. Archibald would cut a pattern from a sheet of metal and hammer it around a rod. Once he had the shape of the barrel, the master blacksmith would heat the barrel in the fire to fuse the ends together. He used long strips of metal to force the edges together and heated the barrel to just before its melting point. It took a very experienced eye to do this. Before the barrel would be cooled in a pool of water, Archibald poured small drops of hot metal into any cracks that did not fuse. When completely cooled, the master blacksmith used a tool he designed that looked a file on a stick. He would file the inside of the gun barrel for hours till it was smooth as glass.

Patrick learns the illegal art of gunsmithing

The gunstock was made from any hardwood the blacksmith could get his hands on. Oak was the most common choice, but Archibald would take custom orders for anything. The twins would work on whittling the oak down to a basic stock and Archibald would step in to do the finishing. He even customized the gunstock, shaving down the grip, a trick he learned from the local savages. With the thinner, modified grip, the musket could now be held with one hand and used as a club when the ammo ran out.

With troops and mercenaries amassing in Savannah, Yamacraw, Uchees, Creek, and Chickasaw war parties were all camping on the outskirts of town. The secret of Governor Oglethorpe's invasion was not a secret anymore. Even Hugh

MacKay's Highlanders, including William McIntosh, were in town and dressed for war. A mixed force of British regulars, the 42nd Regiment of Foot and the colonial militias from Georgia and Carolina were also added to the mix. Five frigates and three sloops were also gearing up for war in the harbor.

When William McIntosh arrived in Savannah, he headed directly to the blacksmith's home. "Is Duncan here, lad?" the large kilted man asked Patrick.

"Who?" Patrick was puzzled.

"Oh right, excuse me. I meant his English Lord, Sir Archibald," McIntosh stated in a sarcastic tone.

"He will be back in an hour or so, do you have a message?" Patrick calmly stated as he continued his work.

"Yes. Tell him da target is St. Augustine and to prepare quickly. We ride out in four days to attack Fort San Diego on our way to da prize. Tell him to get everything in place," the Scot instructed. Patrick nodded and the Scottish warrior ran down the street to join his men.

Later, Patrick took the message to Archibald who, in turn, passed it to Heather. He instructed her to tell Prudence's father to get his savage ready and to join the men west of San Diego in seven days. Archibald explained everyone's role in the family's next endeavor at dinner.

"Sons, you have to stay here and watch the home. If I need to know something important, I want Max to deliver the message." Amos frowned with disappointment. "Sorry Amos, but Max can out run you since you cut your foot. Plus I need you to watch this place closely, keep the lobsterbacks from fishing around the house." Amos nodded as his father continued.

"Marian and Heather, you'll stay with the home. We should be back in a few months. Until then, remain unseen. No socializing and stay the hell away from the reds. Understood? You must not go out at night for any reason and I want you to shut in properly every night. I also want you to carry dirks at all times as well. This is a very dangerous time, so I expect you to check in with Mr. Dandridge and Mr. Quinn every day. They will be staying behind for now.

"We will be going into this war zone under the guise of helping out, but we have no plans on fighting. We are going to scavenge the riches of battle and hope to make this family enough silver to move far away from the British forever. Perhaps if all goes well, we'll head to the frontier where we can live freely. We would only put ourselves in the devil's sight for the family. We will pack light in order to carry back heavy loads. We leave in four days time."

* * *

The three men met quietly on the south side of town. Archibald and Isaac were loaded down with supplies. Patrick thought it odd that this was Freeman's idea of traveling light. "Isaac, I did not know you would be joining us. How did you ever talk the doctor into letting you leave?" Patrick asked.

"Archibald hired my services for the next few months. It is not hard to convince the doctor when he sees the glimmer of silver. Plus, I will be selling medicine and will make a fortune for him. People will pay a good amount of money if you can save them from shitting themselves to death," Isaac replied with a smile.

Archibald belted out, "Lads, best be on our way before the sun beats us down. What I would not pay for a good horse right now but the livery is sold out. I have the map to Fort San Diego around here somewhere." The men slowly wandered down the road loaded from head to toe with equipment as Archibald searched one of his many bags to find the map.

CHAPTER II

LAND PIRATES AND
BATTLE RATS

With a mix of swamp marsh and thick woods, the men moved slower than anticipated. Even the shortest of distances took much time but eventually they made it to the rendezvous point west of Fort San Diego. While Archibald tied yellow and black cloths to his arms, Patrick questioned, "What do you know about the savage sent to meet us?"

"For starters, they don't care much for being called 'savages'," Archibald grinned. "The scout is an older warrior held over from the Yamasee War that ended in the seventeenth year. My understanding is it was a terrible war."

Archibald told the story of the Yamasee War. "The Yamasee hated the Spanish and their evangelizing for Christ and the Catholic Church. The Yamasee joined forces with the English in Charles Towne and assisted in slave raids deep in the Spanish territories. Then something changed and to this day I do not know what. I'd bet the colonials cheated them or took a shite on one of their burial grounds. Who knows? The Yamasee then turned on their former allies, attacking Charles Towne and the surrounding areas. Other tribes that hated the British as well joined the Yamasee cause and attacked. It was a hell of a collection of tribes that convalesced to spill British blood. It was the Yamasee, the Creek, Cherokee, Savannah River Shawnee, Congaree, Waxhaws, Pee Dee, Chickasaw, Catawba, Apalachee, Apalachicola, Yuchi, Cape Fear, Cheraw and others. The English were on the edge of defeat until the Cherokee turned on their savage allies and saved the British."

"Time and bribes heal lots of old wounds," Archibald smiled. "Now most of these tribes are allied with the English. Many of the warriors still hate the British and only pretend to help them until they can spill their blood again. The man we are meeting is one of those. He hates both the British and Spanish and will keep our business quiet. Currently he is spending time with the Creek in a settlement called Eufaula trading deer pelts. Most of his tribe was killed during the Yamasee War and he is one of the last of his bloodline. When he was a young warrior, he spent many years around St. Augustine capturing the enemies of his tribe, selling them into slavery. The British and Spanish would sell those captured men to the Caribbean to work the sugar fields. Sovereign Quinn warned me to show him respect because he is a legend to his people. His skill with a bow is deadly and he is a master tracker."

"This bow has killed thirty-four English, twenty-four Spanish and fifty-five enemy tribesmen. Each bead on my bow is a soul it has captured" said a voice from behind a tree. "I waiting all morning here. You make much noise, you be easy to kill." A white-haired Indian stepped from behind a tree. He was short and muscular but aged. His face looked liked a wrinkled leather satchel with fiery coal eyes. He was bare-chested and had a decorated bow and quiver hung over his shoulder. He was like a proud stone and little expression came from his scar riddled face. On his bead belt hung a strange shaped war club which had been decorated with feathers. The three men jumped back, startled by the warrior's mysterious entrance. "Quinn told to find man who wear yellow and black on arms." The old warrior questioned, "You be him?"

"I assume you are Li Go Che. Your English is impressive. Quinn did tell me what a great warrior you are but he had never told me you were also well educated," Archibald complemented.

"Learning good English made me much silver," Li Go Che replied. "What you whiteskins want from me?"

"We need you to guide us over the next few months. We

need to stay close to the redcoats but staying away from their war. We want to profit from the bloody backs after the battle," Archibald explained.

Li Go Che burst into loud laughter. "You three want me to help you be battle rats? You want to steal the redcoats' fallen warriors' weapons? This disgraceful behavior to my tribe. Will you use these firesticks to kill the English?"

"We want to sell them to people who will use them to kill the British," Archibald replied.

"Let us smoke on this," Li Go Che calmly said as he sat down.

The three white men awkwardly sat down in a circle and watched as the white-haired man produced a small pipe from a bag he was carrying. Archibald watched as the old warrior pulled out a bud of a hemp plant and packed a little in his pipe. He made a small bundle of dead foliage into a miniature torch, then ignited it with a flint rock and a small piece of metal he had. The men passed the pipe around and smoked in silence until Patrick took a smoke and coughed violently. The coughing amused the old man and he broke into laughter. Li Go Che encouraged Patrick to slow down and not suck the smoke in so fast. Patrick failed miserably at smoking, much to the group's delight. Tension lifted as laughter and blue smoke filled the air.

The indentured blacksmith was now turning green and leaned over to spit some brown ooze out. The old man smiled and announced, "I will help you white-skins. The British killed many of my tribe and it would make my tribe's spirits happy to see more redcoats dead."

All the men, except the very green skinned Patrick, sat and smoked in celebration of their union. They puffed the pipe long until they became very hungry and Archibald prepared a dinner of venison and berries.

* * *

Chilly nightfall fell in the new year as muzzle flashes and loud cracks were seen in the dark. The four men were dressed in heavy furs, watching from afar while Oglethorpe's strange mix of troops overwhelmed Fort San Diego. The fort fell quickly the next day with minimal casualties on both sides. The Spanish abandoned the fort in the face of overwhelming odds and fell back into the marshy woodlands. A few loyal Spaniards covered the retreat and were now being run down.

Li Go Che advised, "Battle too one-sided. Now not good for battle rats. Wait till next fort."

Archibald conceded to the old man's raiding experience and followed his advice. "Where do you think the next fight will be?" he questioned.

"Spanish flee to Fort Picolotta not far from here. British follow soon. We follow too," the white-haired man predicted.

The old Creek would be correct. The Spanish fell back and reinforced Picolotta as Oglethorpe's brigade slowly followed, closing in on the next fort. The British were aware of Archibald's party but it aroused little suspicion since it was common for families and merchants to follow armies. To legitimize the ruse, Archibald allowed himself to be employed by the Scottish troops making small repairs on their weapons.

The siege of Fort Picolotta mirrored that of Fort San Diego. Oglethorpe's men, in overwhelming numbers, forced the Spanish to fall back once again. No opportunity presented itself for the band of scavenging battle rats. The next fall back for the Spanish was at Fort Mose. Archibald was ambivalent about the invasion until the siege of this fort. He explained to Patrick he did not want to see the fall of a group of slaves who were now truly free men. He continued explaining to his apprentice that as early as 1687, the Spanish government had begun to offer asylum to British slaves hoping to undermine English control. Around 1693 that asylum was made official by the Spanish Crown making it known that runaways would find freedom in Spanish Florida, but a price had to be paid. The slaves would have to convert to Catholicism and pledge four years of service to the Spanish Crown. Ever since the days the black soldiers aided in repelling a British attack on St. Augustine in 1728, a grateful Governor Montiano abolished slavery in Florida. To cause even more disruption to the English, Fort Mose was set up as the very first free, black settlement. The Spanish governor hoped this would encourage slaves to escape from British settlements and disrupt their economy. Governor Montiano essentially established a free fort of rebels willing to fight against the British and protect St. Augustine. Fort Mose now had slaves from many tribes living free together for a common cause. There were natives of Mandinga, Fara, Arara, Kongo, Carabali and Mina. Tribes that before would never be together now lived in harmony and freedom in this fort. When Archibald finished, he grimaced and confessed, "It hardens my heart to see the British take fire to this fort."

Days later, the three men and their savage guide watched a familiar scene they had already witnessed twice. General Oglethorpe quickly overwhelmed the Spanish fort and the African free men fled into the marshes. The British made an example of the fort, burning everything they found to ashes and sent a clear message to the former slaves. The redcoats only spared what they could use for their own military objectives. Many soldiers laughed as they took great joy taking torches to the homes of the Africans and smashing the artwork left behind. The four battle rats watched in sadness as a symbol of freedom fell to another political power grab. It was decided again by Li Go Che to not make a move. Again, the time was wrong. They would keep following the battle.

The old warrior started to pursue the fleeing black men when a tree next to him exploded in shards of bark and splinters. He turned his head to spot a handful of Spanish soldiers firing at the group. The white men panicked and dove into brush behind some trees as multiple cracks of gunshots echoed. They clumsily started drawing their blades and loading their muskets. The old man had his bow in hand and an arrow was already flying through the air. The aim was true and the colorful feathers of the arrow could be seen sticking from the chest of a Spanish soldier.

With their shots fired, the Spaniards were scurrying to push shot and powder down their barrels with their ramrods. The white-haired, wrinkled old man was dead calm as he knocked another arrow to his bow. Patrick was convinced the calmness of the old warrior in the face of death could only come from a life of battle. Li Go Che was already loading another arrow while his second arrow pierced another soldier's chest. A third soldier raised his musket to fire only to be struck in the neck with a colorful shaft of wood. The forth Spaniard panicked and tried to run, only to be pierced in the back, falling to the ground. The last Spaniard charged at the old Indian using his musket as a two-handed club. Archibald fired a shot that did not find its mark while Patrick and Isaac fumbled with loading their muskets. The old man coolly pulled his war club from his belt and, with a fluid spinning motion, dropped his body and struck the incoming soldier in the knee. The Spaniard dropped and the Indian finished him with a swift death blow to his skull that had so much force it shattered the club. Calmly, the old man picked up the dead man's musket and then collected the arrows from the bodies that littered the field. Letting out a loud Indian battle cry, the old warrior smashed the heads of his fallen enemies with the musket stock one by one. The white men watched in amazement and could not comprehend what just happened. One old man had just effortlessly killed five other men in less than two minutes.

Patrick and Isaac stared dumbfounded as Archibald ordered, "Wake up! Search these bodies and then hide them good." The men nodded and began collecting the weapons of the dead Spaniards. They circled like vultures as they picked the bloody bodies clean. The corpses were soon hidden and the party retreated into the safety of the swamp to tally their swag. Archibald was impressed with the haul: five muskets, bags of shot and horns of powder. Also found were two Spanish blades, three pairs of boots, belts, five water skins and rations. The clothes were bloodied and ruined and not even considered. Archibald then divided the spoils, giving each man a musket. Patrick was handed the musket used by Li Go Che to bash in the skulls of the dying Spaniards. He slowly examined the bloodied Hickory stock.

The warrior quickly started disassembling a gun, freeing stock from the barrel. "Wait what are you doing? That musket is already sighted. Careful or it won't shoot straight," Patrick warned.

"I no want whiteman's firestick. Too slow. I fire ten arrows in time to fire and reload one gun," Li Go Che boasted as the Indian broke down the flintlock, casting the barrel, bindings and lock aside. He took a large knife off his belt and hacked at the stock. He shaved and whittled it until it fit in one hand. He gave his new war club a practice swing and seemed pleased with the outcome. It was only then Patrick realized that Li Go Che's last club was also a musket stock. It made sense to Patrick. From afar, it would look like the Indian was carrying a gun that could possibly deter hostiles. The hard wood in the stock would make for a strong club.

Later that night, Isaac and Patrick found it hard to sleep. Neither had ever seen a man killed as they had witnessed earlier that day and the images were hard to bury. Unsurprisingly, the white-haired warrior and the Scotsman slept well. After killing close to a hundred men, Patrick guessed death no longer bothered the Indian's sleep.

* * *

Almost five months had passed and the Spanish in St. Augustine numbered almost two thousand. Many sought refuge within the wooden walls of Fort Castillo de San Marcos when Oglethorpe's navy began bombarding the town. A mass evacuation of St. Augustine had been underway for days. There were only about seven-hundred and fifty soldiers. The rest were families and merchants, all crammed into the fort, slowly starving to death by the siege. General Oglethorpe's forces had swelled to close to three thousand soldiers at his command. He was finally joined by Ahaya the Cowkeeper and his Oconee warriors. The Oconee had a deep hatred of the Spanish in Florida and were excited to join the British general's campaign. The rest of the British fleet finally arrived, led by Commodore

Pearce, and had blocked the ports while Oglethorpe deployed his batteries on the island of Santa Anastasia. But the Spanish General Manuel de Montiano had an advantage of an impenetrable fort. The British general's cannons were too weak to take down the fort's walls so the armies stood at a standoff. It was now the scorching hot month of July and this invasion had become a waiting game.

"I can't believe we are still in this shit box of a swamp," Patrick whined to Archibald as he swatted another mosquito. "Why the hell hasn't Oglethorpe just given up yet?"

"The general's ego wouldn't allow him to leave. He won't be shown up by Admiral Vernon," Archibald explained. "When he returns to London he wants to be the toast of the town.

"Who's Admiral Vernon?" Patrick asked.

Archibald explained the history, "On the 22nd of November 1739, Porto Bello, a silver-exporting town on the coast of Panama, was raided as an attempt to damage Spain's finances and to weaken its naval capabilities. The poorly defended port was attacked by six ships of the line under Admiral Edward Vernon who captured it within twenty-four hours. It was a very easy battle for the Admiral. He captured a great deal of Spanish treasure and returned to the king as the country's newest hero. Oglethorpe was envious. He desperately wanted to launch his own invasion on the Spanish and return to England as a hero himself. So I don't think we are going anywhere, lads."

"Welcome back, Saw Bone!" the Scottish warrior piped up.

Isaac walked into the camp covered with blood. "That is the third man I amputated that died this week. I can't take any more of the screams. We ran out of spirits and rum weeks ago. Now I have to put a bucket over their head and smash it hard to knock te men unconscious. My bone saw is so dull, it took me almost thirty minutes to cut through the last man's thigh. Half the troops on both sides are incapacitated and dying of the black-water shits. I have never seen such a horrible loss of life just for some man's fucking ego." Patrick gave the brawny man a hug, compassionate of his old friend's frustration, as Isaac continued, "I had two men refuse to let me work on them because I was a Jew, because they thought I would use the devil's favor to heal them. They died in the mud making jokes about my horns on my Yarmucle. I hate this place!" Isaac yelled.

"Today I also treated the hundredth snake bite. I have been out of pulpous for a month. All I can do is get one of their soldiers to suck the venom out and then stick his foot in the cold creek. I am really grateful Li Go Che showed us how to pad our boots, protecting us from bites. At least all the snake meat is tasty," he complimented.

Archibald gave praise to the old scout, "You're the reason we never got sick. We are very grateful you kept us healthy and helped us avoid the bad water. You honor your tribe." He then handed the Indian a leather pouch of hemp bud. The old man grinned a little. He loved compliments from the white man, as he quickly got out his pipe to smoke.

"Lads, I know this has dragged on a long time, but we have to come back with something big now to justify this excursion. Just a little longer. The Spanish are starving and are almost broke. Soon we will have our chance," Archibald persuaded.

"Easy for you to say. You went back to your family for the month of May. Isaac and I are nothing but mosquito welts! How the hell is it they never bite Li Go Che?" Patrick questioned with a laugh.

"I had to go back and sell those guns. My family needed the money to live on. I had to file off all the markings and I sold them for parts. I also worry for the family's safety and had to be sure they were still healthy. Heather did tell me to tell you she has some corn bread waiting for you." Archibald said.

"I am sure it is still good to eat, lad," the Scotsman laughed.

A mottled orange and white dog had adopted the group over the last few weeks. He had shaggy fur with a white nape, white feet and the end of his tail looked as if it was dipped in white paint. He had a long black snout and intense, high energy. He wandered into camp one evening, starving. Patrick had thrown him some scraps from a doe the Indian had killed and now it was impossible to get rid of the dog. William thought the dog looked like an ancient Scottish cattle dog called a collie. The collie was a welcome interruption to the months of monotony as the group debated for days what to name him. The group suggested male names for the dog but after Patrick discovered it was a female, his suggestion won. He named the dog Garland after his youngest sister he left behind in London. In a very short time, Li Go Che had put the dog to work for her meals. He had trained the collie to charge bushes and flush game out. The two seemed a perfect match, like they had been hunting together for years.

As the days passed, the old warrior taught Patrick and Isaac a great deal about tracking and hunting. He showed them how to preserve meat by smoking it over the fire pit. Even though Patrick learned some very useful skills, the one that most impressed him was a trick the Indian did with corn kernels. The white-haired man would take a deep pot with animal tallow melted down and some corn seeds. When the grease grew hot enough, the corn would jump up and turn to white puffs that looked like cotton. The first time Patrick heard the popping sounds, he jumped out of his skin and the old man laughed wildly. Isaac threw some salt in the mix and they really enjoyed the new treat.

Garland would howl at night when the group ate. Patrick would take left over corn meal, ball it up and drop it into the grease. It would turn to round brown balls that tasted like cornbread on the inside. He would throw the cornballs to the collie to keep her quiet. He soon added the term 'hush puppy' when he gave the canine a corn meal ball. The dog learned very quickly to quiet down whenever someone said 'hush puppy.'

It was now the very early morning of June 26, 1740 and was still very dark. The old Indian woke the party up and told them to pack quickly. He reported he had seen a large group of African and Spanish warriors quietly sneaking through the marsh.

"We go Fort Mose now!" the Indian roused the sleeping men. "This army attack Fort Mose soon before sunrise." The parties packed in record speed and within a half hour were on the move deep into the marshes. The small party caught up with the invading force and Patrick was amazed at what he saw. The African warriors looked similar to Indian warriors. They were dressed in war paint and had tribal scars all over their bare bodies. The men's faces were covered with keloid, chevron-shaped scars. Some had muskets, but most had huge spears and small shields they had crafted for themselves. A few Spanish came as well and their weapons were a mix of old and new gunsmithing methods. Some foolish soldiers still wore conquistador metal chest plates with helmets. The heat was unbearable and the soldiers became dehydrated and too weak to be very effective. The rest were a collection of current Spanish uniforms, common clothes and weapons. It was a hodgepodge killing force the Spartans of old would have been proud of as they also numbered three hundred.

Somehow, the free blacks and Spanish managed to sneak out of Fort Castillo de San Marcos during the night, and in just a short time, arrived at Fort Mose before dawn. The Africans knew the inner workings of the fort intimately after living there so long. Using a series of trees as cover, the force was approached by blind spots. They quickly and silently slipped in a small breech in the wall of the fort and assembled inside. The Spanish force almost got a third of its force inside the walls before the shouting started.

The four men watching heard Indian, African, Spanish and Scottish screams of terror erupt as the fighting started. It was then that it dawned on Patrick that the Scottish highlander rangers and the Creek were the only forces the British left to occupy the fort. The group quickly became concerned about William and his clan. The sounds of death were horrible as the fight sounded one sided. A group of five kilted men came sprinting out of the fort toward the four hidden men. Archibald broke ranks and stood up, waving for the highlanders to join them. The Scottish men were already covered with blood and ran to Archibald and his crew. The Scots dove down into the marsh and vanished into the high grass.

William McIntosh's voice boomed, "What da fuck was that,

lads?! I had never seen killing so fast. Dos African savages killed many of our clan while they slept."

"William, are you okay?" Archibald questioned his brother.

"A retreat was ordered to abandon the fort. I have no idea how many made it out. I saw many of me clansmen lying dead with large spears sticking out of der chests." McIntosh shook with nerves while he spoke, "I have done me share of killing but they had the spring on us. There was nothing I could have done to save me brothers. We best get away from this fort and regroup with the clan. Come on, join us."

The four men agreed and followed the bloodied and cussing Scotsman deep into the marsh. After a few hours, the battered war party came to a makeshift camp in the swamp. Men ran out to greet William's group and hugged them. Patrick saw them greet each other in Scottish and then the arguing started.

Patrick quietly leaned over and asked his employer, "What did they say?"

Archibald stoically replied, "Only eighteen made it back here. The fort had one hundred and twenty Scots with only thirty Indians. Over half the clan died and only a few have been captured. They are arguing and debating about going back. We best keep our distance and let the families grieve, lad." The salvaging party stayed in the shadows the rest of the night as kilted warriors grieved for their friends and relatives.

* * *

"Most are going back to Darien. They feel they spilled enough Scottish blood for king and country. I am not going with them. I'm going to stay, see if there be a way to free the captives," William announced the next morning.

"You are welcome to stay with our clan here, brother, and join us," Archibald said with a sympathetic tone. The bloody, kilted man nodded in affirmation.

Following Li Go Che and Garland's careful pace, the group retraced their steps. They got as close as was safe to the fort and waited for an opportunity. A large pile of dead bodies laid strewn on the ground outside of Fort Mose. The Indian counted sixty-eight dead, most were Scottish. He also took note that there were only ten dead African bodies and about thirty captured men.

The party came across a British artillery division involved in a heated debate. The scavengers stayed their distance and listened intently. Patrick heard them arguing about whether or not they should abandon the artillery and escape. Oglethorpe's siege was not holding. The Spanish managed to sneak supply ships through the Royal Navy blockade and any thought of starving St. Augustine into capitulation was lost. Oglethorpe now planned to storm the fortress by land while the navy ships attacked the Spanish ships and half-galleys in the harbor. Commodore Pearce, however, resolved to forgo the British navel attack during hurricane season. The commodore's decision angered the general because he now would have to embarrassingly withdraw his forces. His entire campaign would be for nothing if he called a retreat and he would be disgraced. Now the Spanish were on the attack and driving the British out. The artillery units were running for their lives and leaving the cannons behind. The British soldiers were arguing amongst themselves about leaving the cannon mules behind when a spear struck one soldier in the back. A large group of black soldiers were screaming as they charged out of the woods throwing their spears. The British returned fire with muskets but were caught off guard. They were quickly overwhelmed and the few that were not already dead surrendered without a fight.

The old Indian motioned for the men to leave, but by that time it was too late. Garland barked to alert the group, but when they turned around, they found themselves at spear point. Twelve spears were pointed on the men who then quickly surrendered. Patrick pissed his leg in fear knowing that in seconds they would all be dead. He watched as the African soldiers started bickering and yelling at each other. One black warrior was arguing with the rest of the battle-raged group. The African advocate stepped between the spears and the prisoners and started yelling at his own troops. He waved a familiar looking Scottish battle-axe at his own men, backing them off. The group of five battle rats waited nervously to learn their fate.

"Archibald, no worry you not die today," a familiar voice said. The advocate turned around and was hardly recognizable in full war gear.

"Alick? Is that you?" Archibald replied.

"Yes, friend. Gloria and I make it to Fort Mose. We free now!" the escaped slave smiled. "I tell da warriors here not ta kill you. I tell dem how you risked family's life to help us. I tell dem you hate English. You lucky you're not be dressed like a British. The warriors still want ta kill your Indian and Highlander!"

"Alick, please don't kill these men. They also hate the British and don't want to fight. They are like you Africans and are forced to fight for their freedom. They are used by the white man to do his bidding. They do not want to kill your men. Please help them. They are good men," Archibald pleaded.

A series of translations set in motion. The tribesmen all spoke their own language and each conversation had to be translated many times. There was much heated debate and the infighting between the warriors was lengthy. Finally, Alick explained, "You may return home in peace. No Africans be killing you but we no speak for da Spanish. We keep these British cannon men as prisoners. You stay here. You not run off and warn other British we coming!"

The five men nodded in agreement and sat on the ground, unthreateningly, while they watched the Black soldiers regroup and head out to kill more British. The Africans vanished into the marsh, quiet as ghosts. Patrick's feeling of terror was starting to fade. The pounding of his heart returned to normal as he stopped shaking with fear. He stood up and could not figure out why the rest of the group was smiling ear to ear. "Did I miss something? We all just about met the devil by spear," Patrick questioned.

"Yes, that was a bit close, lad, but you might be looking

around now?" McIntosh laughed. Patrick saw eight cannons completely alone and unguarded. There was a small army of mules as well as artillery carts of gunpowder, cannon balls and supplies. "Fuck this scrounging for muskets, those cannons could make us all rich the rest of our lives. Archibald, we have to take these and conceal them now!" the large Scotsman stated with excitement.

All eyes fell on Archibald. "Li Go Che, can you find us a place to hide these?"

The old Indian reflected and searched his memory. "Yes, a cave I found hunting when I was young warrior, two days into the marsh. We must leave now. All mules in one line. We must take them down river to hide tracks." The savvy men wasted no time seizing the opportunity. They clumsily formed a mule-and-cannon parade and marched the entire lot into the swamp. They slowly moved the line of cannons and carts for hours. The white-haired Indian kept retracing their path and trying to hide the deep wheel tracks. He did his best; his efforts would have fooled a novice, but not an experienced tracker. The party slowed to a crawl as they maneuvered downstream and through creeks to completely erase their tracks. They were even blessed with a hard rain to further melt their prints in the earth. Fear drove them into the night and they did not stop to rest. They knew if the Spanish or Africans saw them, they would be killed on sight. If the British caught them they would be hung as thieves. It was a very dangerous game they played.

After two exhausting days of travel, the group arrived at two large burial mounds hidden deep in the swamp. The Indian man summoned his companions for help. In front of one of the mounds was a large pile of stones.

"Whoa! Whoa!" Isaac exclaimed. "This is not a cave, this is a tomb! I am not digging up a tomb. We need to find somewhere else to hide these."

"No, these mounds are sacred. This mound is fake tomb. No Indian would ever open, it safe. Now move rock, big man!" the Indian gestured.

It took a long time to move all the rocks, but the crew was

amazed at what was revealed. The mound was just an entrance to a large underground room. It still had barrels and some tools in it. The walls of the massive underground chamber were actually buttressed with timber and the cave was very deep. It was in the higher ground of the swamp so it would not flood inside when it rained.

The secret Indian burial mound

"My tribe hide here from Spanish soldiers and slavers. It took many moons to build. Men forget this place for many years. Cannons safe here," Li Go Che said proudly.

The men worked all morning, carefully using the mules to position the cannons and carts. The massive chamber was crammed full. The men would argue and reposition the cannons and carts over and over, trying to make them all fit. Finally Isaac discovered a pattern that allowed everything to fit neatly. They used the oil and canopies in the carts to protect the cannons. The cannons were dried and then covered with oil so as not to rust, and then everything was covered with canopies. The tomb was then sealed closed with rocks to match the appearance of the others. The men were grinning proudly at their hard work. Archibald suggested to push on and camp away from the spot in case they were being perused. The men did their best to wipe clean the area of tracks to appear as if no one had ever stopped there. The exhausted group finally made camp and reveled in their good fortune.

"Lads, it will be perfect if we pull this off. The English will assume they were abandoned and the Spanish stole them. The Spanish will assume the English recovered them and, not go looking for them. It is truly devious of us," Archibald bragged. "I know someone interested in buying these cannons but we will have to come back and move them out to the coast. Great warrior, will you help us?"

"I want profit of four cannons," the Indian replied.

"I will give you the profit of three cannons and all the mules," Archibald negotiated. The old man accepted this with a smile and held out his arm. Archibald locked wrists in the Creek custom.

"I will take the mules with me and hide them. Two months, at full moon, come back to move cannons," the Indian instructed. "Tomorrow take different paths. Draw map for you to return home safe." The men agreed and in a short time all were asleep, even Garland.

CHAPTER 12

ROAD AGENTS AND FLESH PALACES

The swamp heat and stench of warming algae woke the group early. All the men and even the collie were covered with painful bug welts from their trek into the marsh. The poor dog was a miserable mess of fleas, ticks, and tangles. The loud sounds of locusts and frogs overtook the men's conversations. Until now, the seasoned Indian guide had somehow kept the group safe from gators, wolves and other dangerous beasts. Now the men had to venture unguided to Darien and then on to Savannah. They knew they had to move fast to make it by nightfall. Roads were extremely dangerous at night and without a seasoned scout, they were easy prey to road agents and highwaymen that plagued the area.

Patrick wondered how this one old man showed no fear at all while marching off deeper into the forbidding switch grass with sixteen mules and a dog. They were off on their way early when Archibald advised the group to change their musket to smaller shot. The group loaded four smaller balls into the muskets instead of one large ball normally used for battle and large game. He figured boar blast or wild pig shot would give them a better defense against gators or such. The men kept a fast pace but the sounds of Scottish cussing could be heard throughout the swamp. Apparently, a kilt did little to persuade the swamp bugs and sand gnats. Without a guide, the group seemed to almost step on a gator every hour, but they followed the Indian's advice. They would slowly back away and make a large circle around it. The massive reptiles showed no fear of the men and were mostly too busy sunbathing to notice.

The amount of alligators and snakes slowed down their progress, for they were still not close to Darien. Camping this close to the road was asking to get murdered in the night. They only had one unfortunate option left. To get home as fast as possible they would have to move very quickly up the dark road. Soon nightfall had completely set in and the blackness took over. The moon was hidden and the starlight was not sufficient enough to light their way. To travel in pitch black was extremely foolish and even more dangerous than bandits. One wet and slimy stone could turn a foot or a knee. A foxhole or large rut could find a man impaled by his own blade from a fall, but the men valiantly and foolishly stumbled up the road in darkness. The marsh winds were picking up and storm clouds covered the stars.

Isaac heard a soft creaking sound and quietly stopped the group. He encouraged them to listen to the black. The creaking sound seemed to amplify with the wind and it had a consistent rhythm. *Rrrrrrrrrr, rrrrrrrrrr, rrrrrrrrr* was heard about every second. The men drew their flintlocks and lined up shoulder to shoulder. They reached out and touched each other's shoulders to stay within the next man's limited sight. They stood dead still for minutes listening to the noise repeat over and over. William finally spoke up. "Fook this! I still got one dry torch," he impatiently stated.

"Clang, Clang, Clang" pierced the air as bright sparks lit up the ground. The men's eyes went blind as the torch turned the blackness to light. A low-pitched scream was then heard followed by a smashing and a rattling sound. When Patrick's eyes adjusted, he saw Isaac standing next to half of a decaying skeleton. The other half lay at Isaac's feet.

Archibald broke into laughter, "You smashed him good. You look like one of those massive golems out of your Jewish stories."

McIntosh held the torch aloft reveling three other decaying corpses hanging from a tree and stated, "No worries, lads. This is just the thieves' tree. It means we are close to Darien. Come on, it's not far now."

Patrick and Isaac were still in shock, but the two Scottish men pressed forward with no signs of mental distress. Archibald comforted the two men explaining, "Hanging trees are still common in Scotland even today. It is a message to the road agents to steer clear of the town. You should have seen how they used to do it in the moors when I was a child. My town still had human-shaped iron cages that had been used for hundreds of years on bandits." He continued as Patrick and Isaac's mouths hung open. "'Tis true. They would throw the poor bastards in alive and starve them for weeks. I remember hearing hours of screams from men slowly dying. They would scream in pain as their own bodies slowly ate themselves. We are much more civilized here. Now, we just stretch their necks and be done with it."

"Stop talking, you screech owls! Christ, a deaf man could hear you!" McIntosh warned. The men walked very quickly and followed the torchlight. "I hear something. I think this damn torch attracted up some attention. Let's move, lads!" McIntosh commanded.

The four men broke into a fast, clumsy jog. The sounds of their large packs clinging and clanging alerted the world to their pace. "Not much further, through these fields. I know where we are," the kilted man stated.

They knew they were being pursued. The men could hear the sounds of many footsteps behind them keeping pace.

"Me farm is right there, lads! Run!" the Scotsman said in a panic. The men tore up the road to the house in frenzied sprint but the footsteps were closing in on them.

"Lads! Fire your pig shot directly behind us into the darkness," Archibald pleaded. "Trust me! Do it!"

The men slowed their sprint as they blindly pointed their muskets behind them. The dark road lit up with musket fire and group of angry bandit faces could be seen in the flashes. Screams could be heard from the gang of thieves behind them. Throwing his torch at them, William ran toward his home. He

A gang of road agents stalk the men at night

shouted something in Scottish as loud as he could, over and over, as they sprinted toward the house. The wild musket shots bought the fleeing group a few seconds to make their final dash to the house.

The house door flew open and three women and a boy with muskets stepped onto the porch. The women and the boy took fire into the darkness behind the fleeing group and immediately ran back into the house. The exhausted group burst into the house and fell over each other. They immediately got to their feet and barricaded the doors. Angry screams could be heard cursing outside in the night wind. Behind their barricade, everyone reloaded and took positions at the windows as sentries. They sat and listened to the gang yell at each other while one of their men screamed in pain. The screams of agony grew louder and louder until a gunshot was heard and the screaming stopped. By the time second sleep approached, the bandits had finally abandoned their siege.

"Thank you, family, for saving your father's hairy arse once again," McIntosh smiled.

One of the young ladies said, "Gross, Boban! That is disgusting!" The men in the room laughed and the tension at the moment lifted.

"Dis is me bride, Deborah, and our girls, Lindsay and Lauren," the large Scot introduced proudly. "Dat over there is me little wean, Roderick," he said, pointing to the boy.

"Well, we are all indebted to your clan. Thank you for helping save us from those bandits," Archibald said to the family.

"Well you saved me soul with the blacks, so we be level now," McIntosh reasoned.

Lauren, William, Lindsey and Deborah McIntosh

The exhausted men worked out shifts and rotated sleeping. In the morning, the four men emerged from the house slowly, fully armed. It did not take long before they discovered a naked body shot several times. The men cautiously dragged it into the swamp for the gators and wolves to enjoy.

Isaac, Archibald, and Patrick stayed with the family for three more days until they declared it safe. They were eager to get home and see their friends and family.

"I want ya three to wear these for protection against the dark. They will keep away marauders, ghosts, and the Devil. Ya tempt Satan when yas travel in the dark," Deborah cautioned. She gifted the men with three large Rowan wood crosses that were about the size of their hands. The wood was fastened together with switch grass.

"She had dem brought over from Scotland. A very old tradition. Rowan wood is a very powerful and magical wood," William added.

"Thank you so much," Archibald gratefully replied. "It is nice to have something from the moors. I sure miss those beautiful, foggy mornings." The men said their heart-filled goodbyes and then they were back on the trail to Savannah.

Archibald joked, "Sorry Isaac. I guess you could cut that cross up and make it into a Jewish star."

"Well the sentiment was very nice," Isaac replied. "I will keep it. You can't have too many things to keep away evil."

They made their way to Savannah as fast as possible while the sun was up. They left very early in the morning and arrived in Savannah without incident. It was dusk when they arrived at the edge of town and the blacksmiths said an affectionate goodbye to Isaac. "Tell Dr. Nunis to come see me tomorrow and we will settle up on pay for your services," Archibald reminded Isaac.

The indenture and his boss returned home to find it already prepared for the night. The Freemans had already done the nightly "shut in." For hundreds of years, their ancestors used this ancient procedure to protect them from the dangers of the night. The door was locked with a huge key that tumbled the slide locks. The family locked down the shutters and pulled the blinds. Archibald had also installed iron bars on the inside of the windows to protect them from night thieves. He was especially adamant about the shut in procedure when he was not at home. After all, Savannah was made mostly of corrupt soldiers and criminals. Archibald knocked on the door and announced in a deep voice, "We are here for Marian. Send her out in her nightwear!"

Some giggling was heard inside the house and the door flung open as the family rushed out. They embraced the family patriarch and kissed his filthy, bearded face. After the family showed their father the proper attention, they smiled at Patrick. "So glad he did not get you killed Patrick, but I see no swag on you two? I hope you found something of value after being gone that long," Heather stated.

Archibald grabbed his daughter by the shoulder and escorted her into the house. "We sure did but best not to speak of it here, lass." Archibald recounted the entire tale while his family listened intently. After many mugs of grog and much boasting, the men went to sleep.

* * *

Almost two months had passed and feelings in Savannah were tense. Privately people around town referred to the invasion as Oglethorpe's "New Folly." Nobody was brave enough to call it that openly of course. The town was bracing for retaliation from the Spanish. Everyone knew something was coming but nobody knew what and when. Ever since they returned to town, the blacksmiths had been very busy making shot and repairing weapons as the nervous town prepared for a retaliatory invasion. Every few nights Archibald would disappear and not tell anyone where he was going.

The Scottish town of Darien was left in shambles after so many clansmen were killed in the Fort Mose battle. Mr. McIntosh was in negotiations by messenger with Alick and Fort Mose trying to broker a deal for his clansmen's release. He was planning to use his portion of the profits made from future sale of the cannons to buy the prisoners' freedom.

The time was soon approaching for the Indian's return and Patrick still had no idea how Archibald was going to sell the cannons. Who would be daring enough to buy English cannons? It would be a death sentence to anyone to be caught with cannons in their possession.

One evening Archibald closed up early and asked Patrick to join him. The two rushed through their dinners and headed out the door. The patriarch demanded his family to shut in and to not answer the door for anyone but him. The two men followed by torchlight to a familiar looking door. Archibald knocked four times, then five and waited. A flash of red flickered in the torch light as the door opened.

"Welcome to the Red Lady! Enter, you wary men! You look as if you need a bath," the lady in the red dress motioned.

"We need to talk business, April," Archibald said in a serious tone.

She whispered nervously, "Ah, a bath it is then. Come over here. We have two baths ready and they are still warm. We even offer two kinds of soap gentlemen, all for just two shillings each."

The men nodded and went to the private bath area. She had built rooms on to her standard house and now had a building rivaling some of the wealthiest Savannahians. The brothel was very well lit with whale oil lamps and was finely decorated. Patrick assumed this was the upscale whorehouse where the rich came to play.

Patrick had never had a warm bath and he quickly grew fond of it. Exotic women of all flavors were coming in and out of the area. They brought soaps and sponges. April introduced two exotic women dressed in worldly clothes. "Gentlemen, this is Roxanne, the Persian princess. She is not very fluent in English, but she does speak French and Spanish. And this is our import from Paris, Tiphanie. She does speak English, so ask her if you need anything." April clapped her hands and both women pulled their breasts out of their complicated dresses.

The dresses had been modified with flaps so their womanly tools of seduction could be exposed easily. "Enjoy your baths, gentleman. I will be back soon to talk," April Sky said softly.

Archibald was uncomfortable with the whole situation and dismissed Roxanne immediately. Patrick, on the other hand was taking full advantage of the French girl. She scrubbed his back, chest, and hair. His erection kept poking its head through the soapy water. "Archibald, how the hell did I not know about this place? And why are we not here every night?" he asked earnestly. "Down lower. Much, much lower, mon amie! " Patrick instructed with a devilish grin.

"Well...my wife would run me through if she knew I came down here like this, for one. Also, I didn't think you had any money since I have not been paying you," Archibald laughed.

"Well, yes that is true," Patrick conceded before he instructed Tiphanie, "Lower, Lower. Lower down the front."

"Patrick," Archibald lowered his voice grinning. "You have to pay them more if you want them to scrub down there and I am not paying for that!"

A naked black woman named Rose came in with a bucket of hot water and added it to the tub. She looked more Caribbean than African, but the excited indenture thought she was stunningly beautiful and did not care. Patrick had never seen a fully nude woman before and could barely breathe. He gawked openly and she smiled back at him. The black beauty bent over in front of him and hung her full flesh bags of temptation for Patrick to admire as she refilled his water. Archibald waved her off and she left giggling as Patrick's jaw hung slack. When he regained his composure, Patrick stated, "I officially love this place. I know exactly what I am spending my cut of the money on."

Archibald grunted, "And I figured you would buy your contract off me and be a free man."

Patrick scratched his chin, "Hmmm... That is a tough call. I don't think I can unsee what I have just seen. I think I will just keep working for you and spend every shilling here from now on!" Patrick's eyes widened as his smile stretched from ear to ear.

April entered the steamy room and closed the door so they could be left in private. "Well, Archibald," she started, "I did it. I found a buyer for your iron. Two small ketches will be picking them up. I arranged a meeting place on the coast near the spot where you told me. You have to get them to the coast. The buyers will do the rest."

"Can you trust them?" Mr. Freeman asked.

Patrick in the Red Lady whorehouse

"I can trust them to try and steal them," she confessed. "They're pirates."

Archibald queried, "So how can we do this deal?"

"First, I need you to file all the British markings off the

cannons. This captain and I have a history and he *wouldn't* dare steal the war iron from me. Will you trust me in handling the gold for the sale?" she smiled.

"You can broker the deal, but I cannot trust you. After all, my dear, you're a pirate too," he returned.

"You stab a lady in the heart with such venomous words, Scotsman," April snapped back. "So what is our solution?"

"My indentured will accompany you to make sure this deal stays on the level," Archibald resolved.

After a moment of thought, she found this compromise acceptable. "Very well. I would be honored to have this handsome gentleman escort me. In two days meet me here and be ready to sail." April spit in her hand and held it out. Archibald spit in his hand and reached for hers. He had forgotten he was naked in the tub and stood up to seal the deal. He quickly covered his manhood with his left hand and sat back down. April grinned and sauntered over to Archibald and shook his hand. "We have a deal then. And thanks for the show." Patrick burst into boisterous laughter as she left. The Scotsman's face grew bright red with a combination of embarrassment and rage.

"Rinse off. We're leaving," the red-face man pouted.

"No *we* are not leaving," Patrick challenged. "You can go if you want but I am staying till they throw me out."

Archibald barked back, "Fine. But that won't be long after they find out you have no money in your pockets." Archibald rinsed the suds off with a few buckets of fresh water and then dried himself with a linen cloth. He put back on his clothes and mumbled, "Great. Now I have to go throw some dirt on me so my wife doesn't know where I have been all night." The disgruntled Scotsman grumbled then stomped out of the bathroom.

A few minutes after his boss left, April came back in and smiled at the contented man. A fully naked Rose came back in also and helped the scar-faced man out of the warm tub. She started drying him off, being sure she spent extra time drying his genitals while April smiled. A busty blond woman in a bright yellow dress burst into the room and April shot her a look.

"What is this interruption Whoremaster Darden?" April questioned in a stern tone.

"Sorry to disturb you Madam, but we have a problem. That Sergeant Luthor roughed up Carla and now says that since he is in the military, he does not have to pay. He violently took my girl and is not willing to pay for the privilege," whoremaster Darden spit.

April dropped out of her businesslike tone and sounded like a salty sailor. "That arrogant fucker thinks he is going to steal from us just because he is a cock-sucking lobsterback. He is going to pay extra for hurting Carla or I will run him through!" April then hiked her long dress up and unstrapped a large knife hidden on her thigh.

She stormed out of the room while a naked Rose and Patrick stared at each other, trying to figure out what was going on. A loud crash and a ruckus could be heard outside the door. Muffled cursing could be made out followed by a male scream. After a few more minutes went by, April returned, brandishing a bloody knife and a bag of silver.

Patrick ignored the knife and instead luxuriated for a few more blissful minutes in Rose's nakedness. April cleaned her knife and informed him that his time was now up and she needed the room for another guest. Patrick savored every moment of the carnal knowledge he was obtaining. He slowly finished drying off and dressed himself. The French woman then escorted him out of the washroom to the front door. He soaked up all of Tiphanie that he could, admiring her figure until the moment the door was shut. He stood heartbroken outside the door to the palace of magical flesh. "Damn," he muttered to himself. "I am *so* sick of being poor. We got to sell these cannons quickly."

Patrick took in the night air and followed the torchlight home. He saw the night watchman making his rounds, yelling every few minutes about the time, the weather, and all clear. The watchman wanted people of Savannah to slumber, but not too hard. A constant state of vigilance was necessary, especially in the wake of General Oglethorpe's colossal failure of an invasion. "You there!" the watchman barked. "Where are you going and what's your business?" The inquisition was a sobering reminder that Patrick was not free, not even to enjoy the night air walking home. Having to answer questions anytime to a man in uniform was embarrassing and humbling. Patrick tried to ignore him and kept walking as if he did not hear the watchman's call.

"Hey! Stop!" the watchman shouted. "Answer me!"

Because of years of abuse at the hands of prison guards and British soldiers, Patrick had grown extremely resentful of authority. His mind scrambled with angry questions. *What if I do not provide an answer and keep walking? What gives him the right to know my personal comings and goings? I am not harming anybody, why am I assumed a criminal? The only reason I answer him, is out of fear, not respect. I know if I ignore him, his pride will be challenged and he will have to exert his authority. Archibald was right; the only power any government has is force. Anytime I come into contact with the king and his men, it is always only one way. They will use threats and then violence until I surrender to their will. I have to answer him or get the butt of his musket smashed into my skull.*

"I am on my way home," Patrick reluctantly announced. "I will be going now."

"Not so fast," the watchman commanded. "Who are you and where is your home? Step next to my torch and let me get a good look at your face."

The blacksmith refused to move closer but answered his question with a question, "What's your name? Tell me yours and I will tell you mine, good sir."

This angered the sentry and he closed the distance quickly. "That's not how this works," the redcoat angrily barked. "You answer my questions! I don't answer yours, servant!"

"Servant?! I thought a man was free here in the new world." Patrick stood his ground.

"Where did you get that idea? You are a subject to the king. Never forget your place. He owns you, servant, which means *I* own you. Now I am not going to ask again, what's your name, *servant!*" the redcoat now yelled.

"I will tell you my name when you treat me with respect and tell me..." with a crack, Patrick fell to his knees holding his bloodied nose.

"Tell me slave," the bloody back continued. "What's your name?!"

"What's yours?" Patrick spit through a mouth full of blood. "Treat me like an equal and I will tell you."

Patrick felt a thump, saw a flash of white pain, and then his world turned black.

CHAPTER 13

TATOOED WOMEN AND SOULLESS MEN

The sensation of drowning snapped Patrick back to reality. Ringing flooded Patrick's ears and light was painfully spilling in his eyes. He rolled to his side and began to violently cough up water from his mouth and nose. When his heaving chest began to relax, Patrick's eyes adjusted to the light and to the silhouette of Archibald Freeman. He was shouting questions, "Come on! Wake up, man! Can you see? Do you know who you are?"

Patrick weakly grumbled, "Archibald? Where am I? What happened?"

"I'll tell you what happened," a guard hissed. "You assaulted a member of his Majesty's army. You need to thank Jesus I was able to subdue you in your drunken state and did not have to kill you." The guard was standing by Archibald, sneering at Patrick. "Your owner and I reached an 'agreement' and you are now free to go."

"Thanks for letting me take him without getting your superiors involved," Archibald stated humbly as he helped the wobbly Patrick to his feet.

"You need to talk to your servant about his mouth," the guard warned. "Those kinds of words are quick to get a man killed around here."

Archibald nodded and led Patrick away from the guard as quickly as possible. The guard had apparently left Patrick where he fell. He had kicked Patrick off the road until he was out of the way.

"How did you find me, Archibald?" Patrick asked when they

184

were out of earshot.

"I went out looking for you when you did not return home for second sleep. I asked the night watchman if he had seen you and he escorted me back to your body lying on the side of the road, but I could not wake you. I had to bribe the soldier to let me fetch you in the morning," Archibald explained. "But what really happened was you owe me ten shillings for the bribe I had to make."

"I'm sorry Archibald," Patrick apologized. "I am just so tired of being owned by other people that I boiled over when he started demanding answers of me. I was stupid, not drunk. I told him I was no slave and that he had to talk to me like a gentlemen." Patrick rubbed his woozy head. "The last thing I remember was him smashing my head in with a musket."

Archibald laughed, "You're stupid lad, but I respect your dumb courage." As Archibald helped Patrick walk, he continued to explain that working for the king means never having to say you are sorry, that the joy of enforcing arbitrary rules and decrees over another man attracts the worst kind of scum to the job. "These kinds of men have a dark hole in their soul that they try to fill with violence and a sense of authority. They are addicted to the rush of power they get by bending another soul to their will." He continued, "I have heard of people who work to enforce the king's vicious orders will sometimes regret the evils they do. In fact, some of the people with the best grasp of liberty are ones who escaped the system they served. They know in their hearts that it is undeniably evil and vow the rest of their lives to work against it, begging for redemption."

"I think I understand, Archibald, but all this freedom stuff is new to me. It'll take a while to clear my mind of past ideas," Patrick responded. "But I really need to go home and sleep."

"Well you can't work looking like this anyway," Archibald sighed. "And we got to wash the blood out of your hair and beard. You know you're going to have a black and blue face for a few weeks and aren't going to be so pretty for April Sky's lovelies."

Patrick smiled. "Maybe you should take me back to April's

to wash up. I don't mind how I look."

Archibald smacked Patrick in his sore face. "I think you have had enough of the Red Lady for a while, but you will be seeing April tomorrow."

When the two blacksmiths returned home they saw an old Indian with a collie dog sitting on one of the stumps in the yard smoking hemp. The men greeted each other and shared a pipe as Patrick stumbled to his hammock in the shed. "How are the mules?" Archibald questioned.

"In good health. They ask about you!" the old man laughed.

"I need to know of a place where we can bring the cannons discreetly to the coast. Do you know of a place?" Archibald questioned.

"Yes. There was a sacred land to my people." The Indian's face darkened, "The English took it and gave it a new name. Oglethorpe call it 'Jekyl Island' now."

"It has been taken many times and given many names by the Spanish, the French, the Spanish again and now the English," Archibald added. He knew this Island and knew it had an English occupant named William Horton, appointed by General Oglethorpe, to setup a military post to protect Fort Frederica on St Simon's Island. "Last I heard, he built himself a home on that island," Archibald added about William Horton. He reasoned, "We'll have to come in at night so as not to be seen."

"Let me make map and show you good place," Li Go Che suggested. Archibald yelled into the house and Heather appeared with a quill, ink, and a scrap of hemp parchment. Although the Indian could not write his own name, he was excellent at drawing maps. In just a short time, a very detailed map was ready. "Pick up guns, six moons pass. Then meet here," the white-haired man pointed.

"Very good. I will meet you outside of town at dawn." Archibald confirmed. Both men locked wrists and the Indian and the hyper orange canine quickly departed into the marsh.

"Wake up, Patrick" Archibald yelled at Patrick. His face had swollen up while he slept and was now very black and blue. When Patrick was roused, Archibald explained, "I need you to deliver this map to April Sky. I do not want to risk my marriage by being seen there again. Also, I am going to hire Isaac for another week. I will expect you back here in an hour, so no dawdling at the Red Lady."

Patrick's ears were still ringing. He had a horrible headache and his jaw throbbed, but he would not let his master down after he had saved him from the lobster back. He took the map, nodded, and made his way down the street towards town. Although he was in pain, Patrick's mood improved greatly when he knocked on the door of the Red Lady. The door swung open, revealing a smiling April, but quickly her face became very concerned. "Welcome to the... good God! What have they done to you man?! Come in!" April blurted out the invitation. When Patrick was inside the house, April touched his face gently and asked as he winced, "Did Archibald finally have enough of you laughing at his expense?"

Patrick had spent most of his remaining energy on the walk through town in the sun and became very dizzy. He suddenly fell to the floor of the Red Lady's foyer. April clapped her hands and in seconds a group of scantily clad women arrived. April instructed her ladies to pick Patrick up and carry him to a bed. "Ladies, clean him up. I want his wounds tended to as well. Tiphanie, I just received some new yarrow plants. Wash one and bring it to me. Do you understand my English?" The Madam ordered. Tiphanie nodded in affirmation and disappeared to find the yarrow plants.

The next thing Patrick became aware of was being fully erect, even though a wet rag was painfully dabbing at the weeping, open wounds on his face. He smiled as the women tended to his lacerations. He considered going back home to smash up his body, simply so he could come back again to the Red Lady and receive this kind of attention. The French woman, Tiphanie, arrived with a white flowering stem with fingers of green leaves running up it. *Ah,* Patrick thought deliriously, *they're now bringing me flowers.* The madam quickly broke the flower off and instructed Tiphanie to brew a tea with it. April then chewed the leaves until the juices ran from the corners of her mouth. She then took the ball of chewed greenery out of her mouth and applied it to Patrick's cuts. The tattooed woman repeated this process until all of Patrick's cuts and bruises were covered with this green, gooey pulp.

The madam then ordered her whores out of the room and closed the door gently. She turned to her patient slowly and stared at him with compassion. She returned to Patrick's side and carefully brushed the hair from his face, whispering in his ear, "Your face is so scarred from a harsh life. You look like a beast, a wolf that has been in many fights. From now on I will call you 'My Wolf.'"

Patrick reached into his pocket and handed her the map. "He said it is off some sound on the side of Jekyl Island. Be ready to pick up the shipment in six days. He wants to do it by moonlight."

"Well, you will be coming with me early morrow, my wolf. We need to prep the ships tomorrow and be ready to sail. We will sail around Jekyl and fish a few days so as not to draw suspicion," the kind trollop explained. She continued to detail the plan while Patrick's eyes and mind wandered onto April's cleavage. His eyes drifted down her body and appreciated her fantastic figure. Patrick imagined April had been a top-dollar prostitute in her younger years. She had a very attractive face but time had worn her some. When she smiled, deep wrinkles of crows feet lined her eyes and lips, revealing her true age briefly. He had not noticed how striking her green eyes were until this moment while she stared at the injured man with so much care. But even the stunning beauty of her eyes did not compete for Patrick's attention when half-naked women were scrubbing and caring for him.

April stopped speaking for a moment and waited for Patrick's attention to return to her face. Patrick blushed slightly, but she smiled as she spoke, "So that is all the details you need to know right now."

Patrick gingerly rubbed his eyes. "Um...what time do we

leave and where am I meeting you again?"

April crossed her arms under her breasts, frustrated, then sighed. "Are you deaf, my dear? I said sunrise here while you were looking at me tits." She stood up straight and combed the hair from her face with her fingers as she broke into a pirate's brogue, "Christ...men. You all are the fucking same. You cannot keep your cocks in your pantaloons long enough to even make one round of silver." Patrick was taken aback by the sudden accent. He had no words for April as she continued, "Sorry about me unladylike tongue. Me old self comes out when me soul grows a fire. Be here at dawn morrow and come battle ready. And here, take an eyeful with you." She then squeezed her cleavage together and seductively leaned down over his pulp-covered face. The harlot left her breasts close to Patrick's face while she gently cleaned the green goo off with a rag. Patrick did not mind the slight stinging as he enjoyed the sight of April's breasts heaving as she breathed. The Madam was graceful, sexually charged and an utter assault on Patrick's senses. When she was finished, she kissed him on his bruised cheeks and waved goodbye as she exited the room.

Patrick was in no hurry to leave and enjoyed lying in a real bed. He had not lain on a mattress since his childhood and was melting into its softness. He almost fell asleep when the Nubian woman named Rose entered and offered to help him up. He noticed how pretty her smile was now that she was clothed. The scantily-clad, black strumpet showed him out the door of the Red Lady. He stared at the door that had just been closed in his face and again thought, *Damn, I am so sick of being poor!*

Patrick hurried back home, cautious to avoid any soldiers he saw on the way. When he arrived at the Freeman home, Archibald could be heard clanging around in the shed, uncovering his secret stash of weapons. When he noticed Patrick's presence, he smirked, "You seem to lose all sense of time when you go to the Red Lady. Why is that Patrick?"

Patrick grinned, "The lighting is bloody awful. It is tough to find my way out."

"Control yourself, lad," the Scot warned. "Nothing but

trouble, poverty and cock diseases find a man who does not control himself." Archibald put his hands on his belt and gave Patrick a stern look. When he felt his apprentice had understood the gravity of his words, Archibald continued, "Best get your weapons ready. The delicate madam runs with the real scum of the sea. Do not trust anyone you talk to, not even Miss Sky." Archibald then handed him a sawed-off musket, a dirk, a powder horn, shot, and a large Scottish broadsword.

As the weapons seemed to pile up, Patrick exclaimed, "By the Lord's mercy, is there something you're not telling me? What kind of ship is this?"

"Have you not figured out that she is a bloody pirate, lad?" Archibald questioned. "She is going to use her smuggler connections to sell these war irons. Only wanted men would take the risk of buying stolen British cannons. They will cut your throat and take everything you bring if you present yourselves as easy targets." Patrick gulped. Pirates! Archibald could finally see the young man taking his words seriously. Satisfied, he continued, "Go see Heather and get some rations, enough for two weeks. Then say your goodbyes and go sleep off your punch head."

Patrick was ready to pass out but stumbled his way to Heather in the kitchen. She smiled and already had a bag of food packed and ready. "You are going to make such a fantastic wife to a lucky man one day," Patrick complimented.

Heather sarcastically laughed, "Not very likely." She then called out to her father in the yard asking if she could go visit with Prudence and Mari Anna. Archibald stepped into the doorway and told his daughter she could go, but for only two hours. Heather would need to return to help her mother with the evening's cooking. He also insisted that she avoid any redcoats she spotted and her brothers would escort her. With that, she protested, "Father, I am nineteen. I am old enough to go alone."

Archibald crossed his arms and nodded towards Patrick, "Child, take a good look at Patrick's face. You are not going anywhere alone and that is my decision." With that, Heather pouted and stated she was going to go find the twins. Patrick returned to his shed. Archibald was now gone and the inventory was back in place. He passed out from exhaustion on his hammock with dreams of the tattooed woman swimming in his head.

* * *

The indenture woke up before dawn, swatting at the bugs crawling on his open cuts. He was anxious about the morning's planned adventure. He dressed quickly and strapped his arsenal of weapons on his body. He took the sack of rations Heather carefully packed for him and noticed cornbread. He wondered how she kept getting so much of this wonderful manna. Patrick found Archibald already in the yard fully dressed and getting ready to leave. "Patrick, if we are more than two days late, do not wait for us. Assume something went afoul and return to Savannah immediately." He then called for his family to see the men off. The entire family quickly assembled by the fire pit. He informed them he expected a short trip and would be home in two weeks. The same rules still applied. The family was expected to be inconspicuous while in town and they would shut in early. When finished with his instructions, he commanded his family, with a smile and open arms, to hug their father saying, "I love you" to all of them. When he was done embracing the family, he turned to Patrick and solemnly stated, "If something ever happens to me, I expect you to honor me by caring for my family. I ask you to protect them and love them as I would. Do you accept this proposition I charge you with?"

Patrick was honored. "I already love your family and consider them to be my family now. I will watch over them, you have my word." The family embraced Patrick in the emotional moment. Patrick shed a tear. It was the first time since the day his father died that he felt part of a family. He had become so detached and guarded throughout the years because he had lost so much. For a brief moment, the Freeman's embrace broke through his emotional defense and he was overwhelmed.

The blacksmiths finished saying their goodbyes and departed. Patrick watched as Archibald met Isaac on the street and then disappeared into the marsh. He was worried for the men's safety and knew pulling a cannon train through impassable swampland was a brutal task. The trek was difficult enough, but staying invisible the entire passage would be near impossible. Patrick collected himself and his thoughts turned to his own mission. He was about to set sail with real life pirates!

Patrick headed toward the Red Lady and knocked on the door. After a minute, April answered. Not wearing the elegant red dress Patrick was accustomed to seeing her in, she was now wearing a tight red and black corset and a short dress that only hung to her thigh. She had on tight, black stockings that ran into her tall red boots. She would be arrested in the streets of Savannah for vulgarity if she was noticed by a redcoat. April also had a red tricorn hat with a huge red parrot feather adorning it. Black leather gloves belled outward over her wrists. One yellow and one black sash hung off her biceps. She was carrying an extremely fancy blunderbuss and a large cutlass blade was hanging from a red sash around her waist. Jammed in the front and back of the sash were four small flintlock pistols. Patrick stared at her and wondered how she fit all these weapons onto her slender frame.

"Are ya just going to stand slack jaw and stare at me tits again?" April questioned with her pirates brogue. "Well, you can look at them all you want as long as you pick up me bags and follow me." April instructed Patrick to be very careful with one particular bag, making a point that the bag not be dropped or tossed. After a moment she decided to just carry the mysterious bag herself. Patrick snapped to service and collected the enticing pirate's pile of bags. It seemed like an excessive amount for two weeks. The blacksmith's indenture did take her up on her offer and stared at the cleavage spilling out of her low cut top as they made their way to the river. Staying away from well-traveled areas, the two walked for a half hour down the coastline until Savannah was out of sight. When they finally emerged from the woods, Patrick and April gazed upon two tall ships that were much smaller than the *Robin*. On the shore, there was a man waiting in a small jolly boat.

"Well, Captain K.T. Brewer, I did not expect you would be greeting us yourself. What an honor," April spoke with a hint of sarcasm.

"Arrrrr! Aye, lass. I had not laid eyes on ya in a long time," the salty sea captain replied. "I wanted to welcome ya to me ships me self."

"Your ships?!" she questioned angrily. "The *Mary Read* is mine. You're just holding it. Don't ever forget that Captain Brewer!" she threatened.

"Pardon me, me lady. Yes, you be right. Your ketch is the *Mary Read*, but the *Black Hound*, she be mine. I won that trading ketch from you in that game of dice, don't forget that," the captain countered. "Enough with the cordial pleasantries. Let me sail ya over to the *Mary Read*. Ya have four of me most trusted crew waiting for ya." The pirate smiled mischievously as he bowed curiously, removing his hat.

"Let us cast to the waters before we draw too many eyes," April agreed.

The three boarded the small jolly boat and the Captain quickly rowed them to the ship. Patrick got an eyeful when April climbed up the netting and vaulted on the deck. It was not until Captain K.T. Brewer started scaling the rope that Patrick caught a shining, white ankle in the sunlight. After he ascended the net, he tossed down a rope and told Patrick to tie off the little boat so it would not drift away. Patrick did as instructed and then awkwardly climbed the netting, April's bags throwing his weight off balance. Four exotic looking crewmembers helped lift the bags off his back. He ungracefully fell over the railing and splayed onto the deck. The entire crew laughed at his clumsiness.

"I see you are doing quite well for yourself. You got a new fancy hat, and oh look at that fancy new leg. Let me see it," The madam captain commanded playfully.

The old salty Captain pulled up his pantaloons. "Well I traded in that wooden leg a few months back when I had this one made for me in the islands. It is all cut from one elephant tusk. Look at the beautiful scrimshaw work I had engraved. I thought it would make me less of a Jonah to my men." The ivory was carved with a picture of dolphins, turtles and a black cat, for good luck. "I know you're going to be very mad, but I could not find a black cat for your vessel. I figured me scrimshaw cat be a good substitute. I do have some extra turtle bones in me pocket if you want to use those to ward off evil spirits," the captain offered.

"Unless you plan on leaving that leg behind on my ship, it is not going to protect me. You know it's terrible luck to not have a black cat aboard a ship when women be sailing with you. I won't sail without one. It is a good thing I predicted your incompetence," she insulted.

Carefully, April took the mystery bag off her back and reached in. The bag fell to the ground revealing her holding a black cat at arm's length. She held the cat to her chest and it purred loudly. She stroked the cat behind the ears while she warned, "This be me cat Regan. She is named after a character from King Lear. T'was the daughter who wanted to kill her father and sister and take the kingdom for herself. This cat got the same angry attitude. I advise you all to mind her. This cat does what she pleases and sleeps where she likes on this barky. Do you understand me crew?" As if on queue, the cat hissed at the crew and jumped down to inspect her new ship. The wary crew nodded in acknowledgement.

"If some evil falls on this feline, I will kill each and every one of you," she sternly warned, pointing her finger at each man. April then went about making sure all the rituals were taken care of before she set sail. A horseshoe was still secured to the mast to keep storms away and the cat was onboard to make sure the crew would return home safely. All that was needed was for rum to be poured on the deck and in the ocean to offer the sea gods a bribe for safe passage. A crewmember scrambled to find some rum. Once a bottle was procured, April wasted no time and christened the deck and sea.

When all the rituals were properly observed, she instructed

Captain K.T. Brewer to ready his *Black Hound* to sail soon. "I have the map and you will follow me. We will fish for a few days to seem inconspicuous, so make it look good," she ordered.

"Arrrr! Aye, Cap'n Sky. I still not be sure why you use that name out here, but I respect ya wishes," Captain Brewer called as he climbed down to his jolly boat.

"Captain Brewer I want you to come back tomorrow evening and have a drink with me guest. Raise the sails lads and pull the anchor! We be going fishing!" The madam pirate shouted.

* * *

A day had passed and Patrick Willis was relaxing on the deck, watching pelicans in the afternoon sunlight. April sat down with him and offered him a mug of rum. The scar-faced man thought it extremely odd that a woman captained a ship. It was unheard of and he could not figure out why a crew of men would follow a woman captain that dressed so vulgarly. He wanted to know more, but he also saw the small crew respected and feared her. In time maybe, he would find out why, but for the moment he thought it would be best to hold his tongue. Patrick also noticed April's voice and mannerisms changed, depending on whom she was talking to. If it was about business or whoring, she was very polite and educated, but when she talked to her crew she spoke like a salty sea dog.

"So what is Captain Brewer's first name and what is the story behind him? Also, why is his voice so gritty?" He asked as he sipped his mug of rum.

"His voice is like most of us who gave our lives to the ocean. A lifetime of salty air and rum is hell on your voice box. As far as his name goes, I have sailed with that man for years and I still do not know. He refuses to tell anyone because he says when you know someone's full name you have power over them. It is much easier to cast a spell or a hex on them when you know their given name. So he only goes by his initials K and T. He has been going by his initials for so long that I don't think he even remembers his given name." She smiled at her own joke, then continued. "He is the only captain I know more superstitious than me after his encounter. Everyone called him mad and he could not get a crew to respect him, but I believe it really happened as he said. I am the only captain I know that will sail with him now. Ahhh, speaking of him, here he is now."

Captain K.T. Brewer vaulted on to the deck with amazing grace considering he only had one working leg.

"I be here for your rum! Surrender it to me, lass!" The old man laughed.

"We will surrender the rum but only in exchange for a story." The madam captain offered.

"Arrrr, that be a deal, Captain. Which tale would ya like me to spin?" Brewer offered back.

"I want you to tell THE story," she snapped back.

K.T. Brewer became visibly upset and grew deadly serious, "No, Captain! Please! Not THAT story!"

"Good sir, you already accepted a deal for me rum, it would be a curse to break your word."

"True, I cannot breaks me word, but let me at least have the rum first," the salty man said as he sat down.

April ordered her crew to bring him the illegal spirit as the one-legged man told his tale. The crew fell silent and it seemed like even the waves in the ocean quieted just to hear his story. A cold and creepy wind suddenly blew across the deck as he spun his tale.

"The year be 1690 and I was a young man sailing with a Danish crew on a barky called the *Zeebrug*. We were in the Southern Atlantic waters when we found her adrift. She was a Portuguese merchantman called the *Marialva* and had been lost at sea for three years. It left West Africa with a hold full of slaves but never arrived in Brazil."

He started sweating and turning white as he continued, "Our Captain ordered us to board the vessel and salvage anything of value. When we boarded, me crewmates swore they heard noises coming from the cargo hold. I told them it was impossible, the *Marialva* had been adrift for three years, nothing could be alive. To prove it to them, I opened the cargo hold and as I descended, the crew followed. I knew something was not right by the horrible smell in the hold. When I lit my lamp, the moaning started. The slaves were still chained to the floor and violently tried to break loose. Most the crew screamed and scurried up the ladder, but I wanted to stay and help the hungry souls. It was not till I got closer did I see it." He stopped his story and the old sailor started quivering like a child.

Patrick handed him another drink. "Here, take mine. Tell me, what did you see down in that cargo hold, Captain?"

The old man took a sip and nervously looked back and forth. He took a deep breath to settle his nerves. "When I got an eyeful of the slaves, I realized they were no longer of this world. They were not dead, but not alive either, trapped in a state somewhere in between; they be soulless men. Every one of the slaves had a bite-sized piece of flesh missing on their necks. Their eyes were all white and sunken into their skulls. I pissed me leg and ran up the ladder. Me crew was so scared that they had left me behind and were rowing away. With a running jump, I landed in the Jolly boat but shattered me leg. "

The soulless men of the Marialva

He continued while rubbing his Ivory tusk leg. "When we got back, our horrified crew told our captain what was really over there. He believed us because he had never seen such a hardened crew so afraid. He opened fire on the *Marialva* and sunk it into the drink. While I was in the hold, only one other body was found by my crewmates when they searched the rest of the ship. No lifeboats were aboard and only the captain's corpse was found. He had locked himself in his own chamber and blew his own head off."

He stared vacantly at Patrick and reflected. "Matey, I have thought about those poor souls everyday. I can see those undead creatures pulling on their chains and moaning as they reached for me. To think of the horror of what those poor souls saw. Maybe whatever infected them moved through them one by one. As one slave slowly turned, the others could do nothing but watch. When he finished changing, the slave would turn and bite the next slave chained to him. Those cursed souls watched as the infection slowly moved down the line of people. Everyday those images be burned into me mind I can still hear the moans and wails in me sleep."

The young man felt a cold shiver run up his back as the frightened old man drank his rum. April grabbed Patrick's hand to snap him back to reality.

"Thank you for sharing your story. Our agreement has now been satisfied, so drink all the rum you like," the madam captain announced.

"Lass, it seems my whole bloodline has seen supernatural activity. Let me tell you the story of my great grandfather and what he saw on Roanoke Island, North Carolina. It will make your skin crawl right off," the salty dog warned. "In 1587, me kin was there on that island! He witnessed eleven English colonists go searching the mainland for food. Three weeks later only one terrified soul returned. He told the colony the party was attacked by savages who were impervious to shot and blade. He described them as having putrid, worm-ridden skin just like the creatures I saw."

He ordered another glass of rum and continued, "The

survivor said they battled the savages. Only one of the eleven men died, but four of the others were badly ripped up. Those four died the next day and were buried. Their corpses rose from their graves and ate their former party alive. Only the survivor escaped. Me great-grandfather told me that the colony magistrate did not believe the survivor and had him hung. The magistrate ordered a second party to go recover the corpses so heathens would not desecrate their remains. Out of that second party, only five mauled and starched up souls returned. They vindicated the previous survivor by recounting the same story of being attacked by undead savages. Within hours, the five men died and rose from the grave. The local Indians knew about the terror and arrived in the town as the corpses were attacking the colonists. My great-grandfather hid in a bush as he watched Indians from the Croatan Nation round up all of the colonists and the infected and burned them alive. He was the only survivor to tell the tale of why the first English settlement in the New World vanished overnight. Nobody believed him, either, and thought he was cursed, just like people think I am cursed."

Patrick was bright white with fear and his skin was ice cold. "I think this young man has had the piss scared out of him. That will be enough. Go teach me crew a new shanty," April commanded.

The frightened old sea captain did as he was ordered and he shuffled over to the rest of the exotic crew.

The next day the *Mary Read* sailed slowly, stopping occasionally to drop nets into popular fishing holes. Patrick enjoyed the slow pace but found it hard to catch a nap on the deck after such a frightening tale. The ocean breeze was wonderful and he was thankfully free of the bloodsucking bugs who usually feasted on him on the mainland. April found Patrick staring at the sea birds and kicked him on his side ordering, "Well, I am glad you be enjoying your luxury voyage like a king but you got work to do."

"I think your crew has everything under control," Patrick boldly stated. "I am your escort, not your crew."

"*My escort*?!" she mocked with a laugh. "I did not realize I be deserving me own private escort. I really have made it to a queen's life now."

"Well, I *am* a dandy of an escort and you're welcome for your queenly life." he joked back. "I know this is the kind of courting you've always dreamt of." Patrick put his arms behind his head, reclining and commented, "You know, we'd both get beaten by lobster backs for our tongues."

"So, is that what happened to your face, my wolf? You dared break His Royal Majesty's ridiculous laws?" the madam captain queried.

"I guess so. I can't keep up with what's a law and what's not. They are so arbitrary and people who claim they represent the king's law just make up their own laws on top of the king's. So many damn laws, how could a person know all of them?!" the blacksmith pondered.

She solemnly replied, "My wolf, it is not confusing. There be only one law, do you know what it is?" Patrick shook his head no. She sat down next to him so they were touching shoulders. "The only law is obedience! That's all. All law breaks down to obedience and consequences. Do what the king and his men say, when they say it, or suffer their wrath."

"That sure does make it simple," the scarred man smirked. "You are wise for your many years."

She elbowed him in the ribs and her voice changed. "You bastard! I be a hell of a catch. Men would throw themselves in the mouth of a sea monster just to hold me hand."

"If you want to believe that a woman of your age could command that kind of admiration, you go ahead. I know it is important to exercise your mind at your age," the man mocked.

"Fuck you! I am *to* desirable, the most wanted lady in Savannah. You would die in lustful pleasure if I fucked you. I am still as young as I ever was. How old are you?" she challenged.

Patrick had to stop and recount. It had been many years since someone cared enough to ask him his age and he had forgotten how old he was. "I think I am twenty-seven or twenty-eight. I can't really recall. How many years of life have you seen?" he challenged back.

"I am but a lass of twenty years," she smiled back exposing the wrinkles around her eyes and lips. "Do you have a wife or family?"

"I am still an indenture for the next several years. Sadly, I am not even allowed to court or call on a woman," Patrick frowned.

"What?! That be pure blasphemy! You have not wet your wick with a woman the whole time you be here, you poor man?!"

"I am embarrassed to say no I have not. In fact I never have in my life," he shamefully confessed.

"Now I know you be lying to me. You be twenty-seven, you should have many children by now. I know you at least fucked some whores. You don't have to lie to me, my wolf," she pushed.

"No, not even a whore. It makes it very difficult to find a woman when you grow up in a prison full of men," Patrick added.

She looked sympathetically at the pain and embarrassment in his eyes as he shared his dubious past. She reached out and held his hand in her black glove. "I have no children. I spent my early years whoring. It ruined my mothering parts I suppose. By some miracle I stayed clean, but many harlots I know cannot have children because of all the diseases they carry in their privates," she shared. After a moment of staring at Patrick, April finally offered, "Do you want to change that my wolf? Are you ready to spill your seed in a woman?"

Patrick was completely taken aback by this upfront offer. He tried to speak, but just babbled nonsense. Taking Patrick by the hand and leading him below decks, April stated, "I assume that is a 'yes.' Come on, let's go to my private captain's chambers." Before they made their way, April called out to the crew commanding them not to bother her unless the ship was under attack. They were told to make their way slowly to Jekyl Island, keeping an eye out for Spanish ships and to continue fishing.

After lighting a lamp in her cabin, April aggressively pinned Patrick to the bed. She made him watch as she slowly escaped out of her complicated outfit. Patrick gasped. The rumors *were* true. Tattoos completely covered April's skin. Her ink-marked breasts flickered in the lamplight as she undressed him.

CHAPTER 14

SWAMP STAG AND JEKYL ISLAND

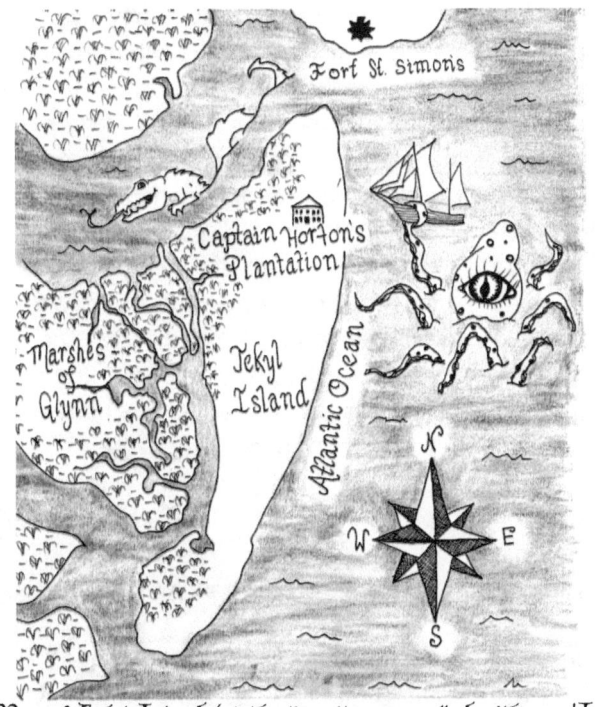

Map of Jekyl Island (at the time it was spelled with one 'L')

*C*rack! *Blam!*
Isaac's pig shot blew the man's foot right off. William's shot finished the man off as it peppered his face. Archibald also blasted his musket to cover Isaac and

William's retreat to reload. Li Go Che stood without fear as bandits closed in on them. Colorful arrows flew through the swamp and into a marauder's chest. The pack mules were frightened by the musket shot and scattered into the swamps. The retreating men stopped in their tracks. Isaac began reloading his musket while William drew his large, Scottish two-handed claymore. He still preferred the traditional two-hand style to the new basket-hilted version, which he considered too English for his liking. The kilted man charged into the mix with a wild Scottish battle cry. Archibald followed suit and pulled his hunting blade as well. The battle-hardened Indian amazingly dropped two more thieves before the party was overrun. William lost all fear. He held his massive blade over his head and charged down a quivering road agent. The thief was paralyzed at the sight of the crazed man and froze. Archibald took advantage of the frightened, distracted man's mistake and pierced him below the ribs with his long blade. The bandit bent over and stumbled in pain. With his full momentum behind him, William dropped his blade on the thief's neck. The head flew from the body as a fountain of blood poured from the neck. The eyes on the head still blinked as it rolled across the ground.

This gruesome display deeply struck fear within the gang of road agents and most of them reversed their charge. William and Archibald then turned on one unlucky thief in striking distance. They struck with deadly synchronicity and it was impossible to block both blows. Archibald's blade sliced deep between the neck and the shoulder. The spray of blood shot from the man, blinding the Scots and making them quickly wipe their eyes.

The Indian used his bow to block a thief's blade. The old man avoided the repeated blows by dodging and weaving. The masked bandit screamed in pain as Garland sank her teeth into his buttocks. As the road agent raised his blade to kill the dog, a colorful war club struck him in the face. A loud cracking noise of a skull breaking echoed through the fight. The old man struck the masked man again crushing his nose deep into his skull. The bandit dropped making a loud gurgling sound. Garland then turned on the man's throat and spilled the rest of his life into the mud.

Only four bandits were left and they were running for their lives. The Indian switched back to his bow and pierced two more men in the back. William finished the dying men on the ground with his blade. Isaac ran back to the line and finally joined the fight ready to fire again.

The old Indian cussed loudly in Creek and kicked the dead masked man on the ground. Archibald panted, "Don't worry I don't think those two will come back."

"Not worried. Masked man's blade chipped favorite bow!" he shouted as he kicked the dead man again.

The group was still at a high sense of alert and a ready state of battle. Li Go Che covered the men as they scavenged the dead like vultures. No guns, just blades and a little silver. They stripped anything worthy of any value and left the dead bodies for the alligators.

"I am surprised they followed us this deep into the swamps," Isaac stated. "Oy vey! I am getting really sick of bandits. They didn't even wait to try and kill us while we slept. They grow bolder and bolder and attack us while the sun is high."

"If we push fast, we can camp at the mounds by night fall," Archibald reasoned.

"Show respect, white man! We sleep outside of sacred burial ground or anger their spirits. No man sleeps near mounds! I am not ready to see the great-spirit horse yet!" the superstitious Indian demanded.

"You are in charge, great chief. We will do anything you ask," Archibald flattered.

"We need find mules. They run off from musket noise," the Indian command.

"Just follow the track, lads," Archibald added. "Let's get those mules back."

The old man relaxed and nodded in approval. The party of blood-soaked men moved quickly deeper into the swamp. Within an hour, the mules were tracked down and they were back on their way to the mounds.

* * *

Patrick did not leave the arms of the naked woman for two days. He ran his fingers on her skin tracing her every tattoo. The two only stopped having sex to occasionally sleep, eat and to use the chamber bucket. For the first time in his life, he experienced euphoria. Nothing else mattered in life but the present moment. April slowly woke and mumbled, "I best be getting topside to make sure the crew has not sailed us to the Caribbean by now."

"You can go after one more time. I want to try you in the dog style again."

As Patrick pounced on the tattooed woman, there was a knock at the door. A muffled voice called through the closed door. "Cap'n. I knows I ain't supposed to disturb ya, but ya best come up topside to see this."

"Very good, crewman," April growled. "I'll be up shortly."

The two naked lovers had a hard time finding all their garments. They were castoff all over the chamber. When the clothes were collected, they dressed as fast as they could but one of April's boots could not be found. After five minutes of searching, the missing boot finally appeared. Both suited up into full war gear and headed deckside.

The sun was setting and a storm was moving off in the distance. Low booms could be heard carrying across the water. "What's that sound? Is that thunder from a coming storm?" Patrick inquired.

"That be cannon fire, my wolf," April answered dryly. She then ordered a crewman to fetch her the spyglass to take a look. A black-skinned, exotic sailor handed her the spyglass and April immediately started to climb up the rigging. Patrick followed and ascended the mast as well. April had a top-of-the-line folding spyglass and it had excellent range. Her vision reached out across the distance to see a galleon firing upon a small trading ketch. She saw a British St. George jack on the galleon and a French jack on the ketch. Within minutes the fight was over and the small ketch was overtaken, so the madam captain ordered the men to fly the British jack so as to avoid the same fate. The crew opened a secret bottom in a rum barrel and pulled the matching jack out of their collection of flags. She then ordered them to set sail and move closer to the fight.

It did not take long and the ketch was now flying a British jack. The two ships sailed away quickly as to avoid the incoming storm clouds. She watched until the two ships drifted away further then barked her orders, "Full Sails. Set the course to the battle waters. Hurry! We must beat the storm. It looks like they lost some barrels. Let us go see what they be dropping."

The crew efficiently carried out her orders and caught the wind just right. They closed the distance in short time and went to examine the area. The wind had picked up and the storm was rolling in. They arrived on the sight of the battle, but Captain Sky was careful enough to leave Captain K. T Brewer's ship in eyesight. Five barrels were rolling in the waves but they were taking in water and sinking. A number of dead bodies were bobbing up and down in the ocean.

"'Elp, 'elp!" was heard over the growing storm.

"Look! Man over board!" Patrick pointed at a man clinging to a sinking barrel.

"Bring the *Mary Read* about, boys, and pick him up," she ordered. The ship swung around and they threw a rope to the splashing man. The crew quickly hoisted him out of the drink.

"Merci, Captain," the soaked man said to Patrick.

"Oh, that was your first mistake!" Patrick cringed.

"I be the fucking Cap'n of this barky! Throw him back in the blue until he learns to show some respect," the true captain commanded.

The four crew men threw the confused, soaked man back into the windy ocean. The poor man was floundering in the choppy water and trying to stay afloat.

"Christ! Throw the rope to him again!" she ordered.

The waterlogged man again grabbed the rope was pulled

aboard.

After coughing up a lung full of water, the rescued sailor begged in a French accent, "Pardon, Madame. I have never seen a lady captain. No disrespect intended, mon amie."

"What da hell happened, sailor?" she questioned.

"We were overrun by British privateers. I was blown overboard with these barrels by cannon fire. The British killed my crew and threw them into the water. I acted dead and let myself bob with the barrels. Thank St. Michael you saved me. I would have drowned for certain with this storm."

"Tell me what is in those barrels floating out there?" she inquired.

"We were shipping salt. That cargo is ruined, Madame, as soon as water breeched them." The French man explained.

"Crew, get us away from this storm! Find me a port. And pull that fucking British jack down! I may need it to wipe me arse," she yelled.

The Frenchman laughed, "Oh thank St. Michael again, you are not the damn British. I would like you to save me some of that jack to wipe my ass with as well, Madame."

"Find this soul some rum," the pirate captain demanded. "Let's have a drink and hear your story. You be safe here now."

* * *

"We don't have time to go traipsing through those damn gator filled marshes just to avoid them. Plus, our luck won't hold that much if we fight them. Those Spaniard troops in our path won't be as easy to slay as those bandits were. We need to find a way through them without bloodshed," the Scotsman warned.

"Well, great warrior, how would your war parties handle something like this?" Archibald asked.

The white-haired man smiled and his wrinkles deepened. He and his collie dog Garland ran into the swamp and disappeared. After twenty minutes he reappeared with a handful of white flowers. The Indian started collecting the seeds and then carefully began cutting up and preparing the roots.

Archibald started laughing, "My god are you going to give them all that Devil's Trumpet? They will be stark mad for two weeks."

"Au Gewalt, I had to use that plant when I ran out of laudanum doing amputations, it did not go well. You might kill those men giving them that much Jamestown weed." Isaac warned.

"As usual, I am the only person in this group that has no idea what the hell that plant is." Isaac complained.

Archibald shook his head, "You really don't know much about the world you live in now, lad. Back in 1676, during Bacon's rebellion in Jamestown, Virginia, Bacon's men slipped a bunch of British soldiers some of this plant's leaves and seeds in their salads. That group of English soldiers went mad for eleven days and had to be quarantined because most went completely out of their minds. They went blind, forgot to eat or could not stop laughing. Most of them were naked and shitting themselves to death. After such a horrible reaction, the plant got the nickname Jamestown weed."

The old man announced that the weed was properly prepared and that he was ready. When he scouted earlier he saw the Spanish soldiers had a small pot of stew brewing. The group watched with admiration as the old warrior slowly crept into the camp in broad daylight. The soldiers were too distracted playing dice to notice the white-haired man drop something into their stew. He vanished back into the swamp as quiet as a cougar.

It took almost two hours before the Spanish men sat down and ate the stew. The entire group ate as they laughed about their dice game. It only took about a half hour before they started acting strangely. A few men started dropping and clenching their bellies in pain, while others just suddenly became amazed at how interesting their own hands were. They stared at their digits, opening and closing them with fascination. When a few of the soldiers got naked and started jumping back and forth over the fire pit, Li Go Che figured it was time to circle around the camp.

They were almost spotted sneaking past because William could not stop giggling at the humorous site of men touched with madness. The group picked up their pace and made it to the mounds without another incident.

The men heard Garland growling and stopped the work of removing the massive pile of stones. The men approached the canine cautiously with their weapons drawn. The collie was growling loudly at a large bush that was shaking. The men crept closer to investigate. The dog yelped as a large, open mouth with rows of teeth stormed out of the foliage. Garland jumped sideways and barely missed the pair of snapping jaws. Isaac showed unusual courage by charging the beast. He unloaded his musket full of pig shot into the reptile's side. It bucked with pain and swung its tail, knocking the hulking man off his feet. It moved in to finish off Isaac when a colorful arrow appeared in the massive gator's side. The scaly beast slowed its approach as another arrow plucked its side. Garland taunted the gator fearlessly and it returned its attention to the yapping dog. Its gaping mouth opened again and then mysteriously stopped moving. It was just lying there with its mouth wide open. The gator's tail was slapping wildly and its body rolled over and over in the mud. Isaac had wearily gotten to his feet when he noticed the head was no longer attached to the flailing alligator body. The group watch in amazement as the body kept spinning for another half minute.

William walked over with his bloody claymore sword, holding the gator head aloft and triumphantly stated, "I am mounting this on me wall. None of me clansman will ever believe I took the head off this beast." As the group inspected the body, they noticed it was riddled with shot, three broken shafts and several stab wounds. "That is one fucking tough beast," Archibald concluded.

"You finish stones. I skin gator," the old Indian man offered.

The men went back to work as the guide skinned the

reptile. The Indian wasted very little time as he carved every little piece of usable meat out of carcass. He even cut the legs off to sell the claws to some tribesman for rituals. All the meat was loaded into a large bag and he hung the hide to dry.

The men finished moving the stones and went into the sacred cave to inspect. The cannons looked like they did when they left them with no rust or browning. They were well preserved considering they were stored in a damp swamp cave. It took most of the day to pull the cannons out and to attach their battle carriages to the uncooperative mules. By sun down, everything was loaded in the long mule train. There were eight twelve-pound cannons, eight artillery and storage carts, and eighteen mules. The Indian thought to bring two more pack mules in case any died during the journey. After readying the mule team, the group spent the rest of the evening piling the rocks back and hiding the entrance to the cave. Li Go Che insisted they hurry and leave before dark. He was worried the white men would anger his ancestor's spirits. The group obliged and finished their work as fast as they could. They were also afraid of being cursed by revengeful Indian spirits.

The men pulled the train in the dark for about an hour and then set up camp. Archibald worried they were already behind schedule. Isaac kept disappearing and coming back with bundles and bundles of wood, more than what was the needed for a fire. The men gorged themselves on gator meat until they could barely move. Even Garland was passed out by the fire with a fat, happy belly. Li Go Che pulled out his pipe, lit some hemp and the men recounted their heroic battle with the green, scaled monster. Unbelievably, they became hungry again after they smoked so much and helped themselves to another course of gator meat. The old man stayed up most of the night curing the hide over the fire and smoking the rest of the meat so it would not spoil during their journey.

The party was woken by pouring rain. It came down so thick and hard, it stung the skin. The swamp was flooding with water quickly and they had to move their muddy train to higher ground. The train slowed as the carts and cannons kept getting

Li Go Che and Garland have a smoke

stuck in the mud. Thankfully, Isaac's massive strength was enough to free the wheels and keep the train moving. To slow the pace even further, the booming thunder and lightning was spooking the mules. The storm was so loud that it even scared their fearless dog, Garland. After one incredible crack of thunder, the dog jumped into a cart and hid under one of the canopies.

It finally stopped raining and hauling the heavy artillery through the muddy swamps took its toll on the carts. Some of them were struggling to stay in one piece. Li Go Che solved the problem by quickly building some Indian travoises, which he quickly attached to the extra mule. He even built one for Garland and loaded it with sacks of alligator meat.

"That collie dog sure has come in useful," William commented. "I really hope ya don't eat the little girl when she gets too old. I will be happy to let her spend her last years roaming me farm, and I can even buy her off ya when the time comes," William offered to the old warrior.

"Eat Garland?" Isaac questioned in shock.

William answered, "Aye, lad. It is a very injun thing to do. They never waste anything. They treat dogs like any other beast of burden. When it gets too old to work, they will eat it. They will use the hide, bones, claws and every other part as well. It would be a damn shame to let a proud Scottish breed suffer a fate like that. It would not be right to let that happen. Lots of Scots brought their dogs with them. She might have even run off from someone I know. "

Garland had a large smile on her muzzle, thrilled to be given a new task to conquer. She pulled the custom travois with surprising power.

An Indian travois is attached to Garland to haul supplies

The men trudged through muck like this for two long days. They fought hordes of fresh, hungry mosquitoes, venomous snakes, gigantic alligators, and were now even being robbed of their food stores by a bunch of raccoons at night. On top of worrying about the beasts of the swamp, the men had to stay constantly vigilant for bandits, as well as Spanish and British soldiers. Being seen by anyone would be trouble, so the old scout took the men through the deepest and least traveled parts of the swamps. That also meant it was the most difficult area to travel through, making the entire trip absolutely miserable for man and beast alike. The exhausted and soaked men had to take shifts when they set up camp. They had scared off a bobcat and the old man swore he even heard a cougar cry the night before. Li Go Che suspected the mules were being hunted by a pack of wolves. The thieving, trickster raccoons had brought the attention of a pack of gray wolves. Since there had been so much hunting of the wolves and their prey, the canines were growing increasingly bold in their search for food. When the sun would set, Archibald could hear the wolves growling just outside the light of the campfire. Luckily, William came up with the brilliant idea of storing dry wood down the barrels of the cannons. If the Scot had not taken this precaution before leaving the mounds, there would have been no hope of starting a fire in all the rain. The men would have shivered and caught ill with no heat and it had the added benefit of keeping those wolves at bay. Surprisingly, the mules had not fallen ill. They were much tougher animals than Archibald anticipated.

Crack. Blam! The sound echoed over the rain making the men spring to life with weapon in hand. Isaac yelled, "That wolf was getting too close to the mules! I don't think I hit it, but the shot scared them off. I heard them running away in the dark." The men then decided to pull the mules closer to the camp and to surround the pack animals with torch light. It was a necessary precaution but William was sure there would no chance of sleep now. In just twenty minutes, the sounds of hungry wolves could be heard just outside of the torch perimeter. Over ten sets of wolf eyes reflected red in the lightning.

"Lads, there be a lot more of them wolves then I reckoned," Archibald said in a panic. "We need a plan." Lighting flashed again revealing that Archibald had greatly underestimated the amount of wolves circling their camp. Now close to twenty sets of hungry eyes could be seen reflecting back. "Get the mules ready to move out. We can't stay here, lads." Archibald announced.

"You are touched in the mind, lad! We cannot be traipsing into the swamp in this black," William protested. "It would be impossible, lad."

The blacksmith fired back, "I count almost twenty wolves out there. We can't be staying here."

William reluctantly lined the mules up to move. Li Go Che took the lead and started to march the train into the foreboding blackness. Isaac appeared holding the large sack of gator meat legs. With amazing strength, he threw the offering deep into the darkness to the pack of predators, hoping to distract them long enough to make an escape. The plan seemed to work. The pack was growling and fighting with each other over the alligator parts as the train quietly moved away.

"Good thinking using the gator, lad!" Archibald complimented. "I hate to give away our prize and that tasty meat, but if we lose these mules, we will be dragging those cannons through the muck ourselves!"

The group did not get very far in the complete blackness of night. The storm had blocked out any star light and it was pitch black. They had no choice but to use the last of the dry wood and set up a new camp. They circled the mules and surrounded them with torches. Sadly, this used up the last of their dry wood. The men were going to need immense luck if they would ever make it to Jekyl Island on time.

* * *

The tattooed woman swigged down a mug of rum and asked, "What do people call you, Frenchmen?"

"Madame, my name is Robert Deaux. My family line is Parisian and from the country side of France. I am a trader merchant who ships spices around the world. I really hate working around the colonies and much prefer traveling to the Orient."

"Was that your ship and cargo the British stole?" she asked as Regan the cat jumped in her lap.

He replied, "The cargo, oui. The ship? No. I rent ships to carry my cargo. I've never made enough to buy my own ship."

"So you are skilled with bargaining and languages, are you? I could use a man of your talents, if you need a job," the captain questioned as she stroked her purring feline.

"Since all my money was just was just stolen and you hate the English as much as me, I would have to say 'oui', depending on the terms," the Frenchman nodded and reached out to also pet Regan. The cat immediately hissed at Robert and swatted his hand. Crimson dots appeared on the French trader palm.

"She is a little particular in who she fancies. Feed her some fish for a few days and then try again. I can pay you five shillings a week and half the profit of any trading you procure. You will have accesses to this ketch and can take her as far as you need to along the coasts and Caribbean. You will have access to my very loyal crew to assist you in any deal you broker," she offered. She spit in her hand and held it out. The Frenchman looked a little repulsed by this custom but spit in his palm and shook.

"I have many great connections. With use of this ship and a good crew we could make much silver, mon amie," Mr. Deaux replied with glee.

"Let us seal the merger in rum and song. Sing me a French sailing song! I be hankering for some entertainment," she demanded.

The French man cleared his throat and started to belt out an old sea shanty. April sat on Patrick's lap and he held her as the man sang for their amusement. Ten minutes of song put the woman in a romantic mood and she whispered something into Patrick's ear.

The madam captain thanked the Frenchman for his song and then ordered her crew, "See that Mr. Deaux is properly fed and give him as much rum as he cares to have. Keep a careful eye peeled for that English galleon and be sure to keep Captain Brewer's vessel in sight." The captain then placed the cat in Robert's lap and it began to hiss. She laughed as she took the smiling, love-struck Patrick back down into her captain's quarters.

The next morning there was a knock on the captain's door and a crewman reported, "Captain, we are at the location, but the land party has not arrived yet."

"Very good, crewman. Report when they arrive," she giggled while Patrick tickled her breasts. She then mounted Patrick and said, "You know, we have much more in common than you know."

"Really? Do those tattoos also give you magical powers to read minds?" Patrick smiled.

"Shake my hand, my wolf," she extended her hand.

Patrick was confused by this but took her inked up hand into his and gave her a firm handshake.

"Not like that. I mean *shake* my hand, Patrick," she hinted.

She slid her hand down toward his elbow and locked wrists. She extended her two fingers in a "V" pattern. Patrick returned the secret handshake.

"How do you know about that? Only men are allowed in that club," Patrick asked, puzzled.

"If you happen to notice, I do as I please. I do anything men do. I run my own business, captain my own little ship and fuck you as I please. Because of my pirating days, people still fear me and the connections I have. I get to do things other women can't even dream about doing. I am also the only woman allowed into a meeting of the Freeman Society," she explained. "I do many clandestine missions to help the cause. I am one of the few people you will ever meet who actually knows what it is to live free. Being a captain on the open waters is the only time when a person can live without anyone else controlling your life. You are free to earn a living as you please, not pay taxes to an unseen master and live by your own rules. It is a life I really miss. I value that freedom over anything else and I am trying to find a way to return to it. The *Mary Read* is a fine ship, but she is too small for living free on the open seas."

"Is pirating the reason you changed your name?" he dared to ask her.

"Any more questions like that, my wolf, and you won't be invited into my chambers the rest of this voyage," the madam warned.

"That question is respectfully withdrawn," he said as he rolled her naked body over.

* * *

It had been three passionate and lustful days since the couple were seen. The naked lovers woke to noisy scurrying topside. "Get dressed quickly, something is afoot," the naked woman barked. The two dressed in a hurry and armed up. They ran up topside and their eyes recoiled from the sunlight. The crew of the *Mary Read* looked down the coast and saw a massive man frantically waving and jumping up and down.

"Let's move it, crew! They need help. Man the sails." The Captain turned to Patrick, "Do you think it's your friends? They are at least two days overdue and it is broad day light."

Using her spyglass to confirm if it indeed was his friends, he spotted Isaac waving his arms on the beach and his clothes were covered in blood. "Yes. That's Isaac but they look like they are in real trouble. Please hurry."

A mule pulling a cannon through the swamps

The *Black Hound* and the *Mary Read* quickly made it up the coast line towards the jumping man. "Isaac, are you in trouble?" Patrick shouted over the water.

"Thank Moses you're still here. I knew you would not leave, even if Archibald told you to. We have a large group of Spanish soldiers about three hours behind us. We have to load these cannons right away." Isaac yelled. The cannon train then came into view and the crew scrambled to get the thick gang planks ready.

Patrick yelled to his friend, "Isaac, these ships have a very shallow draft. Take these lines and tie them to those trees over there. Help us steady the ship and pull her real close." In minutes, both ships were docked against a small cliff. A door on the railing opened and the crew slid the heavy, reinforced gangplank to the top of the little cliff. It was almost perfect, the gangplanks were practically level. The exotic crew poured onto the cliffs to help the exhausted delivery men. They rolled the cannons down the gangplanks and right onto the decks of the small ships. Room was quickly becoming scarce on deck so the cannons were tied to a rope going over yard arm. The line was tied to the anchor pulley and was lowered into the cargo hold. The crew and the exhausted travelers worked in a panicked frenzy to load everything as fast as possible. Captain K. T. Brewer shouted "Take the carts too, to stack them upon the cannons if you have to". Two and a half hours had passed when April shouted to the crews to be ready to cast off.

Li Go Che was visibly upset. Archibald asked him to join them on the ship but he stated, "I need mules, worth good money to my tribe. I try and escape with them."

Patrick overheard this and turned to April, "Please. There is no way this warrior will slip past an army looking for him with eighteen mules. He won't leave them behind. Can we just cram them all on the deck for a day and then drop them off? This Indian has saved our lives over and over. We owe it to him."

She engaged in deep thought and agreed. "My wolf, you are now indebted to me for this. One day I will need a favor and you will return the call." Much to the crew's dismay, nine stinky, flea-ridden mules were loaded down the gangplank on each ship.

Mr. Deaux had untied the lines to the *Mary Read* and rushed down the gangplank before the ship pulled away from the cliff. The crew barely had room to pull in the plank but managed to shut the rail door before Spanish voices could be heard coming near the cliffs. Somehow, everyone and all the cargo had made it aboard the two vessels. It was nearly impossible maneuvering the rigging and the sails around the collection of mules that were in the way. The tiny ships creaked in protest due to all of the weight but they finally turned out into the inlet. The two vessels caught wind and pulled away from the coast just as Spanish soldiers arrived and started firing their muskets at the ketches. The sailors returned fire but both war parties were too far out of range to hit anything. The sails finally filled with wind and they pulled away quickly from the coast, out to deeper waters. The entire crew cheered and congratulated themselves for pulling off such an impossible feat. The wary delivery men sighed with relief and exhaustion. They were given mugs of rum to toast their amazing journey.

Captain Sky came forward and toasted, "Let you recount your tale over some rum."

Archibald smiled, "I would be happy to tell you the story, but first, let's talk gold."

CHAPTER 15

GODS AND FREEDOM

"**D**on't you worry about the gold, Duncan, or should I say 'Archibald?' I forgot which name you be using from time to time. Your payment be safely in the captain's quarters below, although I am told my private quarters is now jam packed with barrels of gunpowder and cannon balls. I will get your money after we celebrate. You sound like you had a very difficult journey," the captain surmised.

"Well top me off with a little rum before I get trampled by all these damn mules!" Archibald smiled.

"So where shall we be dropping your savage off at?" she asked while sipping on her mug of rum.

"There is an Indian trading post he wants to be dropped off at. It's on the mainland just north of Tybee Island. We should be there by sunset if the winds hold," Archibald reckoned.

"He best be taking his dog with him, too. I don't like how that collie is staring at Regan, waiting to make his move. Poor cat won't come down from the rigging."

"Aye. He will take all the animals and his bags of gold," the blacksmith stated. "Speaking of which, I am ready to be paid now. I don't want to know who you're selling these to, but I hope it's not the British. I do hope that you make enough to start saving for a new ship."

"I will not make you wait any longer. Stay here. My wolf, come help me with these bags," the captain replied as Patrick sprang to his feet following the madam below deck.

"'My wolf'?!" Archibald shot Patrick a confused look. Patrick grinned ear to ear at Archibald. He smiled so much that his dimples showed below his beard as he descended down the stairs.

"You had the gold here the entire time? Hell, I even carried it for you and did not know!" Patrick exclaimed.

"Yes, love. A girl has to keep her secrets," she smiled.

"I bet you have more secrets than even you can remember," he teased.

She worked herself carefully though the maze of cannons, carts, and artillery until she found her bag. Even with her skinny frame, April muscled the heavy bag up and shimmied back through the cannon-and-cart obstacle course before bounding back upstairs to where the group of men was waiting for their payments.

"As instructed, I have spilt the gold doubloons evenly into eight bags, one for each cannon." April pulled out eight small bags and handed them to Archibald. He opened the bags and counted the coins as gold sparkled in his eyes and he grinned.

"William, here is your bag of gold. What will you do with it?" Archibald asked the kilted man.

"I hopes it be enough to buy me brethren's freedom from Fort Mose. They still be in dar and da clan is counting on me to save 'em," William replied.

"I am hoping you buy their freedom in haste. Let me know if I can help you," Archibald offered.

"Isaac, what do you intend to do with your share?" the blacksmith asked.

"I will buy off the rest of my contract and finally be free. With the remaining gold I will give most of it to God and try and find a good Jewish woman," Isaac explained as he counted his coins.

"Patrick, what do you have planned with the booty", Archibald inquired.

"I want to spend every last bit of it in the Red Lady, but I will show restraint and save it in hopes that my family in London is finally located. I would like to bring them here when I am freed. I will continue to work for you and honor my contract, saving my money for my sisters and me mum," Patrick summarized.

"And you, warrior chief?" Archibald handed him three bags.

"I find Creek hokti to continue bloodline. One is only Creek through mother not father. I must find true Creek woman. Now rich enough to find way to buy back some scared land. I could have many hoktaki." He smiled devilishly.

Patrick interrupted and asked, "What is a hokti"?

Li Go Che shot back "It is what we call women who can have children, northern tribes call them squaws".

"How can I find you if we need your services again, great chief?" Mr. Freeman asked.

"I come by every full moon to you! You good man to tribe," the old man forced a wrinkled smile.

Patrick finally asked, "What about you, Archibald?"

"I will use the money to move my family as far from the British and Spanish as I can. Don't forget, sovereigns, the remaining bag will be donated to the cause as agreed upon," he reminded the group.

The inked women chimed in "Why is the chief getting thrice the amount as you?"

"He is a great chief. If it was not for him, none of us would have anything at all. The cannons would have been left behind for the Spanish if he had not known about his hiding place. His wisdom kept us safe in the swamp and he is a great warrior," the wigged man boasted.

A proud smile crept on the typically stoic face of the Indian. He loved flattery.

"As much as I love hearing this, we be landing soon to get rid of these stinking mules and the lot of you. So drink up, boys, on a job well done!" April yelled and raised her mug.

"Captain, can I have a word with you below deck?" Patrick asked humbly. April obliged and followed her new lover below the deck when he finally asked, "Are you coming back with us?"

"Hell no! If I don't keep a close eye on me booty, Captain Brewer will steal it all for himself. He would have slit both our throats as soon as we boarded and just kept me gold if he thought he could. But he fears me and fears the people I know that would come in retribution," she explained. "I have to sell this swag to some dangerous fellas but I will make double the gold than what I gave you and your friends. I want to be free again and captain a real dandy of a ship. Ships cost lots of money."

"Well what about our love? What will happen to us?" Patrick asked, clearing his throat.

"You are a sweet man but I got to see this through. I figure you owe me that whole bag of gold for as much sex as I gave you," the madam pirate smiled, but an awkward pause filled the air between them. "Jesus, it was just a joke, lad. I fucked you because it was fun and I think you're a looker. It was free of charge. I could be gone a long time but come see me when I get back to the Red Lady." Patrick seemed to frown a little until April offered, "Come on. Let me give you one more good hump." Patrick nodded eagerly as she bent over one of the cannons.

* * *

The two ships sailed past the Tybee light house in the rosy light of the early morning. It was an impressive site considering it was built so rapidly. It was made of brickwork and cedar piles and was octagonal in shape. It was the tallest structure of its kind in the Americas.

"I had never seen it so close before. It's massive!" Patrick exclaimed.

"Yes it is. A carpenter named Noble Jones from the Wormsloe Plantation constructed it very rapidly. He was rewarded with a lease to this land because he was respected so well by Oglethorpe. He was also a constable and a doctor but he really won favor with Oglethorpe when he laid out the city plans for Augusta," Archibald explained.

"Was a time when it be easy to sneak into Savannah by way of the Skidoway River. Now the redcoats went and build a

The original Tybee lighthouse

fort and plantation on this 'Isle of Hope' making it much more difficult to not be spotted," April injected.

"Did you get a good look at that fort? Since it is so close to the water, Jones had to make it out of tabby," the blacksmith pointed out.

"I am no carpenter. What is tabby?" Patrick asked naively.

Archibald explained, "It is a local mixture of shells, limestone, sand and water. Then, it is covered with plaster and whitewash to keep the sun from weakening the structure too fast. Tabby does very well to hold against foul weather and Spanish cannon balls if it is properly constructed."

"Did you also see how he built wood above the tabby to make it taller and more deadly to assault? See how Jones saved time and money by sharing the fort wall with that large house inside?" the captain pointed out.

Archibald replied, "Yes, it was a wise construction. I also heard after Oglethorpe's failed attack of St. Augustine, he actually commissioned Jones to run a marine patrol out of Wormsloe. We would be wise to keep sailing and avoid this whole area completely."

"Agreed. We be sailing north and out of site of the fort and of Wormsloe," she concurred.

The ships sailed north quietly so as not to arouse suspicion. The *Black Hound* pulled up to the coast first and unloaded the mules as fast as possible. Captain K.T. Brewer was cussing about all the mule shit on his deck. He ordered his sailors to take buckets of seawater and wash the dung away. The *Mary Read* docked next and the crew worked fast so as not to be seen by British eyes. The parade of mules made their way off the gang plank followed by the exhausted, swamp-eaten, bloodied men. The men decided to travel together for safety back to Savannah, except Li Go Che. The old man said his goodbyes and headed to a local Creek village.

Patrick watched with pain in his heart as the *Mary Read* drifted off into the horizon. He was visibly distraught knowing there was a good chance that that would be the last he saw of the mysterious April Sky. "Time to go home, lad," Archibald put a sympathetic hand on Patrick's shoulder. The men treaded into the woods and when they saw the Tybee Island lighthouse disappear from their view, they knew they were almost home. They traveled wide of the Wormsloe Plantation and circled back around to Savannah. They waited until nightfall before entering the town to bring as little attention as possible. Isaac quietly parted ways and the other three men headed to the Freeman house. As expected, it was already 'shut in' and Archibald wasted no time knocking on the door with a secret code. He did not want to shout for Marian to open the door and bring attention to their late night entrance. The door quietly opened and the men rushed in.

The Freeman's were thrilled to see their men healthy and alive but they had many questions about their blood crusted appearance. Archibald knew the inquisition would be waiting but demanded rum before he would share his tale. Heather came out with a bucket of water and a rag and started cleaning the men as they finally relaxed. The twins were merciless with their questions and peppered the patriarch in turns.

"What happened?"

"Where did you go?"

"Did you kill any British, Spanish or Indians?"

"Did you find any treasure?"

"Did you bring us back something?"

"Did you see real pirates?"

"Were you on a ship?"

"Did you fight pirates in the Caribbean?"

When Archibald finally had enough, he demanded, "Boys! I will tell you everything, but remember; the British will kill us all if you have loose tongues with your mates. If you tell this story to anyone, all of us will be run through at sword point. Swear to your family and clan you will never speak of this."

The whole family took the pledge and the father started to spin his tale. The family listened intently to every detail as the light from the lamp danced across their faces. He recounted the close calls and boasted of everyone's bravery.

Heather asked, "How come you're not bloody and battle worn, Patrick?"

"I was sailing and relaxing in the sun but I was with them in spirit," he laughed. Heather threw a wet towel at Patrick's grinning mouth and water splashed all over him.

By the end of the tale the entire room was on the edge of their seats. "And we floated away with only seconds to spare as the Spanish shot at our ships," the father finished.

"Well did you actually get paid? Did she keep her word?" Marian questioned.

"Does this answer your question?" Archibald asked as he poured his gold doubloons on the table. The family gasped. They rarely had ever seen gold and never that much in one place. As the family ogled the coins, Archibald warned, "We will move soon, I hope, because it is only a matter of time before the Spanish seek revenge and take Oglethorpe's head as a trophy. Before then though, I will be leaving one more time with William. Some of our clansmen are still prisoners at Fort Mose. William is using his gold to bribe the guards to let them escape. I am sorry family but we will be leaving again in the morrow. When I come back, we can talk about moving to a new town. Start thinking about a town to move to."

Patrick excused himself and went to his shed. Under the cover of night, he slipped into the darkness and into the swamp at the edge of town. Under the moonlight, he buried his bag of gold under a Spanish moss draped oak. He wanted no one to know, not even his new family, where the gold was hidden. For once in his life, he wanted something that was just his.

* * *

The exhausted men slept late into the morning. The women washed Archibald's and Patrick's clothes while they slept and did a good job of getting most of the blood stains out. After they woke, they ate breakfast and made ready for the road to Darien. Before figuring a way to broker a deal to liberate his clansmen from the free Africans, William first wanted to see his family.

Loud giggling and laughter could be heard as Prudence and Mari Anna came calling with baskets of fresh bread and fruit. The ladies were always in a great mood while shrouded with a hint of mischievous behavior. They both gave heart-filled hugs to the men and were glad to see them. Archibald asked his family to join him and see him off. He handed Marian his gold and told her to hide it well.

"Before I leave, I have something I made a long time ago that I have been waiting to give this group." Archibald opened a bag and took out six mini-dirks he hand designed. "I was waiting to give you these as gifts but I worry that the Spanish are going to answer soon and I want you to be protected. I designed these so you can hide them under your petticoats or vests. I even made leather belts and scabbards you can use to attach them to your legs. I want all six of you wearing these at all times. I even made a couple for Prudence and Mari Anna since they are practically my family. Do you understand?" he instructed while he distributed the knives. The group nodded in understanding. "Remember if things get real heated, go to the shed and retrieve the firelocks in there," he reminded the boys. "I want you to do an early shut in every night and I will be back soon. Stay invisible. No going to listen to music or courting foolish men out of their silver, ladies. Now give us a hug. We have to go if we want to make it before night fall."

The men set off once again down the winding road to Darien. They traveled fairly light but well-armed. Soon, they saw Isaac dressed for travel waiting for them.

"Lad, are you here to wish us well?" William asked.

"No, Sovereign McIntosh. I plan on seeing this through with you. We are brothers and I honor that," the hulking Jew responded.

"What does Dr. Nunis say about this journey? He surely has to be annoyed at all your travel," Archibald inquired.

"This morning I make my own path. I am finally a free man. I purchased my contract from Dr. Nunis and still have plenty of gold left. I have to say, even the air smells different when you're a free man," Isaac observed proudly. The men cheered and embraced him. It was indeed a reason to celebrate. Many indentures died before they were free.

"Well, lad, we sure could use your muscle for this dangerous mission. Bless you," William said.

The four men made it to William's without incident. His family met him on the porch with open arms. Some sweet greetings were exchanged in Scottish and the men sat down for a drink before the sun set. The same scene from the last night at the Freeman's was repeated at the McIntosh's, except that William told their exciting tale in Scottish tongue. Although Patrick had no idea what they were saying, he figured out some of the stories from Williams animated movements. Patrick had a feeling that each time the tale was told, it got more elaborate. He joked with Isaac, "By the time we ever tell this story to our children, it will also involve us sailing around the world and slaying sea monsters and Cyclops."

"William, why did you name your daughter Lauren? It is not a very Scottish name is it?" Patrick asked him after some drinking.

"Lad, we were traveling through Italy trading and we named her after the town she was conceived in. It is old Latin for man from 'Laurentum,' a town in Latium. It was to remember that wonderful voyage together," William explained.

The men laughed and enjoyed the drink as the night wound down. Normally, proper Scottish men slept under a tree, but with so many road agents on the attack, this tradition was no longer safe. The family shut in and carried on into the night. When the men arose in the morning, they ate breakfast and hatched a plan.

"William, how well do you know the men left behind in the African fort? Are they sympathetic to the cause of liberty and personal sovereignty? "Archibald asked.

"Aye, Duncan. That's right, I be calling you 'Duncan,' your real Scottish name. And stop speaking like a goddamned Brit in my house. Use your natural Scottish tongue," William insisted. "But aye, most of them prisoners get it and even come to our Scottish Freeman Society meetings."

"Then I would like to make a proposal. I think the bag of gold marked to help the cause should be used to buy these men's freedom. I can't think of a better investment than freeing souls with this money. What says the rest of you?" Duncan inquired. The men slowly looked at each other from around the table and one by one, nodded in agreement. "Very good. William, keep your gold for your family. We will use this bag instead.

"Now with that done, I have a plan. We cannot just stroll up to a hostile fort with a bag of gold and expect to come out alive. We need to find a Spanish deer pelt trader working around the fort and pay him to take a letter back to Alick. He saved our lives before and I think he would broker this deal for us. The money would greatly help his people and they don't want to have to keep caring for and feeding these prisoners," Archibald surmised.

Isaac voiced his concern, "That will be a very dangerous gamble. I don't like the idea of getting anywhere near that fort. We need to ask Alick to meet us and escort us down to Fort

Mose."

Patrick agreed, "That is the best thing to do but this entire plan is dangerous."

"Say your goodbyes. Time to go free our clansman," Archibald told William.

* * *

In the morning, the mist started to burn off of the swamp and two dark figures could be seen sitting on the rocks in the marsh. The four men approached carefully until they heard a woman's voice yell.

"Archibald! Archibald! That be you?"

"Gloria, is that you?" he yelled through the heavy swamp mist. The four men dropped their guard and walked over to Alick and Gloria. Archibald made formal introductions of the group to the freed slaves. "I am so happy you two made it safely to Fort Mose," Archibald said.

"We lucky. We find Spanish fur trader," Gloria responded. "He take us to da fort. The warriors at fort welcome us and we happy der. Dey great warriors. Feel safe finally."

"I am glad you found peace with your clansman. Did you understand the note?" Archibald asked.

"We be not lettered. Had prisoner read it. The tribe at fort wants your gold. They will say prisoners escape to Spanish. Tribe no trust white man. Yous must pay now. I return with prisoners," Alick explained.

The men looked nervously at each other when William finally motioned to give the bag of gold to Alick. Archibald reluctantly handed the freed slave the gold.

"I return soon," Alick stated as he and Gloria disappeared into the marsh.

"He did save our lives. We have to trust him lads," William tried to ease the nervousness of the men.

"Well anyone think to bring a chess set?" Patrick mused.

Camp was made and the men waited vigil.

"Archibald, how come you never talk about God and

church? I thought you Scots were a religious bunch," Patrick questioned.

"We are. Just not Archibald," replied William.

Archibald sadly confessed, "I lost all faith the day I saw my entire family murdered by the British. What kind of god would allow that kind of savagery? So now I look back and find the whole notion silly. Do you really think there is a king in the sky sitting on a throne deciding who will burn in Hell for eternity?"

Isaac responded, "I would not talk like that. This god is a vengeful god to non-believers. Jews love and fear their God."

"So you think that a being powerful enough to create everything was bored one day and just decided to make man to entertain him? What's the point? If He already knows what is going to happen with everyone before they do it, why would He bother?" Archibald blasphemed.

"It be sorrows I feel for ya, Duncan. Ya carry a great darkness for God around in ya soul. If ya let Him back in, He can make that pain disappear," William injected.

"William, you're an intelligent man. Tell me, why does your god have to threaten me with the worst kind of torture like burning alive forever, if I don't accept His love? Does that sound like any kind of love that makes sense to a rational person?" the blacksmith countered.

"God made man in his own image, so if man gets angry and jealous, so must God, too. He uses fear and love, just like all relationships I have ever known. I fear my father, but I still love him," Isaac responded.

"I am not trying to be disrespectful to you two. I just think these stories were made to control the masses. The two most dangerous ideas on the earth are religion and government. No two ideas have been the death and misery of so many people. The flawed idea that government is necessary and that my religion is right and yours is not. Open your eyes. This dogma was created to control your minds by politicians and priests," Archibald pleaded.

"While I have to agree that church and government have killed countless souls, they are good ideas. Without them, man would have no laws and would kill each other with no accountability. I do not think that is a fair statement; there are many good and righteous people who work for governments and churches. They are just following the orders of bad people, they don't have a choice," Isaac replied.

"That is such shit! Of course they have a choice. Why does a good person just follow bad orders? They simply lack the courage to not comply. It is so easy for someone to say 'I'm just following orders.' That kind of attitude is exactly why a government or religion can kill so many people and still be worshiped and followed. If you can sever someone from the consequences of their actions, they can do unspeakable evil and just blame their superiors." Archibald was getting heated.

"I don't associate with any church, but I still find my peace with God on a personal level. Ya don't need some man in the middle to allow you to have a relationship with the all mighty. Ya simply don't understand. Ya cannot try and poke and prod the good book without first believing in it. Ya have to believe first. Then these questions are easier to answer coming from a position of faith," the kilted man returned.

Isaac interjected, "He is correct: without faith first, this book seems to make no sense. You have to remember to take the message behind it and not worry over all the details. People who believe these teachings will find great reward and inner peace."

Archibald answered, "I will concede that most people who worship are good people. I just don't understand why they submit to control and even create positions of authority. Positions of any kind of authority attract the worst kind of people."

"Unless ya accept the Lord in your heart, ya just can't understand the answers to this question. I don't want to talk about this anymore," William concluded.

"Wait. Isn't that kind of backwards? Why would you first believe something just so you can understand it. One would think you would to need to understand this book first before one can believe it," Patrick pointed out.

"I said we be done. Ya heathens just don't get the line of reasoning we be conveying. I am going to bed," William challenged angrily.

"I guess we are on first watch, lad." Archibald said to Patrick.

The night passed quickly to morning as the night watch shifts changed. The next day grew long as the men grew more and more anxious without the return of Alick.

Until Isaac confessed, "I think we might have just been politely robbed."

"I thought you Jews were all about having faith?" Archibald returned. Isaac shot daggers at the blacksmith from his eyes.

As time went by slowly, the group started second guessing their decision to trust the freed slave with their gold and begun bickering with each other. As the argument became more heated, they were abruptly interrupted by sounds from the edge of the marsh which revealed a group of twenty African warriors dressed in full battle paint and gear. Isaac yelled, "Looks like we have been betrayed! Let us make haste!" The four men agreed with Isaac's assessment and started falling back in retreat.

"Wait! Wait!" a woman's voice called out. Gloria ran into the marsh and was yelling something in her African tribal tongue to the warriors. The warriors reluctantly lowered their spears from their attack position. Patrick stopped running first and waited. The other fleeing men halted as well. Then a ratty, sickly looking group of highlanders and Indians stumbled into the marsh. Gloria escorted the motley gang to Archibald as the warriors cautiously watched the exchange. "Sorry it took long time. Big fight with tribe. Elders wanted keep money and prisoners. Alick had to fight elder and was hurt, but Alick win fight so his promise kept to yous," Gloria said.

"I am so sorry about Alick," Archibald asked. "How bad is he injured?"

"He broke his hand and arm but will recover. Very important to his honor he keep his word true to yous" Gloria proudly said.

The Fort Mose free slaves

"Tell him he is a great and honorable man. Thank him for saving so many souls, but we have a problem, Gloria. We only wanted the Highlanders. We never paid for the Indians," Mr. Freeman stated.

Gloria looked back at the angry warriors and nervously spoke, "I am not lettered. The note said prisoners. We assumed yous wanted all of them. Yous have to take the redskins. These warriors will kill them if you no take dem."

William said, "Duncan, we cannot be leaving these redskins to their death when we can so easily just take them with us. A man deserves to be free."

Archibald nodded, "Come on, you lot. Let us make haste quickly. Thank you, Gloria. You have helped save many lives."

She came to an epiphany with a smile, "Making people free feels good for heart. I help more slaves from Carolina come to Fort Mose and freedom."

"That is very brave. Let me know if I can ever help you.

Now we need to go. Your warriors look angry," Archibald offered.

Mr. McIntosh led the group of ex-prisoners out of sight. The group pushed quietly and quickly toward the town of Darien. When enough distance had been made from the warriors of Fort Mose, the large group started celebrating. Scottish cheers and blessing filled the air while the Indians sat quietly and fearfully. Archibald confronted the sad group sitting on the ground, "Do one of you speak English or Scottish?"

A hesitant Indian stood up. "I speak. We now sold to you. What have us do?"

Archibald looked at his friends and they nodded. "Tell your tribesman yes, we did buy you but, now we are letting you go," Archibald smiled.

"Go? You mean you selling us to Caribbean fields?" The confused Indian asked.

"No. You are free to go. Go back to your tribe and your families. We will not sell you into slavery, now tell the others."

The confused Indian conveyed the message to the other ex-prisoners. With looks of confusion, they slowly got up and cautiously started to walk away. The translator stayed behind and asked, "Why you do this, white man?"

"We do not believe one man should ever own another. All men deserve to be free. Just remember us and if we ever need help in the future, help us," Archibald explained.

"We help you. Just ask Creek tribe near Tybee when you need! Show tribe this when you need us," the Indian agreed proudly and handed Mr. Freeman his family's belt he was wearing. He left with a large group of free Indians whooping war cries of freedom as they departed.

"Duncan, our kin want to get back to their farms tonight and see their families. Let us head out in haste. You have helped do a very good deed today. God bless your heathen heart," William excitedly announced.

In true highlander tradition, the exhausted men ran all the way back to Darien. William parted ways with his excited kin folk and returned to his home with his friends. Deborah met him with tears of joy. The Scottish community had lost so many fathers to the sneak attack at Fort Mose that the town of Darien was in serious disarray. Returning just a few fathers to their families would greatly help with moral. The men celebrated with drinks and old Scottish songs late into the night. When the sun rose, the two hungover men warmly embraced and said their goodbyes. "I am happy I could do something good for the clan again. You are the only family I really have left," Archibald embraced the Scot.

"Aye, Duncan. Don't ever forget who ya are and where ya are from," William hugged his brother. "Thanks for your help, lads. We will see you at our next Freeman Society meeting."

The men were excited to finally be going home to enjoy their spoils of war. They arrived in Savannah in short time. The sun had just set and men said their goodbyes to Isaac as they parted ways. Archibald and Patrick were joking about how they would spend their gold when Archibald stopped dead in his tracks. They noticed from a distance two armed British soldiers standing at attention outside his house. "Why are they not shut in? Go get Isaac, something is very wrong!" Archibald ordered.

CHAPTER 16

THE CRIMSON DOGWOOD AND EXODUS

The Freeman's dogwood in bloom

Patrick ran into the night seeking Isaac's aid. Archibald approached the house cautiously and addressed the sentries at his door. "What is the meaning of this? Why are you at my home at this hour?" he questioned angrily.

"Blacksmith, stay there!" the soldier demanded.

Archibald complied as his soul filled with a mix of rage and concern. After a long, anxious wait, the guard returned escorted by another soldier. Archibald felt a ball of black terror roll up his spine when he realized Commander Byron Kingsley was standing in his doorway. "Mr. Freeman, by order of the King, your house is now being used to quarter his Majesty's Army. We now offer you protection from the Spanish if they choose to retaliate. Your family has been sequestered upstairs while they serve our troops' needs," he coldly explained.

Archibald pushed passed the arrogant commander and yelled up to the loft, "Marian! Are you up there?"

"We are, but Sergeant Luthor is holding us and we have not been allowed to leave for a..." Marian was interrupted.

Sergeant Luthor hissed a threat to Marian, "That be enough accusing tongue, lass."

"Sergeant Luthor, send her down. Let him see his wife is in good health and that his family is happy to be serving king and country!" Commander Kingsley ordered.

After some rumbling and footsteps, Marian climbed down the ladder from the loft. She was crying. "Husband, I am so sorry. They have been here since yesterday, just taking whatever they want. We have been cooking and cleaning by their command. We were just so frightened. I am so happy you're finally home. Tell me you can fix all this."

"Are you and the children unmolested and healthy?" Archibald voiced his concern.

"Our younglings with Prudence and Mari Anna are still crammed up there like livestock under guard since the soldiers stormed the house yesterday. They just barged in. They rounded us up and forced us upstairs. We dared not stop them! The troops searched our home and took whatever they wanted. Just look at it! It's in such disarray," Marian explained through tears as her husband hugged her.

Archibald turned to Bryon and commanded, "You need to leave this house now! I will be talking to Oglethorpe tomorrow and will work all this out. Now it is time to take your men and get out."

"I am sorry, but this is the king's home now and you will need to find a new place to live. You may not vacate until we discuss something curious my soldiers found upstairs in your loft," the commander replied with a grin. "Soldiers take him out back to the tree while I retrieve the contraband." The two sentries pulled Marian and Archibald apart and seized the blacksmith.

"Release me!" Archibald demanded as he knocked their arms away. One guard struck Archibald on the side of his face, knocking the blacksmith down to the floor. "STOP!" Marian screamed through her tears as she witnessed this assault on her beloved. Archibald held his face and feigned injury. The sentry moved over him to strike him again when the blacksmith snapped quickly to his feet. He caught the guard by surprise and the thick top of the skull of Mr. Freeman's head shattered the soldier's nose. Blood sprayed on the floor and the soldier fell to his knees, shrieking in pain. Archibald took advantage of the surprise attack and grabbed the other guard by the neck, moving his leg, behind the soldier's calf. In one fluid motion, he pushed the soldier at his neck tripping him over his leg and viciously throat slamming him to the floor.

"That's enough!" the commander shouted.

The combatant turned his attention to Bryon Kingsley's belting voice. The bloody back now had Marian in his claws and was pressing a large knife to her throat. The husband slowly released his choke hold on the gasping man and cautiously rose to his feet. He raised his hands up and carefully backed up.

"Get up! You two are an embarrassment to my command. Tie Mr. Freeman to the tree outside. You will find him more cooperative now I am sure," the commander ordered. The soldiers were in pain and moved slowly getting up. Brushing off their uniforms, they then manhandled their attacker. They shoved Archibald out the door and dragged him to the large dogwood, whose leaves were now turning a red color for fall. The redcoats wrested his arms back and pulled them around the tree. They tightly bound his wrists with a strong, hemp rope. Archibald tried to wrangle free but to no avail. His thoughts wandered to his captive family in the house and he felt utterly helpless to stop what was happening.

The Freeman's dogwood

The commander walked out like a predator stalking his prey. Byron approached the prisoner carrying a leather bag. Marian ran outside and tugged on the commander's arm, trying to beg him to stop. "Let him go! We can work all this out with your superiors. We can even pay you. Just wait!" Byron lost his patience and struck her in the mouth with the large leather bag, knocking Marian to the ground. She screamed in pain as he struck her repeatedly with the sack until she lay prone on the ground unconscious. Archibald screamed at this abuse and tears welled up in his eyes. He watched for a sign of movement from his love to give him hope she was still alive.

Kingsley then reached into the buckskin bag and pulled out the large, worn-out tomes that were hidden in the loft. "When my men searched your loft they found these books clumsily hidden. I am sure you are very aware these books are forbidden by law. What shall I do with you, Freeman?" Kingsley grinned evilly.

Archibald's eyes made their way to Kingsley's and now, instead of sorrow and fear, they showed pure anger. "How dare you strike my bride! I would kill you where you stand if you were not such a coward to have me bound. Untie me!" Archibald demanded.

"Your annoying wife is fine. I am sure you do the same when she won't silence herself," Kingsley replied.

"You will take me to your commander and answer for what you have done here. I am entitled to a trial and Oglethorpe's judgment on this accusation," Archibald angrily spit out.

"I am able to dispense justice without his input and I have already made a judgment. You are guilty of assaulting one of his Majesty's guards and for reading banned writings," Byron drew his blade and threw the books at condemned man's feet.

"If you use that knife to dispense arbitrary justice for your king, it is only a matter of time until another king's man takes its handle and turns it on you," the convicted man warned.

"Then I will be sure to hold the knife tighter than anyone else," Kingsley smiled as he carved the cold, steel blade into Archibald's throat. A line of crimson turned into a gush of blood as the blacksmith gargled and thrashed. Blood poured down his clothes, pooling and spitting all over the contraband books at his feet.

Byron wiped the blood off his large hunting blade with Archibald's limp body. He turned to face Marian as he smiled. As he pointed his knife at her belly and maneuvered into a killing position, a musket shot rang out in the darkness. Byron jumped for cover as he ordered his soldiers into the darkness toward the direction of the muzzle flash. His guards quickly moved and charged into the darkness. Another loud cracking sound filled the air and the commander felt a shot whiz past his ear. Concluding it was time to retreat, Byron slithered unseen into the darkness.

* * *

Sergeant Luthor smiled. "It appears the commander left us here all alone, sweet ladies. You there, what's your name? I kind of fancy you, lass," Luthor asked, pointing at Mari Anna. Prudence and Heather closed ranks in front of Mari Anna and stood steadfast. The twins then joined in the human wall of defense. The redcoat pulled his long hunting knife and aimed it at the twins. "Stand aside or I will gut each of you until I get what I want," the man threatened.

"Stand down," Mari Anna conceded as she pushed her way forward. "I will just give him what he needs."

"Smart, lass. The rest of you over there, you can watch if you'd like, but move upon us and I skin her like a doe," he threatened while waving his knife.

"Go on," Mari Anna instructed. "Do as he says." The reluctant group moved into a tight corner and started weeping.

"Cover your ears and turn away, boys," Heather demanded of the twins.

Mari Anna started untying her jacket and slipped it off. Luthor slipped the blade under her stay and in one swift motion, sliced the lacing up the front. It immediately fell to the floor. Her breasts were easy to make out in the thin shift and the forceful man grew erect as her large nipples pressed out against the translucent linen. Luthor wasted no time. He ran his blade through the thin cloth, cutting away and ripping the shift. Her hefty flesh poured out of the tear and the bloody back fixated on her large, pink nipples. He put his lips on them and Mari Anna moaned. He gripped hard and crushed her breasts causing her great pain but she continued to feign pleasure as she ran her hand up her petticoats to her thigh.

The Sergeant dropped his pantaloons exposing his erect cock. "Just relax, lass, and I won't stick you too rough," he promised with a devilish smile. Lust now overpowered caution and Luthor lowered his blade to lift Mari Anna's petticoats. She moaned loudly with excitement knowing this was her only chance to seize the opportunity. He pulled her petticoats over her waist and exposed her naked pelvis and gasped.

At that instant, Mari Anna buried her dirk deep into the redcoat's chest. Luthor howled in pain like a pig being slaughtered as Mari Anna pulled the knife out and plunged it in again and again into the rapist's chest. The sergeant cringed in pain. He held up his arms to defend himself from being stabbed but Mari Anna simply stabbed at his hands. The sergeant dropped his knife and yelped as he rolled into a ball. Heather dropped her dirk into his back while Prudence followed suit and pierced his side. The twins continued the assault and plunged their blades into his lower back as the bloody, gasping heap finally collapsed, motionless. Luthor was stabbed so viciously, the children lost count of how many times their knives fell and the carcass was no longer recognizable as human. With ragged breaths, the family finally became exhausted and stopped stabbing the lump of dull, red meat on the floor. They panted in exhaustion as their horrified eyes took in the massive pool of blood on the wooden planks below their feet. They stared quietly at each other in shock at the gruesome display of self-defense they had just committed. Such a brutal group stabbing had not been seen since the Ides of March in the Roman Senate.

"Wake up! No time for this. We have to help father!" Amos finally shouted.

The group scurried down the ladder and did not look back. Blood was raining down the ceiling as it escaped through the floor boards above. Prudence slipped in a pool of liquid crimson that had already formed on the main floor as they ran to the back yard. The family approached the tree to get a better sense of the situation. Heather screamed and cried with grief. The group stood in terror as they took in the brutal scene. Archibald's limp corpse was crumbled up under the dogwood. His arms were still tied behind the tree creating the illusion that he was still alive, but just squatting.

Everyone reacted differently to the severity of the horrible sight. Some dropped to their knees and wept while others screamed in anger. Out of the blackness, Isaac and Patrick joined the gruesome scene. Patrick shook with anger and Isaac stared slack-jawed in disbelief.

"Marian!" Patrick yelled and ran over to her unconscious body. She groaned and moved her arm as a sign of life. Patrick set aside the horror and focused to keep everyone alive. He took charge of the situation. "She is alive! Heather, help get your mother to her feet. Twins, take Prudence and Mari Anna to their families and tell them all to flee immediately. Quickly explain what happened and ask Prudence's father for his horse and cart. Tell the family to take everything of value with them and quickly meet us at the lightning-split tree in Thunderbolt. Also, tell them to take their families making haste and being wary. We'll all be killed if we don't move immediately!"

The shocked twins showed incredible maturity and somehow snapped out of their grieving to handle the task at hand. They followed Patrick's orders and dragged the weeping ladies away to their homes.

Patrick continued commanding, "Isaac, cut down Archibald and carry him as far as you can. Head for the lightning split tree where we dueled. Move fast and quietly." Isaac complied with a face full of tears and threw the bloody corpse over his massive shoulders. The hulking man wasted no time with the grim task and ran into the darkness.

Marian was now sitting up trying to make sense of what she was seeing. "See to your mother, Heather, alright?" Patrick asked softly.

Patrick ran into the shed and threw the scrap metal out the door. He uncovered Archibald's hidden hatch in the ground and flung it open. He grabbed the old dueling pistols and stuffed them into his thick leather belt. At the bottom of the dark hole was a large, woolen cloth. Patrick hastily pulled it out and heard something drop with a jingle. He searched the dark hole and discovered a small heavy bag. *The gold! Oh thank God! I cannot believe I found it*, Patrick thought. He grabbed a wool cloth and wrapped it around the bag of gold. Patrick then stuffed it all into his shirt and headed to back to the matriarch.

Patrick heard yelling in the darkness and assumed the troops were mobilizing.

"We're dead if we stay any longer, Heather!" he said helping Marian to her feet. He steadied her, being careful that she did not stumble. Something caught his eye under the dogwood tree. He quickly snatched up the blood spattered books and stuffed them back into the leather bag that Bryon had cast onto the ground. Patrick and Heather put their arms around Marian and helped lead her half-conscious, wobbling body away from the home. Traumatized, the three disappeared into the blackness, as Patrick heard sounds of motion to at the front of the Freeman house. They quickly stumbled into the pitch black.

* * *

Isaac's back was in terrible pain when he finally sat Archibald's body under the dueling trees. The starlight was barely bright enough to illuminate his exodus. He had twisted his ankle in the darkness but the shock of battle kept him from feeling the pain until just then. He carefully loaded his musket with shot and stared into the blackness keeping vigil.

In a matter of minutes, Patrick, Heather, and Marian came panting in the clearing. Isaac lowered his musket and ran over to help them. He put his arm around the stumbling Marian and positioned himself so she would not see Archibald's bloodied carcass, but it was too late. She saw her husband's lifeless silhouette in the starlight. She was finally conscious enough to grasp the magnitude of what had happened. She pushed Isaac off and threw herself onto her husband's dead body. She rocked Archibald's limp corpse in her arms and wept loud enough for the entire world to hear. Heather ran to her mother and held her while she clutched her deceased husband. The two men held the grief-stricken woman while they clung to the crimson-stained body. The four continued to cry and Marian demanded to know what happened.

Patrick told her that all he had seen was Byron Kingsley hovering with a blade over her. They were too far away to hit them with shot but hoped the noise would rouse his attention. They assumed the lobster back commander was the one who spilled Archibald's soul from his body. The musket shot saved Marian but guards chased after Patrick and Isaac. They were unaware that Archibald had fallen and concerned themselves with leading the soldiers away from her unconscious body. Patrick and Isaac were pursued into the snake-ridden swamps.

After a high speed chase through the night, they lost the soldiers in the pitch blackness. This bought the men precious time to double-back to the house.

"Heather, why are you splattered in blood?" Patrick asked.

Before Heather could tell her tale, she was interrupted by the sounds of a creaking, wooden wagon rolling in. Startled by the eerie noise, Patrick and Isaac pointed their firelocks toward the ruckus. The twins stepped into the starlight followed by a procession of refugees. Prudence and Mari Anna ran over and joined the weeping women holding the corpse. Heather let go of the dead body and silently held her two friends hands.

Mari Anna's and Prudence's confused families were with them carrying all their valuables. The baker and the tailor surveyed the scene. Prudence's father stated in a near breathless whisper, "Dear God, daughter. You speak the truth. The redcoats really did kill him."

Patrick replied, "It is true alright. We cannot stay here. You and daughters are in mortal danger. They were being held and thusly associated with my family. They will be associated with Archibald's crime as well."

Mari Anna's father spoke up nervously, "Daughter, you have done no crime. We should go back and explain your situation to Oglethorpe. Our family does not need to be involved in this."

"Papa, I have not told you everything. We cannot go back. I have indeed committed a terrible crime," Mari Anna confessed tearfully.

"What are you speaking of, young one?" he said with grave concern.

"I am covered with the sergeant's blood. He forced himself on me and I defended myself before he stole my virtue. I ran him through and spilled his life in the Freeman's loft," Mari Anna solemnly confessed.

"You must be confused, little one. Even if you stabbed him, he is probably still alive. Let us go back and throw ourselves on Oglethorpe's mercy," the baker bartered.

Amos's crimson covered body stepped forward and

interrupted, "No, sir. Sergeant Luthor is absolutely dead!"

Patrick looked around at the group of children and realized they were all covered in clumped chunks of red flesh. "Oh, god. It is true. All of you are baptized in blood. It is not safe for any of us now. They probably already discovered the sergeant's body and raised the alarm. We have to get to William's in Darien now. We will figure out our next move from there."

Patrick took charge and ordered the large Jewish man to load the body into the cart. He then commanded the brave group to push into the blackness as fast as they could. The sounds of mourning and sobbing filled the night while the train of refuges marched toward Darien.

CHAPTER 17

THE ARGYLE COLONY

There was pounding at the McIntosh door. "William, please open your door! It's Patrick! We need your help!"

The groggy Scottish man unbolted his large oak door asking, "What's all this racket? I still have an hour of sleep left before rising."

"They killed Archibald, William. The shit-filled coward, Bryon Kingsley, slit his throat!"

Mr. McIntosh rubbed his eyes, "What's that, lad? Me ears did not hear you right, me thinks."

"See for yourself," Patrick grimly pointed. "His body is in the cart."

William stumbled out in silence as he surveyed the cart. His dropped to his knees in the mud and wept. His wife, Deborah, and his girls ran over to him and gawked at the body in sadness. William wiped his tears and angrily belted out, "Let me get me sword! Let us go kill Kingsley now!" He stormed past Patrick and retrieved his weapons in his house.

"William, wait! We will avenge him but not right now. I suspect it won't be long until the whole armies of Savannah come hunting for us. Archibald's children struck down Kingsley's dog, Sergeant Luthor. You have to help us disappear. Archibald's vengeance will be well calculated and delivered when his family is no longer at risk," Patrick pleaded.

"That is not our way. Retribution must be delivered immediately. Every second Kingsley is alive, it is an insult to Archibald's honor!" William barked back.

Patrick grabbed the kilted man by his shoulders, "Archibald

would not want you to risk the lives of his family and friends for vindication. We will wait! Please help us give him a proper Scottish burial and escort us in our exodus."

William collected himself and put his anger on a low simmer and conceded, "Aye, lad. He deserves proper rights!" He turned to his weeping family and ordered, "Lauren, Lindsey, and Deborah, run and tell the village what has happened. Request their aid with the funeral rites. Catch Mr. MacKay as well and tell him to keep his fishing vessel harbored. We need it for passage. Go now! Run!"

William decided Archibald must be buried on his land, in a tract hidden on a hill, which would not easily be found. He felt it would honor Archibald properly and keep his final resting place clandestine. William wasted no time once his mind was made up and retrieved his spade from the house. "Seems proper that Archibald made the tool that we be digging his grave with."

The large funeral procession took the cart up the hill and onto a rocky knoll. The men cleared an area of stones so it would be easier to dig. The honor of digging the grave was divided and the men worked quickly. In just over an hour, a large, man-sized hole laid in wait to accept its offering of flesh. A bell was heard ringing from the town. A priest was crying, "Duncan McIntosh, slain by the British this morrow for illegal writings!" A long funeral procession followed in a single file. The large group approached and took their places circling the now hallowed hole in the earth. The men were on one side and the ladies on the other, watching respectfully. The Darien people were considered very progressive to allow women to attend the funeral, having relaxed many of their rigorous customs since moving to the new world.

Patrick had never seen a Scottish funeral but Archibald had told him about their customs one past evening. The murdered mentor explained how long and elaborate Scottish services were, but how the custom had died out more than one hundred years before. The English had outlawed burial services for Scots and over time, the ceremonies adapted to British regulation.

They were fast and quiet. No words were said and no coffin was used. The body was simply placed in the hole by the clansmen. The ritual occurred exactly as the deceased black smith predicted, except for the addition of an ancient ritual. The clan in Darien observed one ancient Scottish burial rite called "earth laid upon a corpse". The priest laid a wooden plate on Archibald's chest. A small amount of salt and earth were placed onto the plate to represent the future of the deceased. The salt represented the soul which would never decay. The Earth reminded all who witnessed that the body would decay and eventually rejoin the Earth from which it came. The men of the clan quickly covered the lifeless vessel with dirt and then hid the grave with stone and marsh grass. William said something to the funeral goers in Scottish, pointing at the grave and covering it with fallen limbs to hide it. Patrick assumed William told his clan never to revel its location to outsiders for fear of British retaliation. William then nodded to the crowd signaling the ceremony was now over.

Traditional Scottish funeral with no fanfare

The sound of bagpipes filled the air and the men and the women paired off. Patrick and Marian stared at each other in confusion, not sure if the Scottish men and women were dancing. The two watched as the men paired off and sang and danced with each other. The women then followed suit. Patrick assumed that somehow dancing with the same sex after a funeral is not offensive to the Scottish God. He shrugged his shoulders and joined in. After a few minutes, all of the Freeman family were pulled into the celebration and were actually smiling a bit. It was cathartic for the traumatized family to reminisce about Archibald's life with song and dance. People that knew him were telling stories about their fond memories of him and singing old Scottish hymns.

Suddenly, a boy in a kilt came sprinting up to William. He panted, "British be coming! Only about an hour's walk away."

William interrupted and shouted commands in Scottish. Within five minutes, no trace of a funeral could be found. He also reminded the group that this event and grave would never be spoken of to any outsiders. "Time to go, lads. We booked ya a safe voyage. Follow me and hurry." William and his family pushed quickly toward the coastline of the town.

Isaac was massive and strong but it caused him to have shallow lungs while running. "Where are we going?" Isaac asked through his winded voice.

William replied with ease, "You need to run more, lad. Ya be going to a new Scottish settlement up in Cape Fear, North Carolina. It be called the Argyle Colony. It is three-hundred-and-fifty strong. I have good friends there from the clan MacKay. They will take care of ya and hide your families."

After a long jog and lots of sweating, the large group of families straggled onto the coast. In the water was a small fishing sloop. There was no dock but the ship was very close to the shore. William ran into the water and simply swam out to the waiting vessel. In just minutes he was pulled aboard and explaining the situation to the captain. The captain was reluctant at first, but he changed his mind once he realized that the man who was killed was the same man who rescued his clansman from Fort Mose. He agreed to ferry them. William waved at the group to join them. Those who could swim did while the others waited for a small jolly boat to row out and retrieve them. Within just ten minutes, everyone was aboard.

"Take good care of that horse, Deborah! I love that horse and will be back for him someday!" Prudence's father shouted at the women on the shore. William's family waved goodbye then hurried away to hide the horse and cart from the British.

The fishing ship was crammed with passengers and the vessel moved slowly, burdened with all the weight, but luck was on their side. The wind picked up and pushed them away from the shore.

Heather stared into the wind and smiled, "Thanks for the push, Father".

The ship sailed into the afternoon sky and Darien's coast shrank from view. William advised the captain, "Best go into open waters. Be wise to keep distance from Savannah."

* * *

Some more sentimental words were said by the Freemans and their friends as they sailed past Savannah in the night. The family was still in shock but the words they spoke eased the numbness a little. Prudence's and Mari Anna's father approached Patrick and Isaac. The baker stated, "This is a bad time to talk about this I know, but our families are very upset they cannot go home. We have very little money and we left all our tools of the trade back in Savannah. What will we feed our families with now?"

Patrick looked at Isaac with concern. "I am so sorry your daughter got involved with this violence and now your family is displaced."

The tailor replied, "Displaced! You mean wanted! We are fugitives now."

"We all knew the risks of reading those books. This could have happened to either of you. Besides, Sovereigns, these nefarious circumstances affect us all," Patrick reminded them.

"Patrick, I can spare half my gold if you can, we can help our brothers start a new life," Isaac generously offered.

"My gold! I forgot it! Curses! I left it buried in the swamps in Savannah. I had no time to retrieve it. I do have some of Archibald's gold. Perhaps Marian will let us use some of that until I can retrieve my share," Patrick hoped.

Marian interrupted, "Quarters are very tight gentleman and I heard your conversation. I am sure Archibald would want you to have half his gold to get a new start. Think of him when you build a new life for your families." Patrick handed her the wool cloth which contained Archibald's gold. She cried as she unfolded the colorful fabric. She let the gold fall and held the tartan in the moonlight, "This is his clan's colors. Thank you so much for saving this."

The former blacksmith's indenture looked at the kilt with surprise. "I never even noticed it was his colors. I am very happy it was not left behind."

"I think he would want William to have it. It would not be right if you or the boys wear it since you are not bloodline," Marian surmised as she picked up the bag of gold. She then divided the pouch of yellow rounds and gave each of the two fathers one fourth of the doubloons. Isaac then dug in his remaining gold and did the same. They humbly accepted the gifts and went to share the news with their families. The widow then walked over to William and showed him the tartan. He proudly accepted it and pledged to wear it to honor her husband.

Patrick put his hand on Isaac's shoulder and said, "That was a wonderful thing you did. You really honor your God and your people." The large hulk smiled and nodded.

Grief had exhausted the group and by ones and twos, they drifted off to sleep on the deck of the small fishing sloop.

"Ahoy! Cape Fear!" the captain declared waking Patrick from the dead.

"How long have I been asleep, Isaac?" he questioned.

"A day and one half. We ran out of wind and sat for a few hours," the man in the yarmucle explained.

"Take a look at this place. Not much here but a dock. It does look like a good place to disappear though," Patrick sighed.

The crowded ship drifted in but the dock master was nowhere to be found. *Well that be some damned luck! No dock master*, captain MacKay wondered. He then belted his order, "Everyone off as fast as you can! Let's make you disappear before someone comes by and wants to know all your names and your business." The passengers wasted no time. They piled out to the dock and watched as the ship drifted off.

"Don't forget to pick me up at noon in three days," William yelled across the water.

The kilted man led the pack away from the docks as fast as possible. "Let us get to Argyll before sundown. We will find shelter and some excellent haggis with Mr. MacKay."

The troop traveled until they crested a hill and were amazed at what they saw. An entire Scottish town was under construction. Besides the little subtle differences of using local materials, one would think they had just walked into a village in Scotland. The architecture and building techniques were all old world. "William, this is amazing! They made all this in just under two years?" Isaac questioned in disbelief. "You Scottish truly are impressive!" The market place was very busy and people were building structures everywhere. The amount of progress did not reflect the population of four hundred.

"We will look at the town in the morrow," William determined. "Let us go to the MacKay's to find sanctuary."

Many eyes fell on the refuges as they made their way to the MacKay farm. The locals relaxed once they spotted William's tartan as his mob walked by. After a short walk out of town, they approached a small farm house and a barn under construction. William told the large group of friends and family to stay and wait as he approached the house and knocked. He yelled in Scottish, waited, and when the door finally flew open, he was welcomed in. The families waited nervously.

William walked out followed by a tall, skinny, bearded man who was bare chested and wearing only a kilt. The tall man approached Marian and softly stated, "I be very sorry for yar

William McIntosh at the Argyle Colony

loss, lass. William told me about the darkness dat fell upon yar family. He also told me dat yar husband risked his life and fortune to free me clansmen from slavery and death. We not forget loyalty like dat. Yar family will be safe here." The refugees all sighed with relief as the skinny Scot continued, "Ya have a large gathering and we don't have empty homes. Ya can live in the barn until we build ya some places to live. Of course, the men can sleep under da trees like true Scotsmen but you lasses can use the cover of the barn. It is mostly built. We just need more hands to finish it. Ya will have to help work da farm if ya want to eat and help us finish dis barn before winter. Only converse with people I be trusting. No talking to any strangers. You put my family and clan at risk, so I don't want ya all seen much. Can ya family follow des rules?" he asked sternly.

Patrick collected the opinions of the group. They all nodded in agreement to the terms. "Aye, we accept your terms," Patrick stated boldly.

"Very well. Make ya family comfortable in da barn and we will cook up some haggis," Mr. Mackay offered.

The families settled in enjoying the meal and new friendship.

* * *

It was now the fall of 1741 and the refuges had settled into their new lives. The barn was built quickly with so many hands working. Pooling their resources, the families were able to buy a small farm outside of the Argyll Colony. They had even started the construction of two other homes on the property so each family could have their own domicile. News from William reported that all of their homes and possessions in Savannah were seized by the government's men. Warrants were signed for the families but were quickly forgotten about. It appeared nobody missed Sergeant Luthor enough to continue the search for his killers. The troops searched Darien and questioned William but that was the extent of the investigation. Isaac was worried Dr. Nunis would be held accountable for his actions, but William reported that he was unmolested. It appeared Oglethorpe was more concerned about losing a good doctor than carrying out his idle threats. The wanted families used new aliases and kept to themselves. The Scots that knew the truth kept their tongues to themselves and guarded their secret safely.

With the doubloons now all spent, Patrick and Isaac decided the responsibility lied in their hands to make some income until the crops took the following growing season. Mr. MacKay came by one afternoon and offered the men an opportunity to make some silver. "There be an area of sovereign land in North Carolina. Back in the lord's year 1663, the king divided Carolina into eight parts and sold it to wealthy English investors. Over da years, seven of da eight investors, which by the way, fancy being called Lord Proprietors, sold their share back to the king. But one Lord Proprietor kept his land and did not sell it. His name be George Carteret. The property be passed down by family rights to his great grandson John Carteret II, Earl of Granville. He currently owns the land but is stuck in England."

"Wait, I am confused, sir," Patrick interjected. "Are you saying that a large track of land exists in the colonies that is sovereign and not ruled by any government? How can this be? Surely the king would march soldiers in and claim it."

"Well the king would march troops in and take what he wanted if it was owned by common folk but there be rich folk, who own it. The king has to be much more cautious in how he be handling the situation. His majesty needs to look legitimate and if he steals this land, no rich folks would be investing with him again," the skinny man explained. "To answer ya other question, yes, Carteret surrendered protection and participation in the government in exchange for sovereignty. He does not have to pay taxes and he can do as he pleases with the land; he can even make his own laws outside the king's. It is truly a unique situation."

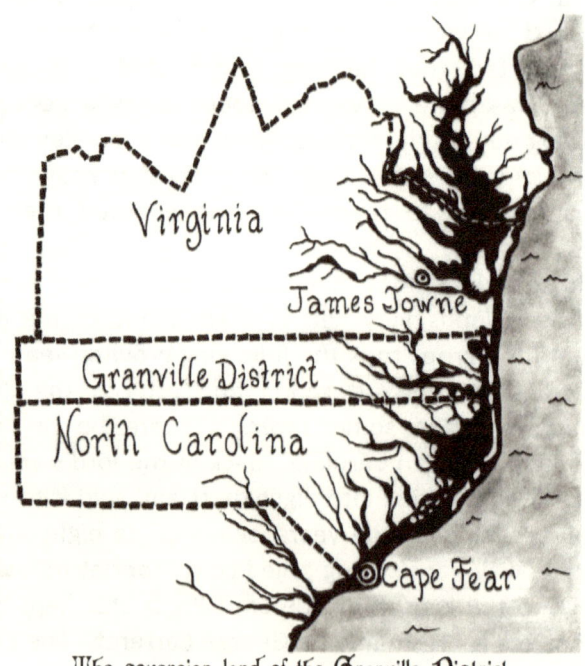

The sovereign land of the Granville District

"That's fascinating. Someone is allowed to live free of the king's rule here in the colonies, but what does this have to do with us?" Isaac questioned.

"Well, he be needing patrols for his land. It is hard, dangerous work but the pay is good. It seems that poachers and timber men are coming on his land and taking what they want. Ya will be guarding the borders of this private land."

"Well, we got to feed our families until the crops take. We will take work," Patrick agreed.

"Excellent," MacKay encouraged. "Come to me farm at dawn in the morrow and I will give ya a map and see ya off."

The men returned, informing the families of the work. As much as they wished Patrick and Isaac to stay, they all understood why they were going to leave to work elsewhere for the winter. The gold had gone quickly and only a few pieces of silver remained. Mari Anna's father would have to sell a beautiful and ornate fowling gun just to feed the group until they returned. The two men said their heart-filled goodbyes in the morning, encouraging the twins to use their excellent fishing fskills to help keep everyone fed until they returned. As always, the three young women were inseparable and making jokes with each other as they wished Patrick and Isaac well. Marian even embraced Patrick while saying goodbye, which by civilized English culture would be considered vulgar.

The lifelong friends waved goodbye and reported to Mr. MacKay's. The men's pack mule was loaded with supplies and food for the long voyage. The tall, skinny Scotsman handed them a map and told them to report to a Mr. Perry. He was waiting for relief at a small estate. The two men and their mule headed out into the wilderness with mixed feelings of hope and concern. The tracking and hunting skills they learned from the old Indian would be extremely useful during their trek. Li Go Che would have been impressed that they even followed the map accurately without getting lost.

Patrick was awed by the stunning colors of the foliage that were turning as they traveled. Carolina had some beautiful trees, unlike London or Savannah. Some leaves had fallen already, which provided wonderful hiding places for local snakes, but both the men were fortunate enough to have thick, deer-skinned boots. Over the years, those boots had saved them from countless snakebites. The two had come across a cougar carcass, but the hide was removed already and the claws had also been taken. The travelers also found two black bears. They stayed safe by keeping their distance and staying upwind as Li Go Che had taught them. The unsettled and wild land was crawling with wildlife.

After a long journey, Patrick and Isaac finally found the small home near a winding creek. Smoke bellowed from the chimney. The weather was finally changing as the mornings were growing cold and the days short. The two friends knocked on the door and waited.

Patrick called out, "My name is Mr. Willis. Mr. MacKay sent me to relieve you for the next six months."

The door sprung open and two men, already packed, shoved past Patrick saying, "Finally! Here are the maps for your patrols. See you in March!"

"Wait! Mr. Perry, what do we do?" Patrick yelled. "We need instructions."

"It is all written down inside. I hope you are lettered and can cipher. See you in the spring!" the man yelled as the pair walked into the woods.

"I guess we should make the best of it. Let us see our home, Patrick," Isaac stated optimistically.

The note with instructions left to Patrick and Isaac was very short. It instructed to patrol once a day and had a map drawn on it. There was a picture of a few other patrol houses on the map, but the patrol area was extensive and would be impossible to cover in just one day. They ignored the note and decided to prepare their new home. The clapboard shack was small and humble, the men knew they had to be ready for a harsh winter or this would be their tomb.

For days they ignored their patrol duties and focused instead on chopping wood. Without plenty of fire, it would be easy to succumb to the coming cold. In days filled with hard work, they had chopped enough wood for three months. When the men reasoned they had enough wood, they finally decided to perform their job of patrolling. The first few weeks of patrol were completely uneventful. Isaac had killed a doe which Patrick had preserved by smoking the venison over a fire like the old warrior had showed him. The weather had chilled some, but no snow had appeared yet. The men found themselves in a daily routine of living off the land. The creek was loaded with bass this time of year and the men enjoyed lazy afternoons of fishing.

"Funny how the owner of this land is worried about poachers, yet we constantly have to hunt to keep fed," Patrick laughed. "We will end up killing more game than the bandits."

The men started to ignore the patrolling duties more and more and simply enjoyed the quiet pleasures of the isolated location. Patrick took the time to carve wooden chess pieces and taught Isaac to play. The two friends chopped many cords of wood before the snow finally dusted the woods. It was January and time had passed without incident. That was until one cold morning, *Crack!*

The shot of a firelock echoed through the woods. The sentries sprung to their feet and dressed for battle.

Crack! Crack! Two more shots rang out.

Patrick and Isaac ran through the pristine snow toward the sounds of musket fire. Isaac picked up a trail in the snow of two men. It took little time to track them down following the fresh footprints. "Freeze or I will burn you through!" Patrick yelled as he and Isaac held the two poachers at musket point. "Drop your knives and we will let you leave in peace."

The poachers were caught skinning a freshly killed bear. They dropped their knives at Patrick's command.

"I will make you a deal to avoid bloodshed," the hulking Jew offered. "You can take the hide of this beast but you have to leave the meat with us. The meat is not worth dying over."

The two Indian poachers stood up slowly and nodded in agreement.

"Finish your skinning then hunt here no more. If we catch

you hunting this land again we will fire on you," Patrick threatened.

The Indians must have understood since they quickly returned to skinning the bear. The poachers were very fast and efficient in their work. They removed anything of value including the claws.

"We want the meat out, too. Keep cutting," Isaac yelled. "No reason we should have to do all that hard work," he laughed.

The illegal hunters sliced the meat out with great skill. Nothing was wasted. One of the Indians pointed at the green gallbladder and then pointed at himself. "Go ahead and take it," Patrick conceded, waving his hand. "Do you remember? Li Go Che said savages use bear gallbladders for medicines. We have no use for it. They can make money with it," Patrick informed Isaac.

The poachers stood up and unthreateningly walked backwards. They took the hide and the other bits and scurried away.

"Don't come hunting here no more," Patrick shouted once more at the men. "That was wise, Isaac. Now we have lots of meat for winter. Let's go dry this on the fire." The men enjoyed bear and fish the rest of the mild winter.

"I have to say," Patrick reveled as he sipped at a hot tea one day. "Not sure what the big deal is. This is the best job I ever had."

Snow was still on the ground in March when Mr. Perry returned. Isaac and Patrick already had the pack mule loaded and were eager to leave. "Take your pay and go," Mr. Perry snorted as he threw two bags of silver at their feet. The two friends took their earnings and headed out.

"I sure am glad I spent the winter with you, Isaac, instead of that master of conversation, Mr. Perry," Patrick joked making both men laugh.

Six long months had passed when Patrick and Isaac returned home to the Argyle Colony. The men were astonished to see all the progress that had been accomplished in their absence. The new houses were finished and the three families finally had their own space. They were greeted with much excitement. The mild winter allowed them to continue working and now they could focus all their efforts on crops for the fall. Isaac and Patrick contributed their new earnings to the group which would buy them enough food until harvest.

Patrick was soon informed that Archibald left one last gift to his family. Marian was gaining weight and even with her loose dress one could tell with she was in a family way. The family was very excited about the unexpected pregnancy and it seemed to help everyone move past Archibald's murder.

Life finally set into a nice quiet rhythm. The families were truly enjoying spending their days with each other. The spring came along with back-breaking planting but the seeds had taken to the soil and were actually sprouting. Patrick remembered the old Indian mentioning a trick to growing corn. They would bury dead fish under the corn seed. The natural fertilizer set up the perfect environment for the plant to take root. All was turning around and going great for Patrick until...

CHAPTER 18

BLOODY MARSH AND SPILLY HOLF CREEK

"You have to come with me back to Savannah!" William commanded.

"You came all the way up here to get me? What is the problem, old friend?" Patrick asked.

"I think yar sister be in Savannah. An indentured servant named Garland just arrived. She is rumored to have mentioned yar name and be searching for ya. Did ya not tell us ya named the Indian's dog after yar sister?" the kilted man asked.

"I did send a letter a while back. Could it really be true that it found her? We have to find her. Who purchased her contract?" Patrick matched William's excitement.

"I have not found that out yet," the Scot explained. "This is all rumor to me. I have not yet confirmed any of this tale. I thought ya would be wanting to know first."

Later that night Patrick called a meeting of the families and explained William's news. "I am going back to a very dangerous situation. I have to go to my sister before she ends up in a life of horror. Being a female indenture is not much different than a being a slave. I've heard the stories around town. Women indentures are routinely beaten and raped by their owners. I can't leave her to a life like that, especially since she came looking for me. I don't want to leave you, but I have to know if it is her," Patrick finished.

The families discussed the risk but after some debate they gave him their blessings.

"I also ask the families' permission to go with Patrick, to keep him alive. He needs a counterpart with a rational mind,

264

not just crazy Scottish warriors," Isaac shot William an eye.

Marian spoke up, "You can go too, but I want you back by the time this child comes calling."

"It's settled. We'll pack up and be ready to travel by first light. I need to cut this beard and hair off so I look different. Will one of you ladies help me?" the indenture asked.

Prudence pulled her knife, "I will be happy to trim down that fooking rat's nest on your face. It's about time. What about you Isaac? You want to cut down that disgusting crumb catcher, too?"

"No, Prudence. My religion forbids it," the Jewish man countered.

"Your religion sure does forbid a lot of shite. Do you all do anything fun? Is it always pray, pray, and pray? What the fook does your God have against a clean face anyway? You do realize, Patrick, that even though you be changing your appearance, people are still going to notice a gigantic hairy Jew traveling with you," Prudence warned.

"I will dress him in a really large women's cloak. He has the ankles to pull it off," Patrick smirked. Isaac's massive hand smacked Patrick in the back of the head causing him to almost fall out of his chair while the families laughed.

"Well, get cutting then!" Patrick barked as Heather and Mari Anna laughed.

William, Patrick. and Isaac all left in the morning and made fast time to the little fishing sloop. The ship avoided the dock and dock master completely this time and had a small row boat waiting for them on shore. The men loaded their things and were ferried out to the waiting Scottish-owned sloop.

"Where to, William?" the captain asked.

"I think it is time to call out a favor, lads! Go to the little Yamacraw village above Savannah. Get us as close as you can."

The men had a blessing of good luck and made it to the little village without incident. Patrick held up the belt made of beads the rescued Indians gave him at Fort Mose. When he held it aloft, the belt was recognized as a sign of peace. Normally, white men would have been killed by mistakenly wandering into the Indian village. Travelers would not know subtle Creek protocol and, unknowingly would offend or threaten the tribe. Even with the belt, the three men approached cautiously and slowly. Hooting and shouts shot across the camp signaling alarm. The men were quickly surrounded by Indian warriors who were inspecting them closely.

"Do any of you speak the king's tongue?" Isaac inquired.

One of the warriors nodded and held his hand out to which Patrick surrendered the family belt to the painted man. The Indian looked it over and read the little bead pictures woven into the belt. "Stay," the warrior commanded with his open palm. He then ran off into the woods.

The three travelers found themselves under guard with nothing to do but wait. While they waited, the men stared at the interesting sites in the village. The village was impressive, but primitive. Nothing was permanent and looked as if it could be folded up and moved in a matter of minutes. Although the camp seemed temporary, it was expansive. It hinted that the tribe had finally stopped moving so much and set up a more elaborate camp with massive fire pits and totem poles.

"Fuck all this standing, lads. I am sitting on me arse," William announced as he sat. Patrick and Isaac looked at each other, shrugged their shoulders, and sat down, too. The Scot produced a fist-sized deerskin pouch filled with hemp. He offered it to the closest warrior guarding him. The painted man looked surprised and slowly opened it. The Indian quickly smiled and beckoned his hokti to bring him a pipe. The feathered woman soon returned with a long ornate pipe and a small torch. The happy Yamacraw packed the pipe and lit the slow burning hemp with the small torch.

The warrior held the smoke in his lungs for what seemed an eternity and then blew a puff of blue smoke out slowly. He then passed the pipe to William and he drew deep trying to match the warrior's time. As the kilted man blew the smoke out, he passed it to the guard standing next to him who in turn smiled and sat down. After only a few minutes, a large group of

Indian men were sitting with the three outsiders smoking. An old Indian passed the decorative pipe to Patrick who over eagerly inhaled. The scarred-face man quickly choked and coughed on the smoke. The group enjoyed a hardy laugh at his expense, relaxing the tense situation.

By the time the original warrior returned with the belt, nobody in the group had noticed. The entire pouch was empty and the guards were laughing loudly as they practiced their broken English on the prisoners.

The man with the belt now was escorted by three familiar looking redskins. "Me called So Lat Ti Kee. You white skins that free us. How we can help?"

It seemed everyone loved the smoke except Patrick. He was green, queasy and had a headache so Isaac spoke up for him. "We need your expert tracking skills to find someone. A white woman named Garland came from England last month as an indentured servant and is now in Savannah. We need you to find her and bring her back to us."

"What she look like?" the Warrior inquired.

"No idea now. She used to have bright, blonde-yellow hair, like straw," Patrick squeaked out.

"You stay here. We find straw hair," So Lat Ti Kee commanded. He then, in turn, spoke to the guards and explained the situation. The three warriors quickly departed in the direction of Savannah as So Lat Ti Kee tied the reunited family belt back around his waist.

"Ya redskins know Li Go Che? He be one dangerous old man!" William asked.

The group of smoke-happy warriors did not understand the Scotsman's brogue or just ignored him. The red men were busy ordering their women to feed their guests. The hoktaki went over to a large bubbling caldron that was always ready. The idea of set meals times was a silly notion to the Yamacraw. Within minutes, the three travelers were enjoying some peaches and deer stew.

The buzzing of a large, black puff of flies woke Patrick who was sleeping on the ground. The other two men were already awake sitting in the dirt trying to gather their bearings.

"Good lord, dos Injuns sure do know how to smoke. I had not seen smoke and grog consumed like that since a Scottish funeral," William chuckled.

"Wake me when those warriors return with my sister. I am going back to sleep over there in the shade," Patrick stated as he stumbled to a spot under an oak with Spanish moss hanging from its branches.

"For the lord's sake, don't let that hanging moss touch ya. It be loaded with little red bitey things," William warned.

Patrick quickly passed out in the shade while the other men went to make water.

He was woken up by someone shaking his shoulder. "Sister sold to group of white soldiers. War break out again. Spanish get revenge and plan to take Savannah from British," the Indian informed him. "Fifty Spanish ships seen near Fort Simons. Oglethorpe be calling back Creek to fight again. Your straw haired sister be with redcoat soldiers traveling to St. Simons. We take you to St. Simons, rescue sister from white soldiers."

"You will be traveling with known men. If the British catch you helping us, they will kill us all. This could be very dangerous for you, my new friend," Patrick explained to the Indian.

"We honor life debt to you. We save sister, you forgive debt?" the Indian asked.

"Absolutely. We will be on the level, redskin," Patrick guaranteed.

"I really do not want to go back into that mosquito and gator infested death swamp, but I really want to find my sister," Patrick explained. "Isaac, William, I do not expect you to go traipsing through such a dangerous place just to help me with my debt I owe my sister."

"We are all family now, even if our blood is different. Your sister is our sister. Of course we are coming, you fool," Isaac smiled.

Patrick stumbled to his feet and hugged the men. "Oh, God, I feel awful! Don't hug too hard or I will unload my guts on your boots," the green man warned.

"Can you trust these redskins not to sell us to the British for silver?" Isaac queried.

"Honor is extremely important to dem in their culture. If this Injun be not honoring his word, his tribe would forsake him and his family. His honor be much more important to him than silver, lads," William responded.

The white men rested and cleaned their muskets while a large group of Yamacraw warriors were preparing to go fight the white man's war again. So Lat Ti Kee rode up with three warhorses wearing English saddles. The appaloosas were painted with yellow and black hand prints. A feeling of panic ran up Patrick's woozy spine. He had never been on a horse before. Although horses were everywhere in Savannah, Archibald preferred to walk or to travel by carriage. The deceased man had been thrown off the back of a gelding and slammed into a fence when he was younger and had never forgiven the beasts. Isaac and William mounted the steeds with ease and the group watched and waited for Patrick to mount. Patrick took a deep breath and placed his foot in the stirrup. He awkwardly grabbed the saddle and pulled. The appaloosa picked up on the man's unsteadiness and lurched forward. One foot followed the stirrup and the other held fast on the ground. The steed quickly ripped Patrick off his foot and dragged him away from the camp. So Lat Ti Kee chased down the horse, laughing. The equine steadied and the white men helped a scraped and bruised Patrick up into his saddle.

"Just relax and don't yank the steeds bit. They hate that. Bend your knees and lean back a little," Isaac advised.

Patrick clumsily steered his painted beast into the line of horses and held his reins in fearsome dread.

"Relax, lad. The beast knows if ya be frightened of him and will test ya. Just stay between us and we will help ya get the hang of it," William chimed in.

"How do you stop this damn thing?!" Patrick yelled as his horse picked up its pace to match the herd.

"Don't worry, Patrick. We will teach you on the journey," Isaac laughed.

The three rescuers rode out and somehow kept pace with the fast moving warriors. The three white men followed the painted men for days deep into the swamps. They veered their path away from Savannah and steered clear of any British inhabitants. The warriors scouted ahead and kept the white men invisible for the entire journey.

* * *

It was July 17th, 1742, when So Lat Ti Kee came back to the men with news. Patrick had discovered through the scout that the Spanish had already seized St. Simons weeks ago and were occupying the fort. A small, one-carriage road named Military Road ran between Fort St. Simon and Ft. Frederica through the dense woods. "We find straw hair. She cook for Chief Oglethorpe soldiers at a camp half day from here. Tomorrow, we go together and take her," the Indian announced. The rest of his tribesman had gone to help the British repel the Spanish so So Lat Ti Kee was able to pass through English lines without suspicion.

"Huzzah! Let us finish this and get the hell out of this damned swamp," Isaac exclaimed.

"Let us enjoy one more lovely night of being dinner for the hungry bugs. We must not rush in blindly," Patrick countered, paying homage to Archibald by flattering the Indian. "We will make a plan tonight. Great warrior, report what you have seen with your hawk eyes." The scout's mood brightened and he smiled. He sat down and constructed a crude model of the camp with sticks and stones. William pulled out more hemp and sat down for a smoke as they hatched a plan.

"Let us get a good night's rest before we move. My arse is still red from all this riding," Patrick complained.

The men took turns at watch while the others slept. When morning rose, one of So Lat Ti Kee's scouts quickly ran into the camp. He reported to the Indian guide for ten minutes. Patrick had no clue what they were talking about, but he could tell from the scouts frantic pointing that something big was happening.

A map of Military road in the Battles of Bloody Marsh and Gully Hole Creek

So Lat Ti Kee approached the white men. "We know much more now about Spanish. Fifty ships sailed through St. Simons cannon fire. Two thousand Spanish landed near Gascoigne Bluff on Frederica River and take fort."

"Oh, that is not comforting. I think if we add up the soldiers, militia, Indians, and Oglethorpe's forces, they are only numbering around seven hundred souls. He won't be able to hold his position much longer. We really need to find your sister and leave this place quickly," Isaac interjected.

The warrior continued, "Spanish starting to move down road. We ride now. Must find straw hair before Spanish kill all the English."

"I am ready. Let us ride. To hell with this swamp," Patrick shouted.

The men broke camp and rode out, kicking up mud behind them. Within hours, the four men arrived at the British campsite. The white men waited and let the Indian coax Garland away from the camp. The Yamacraw ran into the camp and disappeared. After about half an hour, So Lat Ti Kee returned carrying a bloody Indian. The scout propped up the bloody warrior as he spoke, "Straw hair gone. Soldiers move her with camp outside Fort Frederica. We must go closer to battle. Follow!"

The men mounted up and nervously moved closer to the Fort as the sun set. Along the little wagon trail called Military Road, they came across a wounded soldier stumbling back. William stopped and offered the injured man some water. "Sergeant, what be the news?" he asked

The Sergeant went into great detail about the invasion as he drank. The injured man explained that Noble James bested the Spanish General Manitiano's troops up on Military Road in those 'Bloody Marshes.' More Spanish troops descended the little road retaliating their loss. All day the British troops were driven down the road, fighting little skirmishes, until a full retreat was called. The soldier smiled through bloody lips and continued, "When we reached a bend in the road at Gully Hole Creek, Lieutenants Southerland and Macoy decided to stop. Their soldiers and Oglethorpe's Injun allies hid in the thick of the forest. They waited and watched as the Spanish broke rank. They continued to spy, seeing them stack arms, taking out their kettles, and preparing to cook dinner. They had assumed we retreated for good but we had a surprise waiting. Our forces flew from the forest and attacked the Spanish off guard, killing about fifty dead. Truly, I only have minor injuries and I am on my way carrying the news of the victory back to the fort."

"If ya can ride, we can take ya to Fort Frederica to share news of yar victory," William offered the man.

"That would be dandy," the injured man said as he accepted the offer.

Patrick and Isaac shot William a confused look. William nodded to the worried men, assuring them to relax.

Four horses and six riders approached the gate to a group of waiting guards. The injured sergeant yelled in delight,

"Victory today at Gully Hole Creek!" The guards cheered and simply waived the party into the fort without question.

"Well, ya ride ends here, Sergeant. We need to find a wench to do mending for us. Where be the soldiers' wenches?" William questioned slyly.

"Thanks for the lift. You will find all the women in the medical tents right now. Long live the king!" The sergeant yelled and limped over to join his comrades.

Patrick looked across the courtyard and spotted a flash of bright, blonde hair outside a tent sewing clothes. He galloped over to confirm if he was indeed looking at his long lost sister. When he arrived, he just stared at her visage. Her hair was lighter than he remembered and she was now a grown woman. Her eyes were the right shade of green, but she looked so different from what he remembered. Patrick then noticed a small scar drawn across her eyebrow, reminding him of a childhood fall she was once involved in. "Ga… Ga… Garland? Is that you?" Patrick squeaked out.

"Piss off! I ain't got time for washing any of your clothes and I ain't selling my body!" she barked back.

Patrick laughed, "Garland, it's me! Your brother, Patrick!"

She dropped her needle and looked up slowly. She gave his scarred face a long look. "That is you? Oh God, you found me!" she yelled in joy. She pulled Patrick down from his horse and hugged him so hard it left him gasping for air.

"I have missed you so, sister! But we have no time to lose. You have to leave with us now! We are known men and right now we are pilgrims in a very unholy land," Patrick whispered.

"God, yes! Get me out of here, but I have to do one thing first. I will make haste," Garland promised. She disappeared into the medical tent. After a minute she appeared with a tea pot and ran it over to a large soldier's tent. Patrick watched as she switched the teapot and left it hanging over a small fire. She then disappeared into the large tent. After a couple of minutes, she returned holding a bag and wearing a cloak that covered her face and body.

Patrick helped her onto the back of his horse and stated,

"Let us leave this murderous hole and never come back!"

The group started to ride out of the gates when a guard commanded them to stop. "What be ya business leaving at nightfall?"

Nobody in the group could think of a proper response until Garland's voice spoke up. "These men are ordered to escort me to see one of my boys!"

The guard shook his head in disgust, "Carry on!"

"Tell them I will be back very late but I left them their favorite tea brewing on the fire," she yelled to the guard.

The group casually cantered down Military Road until they were out of sight. They then broke off into the dense woods to avoid troops who were on their way back to the fort. Even though So Lat Ti Kee was still riding double with his injured comrade, he made quick time guiding the group back into the swamp. They rode hard all night and wanted to stop but Garland begged the group to put as much distance as possible between Fort Federica and them. Finally, by mid-afternoon, they had to stop for the sake of the exhausted horses and to get some sleep for themselves. The white men made a fire and relaxed while the Indians rotated watch.

Patrick finally got a chance to sit down and catch up with Garland. "I sure did miss you, little sister." He reached out to hug her. As soon as he was in striking range, the back of her hand fell across his scarred-up jaw. The blow knocked Patrick over.

"That is for leaving me alone all these years!" she screamed. She then kicked him in the shin crying, "and that is for not being in Savannah when I landed."

"Garland, darling, I had no choice. I never wanted to leave you. That is why I sent you a letter the first chance I got, asking you to come join me," Patrick pleaded.

"A messenger tracked me down in London. He said he had almost given up but he then he ran across someone from my church that knew where I was."

"Why didn't Mother and our sisters join you? Are they on their way?" Patrick hoped.

"Oh! You do not know, do you, brother? Mother passed away shortly after you left of blood lung fever. She must have gotten it from taking care of Papa. Our other sisters both died from the pox a few months later. I am sorry, Patrick. I am the only family you have left." Patrick grew silent and sad as his sister continued, "Frankly, I thought you were dead. I tried to find you in the prison, but they kept poor records. I was told you must be dead if you were incarcerated that long. That is why I never came to visit you." She sensed his grief, held him as he wept, and promised, "Your family never gave up on you. They were just taken by the Lord."

Patrick had already assumed the worst about his family in London. Somewhere down deep he knew they were dead. He was prepared for the grief and feelings that were now overtaking him. The sting was not as traumatic as it could have been. Sadly, he had forgotten what his mom and sisters even looked like because it now seemed like a past life.

Patrick wiped his tears, "So, sister, what was so damn important that you had to stop and make tea for the soldiers before you left?"

She reached over and held his hand, "Brother, a group of six soldiers purchased me. I was told I would only have to clean, cook and mend for them. I quickly found out they were horrible evil souls. When the tent flaps closed, they took turns forcing themselves on me over and over and they even sold me to their fellow soldiers for extra rations."

Patrick filled with rage; "We will go back and kill these men tonight!"

She held him down, "Brother they will meet the reaper tonight. I have already extracted my vengeance. The six men have a tradition of drinking a hot tea together before they sleep. When I was working in the medical tent I found some Devil's porridge and infused it in their tea."

Patrick repeated in confusion, "Devil's porridge?"

His sister replied, "You know, Beaver Poison, Herb Bennet, Musquash Root, Poison Parsley, Spotted Corobane. I think they call it Spotted Hemlock over here."

Patrick calmed down, "Those rapist scum are going to have a hard time catching their breath when they sleep tonight and the Grim Reaper will come for their souls by the morrow."

"Yes, they have a toasting ritual every night. They salute King George and then they all drink at the same time. If they had a good victory today, they will definitely all be drinking it down together tonight." She grinned evilly.

Patrick had an epiphany, "So that is why you wanted to push the horses and ride as fast as you can, the camp will cry treachery in the morning when the corpses are discovered."

She nodded. Patrick yelled, "Listen up, lads! I need to tell you there be danger behind us. We ride hard at day break to William's home."

CHAPTER 19

PIRATE TUNNELS

Once the group made it to a familiar area the men said their goodbyes and heart-filled thanks to their Indian guides.

"Thank you, So Lat Ti Kee. Your debt is paid to me," Patrick informed him as the group dismounted. "Here, take our horses."

"When the spirit horse comes for me, white man, he will know all my debts are paid," the Indian smiled. So Lat Ti Kee's injured companion stumbled over to Isaac and handed him a battle-worn tomahawk. It had a stunning hand carved cherry handle but the iron blade had chips in the edge from bone strikes. Isaac was grateful for the gift and locked wrists with the injured Yamacraw to show him respect. Patrick nodded his head and the Indians quickly made their exit.

The four walked into Darien and back to William's farm without any pursuers. Perhaps the British would assume the Spanish poisoned them or that Garland fled to join the Spanish. They were just glad to be far away from the war. The group settled into William's home but still kept a nervous eye out. "William, do you think any of the other soldiers recognized you at Fort Frederica?" Patrick asked with concern.

"No, lad. I did not recognize the guards and the camp be pretty much empty. I think we be out of the fire now," William surmised.

"Ouch!" Garland yelled. Patrick smashed a large green horse fly on Garlands arm leaving a smudge of blood and fly parts. "I am still not used to all these biting bugs. Oh, and the heat is brutal! They might as well have built Savannah on the fucking sun," Garland complained.

"Patrick, me thinks da three of ya best stay here for a few days and lay low while I put a word out that you need a ship to Cape Fear," William advised.

"Look at you three men! Come on off with your coats. Look how filthy they are. It will take me all morning to dust these out," Deborah cut in. The three men handed over their riding jackets that were covered with Georgian red clay dust. It would be an exercise in futility to try and wash them, as the dust would turn to clay and stain the fabric. Deborah instead hung the coats on a rope outside and began bushing them with a small hand broom. She called on Lauren and Lindsey to help and with forceful strokes they brushed until red dust filled the air. William enjoyed watching his family do mundane daily chores like brushing. He was settling into the idea of a quiet farming life.

"Patrick, did I tell you? I took some of my gold and ordered me a fold of Kyloe," William announced proudly.

"What are those?" Garland questioned.

"They be Highland cattle; hairy beasts with long horns. They're either black, red, or yellow, but I ordered dun," the Scot explained.

"What is dun?" Isaac queried.

"Fer Christ's sake, have none of ya ever worked a farm?! Dun is a color between sandy-yellow and reddish-brown. Their bodies be lighter than their tails and manes," William explained. "I be figuring Savannah is getting dangerously low on wild game. I could stand to make a killing on cattle here."

"That is a fine idea, William. Just figure out a way to keep Oglethorpe's troops from up and stealing your cattle when they get hungry," Patrick warned.

"Aye. Darien is building a network of spies. We will know hours before the king's men ever arrive. Plenty of time to be hiding the cattle in the swamps and woods," the kilted man explained.

Later, William dispatched word that the men needed silent passage back to the Argyle Colony through his clan network. As the men relaxed, William explained the local going-ons of the Darien colony. "The highlanders have lost their trust of Oglethorpe. After most of the men in this town were killed or were captured at Fort Mose, he changed ancient Scottish law. That angered the old traditional men of the village something awful."

"What did Oglethorpe change?" the Jewish man wanted to know.

"The arrogant bastard changed inheritance rights to 'Tail General,' ignoring hundreds of years of the tradition of 'Tail Male' rights," William pouted.

"I am not following you. What does that mean?" Patrick questioned.

"It means bloody women can inherit and own land now!" he snapped. "Aye, lad. Everything is changing after the Fort Mose massacre. Remember the trustees of Georgia paid for us to move here and be their soldiers. The trustees forgot that Scots don't care for authority none and we are not easily controlled. We fell out of favor rather quickly. In 1739, eighteen of the most prominent members of the Darien colony signed the first petition against the introduction of slavery into Georgia. This was in response to pleas to Oglethorpe because the Trustees and inhabitants of Savannah wanted to lift their prohibition on slavery. Since then, most of the people of Savannah have hated the Scots of Darien.

"Allowing women to own land was a real spit in the eye to us. Many kinfolk be ignoring their soldiering obligation and have moved to South Carolina. If things be staying like this in Georgia, we might be joining my kin as well. Many men, me-self included, will no longer ride with da Highlander Rangers or march with da Highland Independent Company of foot. We feel all the deaths at Fort Mose fulfilled our obligation to king and country."

"Wherever you end up, we will find you and raid your wife's wonderful haggis," Patrick smirked. The men had a hardy laugh and reveled in their fellowship.

A day later, Patrick finally caught Garland alone out by the stream washing the cooking kettle. "So after our family passed, what did you do?" Patrick asked.

"Well, brother, nothing I am proud of. I survived stealing scraps of food where I could. I lived with a large group of homeless orphans who roamed the streets. We got quite good at getting food and clothes but it was a horrible life. Later on, a church going woman took pity on me and gave me a job as a servant in her house. It was nice to sleep indoors again but the work was very hard." She continued, "My benefactor demanded I go to church with her every single day and live a pious life in her home. It was annoying and frustrating but I was grateful to be fed and dry, so I kept working there until I became a full-grown woman. Sadly, her husband, who was a deacon in our church, noticed I was a woman, too. He forced himself on me for over a year until I finally got pregnant by him.

"Right about the time I got your letter, I started to show. The lady of the house was mortified. She accused me of being a loose strumpet. I explained to her that her husband pressed himself on me but she would not believe it. She then forced me to drink a tea that caused me to lose the baby. I lost so much blood, I almost died. She had no mercy for me and threw me into the street, but not before I stole some gold doubloons from her. I used the money to bribe my way onto a ship to find you. Once I was aboard, the captain double crossed me and sold me into indentured service."

Patrick interrupted, "Let me guess. Was the bastard captain named Mr. Gibbons?"

"Yes. How did you know?" she exclaimed.

Patrick then told her every detail of his hard life since they had been separated.

The two enjoyed the next few days in peace catching up and growing close again. Isaac also enjoyed Garland's company as well. Unlike Patrick, she was very interested in his religion and wanted to know every detail about it. She told him how she enjoyed learning about all different religions and wanted to know all about Judaism. Isaac and Garland stayed up late at night discovering and debating the differences in their beliefs.

* * *

A week had passed and William finally had some news. "Lads, I have good and bad news for ya. I think I found a ride to Cape Fear, but you have to go to Savannah to catch it."

"That would be folly. We best just wait for another ship that will come to Darien," Isaac insisted.

"There won't be another ship for months, so this be it, boys. If you miss this, you will be staying the winter with us," William explained.

"We promised Marian we would be back to help them harvest and see her baby born. We have to risk it, old friend," Patrick reasoned.

"Well, I will help ya with your chances. There is a shady tavern they built on the bluff right near the Trustee's garden. The garden is falling apart and they are talking about cutting it up into lots for residents. Some people have already built a few structures over the garden in anticipation. One of the houses has become a den for illegal spirits, illegal trade and a place to bed for known men. Ya will know it by the triple lanterns it has in front and it is made of Savannah brick. If ya go at night, ya should be able to get to dat tavern without being noticed. There ya will be able to barter passage to Cape Fear anonymously," the Scot explained.

"Well, it will give me a chance to get my gold. We have to do it, Isaac," Patrick resolved.

"Fine, but if you get my neck stretched, you will be all alone in your afterlife," Isaac threatened.

"Alone? What do you have some secret that will allow you to escape eternal damnation? Some might pay gold for such a secret," Patrick said in a jesting tone.

Isaac became serious and stated "No secret, Patrick. I merely have faith that God will resurrect me after the Messiah comes. Perhaps he will resurrect you too."

"Sorry, my Hebrew friend. I forget how serious you take those stories. My apologies bestowed on to you, my brother. Let's not wait around for the Second Coming. Shall we pack up and catch this ship tonight?" Patrick inquired.

Garland and Isaac agreed and began packing up immediately.

"William, I am not sure when I will be back this way, but you and your family are welcome to stay with me if you ever need a place. You are family to me and Archibald would have been very grateful of what you have done to help his family. I will miss you, Sovereign McIntosh."

"Aye, lad. Come back soon. I will miss ya and the Jew, too. I will wear Archibald's tartan proudly until it crumbles from me body," William vowed.

The men embraced and Patrick, Isaac, and Garland were quickly on their way back to Savannah. They traveled by daylight so as not to tempt the road agents. By nightfall, the three had made it to the edge of the Trustee's Garden.

Since Isaac had done nothing to alter his appearance, Patrick instructed him and Garland to remain hidden. Patrick assumed no one would recognize him clean-shaven and with new clothes if he was seen from a distance. "I am going to get my gold!" he smiled as he left.

Patrick cautiously scurried around the edge of the town staying out of sight. At one point, he caught a glimpse of the Freeman's house now being occupied by a group of soldiers. They were laughing and drinking under the dogwood and were oblivious to Patrick's movements. He navigated into the swamp and quickly located his buried booty. He used a large oyster shell to dig in the moonlight and the pouch was soon unearthed. He pulled the gold out in triumph and rattled it to hear the jingle of happiness. *This gold is going to change my family's life for the better,* he proudly thought. Before, he could not support those who supported him. Now, however, everything had just changed. He was excited and could barely concentrate as he circled back to his waiting friends.

"Was it still there?" Isaac asked.

Patrick smiled ear to ear. "Let's book us a ship. Come on, let's go to the Three Lantern Pub," he ordered.

It was surprisingly easy to locate after William described

what they were looking for. They spotted the small brick building with three lamps hanging to the right side of the oak door. It was located right in front of the gardener's herb house. The illegal pub also had stone stairs leading down to a rum cellar in the back. They knocked three times, then twice, then once as they were instructed by William. After a minute, the door cautiously cracked open and a ragged old man peaked out the cracked door. "What do ya want?" he screeched with a gravelly voice.

"We are thirsty, good man, and want a drink of course," Patrick replied.

The unkempt man barked back, "Ya can drink but no women or Jews!"

"I really want my friends to drink with me. Are you sure I can't get you to change your policies just for tonight," Patrick asked as he flashed a bright yellow coin before the dirty man's eyes.

"Well, if ya got that much color then I can look da other way just for tonight," he stated as he opened the door for the three of them.

The pub was very small, by tavern standards, and poorly lit. Just two tables and a bar adorned the establishment with a back storage room.

One of the tables was occupied by a stunning blonde temptress dressed in a flashy, yellow, skin-tight dress and a skinny sunburned bearded man who looked vaguely familiar. "I thought you said no women. Well, what the hell is that then?" Garland shrilly asked as she pointed to the extremely large-breasted blonde woman.

"Oh, that is no woman," the grouchy old man scoffed. "She is the whoremaster Miss Darden. I advise just leaving her be."

The three sat at the bar and ordered rum. The old man with the filthy beard went in the back and returned with three small wooden tumblers filled with foul smelling rum. The three made a toast to a new life together and downed the round.

"Just bring the jug, sir. We will want more. What's your name, bartender?" Garland asked pleasantly.

"Me name is Jim Jaques and I ain't be bringing ya no jug till I get paid," the old man barked.

Isaac pulled out his last six silver rounds and ordered, "Keep the rum flowing."

Jim went into the storage room and returned with a dark brown jug with cork surrounding it. He poured the three another rounds.

"Jim, I am told by my friend William that you are a man who knows how to find stuff. He told me you could find the Jewish gardener who used to work in the trustee's garden. He was rumored to grow some real dandy hemp bud." Patrick pressed.

"Ya speak of gardener Goldsmith, he grows the best smoke around. Unfortunately, he is like a bugbear or a ghost, he is almost impossible to find. Sorry I can't help you with that. Dar be anything else I can help ya locate?" The dirty old man asked.

"I am told you could help us procure passage on one of the vessels down by the docks," Patrick inquired.

"That be true. I have been known to help those of wealth from time to time. Where you be wanting to go?" the filthy man inquired.

"We need passage to Cape Fear and we need a vessel to leave as soon as possible, tonight even. Can you arrange it with one of the captains? I will pay you well if you can make this happen for us," Patrick held up a gold doubloon.

The old man drooled at the sight of the gold, but he composed himself quickly and stated, "With that kinda color you get the good rum!" He removed the brown jug and replaced it with a bottle from under the counter. "I think I can help ya but ya will have to wait here for a while. Drink yar spirits and I will see what I can do." The filthy bearded man returned to the back room.

The three had another couple rounds of the good rum and a feeling of relaxation and euphoria came over them. "This is some powerful fire water," Garland slurred. "My brain already hurts." Before her words were finished, she slumped out of her chair and hit the ground. Isaac dropped down and tried to pick her up from the filthy, red clay floor. The goliath stumbled to his feet, holding her in his arms. He wrestled with keeping his eyes open and sat back down. The last thing Patrick saw before his world went dark was Isaac's massive body slumped over his sister's and a bow-legged man standing over them.

"Oh, lord. Jim drugged them. Take them to the tunnels in the rum cellar and go find help. Be fast! We only have minutes," a woman's voice rang in Patrick's ear before he lost consciousness.

The entrance to Savannah's secret pirate smuggling tunnels

* * *

"No, No, No!" Garland screamed. Patrick opened his hazy eyes as her loud voice pierced his ears. He slowly shook off the brain sloth and focused on his surroundings. When his eyes finally became clear, he realized he was in the dimly lit quarters of a ship. "This can't be! This is my mark carved into this wood plank," Garland belted out.

"Where are we? Garland, what are you yelling about?"

Isaac asked as he slowly sat up holding his pounding head.

"Open your eyes, you fools. Look around! Does any of this look familiar?!" Garland screeched.

Isaac and Patrick surveyed their surroundings and at the same time muttered, "No, it can't be."

"Yes, you idiots! We are prisoners back on the *Robin*. I carved my mark into this wood on my voyage over!" Garland exclaimed.

"Oh, God! Isaac, do you think we just got pressed into service on the *Robin*? Oh shite! My gold is gone, too. Damn it!" Patrick yelled and joined his sister's state of panic.

Isaac filled with anger. "I have finally tasted freedom. I will no longer live as any man's slave. I say we make our stand, brother. We die fighting on our feet!"

"Agreed! Isaac and I will throttle the first man through this door. Once he is on the ground, sister, you must stomp the life out of him with your bare feet," Patrick instructed.

"I will not be a filthy sailor's sex slave," Garland resolved grimly.

"I hear someone coming. I will go low. You go high, Isaac and, sister, you stomp. Now quiet until we ambush," Patrick whispered.

The two men's bodies filled with fighting juices and time seemed to slow. The door was unlocked, opened, and the men wasted no time in their bull rush. Patrick bound the man's feet with a leaping tackle. Isaac swung hard and struck the man in the mouth. Since his feet were already tangled, the victim blew backwards hitting his head against the wall. Blood from the man's mouth splattered all over Patrick's white shirt.

"Fuck ya, ya goat-eating, Jew bastard!" the man spat.

"Isaac! Stop! Everyone, stop!" Patrick shouted.

"Damn right! Ya goat-humpers best be stoppin'. I fookin' rescue ya from the certain death by redcoats and this be me thanks. G'damn, ya Jew! Now I only gots four teeth left," Shamus yelled as he coughed out a bloody tooth.

"Wait...why aren't we killing this man?" Garland asked in confusion.

Isaac helped the small, foul-mouthed Irishman to his feet. "I am sorry, Shamus. We thought you came to murder us. So what in the name of Moses is going on?"

"Well, Isaac Swartz, dis best be explained better up topside. Come on," the toothless man motioned.

The small group made their way up the familiar old staircase of the *Robin* and into the blinding sunlight. They could feel the old galleon rocking under their feet and knew they were in open waters.

"Why does me husband have blood all over him, Irishman?!" a woman's voice boomed.

"Ma'am, dese crazy man-humpin' bastards played gladiator wit me. Dat be my blood, Cap'n April Sky," Shamus responded.

A tawdry dressed, tattooed woman stepped out from the crew. "Be known, crew," April announced, "any of you even step on me husband's toe and I will burn you down!"

Isaac, Garland and Patrick questioned April in unison, "Husband?"

"That's right, me husband," April stated. "Our child is not growing up a bastard."

Isaac, Garland and Patrick questioned April again in unison, "Child?!"

As if on queue a small baby toddled over and leaned on to her mother's tattooed leg to keep balance.

"I think I am going to fall down," Patrick moaned as he collapsed into his sister's arm.

"Who is this harlot to be hugging on my husband?" April demanded.

"Wait, Captain! This is Patrick's sister from London," Isaac spoke up. "Her name is Garland."

Patrick started counting the months on his hands. "Well I guess by the age of that youngin' it could be mine, but how do you know?"

April smiled, saying, "Because my dear, you're the only man I have laid with in a long time. It's yours or God's child."

"What's his name?" Patrick asked as he approached.

"Well he is a she and her name is Tracy," the proud mother

smiled.

"She? Tracy? That is an odd name," Patrick stated.

"You uneducated fool! It is an ancient Gaelic name meaning 'warlike and fierce.' She beat me insides up so bad, I figure she's a natural warrior," April explained. "Let us go below deck in the private and talk some more."

The captain left Tracy with a crewwoman named Miss Bias and took Patrick below deck to the captain's private quarters. She kissed him passionately and started undressing him. Patrick enjoyed the kiss but was still rearing from confusion. "I don't remember any wedding when we had our sexual odyssey to Jekyl Island. Did I take a blow to the head and lose my senses?" Patrick asked as his breeches fell to the floor.

"Let me remind you, I am captain and on this vessel I can marry anyone I please. So, I married us," April stated with authority as she dropped to her knees in front of him.

Patrick had noticed her breasts were still swollen from weaning. She had already regained her slender form but her tits now looked much fuller. The tattoo of the alligator on her left breast now appeared to be eating the black cat on the right. "I see. I still think I am supposed to say 'I do' and have a proper ceremony and such," Patrick continued.

"Here, take this," she smiled as she placed ring on top of the tip of his erect penis. "Now say you do."

"I don't think that is how it works," he laughed.

The ring flew across the room as she mounted him and the sex marathon began again. After a few hours of vigorous thrusting from multiple positions, they both became very hungry and thought about stopping to eat.

"You know it is important our daughter not grow up a bastard child. So as far as this crew knows, we've been married since Jekyl Island. I do find you a good man, Patrick, and I would be a great wife to you if you will have me. The sex is fantastic but I think love could eventually bud from this union. I will go down on you one more time if you agree!" she laughed with a devilish grin.

"Well in that case, find that ring and get on your knees

again. Let me warn you of this though, it best not be like all the husbands I know where this will be the last one I get as soon as I accept this ring," he chuckled.

He watched her beautiful, naked body search the floor for the ring. "Here it is, my wolf," she triumphantly announced. She approached him and handed it him. A feeling of sadness overtook Patrick as he realized he had nothing for her. "I know this whole exchanging of rings is a new tradition, but I feel heavy-hearted, as I do not have one to give you."

"Well you're in luck," she told Patrick. "I already have one I like for me-self."

She handed him an odd looking ring. Patrick examined it with his jeweler's knowledge and told April what she had. "This is an antique scribbling ring made in the 16th century for lovers. Do you see these stones set across the top here? They are uncut diamonds. Tradition is you use the stones to etch romantic notes on windowpanes, mirrors or glass." He handed the ring back to her.

"Well it is bad luck not to follow tradition," she stood in all of her naked splendor and carved "My Wolf" into her small pocket mirror. She placed it back in his hands and said, "My love is as fragile as this glass, if this mirror ever shatters so will my heart. Keep it safe at all times". "Can you find anything even more fragile? I want a real challenge," her lover said sarcastically. She flicked him in his ball sack and he yelped. "So let's make this proper. Let us say 'I do' together." She offered.

They both slid the rings on each other's hand and whispered, "I do."

"I guess this means we have to go down on each other at the same time as well," she giggled and she swung her hips toward his face.

CHAPTER 20

SECRETS

Captain April Sky and her black cat, Regan

Patrick woke from his post coitus nap holding April's head on his chest. "Wife, I think it is best I meet my daughter. I could also eat a whale. I have so many questions like how the hell did you end up with Shamus on your barky?"

Patrick's numerous questions were interrupted by a knocking at the door. A woman's voice yelled through the door, "Captain, we need to set up the dining table now for your dinner."

"Very good! One minute," April yelled back. "Get dressed, husband. I am having a private dinner party and all your questions will be answered in minutes."

Patrick dressed as instructed and opened the door. Some exotic looking crewmen rearranged the captain's quarters so a dining table could fit. He watched as Isaac and Garland entered and he quickly whispered to them, "By the way, I have been married for over two years. I will tell you all about it later." Both shot Patrick the devil's eye. He returned their glares with a wink and a giggle. The three took their seat around the table and watched as Shamus and Sam Scurvy walked in joining them. Patrick's jaw fell to the table as he finally recognized the bow-legged man who was in the Three Lanterns Pub. The voluptuous, blonde woman in the yellow dress who was with Sam back at the tavern had also entered in the room, shutting the door behind her. The sultry woman took a seat and then the captain sat at the head of the table.

April returned to speaking in her harsh, common captain's voice, "Introductions need to made. This be me husband, Patrick, his sister, Garland, and Isaac Swartz. Over there is Shamus, Sam and Miss Darden. Miss Darden be me whoremaster and she be running all me business interests at the brothel during me absence. She be the bottom girl or the second in charge. The whoremaster can handle any questions or concerns you might have about the whores."

Patrick spoke up, "Whores? Are there more women on board than you two?"

"There be eight other prostitutes on board and some children," she responded.

"Children and women?! What kind of crew are you running here? I have never heard of such craziness," her husband responded.

"Listen to dis, Patrick Sky," Shamus chuckled at his own joke. "Ya should see all da g'damn cats she got runnin' 'round on here, too. All of dem black. I done lost count after fifteen."

"Do you want to curse this vessel, Irishman?" the captain responded. "Custom dictates you must have a black cat for every woman soul on your barky. Do you want to tempt the fates and not honor tradition?"

"Captain April Sky, I have heard of one g'damn black cat to assure a safe return but never heard of one per lady. Me thinks you just be making yar own fookin' customs up," Shamus challenged.

"That is sea law, Shamus Red. Now you best be minding it before I order the Jew to knock your last few teeth out," she snapped.

The captain continued. "Tonight I am going to tell you about me past. What I tell you never comes off your tongue or your tongue will come off. I be telling you this because I want to make you an offer when I am finished. But first, me husband is dying to ask you two crew men some questions."

Patrick impatiently asked, "Shamus Red, you bastard who never dies, how the hell did you end up serving on the *Robin* again?"

"Well I don't really fookin' serve on it, lad. I own it!" He smiled a toothless grin.

He spun his wild tale. "Ya remember when I last saw ya, dat Captain Gibbons double-crossed us and added more fookin' years to our indentured service? This pissed on me last nerve and I decided I was done bein' 'nother man's fookin' slave. I gathered all da silver I won at dice and sealed it in a barrel. I did not know dat the captain would soon be helpin' me escape and be throwin' me treasure barrel in da drink for me. When he order dos two man humpers keelhauled and cast overboard with me fookin' barrel of silver tied to dem, I knew twas time to make me escape. As all da crew ran to da starboard side ta watch da kook lovers float away, I slipped o'er the larboard side and no souls noticed. I stayed under da drink for as long as I fookin' could while da *Robin* sailed away. Den I swam over to da arse-rammers and untied dem. Da two were so weak that I helped keep 'em from drownin' while the tide carried us to shore.

"When we beached, I helped clean out da canyons dat had been carved into dere backs by the keelhaulin'. I felt bad for the kook munchers and nursed 'em back to da livin'. When dey were healed, dey were so grateful dat they been helpin' me ever since. Da man-lovers were dumbstruck when I pried open da barrel and took me booty of silver out," Shamus smiled as he drank a swig of rum.

"I am surprised you would ally yourself with men so unpure in God's eyes," Garland injected.

"I don't have da same problem as Jesus has wit 'em. As long dey don't affect me coin pouch or me freedom, I could give a pelican's shite who dey be fookin'," Shamus spouted and started drinking again.

The door opened up and an attractive whore-turned-ship's-cook walked in. "Lads, dis be Teresa da scullery wench. She be Italian or Greek or sometin'. All I knows is I can't understand a g'damn ting she says, but she makes some great fookin' food. I also give'er work because I like da way her arse be lookin' when she bends o'er to set out me food," Shamus grinned.

Teresa then delivered the food to the table and the men did indeed predictably ogle her. "How did you come to owning the *Robin*?" Patrick inquired.

The Irishman took the rum down from his lips. "After a very difficult fookin' journey, we boarded at a room in Charles Towne. Dere was a lovely pub called da Pink House Tavern. Dey toss ropes o'r that sea wall so's we can sneak into da city for some food and pleasures. Dey got some decent women dere, but fookin' on those pads wit only a blanket hangin' between me and my whore and the whore and her sailor next to us was a wee bit fookin' awkward. It be tight quarters as it's a tiny buildin', but dey make the most of it wit a whore for every speck of the floor! Shite, I remember havin' to cram into a small space in da roof e'ery time the city's watchmen would come by, lookin' fer trouble. Damn self-righteous men of piety! We know good 'n' damn well dey get a good fook once in a while, too, in exchange for lookin' da other way! Well, the tavern hosted many fantastic games of liar's dice. I quickly found I had a gift for throwin' bones."

"You mean you have a gift for lying," April injected.

"Well, yes, dat too," the toothless man laughed. "Quickly, I built up a good bit o'jingle, but lost it just as fast. I admit, we did go back to Savannah once. I was havin' a spell of bad luck and needed some more o' the color. Da man-shaggers and meself 'eard rumors that Oglethorpe had a very expensive silk winder just sittin' in the trustee's garden wit no fookin' guards or anythin'. Normally I don't go makin' it a habit to be stealin' others things, but I figures Oglethorpe paid for it by stealin' da locals silver dat dey were forced to pay through g'damn crooked taxes. So you could say we 'liberated' bloody winder and gave it back to the people who paid for it, for a small fee of course." He shot a toothless grin across the table.

He continued, "After we sold da governor's prized toy we came back to Charles Towne. We stayed in dat town for years amassing a good amount of color from gamblin'. Twas about last month da locals finally got upset over losing so much and accused me of cheatin'. Dey ran me out o' town and we fled back to Savannah. We come back to Savannah about a month ago and, to me surprise, the *Robin* was in port. I march'd right up to da angry, fookin' kook-sooker Captain Gibbons, and offered him me winnings for da ship. Da greedy bastard immediately took da gold and retired into a life o' high society. Tis all that shite-eatin' captain ever wanted. I mean look how he dressed and talked like a dandy," Shamus paused to take another swig and a bite of fish.

"April Sky immediately knew I bought da barky and came to me askin' if I wanted to hire her as captain. I thought dere was no way a woman was going to captain me ship until I found out who she be. Once I knew da truth, I would be a fool not to take her on. Many of da g'damn crew left because dey would not sail under a woman. You'll see a few familiar faces from da

Robin's crew topside. And of course, a whole lot o' whores, God willin'," Shamus smiled.

April interrupted to change the line of conversation. "I found out from whoremaster Darden about Archibald's grim fate and how your group of friends were now known men. We have been trying to locate you since then. Miss Darden brought me news that your Scottish friends were trying to procure you passage out of Savannah. That treacherous bartender Jim Jaques betrayed our trust and drugged you with high amounts of laudanum in your rum so he could collect your bounty. You were only minutes away from having your neck stretched by redcoats when Sam and the whoremaster summoned help. Fifteen crew members dragged you to the docks through the secret pirate smuggling tunnels we had built below the pub a few years back. It was a good thing Sam recognized who you were. Actually, he recognized Isaac because it is pretty hard to disguise a hulking Jew of that size. We smuggled your bodies on the ship and cast off in the night. Patrick, I found your gold hidden in your pants while you were sleeping," she grinned.

Isaac interjected, "Sam, you still have time left on your indenture-hood. How goes it that you serve on this ship?"

"I purchased me freedom early thanks to a large, gray, stinky waxy ball that I found while fishing," Sam Scurvy proudly stated.

"I don't understand. Why would someone pay you for wax?" Patrick stated in confusion.

"Ya really are da worst sailor lad. He's talking about whale vomit from a sperm whale ya sheep-fucker," Shamus interrupted.

"That's correct. That huge stinking ball of ambergris was worth its weight in gold. It seems it smells very sweet as it ages and the ladies of high society pay a fortune for the perfumes made by it. The smell from it is supposed to also keep the black plague from taking hold of you as well matey. I was blessed to recover such a rare find," the bow-legged sailor grinned.

"Den he runs into me at da docks and I offered him a job as da sailing master. Sam has proven himself one helluva navigator. Now, if we could only find Jessup, we'd have da whole criminal gang again," the sunburned Irishman chimed in.

Sam answered, "Last I saw him was about three years back. He was making a good amount of silver as bonuses killing those whales. I heard a rumor he was lost at sea, killed by an angry right whale he was trying to spear but that could be just a story, who knows the truth?"

"Right whale?" Patrick questioned.

"Arrrr. When you hunt a whale, most will sink when you spear them. They are the 'wrong' kind of whale to harvest. The large baleen whales are the 'right' ones to harpoon. They float to the surface after they die and are easy to tow in," the fisherman explained. Sam then offered a toast, "Here's to Jessup, where ever he may be. Huzzah!"

"Huzzah!" the table repeated as they drank.

Next, Garland told her sad tale and even shared the details of her poisoning her captors.

"Remind me never to take a drink from ya, lass," Shamus taunted.

"Keep your cock out of me and you won't have to worry about it," she snapped back.

Isaac and Patrick recounted their complicated stories next. The table was surprised by how many adventures and near death experiences the two had been through in such a short time.

Miss Darden then explained how she made her fortune throwing private parties and secret orgies for the elite socialites of Savannah. She seemed to know everything about everyone and was an endless fountain of knowledge about Savannah's comings and goings. She bragged that her job really was to keep her mouth shut. The curvy blonde had scandalous dirt and gossip on everyone in that town. April employed her to run the whores and to keep them safe. She said she was threatened with murder many times for the secrets she kept and did not feel it was safe to live in Savannah anymore. She shut down the Red Lady and eight of the prostitutes came with her to the *Robin*.

"Now that all of our dirty secrets are out, tell me, wife, who are you really?" Patrick asked.

The room quieted and the diners pulled their seats closer to hear her every word.

"Let me tell you what I have been up to, me wolf, since we last sailed. We sold the cannons to some Spanish and French privateers and even made enough profit to keep a few. We mainly have been running rum since that large sale, except of course when we ruined Oglethorpe's siege of St. Augustine. If he knew it was my ships that ran the blockade and resupplied the Spanish town, all of us would have walked the plank. Anyways, that is not why I had this meeting, we need to discuss more important matters." Her mood darkened and her tone grew serious.

April began, "A few of you know my real name and a little about me, but none of you know my whole story. I am going to tell you, but only because you need to know the truth for what I am about to ask you."

The captain first explained that all the diners would need to learn a little about pirating history to understand all she was about to tell. She explained England, Spain, and France all used privateers to attack each other. It was legalized pirating; as long as one did not attack their own country's vessels, the government would ignore their murder and stealing. For years, privateers attacked each other and made fortunes. When the countries made peace, they officially ended their privateer programs. This left many privateers out of work. They were addicted to the lifestyle and fast gold and would not stop. The successful privateers took to pirating. She reminded them how when people look back, they always forget that those governments created this problem. Foolish wars and policies gave birth to the scourge of the seas.

One of the most famous pirates was 'Calico' Jack Rackham. Like most pirates of that time, he harbored at Nassau, New Providence, a villainous den of ill repute that April wistfully stated she missed. A rich daughter of a South Carolina plantation owner lived in Nassau at the time with her ex-pirate husband, who turned informant for the redcoats. Her name was Anne Bonny and she was a real daisy. Men tripped all over themselves just to get a look at her. While frequenting the pirate pubs in Nassau, she quickly found herself smitten with Rackham. Since she was still married to a man she did not want, Calico Jack and her ran off together and took to a life of piracy. They were so skilled at this endeavor that the couple made most of their fortune attacking other pirates.

April continued her history lesson by explaining that in June of 1719, the pirate-couple boarded a Dutch merchant ship and, immediately following, the crew surrendered without much fight. All except for one brave soul who would not drop his sword. Jack was impressed with this display of courage and asked the soldier to join his crew and pirate with them. The soldier agreed and proved himself an excellent swordsman and sailor. That brave soul was named Mark Read. As time went by, Calico Jack noticed that Anne had taken fancy to this new sailor, Mark Read. Jack noticed them go off to be alone and in a fit of jealous man-rage, he broke in on their tryst and caught the half-naked lovers in the act. In that moment, Jack noticed that Mark had breasts and was stunned to discover he was actually a woman named Mary Read. Read had pretended to be a boy most of her life and was a successful cabin boy and later, a soldier. Despite Anne's affection for Read, Jack let her stay on the ship. It was even rumored they had a three-way relationship.

Eventually, Rackham's ship was captured in Jamaica because Jack's crew was too drunk to fight. The women were so enraged with their own crew's ineptitude that they actually attacked them before being captured. The whole crew was eventually put on trial in Spanish Town, Jamaica in 1720. All of the male crew, including Jack, were hanged. The two women were spared leniency because they were both with child.

Bonny and Read were both kept in a Jamaican jail where they delivered their babies. Mary and her baby passed away during child birth. It was rumored that Anne had her child there and that her rich father somehow bribed someone to smuggle

18th century wood cut of Mary Read

her back to Charles Towne.

Patrick interrupted April and asked, "Yes, everyone has heard this tale. It was indeed quite the scandal of its time but what's this tale got to do with you?"

April darkened around the eyes and projected a sense of fear in the room, "Husband, have you ever wondered how come the fact that I be a woman captain is overlooked and ignored by so many?　Didn't you ever wonder why I can dress like a tattooed harlot and people still do what I say and respect me? Any other woman dressed like this would end up in the pillory or worse. I am allowed this freedom to be who I am because people fear the rumors about me be true."

"To be honest, I did find that the whole situation around you was out of sorts," Patrick admitted.

"I am the last living pirate of those times that is still at sea. My true name is 'April Read' and I am Mary's younger half-sister. I was one of the bastard children my father left in his wake. Mary knew of me and reached out to me when I was young. Before taking to the seas again, she was married to a nice fellow and they made good money owning an inn located in Holland. When he died young, she was heartbroken and went back to pretending she was a man, taking to the seas again. She sent me money from the profits of the inn and paid for my passage to Nassau. I waited for her and grew up in the roughest, most treacherous city in the world. She never showed and I eventually found work as a whore and made a great deal of money from drunken pirates.

"I copied her ruse that she had been performing her whole life and dressed as a man known as Albert Read. When I heard the wild rumors in the taverns that there were two women pirates on Jack's ship, I knew that one of them must be my sister. I used me whoring profits to barter passage to Jack's flagship the Kingston. It was January 1720 and Calico Jack had a small fleet of ships he captured at that time. They always need able-bodied sailors, so they welcomed me aboard. Eventually, I was able to secretly disclose who I was to Mary. Only she and Anne knew I was a woman and they never told a soul. To this day, it be a secret that only few souls know.

"I only got to spend a few months with them, but Mary taught me a lifetime's worth of pirating during that time. I learned to handle a blade, sail, navigate, and run a ship. I also did some terrible things that I spent my life trying to atone for. We stole from and killed many souls in those short months. One night while we got protective tattoos, she instructed the man to draw a strange design on the inside my upper arm. Later she told me she had stopped at an island and buried all her share of booty there. If anything happened to her, the tattoo would lead me to her swag. She shuttled all that heavy gold from the ship to her secret location, in shifts. It took her an entire day to carry it alone and bury it. She knew she could not trust anyone. Mary convinced Jack to make me captain of two small merchant ketches and deliver some rum to New York. I left at the end of summer and said my goodbyes to my sister. I never saw her again. She and the rest of the crew were captured shortly after and died in prison. I carried on pretending I was a man and focused on smuggling.

"The governments that created pirates knew they had to clean up their mess so a war was declared against pirating. It did not take long. By 1725, very few pirates were left. I turned over my crew and hired a new crew who did not know anything of my past. I hired Captain K.T Brewer and his shady men to smuggle goods on these little vessels. We spent the next eight years making silver any way we could.

"When the colony of Savannah came into being, it was my opportunity to settle down and get away from the seas. I revealed that I was a woman to the crew. They had served under me and trusted my captaining for years so, after the shock wore off, they decided to stay on. They agreed to keep operating my ships while I set up a brothel in Savannah.

"What I quickly learned was how much I hated living under the rules of others. After years of living free, it was neutering to set up in a town under British control. I quickly realized I had made a mistake but had to earn enough gold to get a proper ship to live out the rest of my years on. Unfortunately, the wind be blowing me about in circles. All the gold I make seems to go out to all me employees living needs and such."

The group at the table looked around in stunned amazement at each. The tale they had just heard was hard to believe but plausible. It did fit many puzzle pieces together in Patrick's mind. "That is an unbelievable tale, wife. So what does that have to do with asking us for something?" Patrick queried.

"I am not so much asking you a question but making you men an offer. All of you have been victims of kings, rulers, government and other masters. I had a vision in a dream to make a vessel where all society's outcasts can live free. People are not pressed into service or purchased. They are free to come and go at any time. Those who chose to make a life on this ship can live however they please as long as they do not use force, threats or violence on another. I want a place to live without an authority telling anyone how we must live, a place where all deals are made with each other in a peaceful and voluntarily manner. We will use the teachings of the Freeman Society and have our own culture based on individual freedoms and liberty. Here you only have to answer to yourself. Lads, I offer you the opportunity to join this crew and help me build this vision into a fleet of freedom."

The men were taken back by this bold offer and thought

long and hard until Garland finally spoke up, "Are you not worried that if all of troublemakers live together in one place, that it will make it easier for the British to kill us all?"

"Darling, you're under the illusion that they can't round all of us up now one by one and kill us at any time they desire. I do not want to live a life of fear. I would rather be with the company of other like-minded people and enjoy my days. If the British come for us, they come. At least I lived free until then."

"Well, it is a great offer. What other realistic choice do we have since we are known men? There are very few places we can live without fear of death and the government stalking us. I accept your offer but I do have to go give my gold to Archibald's family and ask them to join us," Patrick answered.

"Garland is right about one thing; having an inexperienced crew would make us an easy target for privateers. We need a more formidable vessel and more crew to live safely in these waters," April continued.

"I might know a ship that could work but we are going to need a pile of gold to buy her," Sam spoke up.

"If I could only find the gold Mary left me, we could buy the ship and then some. If I could only figure out what this damn tattoo means. I have studied it for years and have gotten nowhere," the tattooed captain sighed in frustration.

Miss Darden calmly cut in, "Captain, I have not had time to tell you until now but my sources have finally revealed a name."

April Read's eyes lit on fire and she shot up from her chair.

CHAPTER 21

CHARLES TOWNE

"**D**andridge!" Whoremaster Darden belted out.

"You mean Mari Anna's family?" Patrick questioned.

"Correct. He is some sort of distant relative to them and lives near Charles Towne in South Carolina. He has made a small fortune in indigo and is a brother in the Freeman Society. I sent word to be on the look out to help a fellow brother. Captain, this was very expensive information to obtain," Miss Darden hinted.

April reached into her pouch and handed her a large handful of silver coins. "This should cover the cost. As always, dear, great work. Sam, take us to Charles Towne immediately. Well, husband, it is time you got better acquainted with our daughter and meet the rest of the crew."

The group left the table and headed topside as the scullery wench Teresa came in cleaned up. Patrick tripped over a black cat as it whipped between his legs.

"Lady Bias, please bring Tracy to us!" the captain ordered. A woman with extremely long brown hair and a throng of children following her appeared. She was holding the shy girl with red, curly hair. Tracy raised both arms out reaching for her mother. The child wore nothing but a linen nappy. "This is your daddy, Tracy. Give him a hug and a kiss," April said in a high pitched voice. Patrick leaned in for a hug. The baby was frightened by his scared face and recoiled, hiding her face in her mother's armpit. April sighed and made an excuse for the little redhead, "Well give it time, she is a shy one. We hope she will be talking any day now."

"This barky is mind touched. I would expect this craziness from a transport ship but not a pirate vessel. Look at all the women, cats and children everywhere!" Patrick barked.

"Well these women are widows or unwed mothers of bastard children. They had to bring their children along because they have nowhere else to go. Actually, the older ones are very useful. They help cook, clean, fish, and a few are excellent cabin boys. Over here are some of the whores you already know. This be Roxanne our Persian beauty and you remember the toast of France, Miss Tiphanie. We have six more women around here somewhere but they must be below deck right now." The two women waved at Patrick as April continued, "Of course, you already met the lovely Teresa earlier".

The captain continued her tour, "There are two more ladies who we picked up in our travels. This one here is a German woman with a busy mouth on her. The first time I saw her, I was smuggling muskets to our network in Charles Towne. She was on display in the center of town with her head and hands sticking out the stocks. She was still cussing in German about how evil the king's government was. Then two weeks later, I come back and she was then sticking out of a pillory. She was still cussing at the bloody backs walking by, asking them if they would do this to their children. I knew she was our kind of people and asked her to escape her life and join us. Say hello to Miss Bleish." Patrick waived at the woman who was busy writing in a book.

"I think she is writing a book about liberty and personal freedom in German, but none of us can understand her enough to know for sure. Over here, this attractive blonde young lady is named Audrey Scott. She comes from a family of pearl divers. She be one of the only women on this barky who actually knows how to swim. She been promising teaching the rest of us. She has dived up and down the coast and knows a ton of knowledge about the area. She is fascinated with the dead cultures that used to be here before the white man arrived. Be careful not to ask her about any dead society or she will talk your ear off. She was orphaned when British privateers killed her family and stole her family's ship. The only reason she escaped was because she was diving for pearls at the time of the attack. We took her in and we are glad we did. Even if it is just for the never ending supply of clams and oysters she brings up."

The short-haired blonde threw her muscular arms around April. "I have never heard my own plight told to me. Thank you for all your kind words and nice meeting your husband, finally. If you have the time, captain, there is a fascinating shipwreck around here to dive. "

April responded, "Not right now. We are on our way to Charles Towne to finally get some long awaited answers." Captain Read pointed up, "Up there in the rigging is where Shamus' hammock is, that crazy Irishman gave me the captain's quarters to live in while he sleeps in the wind. Oh, and over there, those shirtless sailors relaxing holding hands are Mr. Michael and Mr. James, the men Shamus rescued." They both waved as they sipped their grog from colorful wooden cups they recently painted.

The captain continued to stroll around the deck and making introductions. Patrick still found it very odd being introduced as her husband but found he enjoyed it after a while.

"Because we have so many ladies, we added two private shit hatches down in the bow of the ship. Anyone can relieve themselves out these small holes. The shit and piss falls right into the water. Of course the stubborn men sailors still use a pissdale. I always found the large lead buckets disgusting and they stink up the ship, too. I told them if they continued on using a pissdale instead of the head, they would be the ones bucketing out all that shit and piss when it is full," April insisted.

She walked by the helm and quickly became out of sorts. "Sailing master, report!" the captain yelled. Sam ran over to discover what she was upset with. April was very mad, "Are you trying to curse us all?! You want to put a vex on this whole voyage?! Why the hell is the compass out of its binnacle box? You know that the compass is run by spirit magic. Need I remind you it always has to remain hidden in its wooden box or its magical properties will curse us all?"

Sam belted back, "Captain, one of the children must have removed it. Hell, I still can't find the sounding weight and chip log. I am pretty sure a couple of those kids are playing with them. You have to keep these children away from the equipment or it will maroon us all."

"I agree," April answered. "Miss Bias needs help controlling these little sea monsters. I will get her some hands to help. See if the whore Margie is available. She seems to have a high tolerance for the wee little ones' antics."

As the sun started setting, Patrick saw his sister Garland and Isaac studying the small Torah the large man always carried on him. *It was nice to be at sea again* he thought as his wife hugged him from behind.

* * *

Half Moon Battery and the Watchtower of Charles Towne

After an hour of morning sex, the captain and her husband

ventured topside. "Look there," April handed Patrick the spy glass. "That is Charles Towne. Do you see the brick wall facing the water? Follow the wall to the middle and you will see the watchtower sitting on the half moon battery. In the bowels of the watchtower is where the pirate prisoners are to hang. This is hallowed ground for us pirates. Lots of souls I knew died dangling from those gallows. I can picture my friends trying anything to steal the keys to get out of their cells. One of my good friends Stede Bonnet was hung in this town at White Point, right there at the tip of the peninsula," she pointed. " was whoring in Nassau when I met him. He was sailing with Blackbeard then, but he went on to get his own barky. He told me he actually bought his pirate ship just to get away from his naggin' wife. Funny, I used to make jest and call him 'The Gentleman Pirate' because he bought a ship instead of stealing one, but now I find meself doing the same thing. Life is funny like that. I really do miss that man. Join me as we throw a shot of rum into the sea to show respect to their spirits." She uncorked a jug of rum, poured a mug full and flicked the liquid into the sea. "Don't ever let me forget to do that, husband. We must do it every time we see that prison," she stated reverently.

"We are going to land on the exact spot that the original settlers landed all those years ago. It used to have dirt ramparts and cannons to fight off the Spanish. All that is left these days are the palisade walls and a plantation. We have paid the owner enough silver to ignore us coming and going on his land. I will put on my more conservative outfit and cover me skin. I will also use my proper lady voice so as not to arouse suspicion. Hell, I might even wear a hat, just for you," she smiled.

The ship sailed in the marsh up a small river to the original landing site of the colony. The two left the ship and April instructed the crew to remain anchored until they returned. After a long walk, Patrick and April approached what was perhaps the oldest tavern and bordello in the southern colonies; it was Shamus's favorite stop in all of Charles Towne. It was a small, three-story building that stood out because of the pink

18th c. Dutch engraving of the hanging of Stede Bonnet in Charles Towne

exterior made with Bermuda Stone, a coral stone with a natural pink tint. Mulatto Alley, in which the Pink House Tavern was located, stunk of booze and urine in the rising heat and humidity. The smells, mixed with the other vivid aromas, made anyone want to vomit. Hung over men, from sailors to gentlemen and plantation owners, stumbled around groaning about having to start their day.

Patrick opened the door to the tavern and the bartender barked at him that they were closed for the next two hours to clean up.

"Good sir, we just need to eat and have a bit of refreshment, then we'll be on our way," Patrick stated as he ushered April inside.

"Alright then, come on in. We have some beef pasties with spiced apples already made," said the bartender as he opened a door to the small courtyard in the back. "Here, 'ave a seat out there. I know it's hot out but it's much hotter in here with the fire goin' fer that stew and more pasties."

"That sounds wonderful, sir," April chimed in oozing her charm to make the bartender loosen up a bit. She had dressed in her best lady's attire, a mantua with a pastel floral pattern and a peach petticoat to match. She noticed he kept looking at her hat and hair and decided this would be how she would work him over, assuming the barkeep had a thing for hair. "Tell me, sir, what is your name?" April asked, untying her hat ribbons and setting the hat down on the table.

"Leo, ma'am," he said as he unabashedly stared at her hair curled and pulled back. Patrick shot April a glance and she gave him a wink to let him know to follow her lead.

"Well, Leo," she began as she unpinned and untied the ribbons holding her hair back. This released her silky mane around her face and over her shoulders, bringing one's eyes straight to her exposed cleavage. "We are unfortunately in a bit of a rush. You see we are looking for someone that lives in Charles Towne." Leo was staring still and his jaw had dropped a bit. April knew she had him right where she wanted him.

"Leo," Patrick interrupted.

"Yes, sir," Leo snapped drawing his attention away from April's luxurious hair and cleavage.

"Might we have some spirits and our meals?" Patrick asked.

"Oh right, of course! Right away!" The bartender disappeared for a moment and Patrick looked at April with a sly grin.

"Oh, my dearest wife, you know how to work us men folk quite well," he said grabbing her hand.

"Living the life I've lived, I had better or I wouldn't be alive now!" she smiled.

Patrick and April surveyed their surroundings in this tiny, sandy space. Some old playing cards were tossed in a corner along with some dice and a broken mug. There were also some ropes coiled up by the wall. Patrick could only giggle, remembering Shamus's story that they were used to sneak pirates and sailors alike over the sea wall into the tavern.

Sounds could be heard coming from the opened windows above of women laughing and patting out make-shift mattresses. *The bordello and whores, no doubt,* April thought to herself. What a shanty compared to her own place back in Savannah. The entire size of the bottom floor was all of a dozen steps. She couldn't, or rather didn't, want to imagine what it was like for them two floors above in those crammed quarters. She, too, remembered Shamus's constant recounts of his trysts up those stairs for a bit of sex and even hiding in a space in the roof.

Leo reappeared with two plates with large pasties and a serving of spiced apples. The smell reminded Patrick how hungry he was. Keeping up with April's sexual appetite required constant sustenance. "Now for your drinks. We have some brew made at a plantation just outside the city. 'Tis very good! Would you like a couple glasses of that to try?"

"Sounds charming, Leo," April replied. "Thank you."

The bartender brought two large mugs full of frothy booze and set them on the table. "Now then. Since you are square with your meal, you mentioned you were looking for someone?"

"Indeed we are, Leo." April sipped on the sweet brew. Patrick looked on and was nearly embarrassed at how the bartender fell for her womanly wiles. He watched her throat move as she swallowed and watched her chest heave for breath in between gulps. Leo took in every seemingly miniscule move she made. Patrick wondered how this man survived working in a tavern and whorehouse if he fell for a woman this easily, but then again, April Read was an intoxicating lady. The scarred face man suddenly caught himself staring at her just like the bartender, as April finished off her pint.

"Oh my!" April exclaimed. "That is good brew indeed! Thank you so very much, Leo." She wiped the froth from her mouth and turned her body to sit directly facing him. "We are looking for a Mr. Francis Dandridge. Do you know him?"

Leo nodded, "Aye, that I do. His brother-in-law is a lawyer that got mixed up in some land dealings 'round these parts. They helped settle a few disputes for us. I think I saw him in town early today. He and John, uh...his brother-in-law John Prue, were paying a visit to the powder magazine."

"Oh wonderful! I'm so glad we will not miss him! But first, I want to sink my teeth into this wonderful smelling meal. Might I have another pint of that brew?"

"Indeed, ma'am. T'would be my pleasure."

"Hey, my love," Patrick whispered to April as Leo walked away to retrieve another drink, "might you get us all this food and drink for free while you are at it?" April cut him a look he didn't care for. "I was just saying...." he trailed off.

The tavern keeper returned with April's refill. "Leo, my boy. Would you care to sit with us?" Patrick asked.

"Ah," he stammered, not knowing how to react. "Ah, I don't know if I should."

"Oh that's nonsense," April stated. "Sit and have some conversation with us. We don't like quiet and working here doesn't make you a leper. Come on now, sit with us." April shot him a dazzling smile and patted a chair next to her, leaning over exposing her cleavage. He complied and sat next to April. "So, how do you know Francis?"

"Well, like I said, he helped with some legal issues and land disputes 'round these parts. Mr. Prue did the official work but Mr. Dandridge did all the leg-work, mediating and making the deals. Really it's because of him, we still have a job. See, most of the rich folk coming over from England don't really like this place, at least not publicly. I see many of their faces here at night but once the sun is shining, they are nowhere near this alley."

Patrick and April listened intently. They needed to get a feel for Francis to see if he was someone they could trust.

"Anyways, Mr. Dandridge checks on us now and again. He likes to know if there are any unjust abuses going on around here. Lots of times the whores take a beatin' from a sailor and it ain't right, but people will look the other way saying they deserve it. Maybe some do, but those that don't never see justice."

April liked the sound of this Dandridge fellow. "Well that is mighty charitable of him, I can't wait to make his acquaintance."

Leo smiled. He was reveling in this type of company. The pair appeared to be well off and people who are well off don't talk much to his kind. April continued using her womanly wiles to coax more back story from the bartender about his life. He was abandoned in London as a child and stowed away on a ship bound for the Caribbean. He was discovered and sold to a plantation owner in Barbados. Leo was bought as an indentured servant and worked with the slaves on a sugar plantation. It seemed that many common folks Patrick kept meeting had come over as an indentured servants, too.

After his seven years of servitude, Leo was released. Then he bartered passage to Charles Towne with the silver his former master gave him. Once there, he found himself at the Pink House Tavern and lost what was left of his silver to a foul-mouthed Irishman. The mistress running the bordello above took mercy and hired him as the bar keep. He has been working there ever since, tending the bar, helping with cooking, cleaning, and serving as the 'counter-watch watchman'. He explained that the rich socialites in Charles Towne kept trying to shut down the Pink House and other places of 'known debauchery'. They used citizen patrols and they started their own watch. When Leo saw a patrolman coming close, he would alert the ladies and patrons up in the bordello and they would hide in a storage space high up in the roof. Patrick and April could only grin as they matched pieces of Shamus's stories with

Leo's.

"So, ma'am," the tavern keeper said, still smiling at the company he had at the moment, "what is your interest in Mr. Dandridge? If you don't mind me askin' that is."

Patrick looked up at April. She had to be careful with her response. "Well, an old friend of ours said he could possibly help us with something. It's kind of private, ya know?"

"Okay, ma'am. No worries, I was just trying to keep the conversation going. I admit I am enjoying speaking with you." Leo looked at Patrick. "And your kind husband, ma'am."

"Oh I'm not worried at all, my dear Leo."

"What is yer friend's name? If he knows Mr. Dandridge, I might know him as well."

Without thinking she blurted out, "Shamus. Shamus Red...." April stopped talking as soon as she saw the bartenders face. He had turned bright red and that soft smile was now pressed into a frown. He began breathing heavily and the blood vessels in his temples and neck began to pop out. "Leo, my dear! Are you alright?" April laid a hand of concern on his forearm but he stared at her hand in disgust.

"Out! Get out now!" Leo screamed as he stood up and swatted April's hand away. "There ain't no person on this earth that can be a friend to that monster! That drunken, annoying Irish bastard swindled a whole lot of good folks out of their hard earned silver. Get out now!" Leo's chest and shoulders were heaving with full, deep breaths and his fists were clenched tight.

Patrick pulled a purse of silver out of his jacket pocket and threw it on the table. "Thank you for your meal and help, good sir." He grabbed April by the arm and pulled her out of the tavern. They could hear crashing sounds and breaking glass as they ran away. They had to leave Mulatto Alley quickly before too much of the wrong attention was garnered from the temper tantrum Leo was now fully engaged in.

"What a damn fool!" April exclaimed as they turned the corner onto Meeting Street and headed toward the powder magazine. "What in this world would cause a man to act like such an infant?"

"Well, April, Shamus is involved so it's very likely justified," her husband replied.

Patrick stopped and turned to look at April. She was trying not to smile, but once Patrick smiled they both laughed and ran to Cumberland Street where the magazine was located.

Once they arrived, they saw a cart pulling away. Fearing it was Francis they ran to the door of the magazine. "Sir, who was that gentleman that just left?" Patrick asked.

"Who is asking?" The proper-dressed man rebutted.

"I'm sorry. My name is Mr. Freeman and I am looking for a Mr. Francis Dandridge. We were told he may be here with his son-in-law, Mr. John Prue."

The gentleman surveyed Patrick and looked at April. She suddenly realized her hair was still down and she had left her hat in the tavern. Not the lady like appearance she had tried to keep while in Charles Towne. "I am John Prue and yes, that was my brother-in-law, Francis Dandridge. What may I do to help you?"

Patrick smiled and extended his hand, hoping to receive the secret handshake of the Freeman Society. John smiled, grabbed his hand and shook. No, John was obviously not in the club and not to be trusted. "We just need to speak with Mr. Dandridge about a business proposition. It's quite urgent we see him as time is of the essence."

"Ah! New business. We are always looking for new business. If it's here in the city, then I may assist you as I handle all of Francis's affairs in the city."

"Oh, no, sir. This is about indigo," Patrick answered. The whoremaster Darden had found out that Dandridge was successful in indigo and it would be a good fall back to keep nosy people from prying for more information.

"I see. That is definitely not my cup of tea then. Here, I'll draw you a map to his plantation in Stono. That's in St. Paul's Parish in Colleton County. Do you know where that is?"

"No, sir. If it's far, is there a carriage we can hire to take us out there?"

"Indeed, sir. In fact, come with me and I'll have a servant

take you there. We renamed him Linus to give him a less African feel. Is that well?"

"Very well, Mr. Prue. Thank you!" Patrick replied. They followed John to his house and he summoned a house slave, not a servant, something Patrick was not accustomed to seeing. "Linus, take them to Francis's plantation straight away. He was with me, but these two just missed him as he left the powder magazine."

"Yessir," the well-dressed slave responded.

The carriage was readied and within minutes the pair was heading to finally see Dandridge. Being from Savannah where slavery was still illegal, Patrick was finally exposed to a typical life of a Carolina slave. The way they were bought, sold and inherited just like cattle did not sit well with him.

April did not care for silence and struck up a conversation with Linus. After a few minutes the slave was feeling more at ease with Patrick and April. As they rode further away from Charles Towne, the slave shared a heartbreaking story of his cousin in Dorchester. Just a month ago, he was hung in a gibbet because he was accused of poisoning his master. The slave owner was a philanderer and his angry wife knew it. Linus dared to think that maybe, just maybe, it was the scorned woman who poisoned her husband and not his relative. His cousin was an easy scapegoat because paranoia against slaves still ran high after the revolt in Stono just a couple short years ago. Patrick remembered that was the revolt that Alick and Gloria had survived and were grateful they had not fallen to a similar fate. April, being a pirate, knew what it meant to be killed in a gibbet. No one should die that way, starving to death in an iron cage, especially an innocent man!

They turned off the main road and began down a road that was lined with planted fields. To their right was tobacco and to their left was the indigo, growing taller than Patrick. The odd plants were filled with what April could only describe as pink and green tiny bananas. Linus laughed at the reference and explained those were the flower buds and later, seed pods. She had to explain to Patrick that bananas were a sweet fruit grown in the Caribbean and even further south. She promised to get her husband some of the wonderful yellow fruit in the future.

They approached a two-story home built up a bit on a small hill to keep it from being flooded by the nearby tidal creek. They could survey about a dozen slaves in the fields and saw a blonde-haired woman on the porch reading to some children of all colors. This woman looked up and smiled.

"Hello, Linus! How are you?"

"Well today, Mrs. Elizabeth. How are you?"

"Very well. Thank you for asking."

"Mr. John asked me to bring these two to see your husband. Has he returned?"

"He has and he will be in as soon as his cart is unloaded. Will all of you please come inside for some water?"

"Thank you, ma'am," Patrick said.

"Children, we will finish this up later. You all get back to your chores now." The children giggled and scattered, some with water buckets to take the slaves in the fields and some with brooms and mops to clean the porches. "Please come in," Elizabeth said, opening the door for her guests.

"You have a lovely home," April said as she entered.

"Oh, thank you, my dear. It's not much to look at now but we work hard to keep a roof over our heads and to feed all those that depend on us. Please have a seat and I will bring some cool water. Linus, you too. Please sit."

"Thank you, Mrs. Elizabeth."

Elizabeth quickly returned with a tray of cups filled with water. "I would offer you some tea but it's so terribly sticky outside I can't imagine drinking something so hot right now."

"No, ma'am," Patrick said after a sip. "This is perfect!"

A tall gentleman in dirtied clothes, unruly brown hair, and bright green eyes entered the house. He was startled by the sight of company, but smiled when he saw Linus. "Linus! Did you miss me already?"

"Yessir! Always, Mr. Francis!" Linus replied laughing.

"And who do we have here?"

Linus stood and gestured toward the pair on the lounge.

"This is Mr. and Mrs. Freeman. They wish to speak with you about business with indigo. They tried to catch you at the magazine and Mr. John offered for me to bring them here to meet you."

"Thank you, Linus, Might you go help Elizabeth with dinner since we have extra company?"

"Yessir," the slave said with a slight bow.

"Feel free to stay for dinner, Linus. You know you are always welcome here."

"Thank you, Mr. Francis, but Mrs. Francis needs me at home right now since Mr. John works late. She don't like to be home alone."

"I understand. Do give her my love again."

"Yessir," Linus replied as he left the room for the kitchen with Elizabeth.

Francis turned to his guests as Patrick and April stood. Patrick held out his hand and was relieved to receive the Freeman's secret handshake.

"This isn't about indigo is it, Mr. *Freeman*?" Francis asked in a hushed tone.

"Can we talk more privately?" Patrick asked in a whisper. Francis nodded and escorted them up the stairs to his own bedroom.

April introduced herself and explained her connection to the former great pirate better known as Anne Bonny. Francis quickly explained that Anne's father had bought her out of imprisonment and brought her and her newborn daughter back to Charles Towne. Anne's father had already arranged a marriage to a local plantation owner by the name of John Burleigh.

Anne's daughter by Rackham was named Mary, in honor of her lost and beloved friend Mary Read. Burleigh had officially adopted her as his own daughter. Since then, Anne and John have had seven more children, the youngest being only two years old. The fearsome pirate had secretly settled into life on a plantation. It was a smaller one, but they frequented parties at the larger plantations due to the large inheritance that Anne had from her father. She enjoyed the attention she gained at these gatherings.

"Can you tell us how to get to her home, then?" Patrick asked.

"I can, but she's not there." April's expression dampened. "Don't worry," Francis continued. "She's not far from here. She is at the Drayton's plantation on the Ashley River. There's a fowling party that started today and will likely last until tomorrow. I will give you directions and a carriage; I'll have to empty it though. It's still got a few things loaded on it from my visit to Charles Towne today."

He wrote out some instructions on how to get to the Drayton plantation just as Elizabeth began to call for supper. "Stay tonight. Eat supper with us, sleep well. Then you may journey in the morning."

"I was really hoping to see her now," April said with disappointment.

"I understand. However, you do not want to be out at night. There is always a risk of running afoul with some thieves in the night. Please, I beg you both, stay for tonight. Had Anne been home you could see her tonight, but I don't want you traveling to Drayton's in the dark."

"He speaks wise words, my dear wife," Patrick said as he smelled the heavenly food.

"You are right, my wolf." she sighed deeply.

Before the four of them could sit down to eat, Patrick could not help himself and had to ask about the Dandridge's slaves. "I have no experience as a slave master, but I doubt any others are as friendly and respectful to their slaves. I even saw Elizabeth teaching the young ones how to read."

"We tell most people who ask that it is because educated slaves are worth more and we are building our investment. Honestly though, it is because we found out if you treat them with kindness and respect they work harder. If you give them just a little taste of freedom and they believe they are free, they are much more productive," Mr. Dandridge explained.

April cut in, "My dear husband, most rulers have used that

line of thinking for years. Everyone who lives in the colonies is a slave to a degree. Being a slave means that someone else takes your labor by threats or force. When any king or government taxes you they are doing just that, taking your labor by threats and force. The only difference between the Dandridge's and Linus is the percentage of their labor that is stolen by someone else. If you think about it, we live on one giant plantation with a few elite politicians owning us all."

"She is dead reckoning with her thoughts, I see why you married her. It really tears at our morality and attacks our conscience about owning slaves. We hope to find another way someday to run a farm profitably without them, but right now I have no idea what that way is," Mr. Dandridge confessed. The rest of dinner was filled with lively debate about ideas of liberty.

He and April slept well in the main house and arose to a large breakfast. They ate and dressed in fancy party clothes provided to them by Francis and Elizabeth. They bid good bye to their new trusted companions and left behind this grand land, heading along the river to the Drayton plantation.

They couldn't believe what they saw when they arrived. There were high society people everywhere and so many slaves they couldn't even guess at how many there were. The fields were expansive and they were growing so many things that neither April nor Patrick could identify most of the crops. A house slave boy offered to stable their horses and cart and Patrick asked him if he knew the Burleighs. The boy nodded and pointed toward the river.

"Is Mr. Burleigh shooting today?" Patrick asked.

The boy laughed. "No, sir, of course not! Mrs. Burleigh always shoots!"

April laughed out loud as the boy led the horses away. "That is certainly not a surprise!" They approached the fowling party along the river and watched as a clay ball was thrown into the air.

On the way to the river, many slaves could be seen beating the scrub brush. Some game would spring out and two aristocratic socialites would fire their fowlers. The firelocks were lighter muskets, but extremely long and fancy. Recently, fowling was all the rage in upper class society and it was a status symbol to own one of these ornate guns. The muskets were loaded with small bird shot and people were absolutely amazed to see a bird hunted right out of the air. April chuckled as she saw a slave holding a very popular book called "Pteryplegia: Or, the Art of Shooting-Flying" while a nobleman socialite was reading it trying to figure out why he kept missing. The two made their way quickly down to the river.

Crack! Bang!

A clay ball exploded in midair. They followed the smoke to its origin of a classy dog-lock musket resting in the hands of a black haired beauty. It was Anne Bonny.

At long last, April was looking upon her adopted sister after all these years. Her heart sang and it was all she could do to hold back the tears now welling up in her eyes. Anne was laughing and certainly enjoying being the center of attention. The ex-pirate had turned to talk to her husband, but her eyes fell on April and the smile on her face dissipated.

April motioned Anne over so they would not have listening ears around them. Anne nodded and graciously excused herself to her admirers as she walked over to join the tattooed woman. She looked at the party-crashing woman from head to toe, trying to assess her identity. She saw a tattoo of a black cat peeping out of her cleavage and smiled. "I thought it was a rumor, but damn me, you're still alive somehow. I can't believe I am standing before little April Read after all these years. I heard rumors of a tattooed woman who pretended to be a man and captained her own ketch. I thought it would be too much to hope that you lived through the great pirate extermination," Anne whispered.

"I thought you died. It was not till recently I found out you and your child were smuggled out and that you be living a new life as a house maiden. I see you in front of my own eyes and I feel like I am conversing with a ghost. Is it really you in there, Anne?" April questioned.

The former pirate Bonny grinned as she pulled down her

neckline exposing a small black feline in her cleavage. Both women giggled and embraced. "Look, as much as I would love to host you for days, you're a known woman and it is not safe for me or my family to be seen with you. I had to leave my past behind. A few people here have figured out my true identity, but I always deny it and they can't prove it is me. I am now called Mrs. Anne Burleigh, mother of eight and church goer," the ex-pirate said proudly.

18th century engraving of Anne Bonny

"I am not here to expose you. I just need some information that only you know. A few months before you all were captured and put on trial, Mary made you stop over for a day at an island to go bury her take of plunder. I think I can find it with your help. I just need the name of the island in the Caribbean she held up at," April pleaded.

"Hmmm..." Anne looked in the air and scratched her head

trying to recall.

"I think you are mistaken. It was no island in the Caribbean she stopped at, but I do remember the island you seek. It used to be called Hilton's Head on my old sea charts. I think these days people call it John's Island after the current owner John Casgoine. I had thought many times over the years of going to hunt the treasure myself, but Mary Read never shared with me where she buried it. Good luck finding it. She never left a map, damn her. I am just dreaming anyway. I could never get away with all my children," Anne smiled as she reflected. The ex-pirate continued, "Speaking of children, I have a wonderful surprise for you. You see the lady over there dressed all fancy like her father, that's Jack's child. I named her Mary after your sister died during childbirth."

April grinned and glowed, "That was a fine thing you did for Mary!"

"Well I have one more surprise for you and it is a big one!" Anne smirked. "It is true that Mary died giving birth, but her baby did not. I became ward of the little girl. I nursed them both and brought them back to Charles Towne with me when my father purchased my freedom. My parents were mortified with the whole jail incident and wanted nothing to do with Mary's baby. They gave the baby to the slave staff to raise and even gave her a name different enough that nobody would ever know it was Mary's child. They named her Nina and she was a servant until she was married recently to an arse of a man."

April stumbled back and held Patrick so as not to fall. "This whole time I have had a little niece, right here in Charles Towne. I want to pinch myself. So many times I have smuggled cargo into this city, been so close to you and Nina and never known."

"She is right over there with her jackarse husband, you need to meet her." Anne shouted towards Nina, "Nina, please join us!"

April sized up Mary's daughter and her husband as she approached. Nina was a lovely thing, donning long brown, curly hair, cute sun freckles, and a rail thin build, just like her mother. As she got closer, Calico Jack's appearance was obvious in her eyes. "My dearest Anne, who are these lovely folks you are keeping all to yourself?" Nina expressed friendliness.

"Dear, I don't know another way to put this so I will just say it. This is your real mother's sister. This is your Aunt April," Anne confessed.

The thin young woman stared quietly at April, walked closer, and took a good look at her. Nina threw her arms around her and hugged, "So it is true, you really are still alive. Please tell me you have come to take me away from this life and my mind-numbing job of serving rude society women."

"You mind your place, woman. Be glad I rescued you away from the slaves' house," her husband reprimanded her.

"It's true, dear. I loved your mother very much and I miss her every day. I just found out about you a minute back or I would have come for you long ago. I had no idea you existed. Hell, nobody did. I am truly sorry." She ran over and hugged Nina.

All three women had a good cry and hugged each other for a long while.

"Well, lass, I am going to make this lost time up to you. Come with us sailing," the tattooed woman offered.

Nina's husband cut in, "I am Julius Chessher and your niece is my property. She is not going anywhere without my say so."

"I am going to hunt down Mary's buried treasure. I figure Nina is due a good share of that gold!" April dangled the offer.

"Gold you say? Well now that is altogether different. I could use that gold to finally establish my family's name in this town," Julius calculated. "Very good, let us go get our gold, wife."

Nina hugged April again and whispered, "Thank you," in her ear.

"Well, lass, you will have to leave your things behind and come with us now," the captain commanded.

Mr. Chessher replied, "We are ready for travel. We will buy anything we need with my gold, I mean our gold, when we return."

"I would love to catch up more, April Read, but we are

already bringing too much unwanted attention to ourselves. You have to go before questions start. Nina, I will explain your sudden departure to your friends. Good luck in your hunt," Anne stated as she gave them one last hug.

The group of four left the party and returned the carriage and clothes to Mr. Dandridge. Mr. Dandridge drove the group back to the original landing site of the Charles Towne settlers. They said their goodbyes as they hastily made their way back to the *Robin*.

Once on board, April introduced Nina and Julius to the crew. It only took a matter of seconds before Julius was condescendingly giving orders to the women crew members to bring him food and drink.

"Sam, we have our heading! Take us to Hilton's Head Island. Sorry. I think people be calling it John's Island now," April ordered.

As the *Robin* sailed into the sunset, Nina and April held hands and shared stories of their lives. Patrick had never seen his wife glow like that before, and at that moment, she was the most beautiful thing in this world.

CHAPTER 22

HILTON HEAD'S BOOTY

The *Robin* could not catch a good wind and was making its way slowly down the coast. The rumor that they were going treasure hunting circled wildly among the crew. Now the captain finally had an island. Hopefully, she could possibly unlock the mystery of the tattoo. Patrick, Isaac, Sam Scurvy, Nina, Julius and Shamus all took their turns trying to decipher it. The tattoo was rather simple. It was three circles near each other with an X marked on the inside edge of one. Under was a symbol that looked like the letter "U" and it had the number "twenty east." The group moved closer to study April's markings.

"Maybe it has something to do with moons and shadows, you know, like a shadow map," Isaac speculated.

Shamus took a guess. "Maybe those circles represent waves, and maybe Mary Read sank the treasure."

Patrick agreed, "Shamus might be right. Perhaps the shapes could be under water reefs."

Sam Scurvy took a stab, "They could be reefs, but I don't remember any shaped liked that on my charts."

"Do you think they are actually the letter 'O'? Perhaps there is something on the island that has a triple 'O' name like the 'Olive Octopus Outcrop' or something," Julius injected.

"I have never heard of such a place. Shut your mouth and stop being an idiot," Sam denounced.

April studied the tattoo for the thousandth time. "The best I can come up in all these years is they represent hills or mounds."

Patrick's attention was stolen away when Audrey Scott started to approach. He noticed her muscular body she had developed from a life of diving and swimming. She was wearing worn out men's diving clothes but was adorned with an extremely expensive pearl necklace she made for herself from her dives. This woman was indeed odd. He had never even seen a woman swim and it was unheard of that one would work as a diver in all those tight clothes. He finally came to accept that if someone was an extreme oddity, they would somehow find a home on this ship. The *Robin* had quickly become a haven to the outcasts of society.

April sighed in frustration, "We are never going to figure this damn clue out. Perhaps we should just go to Blackbeard's island and treasure hunt there instead. It is just south of Savannah anyway and it is rumored he buried a fortune in those sands."

Patrick greeted the young lady diver and invited her to make a guess. The short-haired blonde woman walked up and stared at April's arm. "You say we are going to Hilton's Head?"

The captain replied, "We are, but looks like we will just sail around it aimlessly because we cannot figure out the riddle of these markings."

"Don't let the wind blow your mood in circles. I think I know where to find your booty," Audrey smiled.

The group was silent and stared at the diver in anticipation. She continued, "These circle markings look like the ancient Indian shell ring mounds. The shell rings are laid out just like your markings in your tattoo. Nobody knows who really made the rings but rumor is it was an ancient Indian tribe thousands of years old. Scholars argue that the tribe lived in the middle of these rings and used to throw their waste to the edges. Over time the mounds of shells served as a wall to protect them. If you want my opinion, I think it was a huge midden or garbage mound but..."

April cut her off, "I don't need a history lesson right now, dear. Just tell me if you can take me to these shell mounds."

"I would love to study them some more. I would be happy

to see them again," the young woman chirped.

Excitement swept over the crew, but the captain's experience from her pirating days reminded her to be cautious with whom she trusted. She remembered how large amounts of treasure made normally sane folks go mad with gold fever. She knew the smaller the search party, the better. She picked Audrey, Patrick and Nina. Julius threw a fit and demanded he join the party. "Nina has pirate blood flowing through her, she cannot be trusted. I will escort her or I will forbid her to go."

Audrey instructed Sam of the location to anchor off Hilton's Head Island. The group of five rowed to the beach and started making causal talk.

"So, April, how have you been making profits over the last months in order to keep this crew feed?" Patrick asked.

Julius snickered, "I did not see a crew, what crew? I saw a bunch of women, children, convicts, and slaves."

"You best be keeping your tongue tight when talking about me crew. Yes, most of them might be women, but they have been trained in the ways of sailing now and are getting damn good. These days they be as capable as any pirating crew I ever captained. Speak poorly of them again and you can swim back to Charles Towne," the captain threatened.

Julius was taken back that a woman dared speak to him with such arrogance, but could not respond in a coherent sentence.

"Ah...so 'mum' be the word I see. Wise man," April said condescendingly.

Nina grinned at April. She really enjoyed seeing her husband stood up to by a woman.

"To answer your question me wolf, we made most our fortune running illegal spirits to Savannah and whoring on the open waters. We sail to other merchant ships and mirror their route while the whores go over and shake the gold out of their sacks. In short time, we have turned a respectable profit," the tattooed woman explained.

The small jolly boat ran a beach and the group of five dragged it ashore. Audrey led the treasure hunters through the thick underbrush and marsh. It did not take long for the Island's sand gnats and mosquitoes to discover the new meat. Julius was getting eaten alive by the hungry bugs to Nina's delight. The group slowly made their way to the ancient mounds.

"So, wife, where did you find the male crew on the *Robin*?" Patrick questioned.

April dodged a snake on the ground and causally stated, "A few stayed on when I purchased the barky but most these men are cast offs, too. We have a few slaves on the run, a few political prisoners and some fortune seekers. We will need to find many more as soon as we add the next ship to our fleet."

Indian Symbol for tribe migration

Audrey interrupted, "Look at this ancient Indian marking on this stone." She pointed at a symbol of a round spiral attached to a square spiral. "In most Indian cultures this is a symbol left behind to tell others they have migrated and moved to a new village. That explains what might have happened to them. Ah, we are finally here! We have to walk around it to the opening unless you want to climb a wall three men high made of sharp oyster shells. It's truly amazing to think of how many years of eating oysters this took to make. Think about how these ancient Indians were able to catch and harvest them without any of the modern equipment we have today. All they would have had was a canoe and great spirit. I bet if we look at the other rings we would find..."

The captain cut her off, "We be here to find gold, lass, not to answer age old questions about dead Indian cultures."

Audrey sighed, "I want to come back here soon after you recover your booty. I hope you can drop me off for a few days to study."

They walked into the entrance of the massive ring and took the view in. The tattooed woman gasped, "You are right, Audrey, it is impressive. I will definitely let you come back and look around. Now let's look at this tattoo. Are you sure that this be the right ring, Audrey?"

"Yes, captain, this is it. Where should we dig?" The blonde diver replied.

"That is what this old pirate symbol means, dear. It looks like a fancy letter "U" with a number. That is a symbol meaning we need to look for a seat and we be needing the compass now. Everyone spread out, we are looking for a seat either carved out of the shell or on a rock," April Read commanded.

The group searched for a half hour in the hot sun until Nina called the group over. "I found this large rock and look here, a letter 'U' is carved in it. This has to be it, Aunt April!"

The captain carefully removed the compass out of its binnacle and sat in the indention worn in the great rock. She watched the magical powers of the compass point north and then found dead east. She stood up staring at the compass and started pacing. "...Eighteen, nineteen, twenty! Get your spades out and let's find Mary's gold!"

The excited group dug a large hole at a frenzied pace until Audrey's shovel hit something with a thud. April, Patrick, and Audrey dug vigorously until the chest was free. The three of them joined forces and exhumed the fancy wooden box.

"That will be enough, ladies. Put your hands on your heads and step back," Julius shouted. The three spun their heads around to see the aspiring aristocrat was holding a knife to Nina's neck and pointing his flintlock at April. "Stand up slowly and unbuckle your belts. I want all your weapons piled up over there. Do anything flashy and I open her neck up," he warned.

Julius, Nina and April find a treasure chest!

"You fucking bastard! We would have got our share. You greedy piece of dog shit. My aunt did not have to give us anything at all," Nina spit as she helplessly tried to wrestle from Julius's grip.

"I only married you because I was paid to by your ward. With this gold I can leave you and finally live the life I deserve," he spit back.

The three stepped away from the chest and did what they were told. A pile of pistols and blades were now on the ground. "Step far away from your weapons. Now, *Captain*, go unlock that chest!"

The tattooed woman walked over and kneeled down in front of the heavy wooden box. She slowly pulled out a skeleton key from her dress. She examined the chest slowly until Julius lost his temper. "Just stick the fucking key in the front there!" he angrily ordered.

"That is just a dummy plate. It's not a real lock. It's to keep shit-stains like you from knowing how to open them" April cursed.

Filled with rage, Julius belted Nina across the nose knocking her to the ground. "Keep insulting me, you whore, and I will keep beating your niece!" he yelled.

April capped her anger and kept explaining calmly, "It is an old pirate tradition to hide the lock in the hinge. This key should open any lock." She fiddled with the skeleton key for a moment until a click could be heard coming from the hinge.

"I care not a beaver shit about your annoying pirate traditions. Just open the bloody chest and let me see my gold."

She flung the lid open and a gold light danced across her face. April gazed up at Julius and spoke softly, "It is a shame you don't want to learn about old pirate traditions, as there is one I really like."

Click. Crack! Julius's face filled with confusion as he looked down to see his life oozing down his chest.

April mocked, "Us pirates also have a tradition of burying a loaded pistol with our gold." Mary Read had left April an extremely rare Swedish Boarding Axe Pistol. The weapon was a doglock with a vicious axe head and a spiked tip forged onto the front of the muzzle, making it half-axe, half-pistol.

Julius stumbled and lost his balance. He raised his firelock and was desperately trying to steady his aim when Nina rose up and punched him in his testicles. The captain used this distraction to make her move and swung the axe pistol at the man's firelock. A pinwheel of blood showered Nina and April as the arrogant man's pistol and hand went flying through the air. Julius doubled over in pain, but still tried to move into a killing position with his knife over Nina. April lunged forward driving the spike of the axe head through Nina's husband's eye. The body fell limp into the sand and shells. Nina stood over the dying man and kicked him again. "I hope the devil has his way with you, Julius!" Her husband's hands and feet twitched while

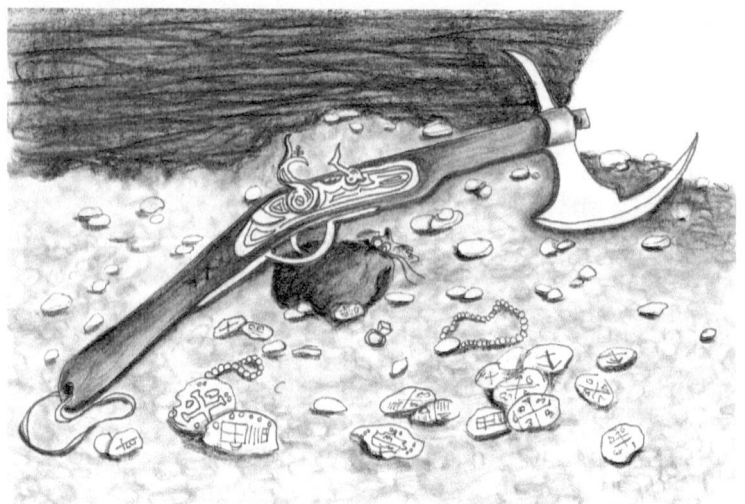

The rare Swedish boarding axe pistol

he lay face down in his own pool of blood. Nina spit on his body as his soul left it.

The niece then ran to her aunt and hugged her as she cried. The two embraced while Patrick grabbed his musket and checked the body to confirm it was lifeless.

Nina's mood quickly changed as she wiped away the tears away with her sleeve. "Leave that piece of shit for gator food. How rich are we?"

The four closed ranks around the chest and their eyes lit up. The chest was filled with a collection of gold and silver coins from all over the world. Leather pouches of pearls and rare gems were buried in the heavy rounds. Fabulous necklaces and rings were found mixed in pokes of pearls. More treasure than they ever imagined would be in this old wooden chest.

The group was giddy, jumping up and down like children. April reached in the pile of jewelry and handed Audrey a large, elegant, ruby pendant. "This would look good hanging on your pearl necklace. Take this matching ring, too. You have definitely earned them. Thank you for helping us recover this booty. Now we return. We must keep this quiet from the crew. Even though I trust them, gold gives people a fever. Just look over there," she spoke gravely as she pointed at Julius's corpse. Everyone nodded and agreed to tell nobody of the contents. She closed the chest and asked Audrey to hide the pendant for now. The wooden box was so heavy that it took all four people to carry it. The group would walk a short ways and then stop, set the chest down, and rest for a while. It took all day to get their booty back to the *Robin*. They talked as they shuffled along.

The niece stated to her aunt, "I can't believe that pistol axe actually fired, the powder had to be primed for over a decade."

"Well, your mother followed another pirate tradition; she stuck a large bag of salt next to it in the chest to keep the powder dry. If you keep asking questions, soon you will know all our secret tricks."

"I have been thinking, aunt. I don't want to go back to that life. I want to stay with you. So instead of giving me a share of your treasure, I would rather you keep it. I would like an interest in the profits of the new ship you're getting. I want to invest this gold back into you," the niece offered.

"That is a very wise idea, niece. Once you spend this gold it will be gone forever, but buy a business and the gold never stops coming. I will work out a fair offer for you," April Read smiled.

The group loaded into the jolly boat and returned to the *Robin*. They did their best to hide the chest and covered it with a large cloth, but the crew obviously saw something heavy being lifted and loaded aboard. The four tried to carry the wood box to the captain's quarters without attention, but failed miserably. Once the swag was safely in her quarters she beckoned for Sam Scurvy and Isaac. The men ran down into her chambers in excitement. Isaac looked around confused and asked, "Where is Julius?"

"Oh it was terrible, the gators got him" Nina smiled slyly.

April cut in "Now, Sam, tell me where I can buy a good ship!"

* * *

Marian was startled at the sound of the pounding on the door. Heather ran into Marian's room and sat on the bed with her, armed with a pistol and a few items from her growing collection of blades. The twins ran to the door. Amos was armed with a musket and cowering behind a chair, while Maximilian stood at the ready by the door. He had his left hand on the door handle and his dirk in his right hand in the air ready to strike. In his best, deep voice Maximilian called, "It be a late hour, stranger! What be your business with us now?"

"Lad, it be your Uncle William! Lemme in before da lobster backs get here!"

Maximilian lowered his dirk and hastily opened the door. "Redcoats?" he asked in shock, "What are the English doing heading here?!"

William burst in and before he could say another word he noticed the twins' positions. The two were ready to take out anything unfriendly on the other side of the door. "Aw, me nephews! Know dat yer dad is proud of you two for being on your toes like dis!" Amos emerged from behind the chair as Maximilian closed and locked the door. "Amos," William continued. "Get yer mum and your sister. Hurry up now!"

Within two minutes, the family was sitting around the table as William explained what had happened and how they were found out. The large bounty on their heads that Kingsley put up attracted many loyalist eyes. Someone had seen and recognized Isaac working on the farm a few months back. A mammoth of a Jewish man in a Scottish village was pretty hard to hide. The redcoats shook down some fur traders who have traveled to the colony of Argyll and they fingered Isaac.

"I got word that the lobster backs were on their way and I came by sea to beat them here. I did not beat them by more than an hour, now hurry!" William explained.

With his story finished, William ordered the girls to pack only the bare necessities that could be carried on their backs. He then ordered the twins to gather the Dandridge and Quinn families. "Make haste, everyone!" he exclaimed as he began to pack pouches with gunpowder and shots.

Maximilian ran to the Quinn house and raised everyone. He spared the details only saying the redcoats were on their way to arrest and execute everyone for murder and treasonous acts. They wasted no time in jumping out of bed and grabbing bags they already had packed. They always feared that at some point this dream life would come crashing to an end. The British intended to ensure the whole world was ruled under England's thumb, no matter the cost.

Amos ran to the Dandridge home and pounded on the door. "It's Amos! Wake up!"

Mari Anna opened the door and yawned as she asked, "What is it, Amos?"

"It's the redcoats, Mari Anna!" Her eyes popped open, wide-awake, as Amos burst through the half-opened door and began gathering their weapons for them. "They're comin' for us for murder and treason. Go! Wake your family and grab only what you need! We're leavin' now!"

Within about ten minutes, all of the fugitive families were standing in front of the Freeman home. Heather looked back at the home she had learned to love and the life of freedom she had grown accustomed to. She began to cry as Prudence and Mari Anna grabbed each of her hands. The inseparable trio walked together as the Quinn's cart and horses began to move to the path leading to the nearby coast. The twins walked out in front, fully armed and fearless, nothing would take them from their solemn duty of protecting this hurriedly-packed group of families. They had lost their dear father and would lose no more!

Marian stood, staring at the moon. William walked up to her side and put a reassuring arm around her shoulders.

"Dat baby o' yours will do fine, lass," he said.

"Oh, of that I have no doubts," she smiled at William. Her gaze turned back to the silvery moon high in the night sky. "I can't decide if I want to bless or curse the moon for being full tonight. I'm grateful for a light for our journey, but I fear it'll make us easier targets for the British."

"T'is a blessin', Marian. Never forget Duncan is always watchin' over all of you! He will guide you when you need guidance and protect you when you need protectin'." The two hugged and Marian fought back the tears welling in her eyes. "It will be alright, lass. Now, let's go." The pair began to walk away from the house when Marian stopped and ran back without a word.

"Marian!" William shouted after her. "Come back! What 'er ya doin', ya crazy lass?!?" He followed her and grabbed her by the arm.

"Turn me loose, William! The books! I left the books! I have to have those books!"

He let go of her arm and nodded. "Aye, but make it quick!" William suddenly felt a chill run up his spine and he made his firelock ready. "Thanks for the warning, Duncan," he muttered under his breath, taking aim at the brush he had first emerged from when coming to evacuate the families.

Marian grabbed the leather bag containing the now sacred books of liberty, baptized in Archibald's blood. She, too, had received the chill, the omen from her dead husband of danger looming. She quietly stepped on the porch to see William aiming at something on the edge of their property.

"William," she whispered.

"Stay put, lass," he said quietly. "I'll draw 'em out. When they get their first round shot, you run fer it and out leg um."

"I'll not leave you, William!" she shouted through a whispered tone.

"No, you won't. I will be right behind you, I swear it!" William stepped off the porch and into the moonlight. Marian watched helplessly and she rubbed her stomach, as if to tell the baby that it was going to be alright. The baby knew something was amiss and would not stop moving inside her. With her other hand, she clenched the bag of books tightly and held them to her chest, as if to tell the books that it was going to be alright, also.

"FIRE!" came a disembodied command from the tree line.

CRACK! POW! CRACK! BANG! There came a series of shots with puffs of smoke rising into the moonlight. William fired his musket simultaneously and heard a man scream in agony.

"Ha!" William shouted as Marian ran past him. "Got one of you pathetic bags of rat shit!" he shouted, taunting his dropped target. He ran behind Marian, with his claymore drawn, trying to escape the next round of shots. Marian and William ran hard and cleared the field in time. As they approached the group, Marian felt a sudden rush of panic as she suddenly realized that she could very well soon be watching her children die just as Archibald had died in front of her. "Run!" she screamed, tears now streaming down her face. "Run! They're here!"

"We heard the shots," Mr. Dandridge said as he met up with William and Marian, carrying an extra loaded musket for William. "Mari Anna, take this and hop in the cart. Get it reloaded quickly," he commanded his daughter, handing her William's musket.

"We've got such a long push to the coast, we'll never make it," Prudence began to weep.

"Now is not the time for panic, dear," her father said as he embraced her with a free hand. "Now, let's get that musket loaded and get these horses runnin' faster."

* * *

Patrick stood in awe of the swamp before him. "I can't believe this, Isaac! Another damn swamp! I will be more than happy to spend the rest of my life aboard the new Ship of the Line and never have to see another bug or swamp again!"

"You really need to stop whining," Isaac said. He was no more thrilled to be traipsing through the swamp than Patrick was but whining was not going to accomplish anything. "We'll all be happy to be together again and to welcome that new child to this world, so let's get moving before we miss the birth."

Patrick let out a big sigh. "You are right, my old friend." With a pat on the back, he began to fight his way through the swamp trying to find some higher ground. April and Sam were back at the Cape Fear dock trying to buy a larger ship. The model was called a Ship of the Line and had aboard it more cannons than the *Robin* did, the *Robin* only being a mid sized Galleon. The two ships would hopefully be able to comfortably fit the increasing number of people that were being taken in by April or, in other words, her collection of social outcasts that she called a crew.

"I do miss playin' 'hush puppy' with our mutt version of Garland," Patrick said. He remembered their days of living in the swamp, stealing arms and cannons from Oglethorpe's clumsy attempt on the Spanish.

"That was a good dog indeed Patrick, but I must tell you, I like the real Garland much better!" There was no concealing the smile on Isaac's face now.

"So I've noticed," Patrick said, half smirking. "I know that should it go that way, you'll be good to my sister."

"I have your blessing to court her then?" Isaac asked.

"My blessing?"

"Yes. Her father, your father, is dead. You are her guardian, her protector, but she would have to convert."

"Ah, good luck getting her to do that!" Patrick laughed. He stopped and turned to Isaac and put his hand on his hulking shoulder. "Yes, Isaac. You have my blessing." They embraced for a moment but were quickly interrupted by the sounds of hooves coming at them.

"Oh, this isn't going to be good, is it?" Patrick asked, getting his firelock pointed in the direction of the noise with Isaac following suit.

"Hold fire, Patrick!" Isaac said as he saw a cart carrying the Quinns approaching in full canter. "Whoa! Sovereign Quinn!" Isaac held up his hand and waved them down.

"No," Quinn stated breathlessly. "No stopping! The bloody backs have found us out! William got us out in time but they are right behind us!" Gun shots could be heard through the swamp.

"Where's Marian?" Patrick asked. His gut filled with worry

about her and the baby. Quinn pointed behind them.

They watched as the trio of girls ran toward them followed by the twins and their mother. The large Quinn and Dandridge families followed next in line. Last, but certainly not least, was a Scot, dancing around in his kilt and shouting in his native tongue as he dropped another soldier.

Amos had a wound to his shoulder, but he shrugged it off. "It's only a flesh wound," he said without skipping a beat, reloading his musket and pistol. Isaac and Patrick ran out to meet William in what was now a battlefield for the safety of their extended families.

"Aye! Be damn good seein' ya, boys!" William exclaimed as he saw Patrick and Isaac run up to him.

"Good thing you are already heading to the Cape," Patrick said. "We have a plan!"

"Good!" William shouted. "'Cause I'm shit out of ideas!"

"Just keep pushing toward the Cape Fear docks!" Isaac hollered at the group in front of him. They began their mad race to the Cape to escape certain torture and death at the hands of a mad and vengeful lot of soldiers.

* * *

Sam buried his face in his hands. Seeing this woman haggle like she was, would have been embarrassing for a man to do, but for a woman? It was not a usual sight. He didn't know if the poor bastard selling his Ship of the Line was tolerating it because he badly needed to sell it, or because she was a woman. Normally, April wouldn't have been looked at twice, but this was Captain Read after all. Nobody messes with her and gets away with it, or so the rumors say.

Sam heard a ruckus in the distance and saw smoke slowly rising over the tree tops. The echo of gun fire was all too familiar.

"Um, Cap'n," Sam started. "Cap'n, I think we better be wrappin' dis up now. I can hear the powder music approaching."

"Quiet, Sam! You'll be cleaning the barnacles off me keel after another outburst like that!" April continued to argue with the man selling the ship and Sam stepped closer and closer to the gunfire, pistol ready and scabbard drawn. He saw a cart approaching with a bloody Isaac driving it hard. He then surveyed a group of people in the cart, some bloodied, some crying hysterically. Following closely behind on foot was Patrick and a cursing Scotsman. The two kept turning and firing as quickly as two younger boys in the cart could reload their firelocks. The refugees finally reached Sam.

"Please, tell me that boat is ours, loaded and ready to go!" begged Isaac.

"No, not yet. Da cap'n be barginin' fierce fer it," Sam replied.

Patrick heard Sam's reply to Isaac and he curtly stated, "Not for long, not if I have anything to say about it!" He ran toward April and stated commandingly, "Captain, let's wrap this up! We need to leave. Now!"

April turned to him, aggravated that he would dare speak to her like that in front of business. "Me wolf, I go when I am damn good 'n ready! Not one moment sooner!" She turned back to the seller of the ship, who had taken notice of the bloodied group and gunshots in the not-so-distant distance.

"Alright then!" the man shouted. "Fine! Just get the hell away from my docks before you cause me grief!" The seller wasted no time and dragged the heavy bag of gold off the ship, disappearing into the darkness.

April grinned and turned to Patrick with a smile of victory on her face. "Nice timing, my husband. So what the bloody 'ell is goin' on?"

"Redcoats! C'mon! We have to get everyone on board now. We have some serious injuries to tend to!"

"No!"

"No?"

"No." Patrick stared at her in disbelief. The British troops emerged and were within range again and the gun fire volley began again. April coolly pulled out a bottle of rum from her purse. "We ain't gettin' on me new ship till it be renamed and done it right. If you don't follow proper tradition, it will curse the vessel for all time!"

Patrick snatched the rum out of her hand and ran to the massive ship's bow. "I name thee *ARCHIBALD'S VENDETTA!*" He smashed the bottle and rum ran all over the side and down into the salty water of the Atlantic Ocean. "There! It's done! Now get on with it! We are leaving NOW!"

"You are so handsome when you try to exert authority, but no not yet. You only poured rum into the sea and never poured it on the deck. We need more rum," she citied.

"For shit's sake, where am I going to get more?" her husband belted back.

As if on cue a British bullet struck a cargo barrel full of rum sitting on the deck. It sprayed the sweet spirits all over the deck boards.

"There! The bloody lobsterbacks helped us out. NOW COME ON! EVERYBODY CLIMB ABORD!" he shouted. April shot him daggers out of her eyes in response.

The rest of the group was already clamoring on board as April and Patrick had what was sure to be the first of many disagreements. Sam and Isaac ran below the deck to ready the cannons as the families tried to take cover from the gunfire coming at them from the dock.

Patrick and April continued back and forth, a heated debate over the name of the ship while the crew prepared to fire a cannon at the dock as they departed. Mr. Quinn unleashed the sails as quickly as he could and Sam joined him. The cannon was loaded and Isaac was ready with the linstock for the command to fire. The large vessel was pushing the limits of the shallow docks as is and the sailing master would have to be very careful not to run her onto a hidden sandbar. The ship creaked and moaned as it moved into the water and April swung the wheel to turn it broadside. "But I wanted to name me new ship for me best cat, Regan! I wanted it to be *Regan's Lore!*"

"Stop it, woman and tell Isaac to fire at them already!" She glared at him. She hated it, but he was right. It was time to end this silly onslaught of British shots coming at them.

"Very well," she said moving her hateful gaze to the shore. "FIRE!"

BOOM!!! Isaac covered his ears from the blast of the 18 pounder Armstrong. The concussive force and vibration knocked him off his feet.

The group on the deck began to shout and celebrate as they watched the redcoats fall and suffer a painful and grotesque death at the hands of such a force. Their muskets were no match and they had no cannons to fire back with. *Archibald's Vendetta* was now too far out of range for their firelocks and they had no choice but to retreat. Patrick surveyed the British men through a spyglass and just for a second he swore he saw an irate Byron Kingsley yelling at his men.

CHAPTER 23

CHECKMATE

"We need to find safe harbor and hide for a bit while we fit our new ship. Do you have any ideas where we could go that is unwatched," April queried.

Sam spoke up, "Cap'n, I would suggest that Spanish chain of islands around the tip of Florida. The locals call it Cayo Hueso."

Audrey added, "Yes, that literally means 'bone key' because the island is littered with unburied human skeletons. Because of its dark nature, I have heard some sailors leave the word 'Bone' out of the title, simply calling the islands 'The Keys'. If you ask me, I have a theory about the culture that left all those bodies. What I think-"

April cut her off saying, "If you want us to shelter there, you best not tell me anymore about the dark energy or presence of a dead culture that inhabits them. Sam, take us to 'The Key' islands right away."

The Vendetta sailed to the island chain in three days without incident and then began its overhaul and refitting. April was very particular about what she liked and started to modify the ship for extra speed. Two weeks had passed when a noise interrupted the work.

The sounds of screams vibrated through the decking. Marian was not having a fast and easy delivery. Miss Bias threw open the door and yelled, "I need more water, quickly!" The dumbfounded group of men tripped over themselves scrambling up the stairs. The midwife laughed at their awkward scramble and then got back to work. Margie waited outside the door, ready to shuttle in the water. Miss Bias had delivered many babies and she knew how dangerous birth could be. Marian also knew the grim reality, too. The longer and more difficult the delivery, the less the chances the baby and she would survive.

Many anxious hours passed until a baby's cry filled the air. As the strength of the new born increased, the mother's strength decreased. The baby boy was placed in his mother's arms as Miss Bias tried in vain to stop the massive blood loss oozing from her. Marian smiled as she stared down onto her new life, "Look how much he looks like Archibald! That will be his name."

She held her baby in her arms smiling as her life bled out from her. Heather was yelling at Miss Bias to save her, but the uterine bleeding could not be stopped. The crowd of women cried as Marian passed on. Heather picked up the tiny Archibald and held him while he was cleaned and dried off. Each person present said a prayer to whomever they prayed to, so as to protect baby Archibald from the islands' curse they feared had struck down Marian.

The crew did a traditional Scottish burial that mirrored her husband's. Her body would be buried on the 'Key Bone' island so that her own bones would not join the rest of the skeletons scattered above ground.

After Marian's funeral, the group reminisced about her courage and kindness. William threw her the traditional Scottish funeral party and the dancing ensued. Fortunately, Margie was still breast feeding and took to the duty of wet-nursing the newborn.

* * *

Two more weeks had passed and life on the ship had returned to routine. They enjoyed exploring all the different islands of The Keys while they foraged for supplies. Audrey Scott was bursting with excitement and spent hours doing her own research at every spot they stopped at.

A group of children prodded Margie into approaching April and asking her a question. "Captain, you know All Hallows Evening is approaching...the children want to know if we will be participating."

A cold wind blew in as the mood on the deck darkened. April turned to the kids hiding behind Margie's legs and spoke to them directly, "I celebrate Samhain, not All Hallows Eve. Do you children know what that is?" The little ones shook their heads no. "The year is divided into two parts, a light half and a dark half. On October 31, the light half gets over taken by the dark half. On that night, time and space become muddied and the veil between life and death is at its thinnest. The living world and the dead world can mix together. It is rumored that the elders could do sacred rituals to make people swap worlds. The living would be transported and lost in the world of the dead, whereas the dead would come back and walk in the world of the living. You need to be extra careful you do not accidently invite a dead spirit onto our ship."

William interrupted and took his turn scaring the children, "To us Scots, that night is very frightening. Bogeys or Bogeymen come from the ghost world and will hide under your bed or tap on your window. On that night you must never cross a gate, stile, or a fence because the bogeymen are always hiding on the other side, waiting for you."

Sam cut in to keep April and William from continuing to terrify the children, "Why don't we just celebrate a nice Christian's holiday and go souling on November 2nd for All Souls' Day."

Patrick questioned, "I never understood what knocking on strangers' doors and begging them for soul cakes had to do with heaven."

"Well, we Catholics can get stuck in a place called purgatory. It is an empty holding land between hell and heaven. If your loved one gets trapped in there, the only way out is if they receive enough prayers," Sam explained.

"Oh I get it! So you bribe these beggar children with raisin spice cakes and in return they pray for your loved one's soul to help them escape purgatory," Patrick summarized.

"Correct, you got it! Although I have to admit the church just took this holiday from the Roman pagan festival of Lemuria. They thought it would be an easier transition for pagans if they repackaged the All Hallows Day holiday and moved it from May 13th to November 1st. I thinks da church figured if they put it close enough to Samhain it would bleed the life out of the celebration. The church don't like you knowing this history none and I got a swollen lip for asking a nun about it once"

Patrick turned to the children. A cold wind blew back up and darkness grew around him, "I think these children should be more worried about keeping away Jack-O'-Lantern. Jack was such an awful evil soul that not even hell wanted him and the Devil sent him back to walk the Earth. The Devil took a burning ember from hell and gave it to Jack so he could search for souls at night. The only way to confuse Jack was to carve a turnip into a scary face and put a candle in it. I don't think we have any turnips onboard but I saw we had a squash and a pumpkin that might work. If you could carve them and light them up, it will protect our barky." The children grew excited about designing, carving, and illuminating the gourd.

Shamus offered his thoughts, "I says ya skip this whole fookin' spooky holiday and put all our fookin' energy into celebratin' hatin' da British government. Let's have a Guy Fawkes bonfire night on November 5th, dat is close enough to your creepy, goat-humpin' holidays."

April spoke up, "Oh no, I just got this barky the way I like it. I won't tolerate a bunch of children wearing masks, starting fires, and breaking the ship up!"

Patrick interrupted, "I never understood what that holiday is all about. Someone tell me who Guy Fawkes is and why all the children burn and destroy the town on that night."

Shamus replied, "In 1609, a fookin' Cath'lic rebel, Guy Fawkes wore a theater mask and tried to blow up da House of Lords wit thirty six g'damn kegs of gunpowder. Da angry British hung 'em, drawn, and quartered 'em, den dey threw da pieces of his body into a bonfire. E'ry fookin' year after dat, da g'damn chil'ren of London half-mocked, half-hon'red him by taking to da streets and causin' chaos. Dey wear masks, beg, parade, vandalize, and set fookin' bonfires e'rywhere."

"So you want us to celebrate a pro-Catholic terrorist who dresses like a harlequin?" Patrick replied.

"Yes, sorta, but you're not allowed to fookin' say it like dat! I want to celebrate his spirit of standing up against oppression."

Isaac interjected, "No, he didn't stand up against oppression or the idea of tyranny. He wanted to supplant one tyrant with another, to remove the Protestant king with a Catholic king. I will not celebrate such an act."

"Fook you ya rat-dicked bastard! Dat man be a hero! Your tiny Jewish brain just be incapable of understanding tings like this," the Irishman pouted.

April stepped in front of the children and delivered her decision. "Keeping with the spirit of this ship, you children can celebrate anything you want as long as it does not harm someone's liberty or their possessions. Enjoy yourselves!"

The group continued debating over Guy Fawkes while the children ran off to find the pumpkin.

* * *

Sam Scurvy could barely steer *Archibald's Vendetta* straight because he was so distracted. Mari Anna, Prudence and Heather looked lovely in the afternoon light as they passed the newborn back and forth. After a while, they handed Archibald back to Margie for feeding. He was then hypnotized as they combed each other's hair. April slapped Sam on the back of the head and commanded, "Mind your wheel, sailor."

"Sorry Captain, but they be like sea sirens to me. I am falling under their song. How do three women reach this age without being married already? I do not understand," Sam Scurvy pleaded.

"Men are so thick in the head. Do you really not know, sailor?"

"Captain, you have only known them a few weeks. What did they tell you?"

"They did not tell me anything. It is as obvious as the wart on your nose, sailing master."

"I do not understand, what is so obvious? I must know what they are thinking so I can steal one's heart, Arrrrrr."

"You fool. You are trying to sell a dog to a woman who prefers cats."

"I am so lost, which one of them is selling a dog?" Sam Scurvy was confused.

"Christ, take a good look at them right now!"

Sam surveyed the women. All three were standing side by side and Heather had both her arms around their waists. She slowly slid both hands down their buttocks and gave them a playful squeeze. Mari Anna and Prudence smiled and the three women squeezed closer together.

"Oh. Oh...OH! You mean those lasses only like other ladies and the *three* of them are in love? Curse my luck! Ya know ya run the strangest barky in the world. I don't think this ocean will ever see such a collection of oddities again. Great, now that baby has three mothers and I get go to bed again with swollen cherries!" Sam exclaimed shaking his head.

She belted out a great laugh and nodded her head in agreement until her mind started to wander.

Captain April Read quickly realized she was in trouble keeping both ships afloat and sailing the same direction. Since taking on *Archibald's Vendetta*, both ships were horribly understaffed. The crew was exhausted from working double shifts for a week and she knew she had to find some extra hands. Not just any hands would do though. She only wanted a crew that would live under her philosophy of liberty. *Where would I find such a crew*, she thought.

Everyone was at his or her breaking point; both crews needed sleep. The weather finally looked safe enough to drop anchor, allowing for everyone to get some much needed rest. The captain gave the order and within an hour, the only souls awake on either ship were the watchmen.

The crew got a very long sleep in, including a day of relaxation on deck and on one of the Key islands.

Patrick ran up topside of *Archibald's Vendetta* and announced, "Look what someone left behind in the captain's quarters!" He ran up to Isaac with a wooden box. "Sit down; we are going to have a game."

Isaac humored his excited friend and sat down. The wooden box opened up into a painted chess set with the wooden pieces stuffed underneath. Patrick beamed with a smile, "Now is your chance to finally beat me after all these years."

Isaac laughed, "I will part your pawns like Moses parted the Red Sea, old friend!"

The men wasted no time getting started and after ten minutes, a large crowd gathered round.

"Checkmate, Isaac. You really have to remember to watch the bishop pins. Who's next?" challenged Patrick, to the crew.

Sailor after sailor played and Patrick quickly and effortless destroyed them all. Shamus was cussing at Patrick accusing him of making up a move. "No really, Irishman. It is a real move called en passant. If you move your pawn to the fourth rank in one move and my pawn is one file over, but also on the fourth rank, I can slide behind your pawn on the third rank on your file and capture it," Patrick explained. Shamus knocked the board over and stomped off, mumbling. April finally sat down and questioned, "I never did understand this game. Can you explain it to me?"

"Chess is a war and each side is equally matched. The game is over when you capture the king." He picked up the king and handed it to her. "But the funny thing is, your king is your weakest piece."

She smiled and asked the question she already knew the answer to, "Then what piece is the strongest?"

Her husband smirked back at her, "That would be the queen, my love. She is the most dangerous piece on the board. The chess board is setup much the same as this ship, my wife," he laughed.

Chess King

"So, husband, I did not know you had such a gift for strategy. Do you think you can apply that to pirating?"

"I am excellent at chess by setting traps and swindles. Perhaps I could use the same philosophy and such and apply it to bigger pieces."

"Well, me wolf, I need you to find me a crew and soon."

Patrick sat back and pondered the question. "I do have an idea. It would take our weaknesses and turn them into our strengths!"

"What a fine catch you were, husband," April beamed at him. "Do explain."

* * *

BLAM! BLAM! BLAM! The concussion of the cannons firing vibrated through the *Robin*'s deck.

"Hurry up and raise the English Jack. Make sure they can see we are fellow countrymen. Garland, throw some more sand down so we don't slip in all this blood on the deck," April shouted orders over the ruckus of battle.

The large Spanish vessel bared its cannons down on the *Robin*. *BLAM!* A large gray cloud hung between the two ships.

Orders were shouted over the noise, "We have to head for that British slave ship. Sail us right up to her broadside."

The *Robin* swung her bow around and went full sail toward the English slave ship. The large pursuing Spanish vessel continued its merciless assault by cannon. The English slave ship turned and plotted a course dead through the battling ships. Seeing this, the Spanish vessel broke pursuit and started to flee.

April pushed Sam's lifeless body off the helm and took the wheel. She was closing too fast and ordered the wind be let off her sails. She looked across the deck and sadly spied Isaac and Patrick's bodies also in a motionless, bloody heap.

The English slave vessel was now in shouting range. The whores and children, covered with copious amounts of crimson, ran to the rail. "Please help us, help us! Spanish privateers murdered my husband!" a skinny woman named Carla shouted. A group of cackling women joined in and yelled to the vessel to stop.

The slave ship captain surveyed the *Robin*'s bloody deck. He snapped shut his spy glass and ordered his crew to stop and help the women. In under a minute, grappling hooks tied the ships together and the slave ship's crew dropped a gangplank between them. The hysterical women stormed across the wooden bridge and poured onto the deck. They threw their arms around the English sailors. "Thank you for saving us," Miss Bleish said as she kissed a man on his cheek. The scullery wench Teresa shouted something in Greek or Italian and flung herself into the arms of a surprised officer.

April ran over to the captain and hugged the man, "Thank you! They killed my husband!" A crooked smile came over the slave captain.

"So you lasses be all alone. Hey, lads, these women be sailing all alone now. Let us go over and examine their ship to see if we can help!" His mind was already plotting. He flung the grieving woman to the deck, "Fuck it, lass I am going to help myself to your ship and then I am going to help myself to you. Crew, take their vessel!

"Belay that order," April yelled as she slid her knife up to the captain's testicles. The women, who were hugging the crew, pulled their hidden knives and held them to the rescuers' throats. "Nobody has to die. Just do as we say and we will let ya sail away." April pressed the knife up hard against her capture's crotch as she stood back up.

"Stand down, lads! Do what she commands!" the captain shouted in a panic.

April let out a belting, high-pitched whistle and the deck of the *Robin* started to stir. The bloodied men rose from the dead and stormed the gangplank with pistols drawn and cutlasses in hand. The sight of the walking dead storming their deck terrified the slave ship's crew. Patrick had four flintlocks tied around his neck, hanging down his chest. Isaac armed himself with the short blunderbuss jam packed with pig shot. Wooden bandoleers filled with pre-made wads of shot and powder hung across him, shoulder to waist. The men trained their guns on the rest of the slave ship's crew.

April shouted more orders, "Isaac, take Sam and fifteen men and clear the cannons below deck."

"Aye, Captain!" the hulking man said as he began to gather his own war party.

BLAM! Both ships shook as a hole opened on the side of

the *Robin*. Smoke and shivers from the hull hung in the air.

"Isaac, stop those cannons, now!" the captain ordered.

Isaac's party stormed down the stairs as screams of agony came from the new hole that was blasted into the *Robin*.

When the men found the cannons, they noticed three men desperately loading for another shot. Isaac's party quickly overwhelmed the slavers and subdued them. "Men, search well and make sure there are no other souls manning a cannon!"

By the time anyone noticed, it was too late. The large Spanish vessel took advantage of the situation and approached with their cannons trained on them. As they got broadside with the slave ship, they pulled their Spanish jack down. Mari Anna's father yelled from the deck of *Archibald's Vendetta*, "We heard cannon fire! We have you covered!" Some loud Scottish cursing could also be heard from a man in a kilt. Now that the ruse was over, the *Vendetta* loaded their cannons with balls rather than just powder charges.

Isaac dragged the three gunners to the deck as he returned topside. "Just these three gunners, captain. No other cannons were manned."

"Tie them to the rail until we know what their judgment be," the tattooed woman barked. The women stripped all of the sailors from the slave ship and took their weapons.

Margie was an ex-whore turned brood-mare. She currently had nine children on the *Robin* and was wet-nursing Archibald. The mother ran across the gangplank screaming, "Murderers!" Her dress was so soaked with blood it was dripping a trail behind her as she ran. She was crying so loudly, April could barely understand what she was saying though the sobbing.

"Did you say the cannon shot killed three of your children below deck?!"

She hugged the balling Margie. "Come with me," the captain mumbled stoically.

Captain Read stood over the three men and demanded, "Which one of you gave the order to open fire on a vessel of women and children?"

Two of the frightened sailors both yelled, "He did!" as they pointed with their heads to the man in the middle.

"I ordered the cannon to be fired and I wish I had time for another shot at you pirates!" The slaver in the middle arrogantly exclaimed.

Margie screamed and snatched Isaac's blunderbuss out of his hands. Before anyone could stop her, she held the firelock to his face and pulled the trigger.

CLICK. BOOM! The large mouthed gun erupted in a huge cloud of gray. When the smoke cleared it revealed a headless body.

"Fuck me! Crazy bitch blew his face right off!" one of the other two men yelled as the third pissed his pantaloons.

"Wait! Wait!" one of the restrained men begged, "I was just following orders. I am a good man. I am innocent."

"Innocent?! You piece of dog shit. You loaded the cannon that killed my three wonderful children! You think you're not responsible if you just load the weapon and pack the powder? You should've had the courage to not follow an evil order. Good men following evil orders are still evil, you son of a whore!" Margie yelled. She grabbed two pistols from April's belt and unloaded them into the man's eyes. The bullets pierced on both sides and brain matter splattered back out of his gaping eye sockets.

The remaining man wept out load, "Please, show mercy! I should have had the courage to say no to the master gunner, but I didn't. I am a coward. Please, do not kill me."

April stepped in front of Margie as she pulled her knife to kill the remaining assailant. "These were your children and by right, these men's lives are yours to take, but consider mercy and a less hasty decision. Instead seek for restitution to your family. It might feel good to kill this man but that doesn't help you raise and feed the rest of your children. Consider, instead, restitution. This man will work and serve your family until you feel you have been made whole, which might never happen. We will make this man work to replace the labors and profits your children would have contributed to your family."

Margie stomped back and forth fingering her knife,

thinking out loud and reasoning, "I want to kill him and send him to hell to get raped by devils. You know that's what happens to children murderers, they get arse fucked by devils! Captain, what you said rang true in me ear. Take him over to the ship and tie him up until after I bury my children. But I will kill him later if I change my mind!"

"Thank you for your mercy! I will make this right. I am so sorry," the man cried as Isaac dragged him across the gangplank. Margie followed Isaac, kicking the man and warning him to hold his tongue.

April turned her attention to the slave ship captain. "You stole these men and did unspeakable things to them. We are here to free them and if you behave, you can take your ship and sail off when we be done. Do you understand?"

The terrified captain nodded his head in understanding.

The tattooed woman ordered Teresa, "Go fetch Mingo. He is an African man with tribal scars all over his face." The Greek or Italian, brown-haired woman nodded and ran to retrieve Mingo, returning with him in short time.

Audrey cut in, "Mingo speaks almost every African dialect and has been teaching me. He is definitely the best choice, Captain."

A tall black man stood in front of the captain and asked, " What you have me do?"

"I want you to translate my message and make these slaves understand. Okay, open the hatch to the cargo bay."

Mr. Michael and Mr. James flung the hatch open and vomited on each other. The putrid smell overtook the lovers before they could get away from the hatch. Even Shamus, with his disgusting odor, was repulsed. Screams and yells erupted from the hole.

"Mingo, would you shout this down into the hold?" April asked. "We are here to rescue you. Please do not attack us, you are safe. You will be free to go back home. If you have no home to return to, then please consider working for us on our ship."

Mingo had to yell a few times until the frightened slaves

quieted down and listened. It took some time to yell the message in so many dialects. Shouting of excitement resonated up the hatch.

"They understand, captain! They ready!" Mingo smiled.

"Get the gangplanks ready for the *Robin* and the *Vendetta*. Okay, lower the ladder."

Mingo lowered the ladder down, but nobody came up.

"What the hell is going on here?" April demanded.

"Captain, they all still be chained," Mingo said.

"Give me the keys now!" she threatened the slave ship captain.

The captain complied and then April threw them to Patrick, "Go down and unlock them with Mingo."

Patrick and Mingo wrapped a cloth around their mouths and noses and descended into the dark, ammonia-filled hole. Patrick's eyes immediately burned and the smell brought back terrifying memories of the king's debtors' prison back in London. It took a minute for his eyes to adjust until he realized there was no floor. It was shoulder-to-shoulder filled with bodies chained to the floor. Patrick wanted to vomit, but could not find an open space on the deck. Many of the slaves were locked down with one long chain. Mingo had seen this before when he was a slave and he knew how the chains and locks worked.

Slaves screamed and begged to be released first. Mingo carefully stepped over bodies and unlocked the chain. Patrick pulled the long strand up and the prisoners tried to jump to their feet. So weak and malnourished were they that many of them had to be lifted out of the shit and piss soaked floor. Their skin was raw from urine burn and some were missing patches of flesh that stuck to the deck when they pulled them up. Mingo and Patrick slowly helped them up the ladder one by one while Shamus and Sam helped from the topside.

The *Robin*'s crew expected to see elated throngs of captives pouring out of the hatch in excitement. Instead, they saw a sad and depressing site of men, women, and children too weak to walk. Sam Scurvy helped a man take very painful steps up the gangplank. He sympathized with his scurvy pain. It reminded him of his long walk to the *Robin* all those years ago. The process took hours and April was growing irate from watching this parade of skeletons slowly board her ships.

The crew imagines how the slaves should come out of the hold

Patrick reported back to April, "I would say there are about one hundred and thirty that we saved, Captain. They are all aboard and are ready to depart, but there are about fifteen dead bodies that had been chained to the live ones. I also saw some of the mothers refuse to leave the bodies of their dead children and they carried the corpses to the *Vendetta*."

Anger came across the captain's face, "Husband, throw these prisoners in the same hold they made these slaves live in." The *Robin*'s crew started forcing the prisoners down the hatch.

"I thought you said I could sail away and you would leave us in peace?!" the slave ship captain yelled.

"I changed my mind after seeing what you did to these poor souls. I will leave you with your lives, but I am giving your ship to these slaves for restitution. Because of your crimes against them, you owe them much more than the price of that ship. Count your blessings I don't let them press you into being their slaves! Now climb down in the hold with all those rotting bodies ya killed," April commanded and trained a flintlock on the men.

Mr. James and Mr. Michael battened down the cargo hatch after the prisoners were loaded.

"Ya should chain 'em to da shite covered floor like dey done to dose fookin' Africans," Shamus snapped.

"I want guards on the hatches. Audrey, where is an isolated island we can maroon these men on?" the tattooed woman questioned.

"Hmmm...there is an island close to Charles Towne that would work. I will show Sam where on the chart," Audrey answered.

"Very good. Let us dump these slavers, clean up and feed these poor souls. Nina and Teresa, you are in charge of nursing them back to strength. Find Rose, she still speaks many African dialects and should come in useful"

April walked up to her husband, "I think they will make a fine crew. Who better to embrace the ideas of liberty than a group of former slaves?" She reached out and handed him the wooden king from the chess set. She smiled at him and announced, "I rather like this game called 'chess.' I think I am supposed to say 'checkmate' now!"

* * *

All members of the three ships watched as the crew of the slave ship swam to the shore. April showed mercy by giving them some barrels of fresh water till they collected their own rain water. She also sent them off with some fishing hooks, bait, and a few knives.

"Muster all three crews and the ex-slaves as well," April command her husband. She had decided she would train Patrick as her quartermaster and even made up a title position she bestowed on him called Master Strategist. It took some time to bind the three ships together so all ears could hear. Mingo and the whore Rose would translate the captain's words to the freed men. The boatswain's whistle blew and the crew started to settle down.

"All, quiet down! Admiral Read wishes to address her crew," Patrick barked out.

"Admiral?" she whispered to her husband.

"I know. I don't have the same seafaring knowledge as you, but I am pretty sure you call anyone who commands more than one ship an admiral," her new quartermaster replied.

She smiled at him, "I think you be right, my wolf."

"I be going to explain to ya the rules of this small fleet. Unlike the rumors ya hear in pub tales, most real pirate ships are not run by an iron fist. Each of ya crew gets a vote on major decisions. If ya don't like the way the vote went down and ya are uncomfortable with it, ya will be free to leave the fleet and rejoin us when you're comfortable. Unlike military vessels, you are free to leave anytime ya want. We are trying to create something so special that ya don't want to leave. This fleet will be a symbol of freedom to the world. We will not interact with each other using force or threats. I want this to be the only place on this world you can be truly free. Ya will get paid for work. If ya lazy and don't contribute to the crew, then ya won't have silver to eat.

"We will not be the pirates of old. They were hunted down and murdered because they got too greedy and attacked everyone they saw. We will not steal from other innocent sailors. The only vessels we will take will be that of the government's; vessels who owe us restitution and payback for all the damage they have done to our lives. These military vessels were paid for by money they stole from us and the lives of our loved ones who they murdered. We will take all of our stolen money back that we can.

"To the slaves we liberated, I offer ya this. I will give ya the slave ship to return to your home but if you have nothing to go back to, I ask you to join our fleet of liberty. You will be free men, treated as equals and you can help us free more slave ships. We will train you and pay you well.

"We also will offer you access to a security fund for your injuries if you choose. A portion of every share you take in will be placed in a central fund. The quartermaster has a list of the amounts ya be paid if ya injured. Ya get as much as six hundred pieces of eight for a leg all the way down to one hundred pieces of eight for an eye. Yar welcome to see the list anytime.

"Even the captain can be removed if the crew loses faith in me. If ya vote me out, I will step down and find a place in the crew. Ya have till the end of the day to decide if ya want to live by these customs. Ya are here on your own free will and accord and we will drop ya off in Charles Towne if yar not interested in my offer. That is all."

She stepped down and the decks erupted with chatter. The chatter went on all night long and even until sun up.

The boatswain's whistle blew the next day and the crews mustered to deck. The new quartermaster spoke up, "Now is the time to choose! Board the ship you want to work on!"

The crew scrambled around. The Africans were moving much better. Their full bellies and the sunshine agreed well with them. After a few minutes, the crews were set. Patrick counted the heads.

"What is the headcount, Quartermaster? How many Africans will be leaving with the slave ship?" the admiral asked.

"The count is thirty-two. Then there are eighty-seven new crewmembers: thirty-seven to the *Robin* and fifty to the *Vendetta*," the quartermaster replied.

"Let us make sure they are properly trained and wish them well. Get to training!" April belted.

The crews pitched in to help with the training and to give the African vessel a chance.

"Admiral, why do ya keep calling us 'pirates' instead of 'privateers'? Pirates are associated with stealing, theft and brutality, but privateering has the legitimacy of the king behind it." Sam Scurvy asked.

"You answered yar own question. This fleet is to show the world we don't need a government to live in peace. It doesn't make sense to seek out some king's blessing so we can steal and not actually call it stealing. No, the word 'privateering' is associated with begging a government for permission. Instead, we be the 'Pirates of Savannah'. Arrrrrr!"

CHAPTER 24

HUNTING PIRATES

eather went through her mother's belongings and was taken aback when she opened the leather bag containing Archibald's books. She pulled out Locke's tome and surveyed it. The cover was splattered with her father's dried blood and the book was worn. She carried the bag to April and showed her, "Do you think the crew would enjoy being read these books?"

April smiled and replied, "That is a dandy of an idea. I would be honored to hold them for you until you want them back."

"I think my father would be so happy to know that a multitude of ears will be hearing the messages from out of these illegal book that he died for," Heather replied.

She pulled the books out of the bag and noticed something was wadded up on the bottom. She dug around and pulled out a group of yellow and black strips of fabric. "Oh, look here. It is Father's armbands for his meetings," she said as she pressed them to her face. Her eyes suddenly brightened and she announced, "I am keeping these. I have an idea for them."

A few days passed and each night the *Robin* and the *Vendetta* would be lashed together. April would pick a chapter in one of the books and read it loudly so both crews could hear. Mingo and Rose translated so even the African crews could enjoy it and discuss the ideas of liberty. Much like a meeting of the Freeman Society, a passage would be read and it would be opened up for discussion. Heated debate and ideological arguing could be heard most nights. The crew loved the new tradition.

One night, Heather finally revealed her surprise project she had been working on. "Admiral, I present this to you to remind people to enlighten themselves. I made this with the set of Father's collection of arm bands he used in his meetings."

April unfolded the cloth and it revealed black and yellow colors, set at a diagonal. She saw the hand-woven fabric and figured this must be a flag. "I thought that *Archibald's Vendetta* needed its own proper jack," Heather said as she smiled.

"I love it," April said softly, placing a reassuring hand on Heather's shoulder. "Let us raise this in proper ceremony tonight!" she commanded.

Miss Darden ran up and interrupted them, "Admiral, your cat is having kittens! I have counted four black ones in total."

"Aye! Very good, lass. That should counter any bad luck from having a baby born at sea on our barky. A baby black kitten should balance a new born."

Sam Scurvy cut in, "Ya know, I have been sailing me whole life and never heard of these traditions. I thinks you make some of these up."

The admiral snapped back, "You must have sailed different waters then, or ya would know how rituals be done proper!"

* * *

One year had past at sea and the crew's numbers grew. When the fleet dropped off William, they increased their ranks with some disgruntled Scots. They managed to find like-minded individuals everywhere. Every smuggling run they would pick up new sailors. Profits had been exceptional and the crew was happy. Miss Darden had expanded her floating brothel idea and recruited new prostitutes so, of course, April recruited many more black cats. A healthy profit was being made due to her clever ideas of new ways to whore.

The Admiral had also used the same ruse Patrick had created to liberate three other slave ships. She knew she could not keep using it because word of her little fleet of outcasts was spreading quickly. The freed slaves bolstered her numbers and the ships were finally at respectable numbers. April started spending large amounts of time training Nina and Audrey in the ways of commanding a ship.

One thing the admiral was very strict about was drilling. Many months of intense drilling took place during that time period. The gunners could fire the cannons, reload and fire again in just over a minute. Some of the ex-slaves became excellent shots with the long muskets. Many of the Africans fashioned traditional spears and clubs and were deadly proficient with them. April trained the officers in the art of blade play. Each was given a cutlass and was expected to practice daily. In just a few months of hard work, Sam and Patrick had become decent swordsmen.

All things were going very well until a rum running to Savannah. During one of the *Robin*'s late night deliveries to the secret pirate tunnels, the admiral was delivered a message. The messenger told her Byron Kingsley had been chasing them for a year and that he finally convinced the board of trustees to take out a British man-of-war to hunt the fleet down. He was only hunting the *Vendetta*, as he did not know about the *Robin*. He saw the *Vendetta* fleeing in Cape Fear and had his sights on her ever since.

April called a meeting with her officers that night to discuss the situation. "What are our options, gentlemen? We are making a fortune staying local and smuggling, but the risk is great. We could move our operation to South America but it won't be nearly as profitable. I am looking for ideas."

Sam Scurvy spoke up, "I vote for running. Even with both our vessels at full guns, we would need a miracle to take a man-of-war."

"What do you think, my quartermaster?" April questioned Patrick.

"Of course," he replied, "I want to stay and get a chance to kill Kingsley for what he has done, but that is my heart talking and not my brain. I would not put the lives of my friends and neighbors at stake for my lust for revenge."

Isaac injected, "I agree, had Kingsley is an evil man who the world would thank us to rid them of, but I have to throw my vote in with Sam. We should run."

The consensus around the table was to remain safe over profit. For the first time ever, people had experienced freedom and had already gotten hooked on their new way life. They would do anything to remain this free.

"Experience tells me we better at least have a backup plan. My wolf, you will be in charge of our strategy in case we have no choice. It is decided. We make one last run to Cape Fear and then we sail to South America, for a little time. I will inform the crew tonight," April stated with authority.

The crew unloaded the crates of illegal muskets to the purchasing parties at Cape Fear. They took their payments and explained it would be awhile before they could deliver more guns. They cast off and headed down the coastline at full sail. A fishing vessel intercepted them and delivered a message. Kingsley knew their location and they were told they better prepare. The admiral knew she could not just take to open sea because eventually Kingsley's ship would overtake them. She thought, *We're going to have to fight him eventually. We should fight him on our terms.*

* * *

"So this is where we make our stand? This cove has lots of great hiding places, but it is a dead end. There is no way out if your plan does not work," April said nervously, thinking aloud. "They call this place Long Bay. A few families own this land but most people call it Myrtle Swash because of all those Southern Wax Myrtles. A couple of us pirates used to call it 'Myrtle Beach'. Almost nobody is out here. It should be remote enough for what we need to do. Plus, it has a sandbar over there for what you need to do."

"Everyone is in position. If this goes right, none of us will have to fire one cannon," Patrick replied.

Isaac interrupted, "Admiral, man-of-war approaching. She is just coming into view. Do you want to send out the jolly boat and terms to meet them?"

April's breasts heaved as she breathed in deep. "Aye!" she

commanded.

Sam nervously rowed the small boat out toward the man-of-war. As he got closer, he ran up a white flag and waited off its starboard side. "I seek audience with Commander Byron Kingsley," he yelled.

The soldiers on deck kept their muskets trained on him while they mustered Kingsley. An officer claiming to be Byron Kingsley shouted down to Sam.

Patrick watched nervously as Sam rowed back to the *Vendetta*. The bow-legged sailor climbed some netting that was draped over the side of ship and made his way to Patrick. "You were right, he is an arrogant piece of shit and took your challenge. He accepted the duel and his terms are single combat without seconds. He chose a traditional night duel with blade and lantern. He will meet you on the sand bar an hour after sunset. If you win, the *Vendetta* is free to go. If you lose, we will surrender the *Vendetta*." Sam concluded grimly, "And Patrick, there will be no quarter given."

"I am grateful for the duel, but I am not happy he chose sword and lantern. I am not as good of a swordsman as I want to be," Patrick murmured.

April hugged her husband and comforted him, "Be brave. Remember what I told you, sword fighting is mainly about stamina. Whoever gets tired first dies."

She ran her hand across his groin and reminded him, "Now, I know you have excellent stamina, my wolf!"

The crew rallied around Patrick as April gave him some last minute tips on fighting in sand and how to use a lantern for defense and attack. After drilling, Patrick wanted to be alone in his quarters to get focused. April sat as she watched her husband shave off his beard. As he carefully guided his large hunting knife across his battle worn face he spoke, "I only grow this beard because my face makes most people uncomfortable. The scars used to really annoy me, but now I am older and I have learned to just accept who I am. This face is part of me and I need to just be comfortable in my own skin. I am tired of hiding my face because of other people's feelings, fuck them! If

I am to die tonight, I will die how I want to look!" Patrick reflected. "Well, it is smart to shave it off before battle. The Romans used to do the same thing so their enemies could not grab it in a fight. You look so nervous, husband. Come lay with me on this bed and I will relax you." She climbed on top of him and gave her husband a proper send off.

As the sun set, Isaac distracted himself by watching two small fishing vessels off in the distance. He was very worried about his best friend, as was the rest of the crew. His life now depended on Patrick's mediocre swordsman skills against a lifetime soldier.

The new quartermaster emerged from the captain's quarters slowly savoring every step. There was a good chance this was the last hour of his life and he was trying desperately to slow it down. His friends encircled him and hugged him. They all knew he was taking an enormous risk to keep his crewmates safe.

"This be one of the finest cutlasses ever made. I have taken eight souls with this blade and it has absorbed their powers. You will fight with the strength of eight men and it will protect you," April said before she kissed him on the cheek and handed over her blade. The cutlass had a shorter blade, thick and curved. It had many notches in the edge from striking blades and bones. The hilt had an ornate sword guard shaped like an octopus. Its tentacles came down and wrapped around a large ruby encrusted pommel. Etched in the blade was a picture of April's black cat to add to the luck of the sword. The cutlass seemed more a work of art than a weapon.

"I added extra wick and oil to this lamp so it should give you the advantage of more light. Just remember to watch your foot work and you will do great, old friend," Isaac smiled and handed Patrick the lantern.

It was time. Patrick said goodbye once more and climbed down to the jolly boat. The crew watched in anticipation as the lantern on the boat slowly grew dimmer and dimmer as it drifted further away. Patrick's mind was racing with what-ifs as he slowly rowed to the sandbar. What if Kingsley thrusts high right? What is the correct response if he parries down left? He knew he had to settle his mind and focus as he approached. True to his word, Byron was already on the sandbar waiting.

"Ah, took your time coming to your funeral, boy! You're a troublesome cuss. I have been trying to catch up with you for some time now," Byron yelled to Patrick.

Patrick cautiously and slowly stepped on to the damp sandbar. He tested his footing in the wet sand. His bare foot stuck. This was promising he thought. It should even the odds in Patrick's favor if Kingsley cannot be quick with his foot work. Courage filled the amateur swordsman as he stepped closer.

"You're a blight on this world, Kingsley. I hope Archibald can piss on you from heaven while you get raped by the devil dogs," he baited.

The final duel on the sandbar

Kingsley answered Patrick's insult by stepping closer into the light of the lanterns. He was still wearing his standard issue red coat made by the famous South Carolina Independent Company. He chose to fight with his military hanger. It was a long, thick, straight hunting sword with a double-edged blade and a simple hilt, a very popular style blade in Savannah.

As the men approached each other, both ships exploded with cheering. Although tough to make out details in the darkness, the crews could clearly see the duelers' silhouettes in the moon and lantern light.

Bryon gave no more warning and ran at Patrick. The new quartermaster planted his feet and braced for the blow. "Clang! Clang! Clang!" The sounds of steel clashing rang out over the waters to thunderous cheering. It was already hard to see and Byron was swinging his lamp by Patrick's head, wrecking his night vision. The pirate focused hard to keep track of the blade in the darkness. The inexperienced swordsman knew he made a mistake the moment he got off on his footwork. Kingsley feigned to the left and Patrick parried too hard. This shifted his weight and presented his right side exposed. The soldier took advantage of the rookie mistake by slicing him across the ribs.

Patrick's side burned with pain, but he refused to let it distract him. The pain woke him up and reminded him to stick to April's training. It was then that he decided to stop trying to fight like a gentleman and fight like a pirate. He changed his style to that of a good, bare-knuckled swordsman and pushed in tight. The pirate locked blades with the redcoat and swung his sword guard into the soldier's teeth. A spray of blood erupted to thunderous cheers.

Bryon focused his anger and turned to Patrick with a mad flurry of skilled strikes. The rookie answered the fast blows with parries until the last slash broke the tip off his cutlass. A shard of broken blade pierced his right eye. Patrick recoiled in pain and swung wildly, backing up. Kingsley was amused by this and taunted his crippled foe. He attacked the blind side thigh, dropping Patrick to his knee with a scream of pain. The pirate dragged himself backwards as Byron nicked his right arm and laughed. The arrogant solider stopped to admire his work, enjoying the sight of blood rolling out of Patrick's eye, leg, chest, and arm.

"I want to drag this out more boy, but my men are anxious

to hang your crew. To your credit, you did last longer than Archibald, so good show. We are going to have a good time poking your captain before we...AHHHHHH!"

Kingsley ran for the water as Patrick reached out with his broken cutlass and sliced through the commander's Achilles tendon. Archibald's murderer immediately fell, yet continued crawling for the water. The pirate crawled after him and sliced the burning man across the ass. Bryon rolled into the water, dousing the flames, as his dueling partner continued to crawl after him. Patrick made no speech nor said a clever curse before extinguishing the soldier's life. He brutally skull-bashed Kingsley with the ruby encrusted pommel. The pommel fell multiple times to the cheers of the *Vendetta*'s crew until Bryon's face was no longer recognizable as human. The exhausted Patrick sliced the throat of the corpse to ensure he was dead.

A faint cracking sound could be heard and then the victorious man noticed the sand exploded next to his leg. Another musket shot rang out from the man-of-war and splashed into the water. The woozy Patrick slid into the water and dove under as more shots rained down on his position.

"Lying bastards! Bring us in! Man the cannons!" April commanded.

She turned to Audrey Scott, "You are the only one strong enough at swimming to save me husband. Take some bandages and go save him please!"

"I am not a surgeon but I will do what I can." She grabbed a small medical pouch and dove off the *Vendetta*.

"Nina, when I let go and board, I need you to hold this helm straight. Do you understand?"

Nina barked back, "Aye, Admiral!"

The *Vendetta* had never anchored and was now dropping its sails. The crew knew they had to be very close or the cannon balls would never punch through the tough hull of the man-of-war. Both crews scrambled to their stations. "Can you get a clear cannon site to their bow? It is our only hope to stop this ship," April questioned Sam.

"It's going to be close, Admiral. It depends how drilled their crew be," Sam shouted back as he frantically helped April steer the *Vendetta* into proper position.

"We only are going to have one shot at this! Let us wait," she shouted calmly.

BLAM! BLAM! BLAM! Three cannons on the man-of-war fired. Two shots overshot the deck ripping through some sails while one struck a jolly boat tied to the side of the ship blowing it to shivers.

"Finally, the cannons are in line! Fire!" the Admiral screamed. The order was repeated across the deck. Shockwaves cracked through the air as large gray puffs of smoke filled the space between the vessels. When the smoke cleared, the bow was smashed in some but it was still holding.

"Damn, she is a strong barky. Reload!" April barked.

The *Vendetta's* long musket men were perched in the riggings. They started taking long shots at the British deck officers and struck two down.

The man-of-war's retaliation was terrible. Multiple cannons tore through the *Vendetta*. The main mast was keeling and pulling the ship over. Multiple holes were blown in the side of the smaller vessel and a few of the *Vendetta's* snipers in the tops fell to their death. The British had no intention of capturing this ship. They were firing to sink it.

"Damn it! If we don't punch a hole in that bow, it won't take them much time to out maneuver us. Where is everyone else?" April wondered aloud.

Nobody had paid any attention to the two inconspicuous small fishing ketches that had sailed into position. They unveiled their cannons, which had hidden under piles of nets. "The *Vendetta* softened her bow up, lads! Let's punch through!" Captain K.T Brewer shouted.

"Oui! Viva Liberte!" Captain Robert Deaux shouted.

The *Black Hound* and the *Mary Read* fired their four cannons together. The sight of shivers and planks of wood filled the air as the crews of the tiny vessels celebrated. They finally punched a small hole in the bow of the British ship.

"Fire!" was repeated on the deck of the *Vendetta* as the cannons focused their fire power on the exposed hole. Shouts of terror came from the belly of the British vessel as a section of gunners were blown apart.

In all the excitement, the crew was too busy to notice another vessel approaching from her backside. The *Robin* had quietly hidden behind a small island in the cove, waiting to make her move in the dark. Their stealthy approach was easy due to the confusion of the battling at night.

The *Robin* sneaks into position during the night battle

Shamus shouted, "Clear dere decks wit da g'damn grape shots, lasses!"

Heather, Mari Anna, and Prudence worked together aiming the small deck cannons of the *Robin*. The twins and the girls' families all manned the other cannons in teams. The group lit the war irons simultaneously. To the soldiers' surprise and confusion, many of the bloody backs on the decks where cut down by the brutal shower of shot.

April nodded at Sam as he swung the wheel hard. The

Vendetta's stern drifted quickly next to the enemy vessel. The fast movement caused the *Vendetta*'s teetering mast to crash down upon the British ship's deck, crushing two of its members to death.

The admiral pulled out Mary Read's Swedish Boarding Axe Pistol and screamed, "Boarding parties!" Grappling hooks flew in from all directions as the four vessels latched onto the man-of-war. Cannon fire rocked the *Vendetta* at such close range and her crew screamed. She had many holes, but none were yet low enough to have her take on water.

Isaac led the charge from the *Vendetta* with a blunderbuss in each of his hands. He fired both guns down the gangplank they had dropped, clearing out a group of five unsuspecting British soldiers. He then picked up a spent musket and stuck his plug bayonet into the end of the gun. The dagger had a tapered end and slid into the barrel with a tight fit to make a lethal spear. He stabbed any fallen English soldier posing a threat, clearing a space on the deck for others to follow. The bayonet quickly got stuck in a redcoat's rib cage. The hulking man switched over to the boarding tomahawk the injured Indian had given him and he continued whirling around the crowded deck dropping bodies. The rest of the British crew was too busy to notice that Shamus and a group of whores were boarding from the *Robin* as well.

Miss. Darden used a linstock to light the fuse to her cast iron ball that was packed with gunpowder and shot. The whoremaster then rolled the grenade down the stairs to the lower decks. Shouts of pain were heard below deck as it exploded. The other whores followed suit and dropped their grenades in any hatch they could find. As Margie dropped her grenade down a hatch, a redcoat hit her across the head with his musket butt. As he lifted his firelock over his head to deliver a deathblow, his chest exploded with red. The dizzy woman looked up to see the man whose life she spared had just returned the favor, fatally shooting her assailant before he could ever deliver that final blow to her head.

In an intoxicated stupor, Shamus threw a grenade onto a

closed hatch. By the time he realized his drunken mistake, it was too late and the bomb went off. He looked down to find out why his foot would not move and noticed it was no longer there. He fell over in shock.

An angry lobster back officer swung his sword at Teresa's head. She barely ducked the blow but fell on the ground. When she looked back up she saw the soldier stumbling backwards with two arrow shafts sticking out of his chest. Amos and his twin had both made unbelievable shots with their hunting bows from the *Robin*.

African warriors had already run across the downed mast of the *Vendetta* and were swarming the deck in droves. The English shot a few with their muskets, but were poorly matched against their melee fighting skills. Very few foes could withstand their up-close spear fighting. Even with such a crowded deck, the warriors were able to skewer the redcoats with great agility.

April and Sam stormed aboard with the ex-slaves and headed below deck. Sam had a string of four pistols tied around his neck and would rotate them as he fired. He covered April's backside while she charged down the stairs. The admiral cleared the hall with a vicious spray of shot from her axe pistol. An unfortunate soldier turned the corner and the lady pirate buried the spike of the axe pistol into his chest. The vicious metal point went in so deep that she could not recover the weapon. The swordswoman changed over to cutlass and main gauche. April had killed many men in the past with this two-handed style. The main gauche was perfect for the tight quarters below deck because it was a short, thin, left-handed stabbing blade with a large hilt and hand guard.

She quickly found herself ambushed by two attackers which would mean a quick death to most. April knew that very few swordsmen practiced attacking in pairs and she could turn their inexperience against them. The admiral knew that with some basic maneuvering she could use them to get in each other's way and open up an easy opportunity. Her opponents found themselves hitting each other with parries and knocking each other off balance. April's attackers stepped on each other's feet knocking them both off kilter. With a double thrust using both hands, the two men simultaneously fell in pain and she quickly cut them down.

Back on the *Mary Read*, Mr. Michael and Mr. James loaded their slings. "For the Lord's sake, be careful not to drop those on our ship, monsieurs," Captain Deaux pleaded. The men loaded the glass pots filled with rancid meat, shit and oil in their slings. They lit them and brought the slings to full speed. They let the stink pots fly into the hole of the bow and cheered. When the glass bottles exploded, the stinky smoke was so horrid and foul and sounds of retching could immediately be heard.

A group of six bloodied redcoats stumbled out of the hole in the bow coughing and moaning. The sight of the men slowly stumbling and moaning caused such fear in Captain K.T Brewer, that he forgot where he was and even what year he was in. The peg-legged captain fired his pistol at them from the *Black Hound* and yelled, "Ya walking dead will never eat me soul! Arrrrrrr! " The confused British sailors threw their hands up and dropped their muskets when the saw they were staring down the barrel of a cannon.

The crew of the *Mary Read* took the prisoners aboard.

"Mr. Michael, I don't believe what I am seeing, do you?" Mr. James asked in stunned tone.

"We must be the luckiest men on the seas today. Look at the stinky fish we caught!" Mr. James exclaimed.

A Greek man coughed and then the color ran out of his face when he realized who he just surrendered to.

"Remember us, Mr. Mandrik? Because we remember you every day when we dress. We both still have to look at each other's scars and think of you and Gibbons keelhauling us," Mr. Michael grimly reminded him.

"That was Gibbons order, I did not want to do it. You forget, I said we should beat the man love out of ya, not keelhaul ya," Mandrik coughed out.

Mr. Michael continued "Ah yes, captain Gibbons, We

caught up with him about a year ago in Savannah and showed him how much we appreciated his 'discipline'." The two men giggled evilly.

Mr. James barked, "You shouldn't have followed that order. Now, we are going to teach you something about man love and beatings. Take him below deck!"

As soon as the African warriors stormed the lower decks, the English surrendered in droves. Within ten minutes, all the prisoners sat topside with their hands on their heads. The smoke started to lift off the deck and the admiral surveyed her bloodied crew and wondered if her husband was still alive.

* * *

The *Vendetta's* jack now has the emblem of the gentleman pirate Stede Bonnet

The graying admiral looked back at her ships at the docks and smiled when she saw the tattered yellow and black jack blowing in the wind over the *Vendetta*. The flag was now adorned with the emblem of the gentleman pirate Stede Bonnet. April wanted to honor her dead friend but really knew she was the last of her kind and modified the flag so she would never forget her past. Nina put her hand on her aunt's shoulder and reassured her, "Relax, Captain! Audrey Scott will keep our little fleet safe while we are gone."

Patrick lost his balance on the cobblestone roads as they made their way to the bar. "It has been over ten years and I am still not used to seeing out of only one bloody eye."

Tracy grabbed his hand and smiled, "I will help you, Daddy." He reached down and held the blue-haired girl's little hand.

"I know it has been a long time but do you think it is safe to be back in Savannah? People might recognize us," the scarred up man with the eye patch asked.

"Relax. Ever since Oglethorpe got promoted to Brigadier General he returned to England. Nobody cares. People hated Kingsley and with him gone, our shenanigans became such a low priority. They've forgotten us by now. Trust us," Captain Nina Read smiled.

Patrick was completely surprised by how much Savannah had grown over the last decade. Ships from all over the world used stones to balance their ballasts, which they would dump in the port of Savannah when they picked up cargo. The city came up with the solution to use the growing number of ballast rocks in their ports. They used the piles and made cobblestone roads around town. Patrick also saw huge churches, multiple-level tabby buildings and brick buildings. He even saw a brickyard in full production down by the bluff. There was no doubt about it; Savannah was really jumping now.

The couple, their daughter, and Nina made their way to where the Trustees' Garden used to be. A large inn now sat over the entrance to the secret pirate tunnels, adjoining itself to the gardener's herb house. The establishment had a reputation for shady costumers.

"You're going to love this inn, husband. They already nicknamed it the 'Pirates House' because of all the undesirables it brings in like us. They should at least have a drink named after me!" she chuckled.

They entered the inn and a wench yelled, "We are all booked and out of rooms. Go someplace else!"

"We are meeting friends for drinks," Patrick informed the wench.

"Well, you can watch the equinox harvest moon come up tonight out back. It should be a good crowd tonight, if I can get these dead beats to buy anything. Follow me out back, your party is waiting for ya, Admiral Read," the cantankerous wench barked.

Patrick shot his wife a look. "So much for this town forgetting about us!"

As they walked outside, cheers erupted from a large table. Many of their old friends were present. Tracy ran over to the large Jewish man and flung her arms around him. "I missed you, uncle!" The man was a little slower, but still very strong. He lifted Tracy off the ground with just one hand. She giggled and tried to escape from his grip. "When are you going to tell me why you are missing a finger, uncle?"

"When you tell me why you keep dying your hair strange colors," he snapped back.

Patrick hugged his old friend and said, "She keeps getting into the indigo when we are not looking. She is very headstrong and independent," Isaac laughed and dropped the little indigo-haired girl.

"Where is your wife, children, and Archibald, uncle?" Tracy inquired.

"Archibald is over there playing with our son Tobias and I think my wife is gossiping with those three old maids," he smirked. Tracy ran over to the boys to show off her new hair.

"How is Garland taking to the whole traditional Jewish lifestyle and having to go to temple and such?" Patrick smiled.

"She studies hard, but it annoys her we study separately now. Men and women should be separated for worship, but we could not really do that well on the ship. Now that we had some time in a proper Jewish community, she is not adapting very well. She never believed our religion, but she enjoyed reading our stories for entertainment. She kept asking difficult questions and the rabbi asked us never to come back. I think she will be much happier back on the ship. It has been a lonely two years without you," Isaac hugged him again.

Isaac asked, "So what have you been doing since I last saw you?" His best friend replied, "During some of our long voyages, I decided to write a book about our adventures." Patrick pulled out a journal from his vest. "Look, I even have drawings of all of us in it. Here is my drawing of you on the auction block, see?" Isaac smiled and was touched to see his lifelong companion attempt to draw him.

The twins were barely recognizable as full-grown men. Patrick shouted, "Max, Amos!" and gave them a friendly wave. They returned the wave but were much too interested in talking to William's beautiful daughters Lauren and Lindsey.

William approached with his wife Deborah. "I brought some of the finest steaks you will ever have, lad! They are from my prize cattle. I am going to get that wench to cook it up if I don't choke the life out of her first."

Hugs were exchanged and Patrick said, "You look good, William. I can't believe Archibald's kilt still fits you. I meant to tell you, I ran into that crazy old Indian scout a few weeks back. Li Go Che has himself a good bit of land, a young wife and a few children. Can you believe that dog is still alive, too? He said she has had many puppies. Let's sit down over there with your old crew and drink."

With a loud whistle from William, the crew gathered around the table.

"Well, monkey-hump me! You're still alive, Shamus!" Patrick laughed. Shamus looked very aged. He was completely bald, toothless and had a wooden right leg. He was gaunt with yellow eyes and had a huge, bloated liver, which looked like a large bulge under his shirt. He was adorned with hands full of rings and had a parrot sitting on his shoulder. Patrick pointed at the colorful bird, "I see you finally got married, too."

"That not be true you, goat-humper. I have a different wife every night now," he laughed as he slapped Teresa on her ass as she walked by.

Sam interrupted and kissed Miss Darden, "Thanks to this lovely lady, our floating whore house has been a smashing success. She is a damn whoremaster genius! She might as well take sailors, turn them upside down and shake the silver out of their pockets."

"How was South America, lad? I heard it's all fookin' savages and heathens down dar," Shamus inquired.

The man wearing an eye patch responded, "People tend to leave you alone when you got a ship as big as the *Vendetta* and having a man-of-war doesn't hurt either. We made a fortune trading exotic goods from all over the world, including bananas, my new favorite fruit. The merchant life is not too bad. By the way, Shamus, I love your parrot. What did you name him?"

"Well, ya can't understand a ting he be sayin' and he got a grouchy g'damn attitude, so I named him 'Mr. Mandrik'." The men burst into a hardy laugh.

The bar wench interrupted, "Is one of you cheap patrons Patrick Willis? I gots a note here for ya. Things been here so long I almost forgot."

"A note for me? Who from?" inquired Patrick.

"Jack-o-Lantern, how the fuck should I know, here take it. I expect a bloody good tip for that!" The tavern wench barked.

The scar-faced man tore open the wax seal and read the note. An extremely puzzled look came across his face.

"Well, my wolf, are you going to tell us what it says?" April questioned

Patrick shook his head. "All it says is 'I will be seeing you soon, Jessup'."

Shamus belted out, "Fook, I forgot all about dat guy! I thought he be killed by a pissed off whale!"

Isaac spoke out, "That mysterious bastard has not talked to us in over a decade, and that is all he says in the letter. I think I hate that man!"

"I am sure in time this note will make sense; I am not going to worry about it tonight when I am in such great company." Patrick dismissed.

April interrupted, "I am glad we all agreed to have a

reunion when we have issues to discuss. But before we get down to business, let us make a toast. Even though it is 1756, let us never forget the twenty-eight souls we lost the day my husband struck down that bastard. Those men and women barely experienced freedom and gave their lives for it!"

"Huzzah, Huzzah, Huzzah!" The group drank their rum.

"Everyone keep an eye on each other. Don't trust what you drink here. The Pirates House has a devious reputation for drugging their patrons and selling them to ships. They drag the bodies into the rum cellar and out the smuggling tunnels. They sell the poor souls to be pressed into service for ships going as far across the world as Shanghai. I don't trust dat shady serving wench!" Sam warned.

April interrupted again, "Very good, mind your rum, boys. I have returned because I heard there is a change in the wind. The ideas of liberty and personal freedom have made their way deep into the culture of the Lowcountry. Something big is brewing and I can feel it stir. Tell me, what do you know and what be your plans?"

William spoke up, "You are not imagining this wind of change. Our message has sunk deep. It is growing roots and I see it blossoming everywhere. We are hearing rumors from our Scottish kinfolk from up north. They are talking about going over the mountains and living their lives out of reach of the king. It is a harsh difficult journey, which keeps them just outside of British control. They are speaking of settling in a land west of here, called Watauga then setting up a free society independent from any oppressive government's rule. Our family is planning on going. All three of Archibald's moms want to go and the twins want to come, too."

Shamus interrupted, "Well since I blew through dat six hundred shillin's I got for me leg in one night, I guess we'll keep fooking runnin' whores. Oh and we be runnin' gamblin', too. But don't be worryin', we will remember to think of ya fooks while we live it up."

Shamus pointed at his stump of an extremity. "Ya just wait ya shite eaters. Sam and I are starting to make some real fookin' jingle now. One of dese days soon I'm going to get meself a leg made of solid gold. Ya fooks just watch me; I am really goin' to get a grand, golden peg leg for all da whores to fancy."

Sam cut in, "Ya shouldn't have got a damn round of silver from the ship's fund. Ya blew your fooking own leg off, you drunk!" He turned to Patrick and April and continued, "We also have plans beside whoring and gambling, Shamus! I know we have had many debates about if a violent revolution is the only way to rid us of the king and his government. Shamus and I feel there is no other way. Even if we wanted to be peaceful, the English will not let us be. Force is all they understand and unfortunately it is the only real way we will ever be free. Other secret liberty societies are developing all over the country. We have heard of one called the Sons of Liberty and we want to locate them. When the fight for this country finally happens, the colonists will need a navy. We want to help organize and build a fleet to rise up against the British someday."

Isaac spoke his part, "Your sister and our family have decided to stay with you, Patrick and April. Whatever you decide, we will follow."

Patrick chimed in, "We would love it if your family joined us, old friend. Friends, those are all fine ideas. We may all be on different paths toward liberty, but hopefully we will meet up at the same destination. We wish all of you luck and will be here if you ever need us. As for our family, we are going back to sea life to continue living freely, doing as we please, when we please. We will be easy enough to find if you ever need us. Just leave a message at any major port and it will find us. We plan on staying on the coast a little longer to scout new opportunities to make some gold. April and I have heard rumors of a French and Indian conflict starting and I bet some color is to be made in that mess somewhere. "

Patrick, Nina, April and Tracy toast!

Patrick lifted his mug. "Like my wife said, liberty is heavy in the air these days and I want to take a moment to breathe deep. I am not sure what our future holds for us, but as for me, I am just going to take a good drink and enjoy living free tonight!"

AFTERWORD

I hope you enjoyed the book and recommend it to your friends. There was much demand from readers and listeners to know which parts were based on fact and which were fiction so I wrote this chapter. Now I will spill the beans and tell you the facts and where I used my imagination.

Patrick reflects after a hard life of pirating

Chapter 1: Debtors' Prison

<u>Fictional</u>
Patrick Willis
Shamus Red
Isaac Swartz
Jessup
Sam Scurvy
William Potts
Garland Willis

<u>Real</u>
Filth and utter lack of hygiene
Debtors' prisons (both private and Government run)
Small Pox and Consumption, a.k.a. Tuberculosis, were rampant
James Oglethorpe
King George the II
Robert Castell

Oglethorpe did have a friend named Robert Castell who died in debtors' prison after incurring publishing debts for *The Villa of the Ancients*.

Oglethorpe called for an investigation after Castell's death and the accounts of the crooked guard were published in the local paper.

Oglethorpe did have a meeting with George II and convinced him to start the Georgia colony using convicts.

The first ship to settle Georgia for the British was the *Anne*; she landed in Savannah on February 12, 1733.

Chapter 2: Out of the Muck

<u>Fictional</u>
Peasant stain pantaloons —I extracted that and assumed this is what would happen if you only owned one pair of pants and were rarely able to wash them.
The Robin
George Mandrik
Captain Gibbons

Mr. McLain

Real

Quaker Cannons were fake cannons or decoys that were used to make ships appear more dangerous.

Ship captains secretly bought prisoners to resell as indentured servants.

The Greek Mati, or The Eye, has been used for hundreds of years.

Icons were very import to Greek sailors.

Most ship's carpenters were also the surgeons.

Most indentured servants served 3-7 years.

All the positions and jobs on the ship were real including the powder monkeys.

The "Yellow Jack" was a flag flown to signify a ship had persons aboard infected with yellow fever.

Enemies' heads were regularly hung from the Bowsprit.

Very few grown men had healthy teeth and hair.

Grog was water diluted with rum to keep bacteria from growing in the water stores.

Chapter 3: Pirates AHOY

Fiction

The privateer attack on the *Robin* never happened.

Real

Most pirates were dead by 1722 but privateers were still a very real threat.

The crow's nest was used as punishment because of the amplified motion.

All the navigation devices mentioned are real, but some of the ones the Sailing Master used in this book would have been considered very outdated.

Sailing Masters of that time would have had massive sun damage to their eyes.

Many sailors are still killed today by being blown overboard in a storm. Sailing in stormy waters is never safe.

All the cannon firing procedures are accurate.

"Shiver me timbers" meant a mast was blown to splinters.

It was also a term used if the ship ran aground and the mast vibrated because of the impact.

A "jolly mast" was an emergency mast made from a broken one.

A sloop was a very popular vessel during that time period.

Chapter 4: Passage to a New World
Fiction

Mr. Michael and Mr. James

The high stakes dice game

The Keelhauling incident

Real

Heavy salting preserved most of the food onboard but also made it very hard to eat.

Having enough fresh clean water was usually the biggest concern of a voyage.

Sailing luck rituals included: a horseshoe on the mast, cats – black cats were considered the most magical, pouring rum on the deck and in the ocean, protective tattoos and earrings. Despite the believe that a woman on a ship was bad luck, a naked female figurehead was believed to calm story waters and also gave a sort of "life" to a ship, so that it can see its way. Often figureheads also reflected the name of the ship, so that illiterate sailors could identify them.

Seeing dolphins following your ship was also considered good luck.

"Liar's dice" was the gambling game of choice. Dice were usually made from bones, hence terms like 'throwing or rolling bones'.

Paper monies of the world were not trusted and very few people would take them as a form of payment. Gold, silver and copper were preferred for transactions.

Savannah only had four laws when it was settled:

No hard spirits, including rum.

No lawyers were allowed to practice.

Owning slaves was illegal.

No Papists, Roman Catholics and Spanish Catholics were

allowed to practice their religion.

No Jews was an unofficial rule, but this was ignored because the town liked Dr. Nunis.*

Homosexuality has always existed in navies and militaries.

Punishments aboard a ship included flogging by the cat-o-nine tails, tying someone to the mast for days without food and water. The most extreme punishment was keelhauling.

Indentured servants were bought and sold in a way very similar to slaves. The advertisement for Patrick was based on an actual sales flyer I discovered from that time period.

Chapter 5: Savannah
Fiction
The auction
Archibald Freeman
Real

The description of Savannah is based on the map from 1734 at the front of the chapter.

Savannah did have a dock, bluff, and palisades. It also had a ratcheting crane to pull cargo up the bluff and houses that were all built the same style.

The Thunder Mug cannon was real and was initially used to test gunpowder as it was being manufactured; however, it was adapted for many uses, such as signaling.

It was not uncommon for a ship's crew to be inspected for disease before being allowed to port.

Savannah was this country's 1st planned city.

The town was under a heavy military presence the first few years.

Auctions and most commerce went through Market Square.

The Carolina's were famous for their tobacco and it was a highly sought after commodity.

The Indentured servant contract in the book is based on a true contract I discovered from the time period.

*Dr. Nunis (also seen spelled Nunes) was an actual Jewish doctor that the residents loved.

Whaling was the most dangerous profession of the time. The death rate for just two years of service was over 50%. The profession was also known to have many black whale hunters because it was one of the only jobs that ignored skin color.

Chapter 6: A New Life

Fiction

Marian Freeman

Heather Freeman

Maximilian Freeman

Amos Freeman

Mari Anna Dandridge and family

Prudence Quinn and family

In Percival Ward it was extrapolated that this was where the whorehouses would have been. For some reason no official records exist on Savannah's whorehouse locations. (Hmmmmm, I wonder why?)   Most of the first Jewish settlers are rumored to have lived in that ward but this could also not be confirmed.

The Red Lady whorehouse, sadly, never existed.

April Sky

The bard, Wes Loper

Real

Savannah's community helped George Whitefield found the famous Bethesda Home for Boys orphanage in 1740. It is still in operation today.

The Military would restrict and seize firearms from commoners if they suspected the use would be for other purposes besides hunting. Also the government would want the guns for themselves or for their troops.

Cornbread was all the rage in the early colonies. New uses for corn were always being found such as corncob pipes, hats made of husks and using cobs for cattle feed.

The heat in the south forced many heavy labor activities to be done at night.

Most cultures in the world split the night into first and second sleep until after electric light became prominent.

Bugs and snakes were everywhere; Savannah was basically

carved out of a swamp.

Savannah was nicknamed the "Scoundrel's Haven"

The layouts of wards, squares, trust lots and tything lots are all accurate.

Settlers were also given up to five acres on the edge of town to farm.

There are two legends surrounding the naming of the area known as Thunderbolt. One is that a bolt of lightning split a tree. The second is that a bolt of lightning created a freshwater spring on the Wilmington bluff. Both legends were found in my research, but I chose the tree because I found it fit the story better.

"The Strand" is now called Bay Street and "Thomas Broughton's street" is now simply called Broughton Street.

Decker Ward and Market Square, which is now called Ellis Square, are still there today. This was the center of activity for trade. White business owners used the square while black owners used carts in the surrounding streets.

During the first few years of Savannah, the government did distribute most of the food.

Derby Ward and Johnson Square had the Christ Church, the first Anglican *(Episcopal)* church in Georgia.

The story of Pastor John Wesley, who went back to England and started a Methodist movement, was accurate.

Henry Herbert and Pastor Quincy were real residents of Savannah. The Sophia Hopkey scandal was an actual event.

Heathcoat Ward and St. James Square, which is now called Telfair Square, are still there today. This ward and square contained the most fashionable and expensive residential areas. It was also the center of art and music culture in Savannah.

Percival Ward and Percival Square, which is now Wright Square, are still there today.

Tomochichi's burial ceremony and tomb takes place in Percival Square.

Deer skin was the prominent choice in leathers in the south.

The drawing and forging procedures for blacksmithing nails

are accurate.

The Upper New Squares mentioned in this chapter became Reynolds Ward and Square, Anson Ward and Oglethorpe Square.

The Trustee's Garden and garden tender, Francis Moore, were real, as well as a Yamacraw pyramid burial mound located in the garden.

The soldiers' red coats were made by a company out of Charles Towne, the South Carolina Independent Company.

Courting a woman was usually a long complicated procedure which could involve the giving of many gifts.

Chapter 7: Angry Lobsterbacks and Tomochichi
Fiction
Byron Kingsley
Sergeant Luthor
William McIntosh
Real
Queen Anne's dueling pistols were a popular style the century before.

Traditional Scottish weapons were claymores, targs, dirks and large axes.

In exchange for their military service, the Trustees set up the Scottish town of Darien. The Scots in Darien mainly made their fortunes in timber and cattle.

Fort Argyle was set up as a defense against the Spanish and Indian raiders from the south. It was built in 1733 along with a string of other small forts circling Savannah. It was abandoned by the 1750s but would be used off and on again.

Captain James McPherson, a Scot from South Carolina, garrisoned Fort Argyle with a small force of Rangers.

Oglethorpe did try and make silk in the Trustees' garden until the winder was stolen.

Certain Jewish sects would only eat unleavened bread.

Savannah was a huge melting pot. It was made of British, Irish, Scottish, African, Redskins, German, Polish, Portuguese and a collection of stragglers from all over Europe.

Tomochichi's burial ceremony surprisingly had very little written about it, some parts are embellished but most of it is accurate.

Oglethorpe, Tomochichi, his wife and nephew all traveled to London together in 1734.

The Yamacraw and Coweta, Senauki and Toonahowi are actual Indian tribes. Edward Griffin, Brims, and Mary Musgrove were real people.

Mary Musgrove was later arrested for being a woman who dared interrupt a conference of men. She was so mad about not being chosen as a translator for the meeting that she got drunk and barged into the meeting claiming she was the Empress of the Creek Indians and she would command them to rise up against the council. Later in life she received the Yamacraw land of St. Catherine's Island as compensation for her translating work.

John Wesley, Benjamin Ingram, Peter Rose and the Salzburger community founded the Indian school at Irene.

Oglethorpe swore to the Yamacraw that Tomochichi's pyramid would never be touched. Of course it was moved and the actual location of his grave is unknown. Currently there is a large rock randomly placed in Wright Square to remember him.

Tomochichi claimed to be the proud age of 97 but eyewitness accounts say he lied about his age and was not over 60.

The murder triangle of John Musgrove's servant Justice, Skee and Essteeche was scandalous news of that time.

Chapter 8: Fort Mose, Liberty and Honor
Fiction
Alick
Gloria
Duncan McIntosh aka Archibald Freeman
Mr. Edgeington
Real
During The Stono River Slave Uprising 60 slaves and 20 whites were murdered.

Francisco Menendez helped establish Fort Mose in Florida, the first free black establishment in the New World.

Fort Mose was a beacon to run-away slaves and is considered the start of the Underground Railroad movement by some historians.

England did forbid Scots to own weapons and even have traditional burial services. The English wanted Scotland to assimilate and become British so they outlawed most Scottish traditions.

The Flintlock loading and firing procedures are all accurate.

Worm removal was big business back then, in fact modern day Caduceus symbol (the snakes wrapped around a staff) derived from old advertising signs for worm removal. The worm winding stick became the staff and the worms became the snakes.

Chapter 9: Dueling at Noon
<u>Fiction</u>
The duel
<u>Real</u>
Oglethorpe had mixed feelings about dueling. He was losing soldiers and doctors in town over petty duels so he forbade it. Personally he supported the right to duel even into his old age.

Fascinating facts about dueling: up until 1800 many duels were fought with the first and seconds all attacking at each other at the same time. It was not till near the turn of the century that single combat became stylish.

Oglethorpe had a huge tent on the old maps of Savannah so I used it in the story.

With lawyers being illegal in Savannah, anyone accused had to make their own case.

Chapter 10: Jenkins' Ear
<u>Fiction</u>
The Freeman Society
<u>Real</u>

Treaty of Utrecht did grant England a thirty-year Asiento to sell slaves to Spanish colonies.

Captain Fandiño did slice off Captain Jenkin's ear and the incident was used as propaganda to start a war.

Books and papers with anti-government themes were outlawed and very dangerous to own.

John Locke, Algernon Sidney, Trenchard and Gordon from Cato's letters, were some of the first people to write about the ideas of individual liberty in colonial days. These writings were not perfect by any means but they would highly influence the colonial liberty movement.

Gunsmithing procedures were accurate for that time. Most colonial guns a blacksmith made would simply be copies and knock offs of existing guns.

The process of "Shutting in" every night was a centuries old tradition from Europe. Nighttime was very dangerous and folks avoided going out at all costs. They locked down their houses very tight and usually slept on different shifts so someone was always keeping watch.

Hugh MacKay was a well known Highlander warrior, chosen by Oglethorpe (along with John McIntosh Mohr) to found a military town and outpost closer to Florida. This was the town of Darien.

Chapter 11: Land Pirates and Battle Rats
Fiction

Li Go Che -but I did find the name in a list of actual Yamacraw warrior names.

Swamp Indian burial mounds, although they do exist, I could not determine if any were located close to St. Augustine.

Garland the Collie

Real

Fort San Diego, Fort Picolotta and Fort Mose were captured and recaptured.

Scavengers or battle rats made good money following skirmishes and picking bodies clean.

In the Yamasee war the combined Indian tribes came very

close to wiping Charles Towne off the map until the Cherokee switched sides and saved the white man. I bet they now regret that move.

Hemp was smoked as much as tobacco in colonial days, a fact most history books completely erased. Hemp was extremely useful and the colonists used it for food, paper, clothes, ropes, and, of course, recreation. It was such an important plant to the colonists that some towns required residents to grow it.

Governor Montiano was so grateful for black soldiers repelling a British attack on St. Augustine in 1728 he abolished slavery in Florida.

Indians of the south routinely made their war clubs out of gunstocks.

Almost half of Oglethorpe's troops died from swamp sickness and snake bites during the long campaign.

Although Collie dogs were not bred to a standard till the 1800's, the dogs have been used to help with cattle in Scotland for hundreds of years.

Popcorn was very popular in southern Indian tribes and they are credited for introducing it to the colonists.

The invention of "Hush Puppies" to keep hunting dogs quiet was also credited to the southern Indian tribes. Since only oral Indian history exists on this topic, the origin of Hush Puppies is still debated in the food world today.

The free African warriors of Fort Mose did take back their fort with a sneak attack killing many Scottish highlanders from Darien and Yamacraw Indians.

A Spanish vessel did sneak past the blockade and resupply St. Augustine, ruining Oglethorpe's siege. This caused Commodore Pearce to withdraw the British Navy because of Hurricane season and Oglethorpe had to quickly retreat leaving all his artillery behind.

Chapter 12: Road Agents and Flesh Palaces
Fiction
Deborah McIntosh

Lauren McIntosh
Lindsey McIntosh
Roderick McIntosh
The whores: Roxanne, Tiphanie, Carla and Rose.
Whoremaster Darden
<u>Real</u>
Old writings talk about the large populations of alligators, wolves, snakes and cougars. Also I found writings mentioning Georgia even had forest buffalo at that time.

Again, nighttime was extremely dangerous to travel. There were no lights or paved roads, so it was very easy to twist an ankle or break a foot. Even light injuries were life threatening.

Another reason not to go out at night in the colonies was the growing problem of organized gangs of thieves. Remember, Georgia was a dumping ground for prisoners and they quickly returned to practicing their craft.

Different size shot was just starting to be used for different purposes in the colonies. The shotgun had not been officially invented yet but people filled their muskets with all sizes of shot, using them as makeshift shotguns.

Rowan wood crosses were a common protective charm in Scotland and all over Europe. Rowan trees were considered very magical.

Whorehouses in port towns had many ethnicities of women. Many women from around the world were forced into service and sold to whorehouses.

Towns did have town watchman to deter crime and watch for fires.

Chapter 13: Tattooed Women and Soulless Men
<u>Fiction</u>
The Mary Read
The Black Hound
Captain K.T. Brewer
Regan the Cat
<u>Real</u>
Jekyl Island is now spelled Jekyll Island and was the

playground of the ultra rich. It is best known as the secret meeting place where the Federal Reserve was established. Establishing the Federal Reserve is considered the most damaging event to ever happen to the American economy. Since the U.S.A was forced off the gold standard by the Federal Reserve, the dollar has lost over 97% of its buying power.

William Horton set up the first English home on Jekyl Island.

Yarrow plants were used as an antiseptic and painkiller.

The stereotype that pirates had hooks and peg legs was well founded. Amputations were rampant in a sailor's life. Hooks were very expensive and most sailors just made do with a stump.

Scrimshaw was a very popular art form back then, as well as using bones to build model ships.

The tale of the zombies on the *Marialva* is taken from real historical eyewitness accounts.

The tale of the first settlement in the New World on Roanoke Island, North Carolina, vanishing by zombie attack was passed down orally by the Croatian Indian nation.

Chapter 14: Swamp Swag and Jekyl Island
Fiction

Robert Deaux, although an actual Savannahian, he was not alive in the 1700's. The real Robert Deaux passed away in 1993 and his ashes were spread into the air ducts at his favorite bar in the 1790 Inn and Restaurant. It is rumored that patrons and employees of the bar see his ghost drinking in the corner from time to time.

Real

Privateers routinely attacked ships of the southern coast during this time.

"Jamestown weed" got its nickname when it was used on soldiers during Bacon's Rebellion to incapacitate them for over a week.

Accounts of massive packs of wolves eating people were common.

Just the amount of the iron content in a cannon was worth a good amount of gold back then, but an actual cannon that worked could sell for a fortune.

Chapter 15: Gods and Freedom
Fiction
Although battle rats could have salvaged a few cannons, it is assumed that the attacking Spanish force captured them all.

I could find no records of what happened to the Highlander and Indian prisoners at Fort Mose. I took liberty that someone bought their freedom.

During the time period of the book, Tybee Lighthouse was not really a lighthouse at all. It was just a daymark and actually did not acquire its light until the 1800's. I took liberty and gave it a light because I thought it would be a nice picture in the book.

Real
The first Tybee lighthouse was the tallest structure of its kind in the America's at the time.

Nobles Jones was a real person and the Wormsloe plantation, Skidoway River and the tabby fort were all real places.

There have been a total of four Tybee lighthouses. The first two did not last long and were blown down in storms. Part of the third lighthouse still stands at the location it is currently in. During the war for Southern Independence, a.k.a. the civil war, confederate soldiers burned down part of the third lighthouse to keep union soldiers from using it.

Chapter 16: The Crimson Dogwood and Exodus
Fiction
The murders of Archibald Freeman and Sergeant Luther
Real
Having anti-government books could easily cause a person to be labeled a traitor to the crown and executed.

Chapter 17: The Argyle Colony

Fiction
Captain MacKay
Farmer MacKay
Mr. Perry
Real
The Argyle Colony was a large Scottish community located in Cape Fear, North Carolina.

The Scottish funeral rights and service were accurate for that time period.

George Carteret and John Carteret really were Lord Proprietors of a sovereign section of land in North Carolina on the Virginia border known as the Granville District. The free land was stolen by the new U.S government immediately after the Revolutionary War and was enveloped into North Carolina.

Most Indians did not understand or did not care about the concept of property rights hence the frequent complaints about them poaching on private lands.

Chapter 18: Bloody Marsh and Gully Hole Creek
Fiction
Garland Willis
So Lat Ti Kee
The poisoning of English troops in Fort Frederica
Real
Some Indian belts were much more then decoration, they were a pictorial family history. The bead belt would have been considered very important to a warrior.

The retaliation of the Spanish and the Battles of Gully Hole Creek and Bloody Marsh really happened. Fort St. Simon, Fort Frederica and military road were real and the accounts of the battles were accurate.

Spotted Hemlock can cause death by affecting the nerves and breathing.

Chapter 19: Pirate Tunnels
Fiction
Bartender Jim Jaques is fictional, but the Pirate House

bartenders did really drug unsuspecting victims and sell them.

The Three Lantern Pub is fictional but there was rumored to be residential houses built in the Trustee's Garden before the Pirate's House existed. Since most buildings were never knocked down, I took the liberty in making this the illegal tavern the predecessor of the Pirate's House.

Gardner Goldsmith

Tracy Sky

The caregiver Mrs. Bias

Real

The Pirate tunnels under the Trustee's Garden. Lots of debate and speculation have occurred about when these were built. Since they were used as illegal smuggling tunnels, no records of them exist. Official records from Oglethorpe's letters to England do state he commissioned other tunnels be built under all of Savannah at a later time, however, I am taking liberty assuming these smuggling tunnels appeared earlier with the introduction of his alcohol prohibition. The tunnels under Savannah were later used to keep women out of the brutal weather, moving cargo and for military movement. The darkest purpose of the underground passage was as a mass grave for victims of yellow fever. Over 150 sick souls were buried alive in tunnels to quarantine the outbreak and it is rumored the tunnels are one of the most haunted areas in Savannah.

Scribbling rings were all the rage in the 16th century.

Chapter 20: Secrets

Fiction

Closing down of the Red Lady, although very sad, it was not real.

April Read and her male persona Albert Read

Real

Sperm whale ambergris was worth a fortune; it was used to make expensive perfumes which supposedly protected one from the Black Plague.

Baleen whales were called "right whales" because they

would float and not sink after being harpooned.

A combination of English, Spanish and French government policies created the great pirate scourge.

Anne Bonny ran off with "Calico" Jack Rackum from Nassau and took to a life of pirating. Mary Read was the most famous cross dresser of the time, pretending to live most of her life as a man. The capture and trial were accurate, but the fate of Bonny and her child are unknown. No records were ever found confirming she was executed. Accounts also state Mary Read either died in prison from fever or during childbirth.

Chapter 21: Charles Towne
Fiction
The Italian or Greek Scullery wench, Teresa
The German political dissident, Miss Bleish
The pearl diver and amateur archeologist, Audrey Scott
Leo, the Barkeeper
Linus, the slave
Mary Burleigh, Anne and Jack Rackum's prison born child
Julius Chessher
Nina
Real
Francis and Elizabeth Dandridge did have large acreage in Stono, within St. Paul's Parish in what was then Colleton County.

John Prue was real and related to Francis Dandridge through marriage of his sister, also named Frances.

The Charles Town Fortification brick wall with the half-moon battery really did have a pirate prison above it. Later a dungeon would be built under it to store cargo and eventually prisoners. It is now called The Old Exchange and Provost Dungeon; there is a fun tour to take.

The gentleman pirate, Stede Bonnet, did sail with Blackbeard and was hung in Charles Towne.

All accounts of The Pink House Tavern are accurate. It is currently an art gallery and continued to serve as a brothel into the 20th century.

Pasties (plural for pasty and pronounced as păs'tēs, not pās'tēs) is a food that is a pastry usually filled with beef and vegetables.

The Powder Magazine was real and is still there today serving as a museum.

Fowling parties were very popular in upper crust society and would last for days.

Pteryplegia: The Art of Shooting-Flying is a real book that introduced sport shooting. It became a best seller and was wildly popular.

Anne and John Burleigh were also real Charles Towne residents. The tales of Anne Bonny and her new husband are most likely accurate. Many historians now believe that her father brought her back to Charles Towne where Anne married John and had many children.

Chapter 22:   Hilton Head's Booty
<u>Fiction</u>
Mary Read's treasure
<u>Real</u>
Hilton Head did have an ancient Indian tribe inhabit the island who built huge circle shaped mounds out of shells. Remains of the shell rings can still be seen at Sea Pines Forest Preserve.

The Swedish Boarding Axe pistol was only made between 1703 and 1709. They are extremely rare. Only one place in the world I know of makes a replica. Check out the real pictures of it and buy the real weapon at www.kingsforgeandmuzzleloading.com.

Before pearl farming existed, pearls were rare and very valuable.

A ship of the line was a large vessel but not as large and powerful as a man-of-war.

Chapter 23: Checkmate
<u>Fiction</u>
The attack to liberate the slave ship never happened.

Mingo

Margie, the wet-nurse

Real

The Florida Keys was originally known as Cayo Hueso because of the large amounts of unburied skeletons originally found by the Spanish.

All the accounts of Samhain, All Hallows Eve, Bogeymen, going souling for soul cakes, Lemuria, Jack-o-Lantern and Guy Fawkes celebrations are all accurate and prominent beliefs of the time.

An en passant might be unknown to many players but it is a real move in chess.

Accounts taken from real slave ships are even more inhuman than I describe in the book. Slaves ship cargo holds were horribly disgusting and cruel.

Pirate ships absolutely attacked slave ships and liberated their crews. I found estimates that 40%-60% of pirate crews were made up of ex-slaves.

Pirate ships were considered the first true forms of democracy in America. Their crews voted on all the major decisions about the ship.

Pirates really did have one of the first known examples of disability insurance through the use of mutual aid funds.

Pirate captains did not usually rule with an iron fist because they could get voted out and removed from their position at anytime.

Chapter 24: Hunting Pirates

Fiction

The final battle and duel at Myrtle Beach.

The Pirate House wench

Isaac's and Garland's son, Tobias

Real

"Long Bay "or "Myrtle Swash" eventually was renamed Myrtle Beach.

Man-of-war ships were terrifying vessels usually carrying as many as 40 cannons.

During my research on dueling I discovered that duels by blade and lantern at night were popular during that time period. The history behind dueling is fascinating and I could write another book just on the subject.

All the pirate weapons including grappling hooks, boarding axes, blunderbusses, plug bayonets, grenades, stinkpots, blades and firelocks of all kinds are all accurate.

Savannah did use ships' waste ballast rocks to make cobblestone streets.

The Pirate House did exist in the time period of the book and is still in operation as a bar and restaurant today. You can see down into the real Pirate tunnels from inside the restaurant and take a tour. It is also world famous for being haunted by the ghost of Captain Flint and its history with the novel Treasure Island. The Trustees' gardener's house called the, Herb House, is part of the restaurant and is the oldest existing structure in Georgia. Order the steak at The Pirates House. It's great!

Thanks for reading the book, I hope you enjoyed it. I hope it encourages you to visit and see some of the locations. Please remember, I am self-publishing so I could really use your help with marketing. If you enjoyed it please tell your friends and have them checkout www.PiratesofSavannahBook.com. Who knows? If I get enough support I might be talked into writing a sequel.

As always this is Tarrin P. Lupo and GOOD HUNTING!

Tarrin's Links

email: Luporeport@gmail.com

Facebook: https://www.facebook.com/tarrinplupo

Goodreads: http://www.goodreads.com/author/show/4870497.Tarrin_P_Lupo

My Kindle and Paperback books: http://www.amazon.com/Tarrin-P.-Lupo/e/B005CDUB3Q

All other eBook readers goto Smashwords: http://www.smashwords.com/profile/view/tarrinlupo

Wattpad: http://www.wattpad.com/user/TarrinLupo

Website: www.Lupolit.com

My Free Audio Books http://lclreport.podomatic.com

Twitter: @TarrinLupo

www.ingramcontent.com/pod-product-compliance
Lightning Source LLC
Chambersburg PA
CBHW020928020726
47495CB00002B/397